continued . . .

"A fabulous action-packed thriller that hooks grateful (except for the lack of sleep) subgenre fans from the moment Kel rushes into Corine's store and never slows down until the final confrontation with the Montoya mob of hit men and magical mobsters."

—Genre Go Round Reviews

HELL FIRE

"Riveting. . . . Full of well-drawn characters, a nearly tangible setting, and the threat of death around every corner, this spine-chilling paranormal mystery is sure to keep readers turning pages—and glancing over their shoulders." —*Publishers Weekly* (starred review)

"Fans of the first book, never fear: This is a good, solid follow-up that left me hungry for more."

—Calico Reaction

"Reading *Hell Fire* is a completely sensory experience that would be half as immersive in the hands of a lesser writer." —All Things Urban Fantasy

BLUE DIABLO

"Ann Aguirre proves herself yet again in this gritty, steamy, and altogether wonderful urban fantasy. Outstanding and delicious. I can't wait to see what she comes up with next."

—#1 *New York Times* bestselling author
Patricia Briggs

ALSO BY ANN AGUIRRE

CORINE SOLOMON NOVELS
Blue Diablo
Hell Fire
Shady Lady
Devil's Punch

SIRANTHA JAX NOVELS
Grimspace
Wanderlust
Doubleblind
Killbox
Aftermath
Endgame

ANN AGUIRRE

AGAVE KISS

A CORINE SOLOMON NOVEL

A ROC BOOK

ROC
Published by New American Library, a division of
Penguin Group (USA) Inc., 375 Hudson Street,
New York, New York 10014, USA
Penguin Group (Canada), 90 Eglinton Avenue East, Suite 700, Toronto,
Ontario M4P 2Y3, Canada (a division of Pearson Penguin Canada Inc.)
Penguin Books Ltd., 80 Strand, London WC2R 0RL, England
Penguin Ireland, 25 St. Stephen's Green, Dublin 2,
Ireland (a division of Penguin Books Ltd)
Penguin Group (Australia), 707 Collins Street, Melbourne, Victoria 3008,
Australia (a division of Pearson Australia Group Pty. Ltd.)
Penguin Books India Pvt. Ltd., 11 Community Centre, Panchsheel Park,
New Delhi - 110 017, India
Penguin Group (NZ), 67 Apollo Drive, Rosedale, Auckland 0632,
New Zealand (a division of Pearson New Zealand Ltd.)
Penguin Books, Rosebank Office Park, 181 Jan Smuts Avenue,
Parktown North 2193, South Africa
Penguin China, B7 Jiaming Center, 27 East Third Ring Road North,
Chaoyang District, Beijing 100020, China

Penguin Books Ltd., Registered Offices:
80 Strand, London WC2R 0RL, England

First published by Roc, an imprint of New American Library,
a division of Penguin Group (USA) Inc.

First Printing, March 2013
10 9 8 7 6 5 4 3 2 1

ALWAYS LEARNING   PEARSON

For Laura Bradford, who said, "A series set in Mexico? Really? Well, let's see. . . ." Told you I could make it work. Corine's HEA is for you.

ACKNOWLEDGMENTS

I'm starting with Anne Sowards. I've mentioned her before, but I'm not sure if I've encompassed the depth and breadth of how much joy there is in working with such an amazing editor. Her notes make my books exponentially better, and I'm thrilled she acquired me. My gratitude extends to her assistant, Kat Sherbo, a woman of marvelous acumen and endless patience. Actually, I appreciate the entire Penguin team. Everyone who works on my novels has my deepest appreciation.

There's also the Loop That Shall Not Be Named. I can't say much, or the ninjas will get me, but trust me when I say they're essential to my survival. I heart them. They're my best friends and the wind beneath my wings, the spicy taco sauce on my cheese enchilada. Hm. Yeah, I'm stopping, before this goes too far.

Next, there's Suzanne McLeod, who generally has first eyes on my books. I'm not sure how she became my crit partner, but it works beautifully, and my books are shinier because she's so clever.

Have I mentioned my kids? They've grown into such magnificent people, and I'm proud of them. Their imaginations are so impressive; they can usually dream their way out of the awful situations I devise. Thanks for all the hours spent listening to me.

Finally, I thank Andres for . . . everything. I've never had a dream he didn't help me build in some fashion.

Ghost Cottage

We had been in London for a week when my cell phone rang, an early call. My best friend, Shannon, had just talked to her boyfriend, Jesse, the night before, so it probably wasn't him. It might be Tia, I supposed, concerned that I needed more money, but she had already wired me plenty.

I didn't blame my teacher for being worried; it wasn't every day that a pupil went to Sheol to rescue a friend, staged a minor coup, lost her lover, and then returned via demon gate to a different continent. The journey started on a remote mountaintop in Mexico and ended in a London alley. For obvious reasons, I was struggling to find a way for us to get home. Official channels were out, as the U.K. would ask too many questions about how we'd arrived without passports. A fresh headache throbbed, a vise around the back of my skull.

My gifts were complicated. Once, I only had the touch, which permitted me to read charged objects; they could tell me secrets people didn't want me to know. Then I gained my mother's witchy skill, but I burned her white magick out in Sheol, channeling demon energy at a ferocious rate. I could probably still read objects, and the demon magick lingered, an echo of the demon queen's possession in Sheol. If I had any choice, I wouldn't use that again. To make matters worse, the trouble probably hadn't ended with my exit. Demons had long memories, and I still owed a debt to Sibella, the Luren Knight. With my luck, she would hunt me down.

The phone rang for the fourth time. My dog, Butch, nudged me. He was curled up on the bed beside me, and he looked worried as only a Chihuahua could.

"Hello." I didn't want to talk to anyone, but our friends in Texas were worried, wondering when we'd hop a plane. That depended on a number of factors.

"Are you all right?" Booke asked.

No, I thought. *I never will be again.*

The love of my life, Chance, was gone; he'd sacrificed himself so Shannon and I could escape Sheol. Shortly after our crossing, we'd raised him on Shan's spirit radio, which meant his soul hadn't been destroyed by the demon gate, but . . . Shan's gift permitted her to talk to the dead. So he wasn't here anymore.

It was hard for me to think beyond my own pain, imagine what the future might hold. But for Shannon, I had to get things straightened out. Life went on whether I wanted it to or not.

"Fine," I managed.

"I'm sorry if this is a bad time."

"It's not. Why?"

"I thought it might be because I haven't been able to find you. Not online. Not on your cell. Not even in dreams. Where did you go that I couldn't touch your dreams?" He sounded terse. Worried, even. Which wasn't like him.

The Booke I knew was an unflappable scholar, better suited for research than human relationships. There was doubtless a reason. Maybe I'd learn why, at long last. Any other time, my curiosity would be piqued beyond bearing.

"I'd rather not talk about it." My secrets matched his, though I hoped his didn't come with such awful, aching depth. "You were looking for me, I take it?"

He inhaled sharply, his distress plain. It might be tough for him to ask for a hand, but I needed the distraction, so I waited for Booke's request.

"I need your help rather desperately, Corine."

Mentally, I was already packing my bag; I didn't have as far to go as he imagined. "I'm listening."

"It's a bit complex to get into long distance. Can you come? I'll pay for the ticket. I know it's asking a lot—"

"I'm in London," I cut in, hoping that would stem the apologetic tide.

The pause said I'd surprised him. I imagined he was weighing whether to ask what I was doing there, but in the end, he opted not to pry. He had been guarding his own secrets so long that it probably felt awkward to poke at someone else's. And it wasn't that I'd refuse to tell him; I just wasn't ready, particularly over the phone.

"You already know I live in Stoke . . . it's not far on the train."

"Give me your address."

He did, and I scrawled it on the cheap pad of paper provided by the economy hotel where Shannon and I had been staying. I hadn't been looking forward to living here for an extended period anyway. The amenities were basic, at best.

"I suspect the cottage will strike you as a tad ramshackle, but inside it's not as bad as it looks. I'll leave the door unlocked, so just come straight in."

"I'll see you later today," I said, and then rang off.

Maybe it was just as well we had a side trip, as I needed time to pull together our exit strategy. Our cooked passports would pass cursory inspections for national rail travel, but if we tried to leave the country, and they scanned them, well, that would be a problem, one that required a solution, and I was working on it.

Though I tried to stay out of the system, I had no outstanding warrants. I'd been questioned a few times over the course of my work with Chance, but mostly I had enemies I'd pissed off by discovering the very bad thing they'd done. Many of those people were in prison, but caution had become second nature; I worried about people finding me who shouldn't, flagged by governmental forms.

"Who was it?" Shannon asked, as I started packing.

"Booke. I think he's in trouble."

She straightened from her lounge on the twin bed, covered in a rumpled black and white spread. "What's going on?"

"He didn't tell me."

"You sure you're up to working?" As she hadn't put on her Lolita makeup yet, I could see the faint worry creasing her brows.

I thought about that as I packed my few belongings. "No, but the alternative is sitting here, staring at the walls. I don't think that will help my state of mind."

Shan made an openhanded gesture that I took for agreement; then she gathered up her stuff too. Neither of us had much, so it didn't take long. I shouldered my purse with Butch inside it, then picked up my backpack. Booke needed my help, and as many times as he'd saved my ass, I owed him.

It didn't take long to check out, as we had been renting day by day; fortunately the hotel was booked light enough to accommodate this laissez-faire strategy. On the street, it was cool and damp, not quite raining.

I liked the ready access to public transportation here, however. We made our way to the tube, and with minimal effort got a train to Stoke. They ran regularly, faster than driving, according to Shan's Internet search. In short order, we settled into the car along with the other passengers. Some looked like commuters; others were sightseeing, based on their luggage and camera addiction. Shan settled in the window seat, which left me on the aisle. The car was three-quarters full. I said little as we pulled out of the station. Butch stayed hidden in my bag as we hadn't checked the pet policy before we traveled. But it was a short trip, so he could nap for that long.

"You want me to find somebody to pick us up?" She pulled up Booke's address on her smart phone, mapping it online.

I leaned over to scrutinize the distance. "That would be good. Looks like it's not in town."

Shan was already searching. "So a car service, not a taxi."

"Good call."

The girl was remarkably efficient at finding information on her cell, and after a few moments of clicking, then one call, she arranged a ride for us. "See, Corine, technology is your friend."

Because it was Shan, I dredged up a smile, even though my throat was always, always tight, as if the tears could start up at any minute. Sometimes it was hard to look at her, knowing I'd brought Chance with me, then he died saving her. *It was supposed to be me,* I thought in the heaviest despair. The sensation didn't dissipate. Instead with it rose a profound nausea, possibly caused by the movement of the train.

I barely made it to the lavatory before emptying my stomach. Three more heaves and I had nothing left. *Great.* Though I'd never heard of grief making somebody physically ill, there was a first time for everything, right? Unsteadily, I pushed upright, then rinsed my mouth repeatedly. Washing my face and hands didn't seem like enough so I used antibacterial gel when I got back to my seat.

"Everything all right?" Shan asked, her gaze skimming my face.

"Just not feeling well." *In so many ways.* "I'll get over it."

"Do you want something to eat or drink?"

"God, no. After I catch a nap, I'll be fine." Listless, I turned my head against the window, saw nothing of the countryside, and willed myself to sleep.

I woke to Shan's hand on my shoulder. "We're here. Feeling any better?"

"I think so." Blearily, I followed her to disembark.

We had no baggage to collect, so we moved quickly through the crowd of milling passengers. The train station was busy with people collecting friends and relatives, tourists poring over maps to figure out the way to their hotels, commuters striding with bold confidence.

A few paces on, the driver was waiting for us with a small sign. He was around forty with a crop of ginger hair and a generous sprinkling of freckles.

Shan nudged me. "Is it weird that I feel shiny over that placard?"

"No. It's a first for me too. Very VIP." I managed a smile.

He wasn't wearing a uniform, but there was no question we were the Cheney party. At our approach, the driver reached for my backpack, but I shook my head. "I'm fine, thanks. Just lead the way."

"As you like, miss. The car's parked over here." He led us out to a gray sedan and opened the door for us.

I climbed in, Shannon after me. As we settled, he checked the address. "You've rented the ghost cottage, then? I didn't know it was to let."

Raising a brow, I exchanged a silent look with Shan, before replying cautiously, "It should be an adventure."

The driver cast us a look as he pulled into the stream of traffic. I'd *never* get used to driving on that side. "The place is quite isolated. Are you sure it's habitable?"

"We're used to roughing it," Shan said, hefting her backpack.

"Are you ghost hunters? Will you be doing EVPs?" It seemed like an odd logical leap until I remembered the reality shows devoted to that pursuit. Maybe it was mainstream enough these days that this became the natural assumption.

It seemed safer to play along. "Strictly on an amateur basis."

He turned down a busy street with the confidence of one who had lived someplace his whole life. "Have you ever found anything spooky?"

"You wouldn't believe me if I told you." Shannon's grin took the sting out of the rebuff.

"What's the legend behind the ghost cottage?" I asked.

"You didn't research it before coming all this way?" He sounded surprised.

A valid question, but I covered. "Of course. But I'd like to hear how local stories differ from what's online."

"Oh, good point. The story starts back in the early nineteen hundreds. The man who lived there was odd. Reclusive. People whispered all kinds of things about him . . . that he was a murderer, a wizard who practiced the dark arts." The driver's tone became self-deprecating, as if he was embarrassed to repeat such rubbish.

"What happened to him?" Shan asked.

"Nobody knows. He simply vanished one day. People say he disappeared on the day Aleister Crowley died, but I suspect they've embellished the story."

I thought about that. The mysterious, vanishing mage must've had heirs. "Since then, what's become of the property?"

"No relatives were found, so I hear. The land was auctioned, and it's been bought and sold half a dozen times since. People can't seem to live there. The last owner tried to renovate, turn it into a bed-and-breakfast, but eventually she went back to Ireland in tears. Nobody from town will step foot inside the place, not to clean or keep watch, not for love or money."

"That's super creepy," Shan said.

Belatedly, I realized he had been waiting for some response to his recitation. He nodded, as if gratified by Shan's reaction. I didn't know what to make of his account, but local lore wouldn't stop me from seeing about Booke.

"I suppose the owner's trying a turnkey business to recoup her investment?" He was definitely fishing, probably so he could report his findings at the pub later.

"Who could blame her?" I murmured with a friendly smile. "It can't have been easy abandoning her dream of a bed-and-breakfast."

"No, indeed," the driver agreed.

Shannon and I made noncommittal noises, encouraging him to point out attractions that might be of interest, if we got a chance to explore the city at all. I didn't think that was too likely, given my track record. The drive took us through town, which was probably charming, but I was too numb to appreciate such things—and out the other side, where the tighter streets gave way to country roads. Shannon watched the scenery with a permanent smile in place; like me, she had grown up in Kilmer, which meant she had never been anywhere. Chance had taken me to Europe once in celebration of solving a particularly difficult case, but that meant I saw echoes of him here. He haunted me.

The driver's store of small talk dwindled the further we went from the city limits, and as we turned toward the countryside, he focused on driving. No more polite chat. He seemed tense too, as if he regretted agreeing to convey us out to the ghost cottage. I didn't mind the silence, as it gave me a chance to evaluate what, if anything, I knew about Ian Booke. It wasn't much. I didn't have any idea of his age or appearance; at this point, I could only be sure that he was male and English. And he lived in a place the locals called the ghost cottage.

Which they believe to be vacant.

After half an hour in the car, the driver turned down

a rocky, rutted lane, overgrown with tall grass. Seeing the route, I understood why he'd questioned our destination; it didn't look like anyone had passed this way in a long time. With darkness falling, the terrain became even eerier. Trees gained claws, and the ripple of the wind through the leaves seemed ominous.

"A tad ramshackle" is quite the understatement.

Shan slipped her hand into mine as if she sensed my courage needed bolstering. I gripped tightly as Butch whined. This little dog had saved my bacon more than once . . . and if he sensed trouble, then it was definitely on the way. But then, I had known as much already from Booke's tangible fear during our phone call; he wasn't the sort of man who cried wolf. Whatever his personal problems, he'd never shared them before, never asked for help.

The road was barely passable for a normal vehicle, with steep drainage ditches on either side; it would be impossible to pass if another car met us head-on. The possibility of a collision sent a chill through me, burying my less mundane fears. Two pale, freckled hands gripped the steering wheel as the driver peered into the darkness, made more opaque by the brightness of our headlights. The shadows didn't feel like they came from a normal sunset—no, it was more like we'd passed some barrier that kept the light at bay. Ahead lay a weathered stone bridge, worn from years of exposure to wind and rain; it didn't look as if anybody maintained it.

Abruptly, the driver stopped the car. "This is as far as I'll take you. If you peer hard, you can see the cottage from here."

Yes, there it is.

As he'd said, I glimpsed our destination, nestled amid a thicket of thorns, across the dark arch of the bridge. I didn't protest. His tone made it clear it would be a waste of breath. So I tipped him and slid out of the vehicle. My belly roiled, an echo of the upset from the train. The house did have a haunted, run-down air, justifying the stories that circulated about the place. Before we'd moved off more than two steps, the driver was already maneuvering the car in a slow five-point turn, being careful not to back into the ditch. I could pretend that was why he hadn't wanted to come further—he didn't want to get stuck—but that wasn't the reason.

Shannon's face was pale in the half-light, still unpainted from our hurried departure, and her cosmetic-free countenance offered stark contrast to the punky streaks in her black hair. "Shall we?" I asked her.

She squared her shoulders. "This idea seems worse all the time. But yeah, *obviously*. When have I ever let portents of doom discourage me?"

That time, my smile was real. "I knew you wouldn't let me down."

"Hey, you went to hell and back for me. The least I can do is check out a little ghost cottage." In her tone, I heard awareness of what that rescue had cost me.

I didn't want her to feel guilty, but a dark, uber-creepy road at night wasn't the place for a heart-to-heart.

My head whirled with potential explanations. Maybe Booke was squatting here. *But no.* He'd told me once that he was *stuck* in Stoke; he couldn't leave to help me even if he wanted to. Well, whatever the solution to this riddle, it lay inside the ivy-wreathed walls of the ghost cottage.

As we had been traveling a while, I set Butch down to do his business. "You can walk if you stay close."

He responded with an affirmative yap. Since he held the title of world's smartest Chihuahua, it was unlikely that he would go exploring in a place like this with night rolling in. I noted that Shan still hadn't relinquished my hand, not that I blamed her. This place was spectacularly spooky. There were no normal night noises. No traffic. No signs of human habitation. Though it might be the time of year, I didn't even hear birds or insects. It was

like stepping into a dead realm, where you were cut off
from all other life.

"This reminds me of Kilmer," Shannon whispered.

Earlier in the week, I'd failed to access my mother's
magick, which meant I wasn't a witch anymore, so it was
no surprise when I couldn't assess the place with my
witch sight. That was the price ambitious witches paid;
their power wasn't compatible with the greedier pull of
demon magick. I *might* be able to summon and bargain
with demons, a power I didn't want. I'd had enough of
the creatures in Sheol, where I had learned they weren't
all good or evil, just like human beings. The realization
weighed on me, but it didn't make me want to get to
know them better on the chance they were as honorable
as Greydusk, the demon who helped me in the nether
realm.

I sniffed the air. "I don't detect the same hint of brimstone and decay, though."

"I don't think it's demonic. It's just . . . not right." I
could tell by her frustrated expression, that wasn't what
she wanted to say.

But I couldn't pinpoint the precise word to describe
what I was feeling either. It was a creeping sort of dread,
like it could suck the life out of you, given sufficient time.
If I let myself be dramatic, I'd call this limbo, a place
where unmoored souls drifted in mournful silence. I
didn't articulate the idea out loud; there was no point. If
the dead surrounded us, they'd make themselves known
soon enough. Hell, they might announce themselves on
Shan's radio.

The mist deepened as I crept over the weed-choked
stones. My shoes made little sound, just a rasp and scrape
when I went from the rutted road to the bridge. I felt
none too sure it would bear weight. I could imagine the
masonry giving way, tumbling us down into the murky
water below. Shan's hand tightened on mine.

Somehow, we made it across the stonework onto the

other side, where it felt colder. We shared a glance. Then Shan and I crossed the remaining distance to the front door. The ghost cottage radiated menace, as if the empty windowpanes were malevolent eyes; there were no lights inside. Cobwebs hung from the eaves, drifting in the chill breeze like the tattered pennants of a long-ago war. Here and there, bits of the outer wall had crumbled away, littering the yard like broken gravestones.

"I'll lay odds if I turned on my radio, it would light up like the Fourth of July."

I swallowed hard, unnerved by the prospect. Oh, I accepted the idea that the dead were all around us—and Shan could talk to them using said radio—but I had seldom sensed their presence so strongly. Her grip tightened on my hand as Butch nudged up against my shins, demanding to be picked up. Great, the atmosphere was affecting my dog too.

At least that means you're not imagining it.

Obligingly, I scooped him up and tucked him into my purse, his safe space. He hid his head, like the bad stuff was about to commence *right now*. Shan spun in a slow circle, tracking the horizon, but there was only silence, and the thorn thicket, and then the darkness over distant fields dotted with quiet trees. The wind blew through the greenery surrounding us, and it whispered with a host of voices. Soft, sibilant, I couldn't make out the words, but the tone raised the hair on the nape of my neck.

She stared at me, eyes wide. "*Tell* me you heard that. I'm too young to go batshit. I bet the asylums in the U.K. aren't as posh as they could be."

"I did," I muttered. "And we're not standing around to see what else happens. Time to get this party started."

Six Impossible Things

I tried the doorknob and found it unlocked, as promised. It seemed hard to imagine that Booke actually *lived* here. The place was a ruin. Though the driver hadn't said when the owner went back to Ireland, I could tell by the air of neglect that it had been years.

"He said it's not as bad as it looks, inside."

"It couldn't be," Shan muttered, "or we'd fall through the floor."

Without further debate, I turned the handle, then nudged the door open. Old, unoiled hinges squeaked loud enough to announce our arrival. Peering through the door, I made out scuffed floors and rough walls, some with holes large enough for something scary to have crawled inside.

"This just gets better." Shan stayed close as I eased over the threshold.

The moment we stepped in, heat sparked over my skin, like passing through a dense, hot fog. The temperature spike blanked my vision for a few seconds, and in that time I heard Butch howling, but I couldn't see what was distressing him. Shannon held my hand tightly while we waited for the inexplicable blindness to pass. Eventually, the dog fell quiet, but I couldn't be sure if that was good or bad. Finding him in my purse, I stroked his head to make sure he was all right; he stilled after a few seconds.

When my head cleared, the house was . . . different; it looked dated but cozy enough, full of esoteric tomes and a jumble of arcane implements, more or less, I realized, like the cottage Booke had showed me in one of our shared dreams. A calendar on the far wall showed December 1947. In a way, it was like time had stood still here, capturing a moment.

As the thought occurred to me, movement sounded down the hall. I tensed, taking half a step in front of Shannon. The gentleman who came into sight didn't look dangerous, however. He was tall and thin with a shock of rumpled silver hair; his face was lean, pale from years of eschewing the sun, and he had gray eyes full of boundless sorrow. Artistic fingers showed their age in a slight thickening of the knuckles and a light dusting of liver spots. As I took stock of him, he extended a hand toward me for a polite greeting. On automatic, I accepted the gesture. Afterward I realized I knew this man. I'd seen his face in lucid dreams, but with thirty years pared away. He had shown me an echo of his youth—clever rather than handsome, but relatively unlined.

"Booke," I said softly. It wasn't a question.

"What happened? This better not be Sheol." Shan knew as well as I that one didn't pass into the demon realm without sacrificing a soul, so we couldn't be there.

On the other hand, I did suspect we weren't in England any longer.

At least, not exactly.

"I wasn't certain I could get the spell to let you in. It's been successful at keeping others out—and me in—for quite some while." His weariness was apparent, and I smelled the magick on him, crackling ozone that raised the hair on my arms.

"You look tired," I said.

He didn't deny it. Instead, he gestured toward a grouping of chairs. "Won't you both have a seat? I expect you have a number of concerns."

"To say the least," Shannon murmured. But she chose an armchair before the fire, which crackled merrily.

I had so many questions I didn't even know where to begin. First, how did he get modern technology, when he was trapped inside some kind of spell? And how did he use it to contact the outside world? But those issues were more my own curiosity, so I put them aside for the moment. Oh, I'd get satisfaction at some point, but his problems took precedence.

"I'm happy to let you explain why you need us," I said then.

"I feel as though I owe you a story first. Can I offer a bit of something to take the edge off? Tea and sandwiches, perhaps?"

From Shan's expression, she was relieved that he *ate*. I didn't blame her for wondering if we'd stumbled into a ghost story, but things seemed very real here. I nodded, setting Butch on the floor to explore. The dog trotted over to Booke, sniffed him cursorily, and then licked his hand. To my surprise, tears sparkled in his gray eyes as he picked my pet up and stroked his head gently. I could only imagine how lonely he'd been.

"Why don't you just hold Butch for a minute?" He looked exhausted, trembling with it, and Booke didn't demur when I added, "If you don't mind my rummaging in your kitchen, I can fix the food."

"By all means," he said quietly.

I supposed it was time to learn all his secrets. When I moved through the cottage, I found the layout of the rooms to be exactly as he'd shown me in our shared dream, even down to the furnishings. It was a little eerie passing through places I'd only seen before in my mind's eye. Shannon followed me, ostensibly to help, but I think she wanted to stay close to me too. If I passed through another trigger spell, she didn't want to wind up stuck here alone. Not that I blamed her. After Sheol, I was lucky she was still talking to me. Not only had it been my fault that she was kidnapped, but I'd gone mental due to the latent presence of a demon queen. Now I had a hole in my soul where evil used to be. On top of the pain from losing Chance, I didn't feel like myself anymore. Even the dream of returning to Mexico and launching my new pawnshop tasted like ashes on my tongue.

In silence, Shannon and I put together a light meal. The mystery remained, but at least we weren't stranded in an abandoned cottage full of ghosts, rats, and spiders. Frankly, the latter worried me more than the former, as Shannon could command spirits, but rodents and arachnids did as they pleased. When we came back into the sitting room, Booke had his head tilted back, eyes closed, and Butch had settled into the crook of his arm. I let him rest while I prepared my tea with milk and sugar. Shannon and I ate in silence, and as we finished, he straightened in his chair.

"Thank you for that respite. You'd think after so long I would be eager to see people, but it is . . . more difficult than I expected."

"What is?" I prompted gently.

"Making my deathbed confession."

"You don't mean that literally?" Shan asked.

"I'm afraid I do. And it is awful trying to find the words to explain how I came to this pass . . . and what I need from you now."

If he suggested euthanasia, I was out of here. But I owed it to him to hear him out. So I said, "Don't worry about framing it. Just tell us."

"Very well. Long ago, longer than you can credit, I was a vain and foolish young man. I thought I could have anything I wanted . . . without consequence. My father was powerful, steeped in hermetic tradition."

I nodded. "You mentioned the last part."

"Did I? He encouraged me in this narcissism, until I became quite intolerable." He paused, not so I would dispute his claim, but to reflect on some long-ago memory. For a few beats he stared into the fire, and then gathered himself visibly to continue the story. "Eventually, I came across a woman I wanted . . . who would have nothing to do with me."

Shan eyed him worriedly. "Tell me you didn't . . . ?"

"No, but that would have been cleaner. I wooed her with expensive presents and minor charms that lowered her resistance. Eventually, I had her."

"When was this?" I asked.

"1939."

Eight years before he vanished from the real world. I made a mental note, wondering if it had been shocking for a woman to take a lover during that era. "I don't see the problem."

"She was married to my father's greatest rival."

Okay, now I see the conflict.

Shan leaned forward, interested by the story. "How long did this go on?"

"Seven years. At first she was a conquest, but to my dismay, I fell in love with her. I tried to get her to leave her husband. I promised her all sorts of things . . . and I considered using magick to suborn her will."

"Did you?" I asked through a tight throat.

That was one of the darkest sins a practitioner could commit, almost worse than trafficking with demons. If you used your gifts to enslave someone else . . . I shivered at the thought. If Booke had done that, I wasn't sure I could help him, no matter how much assistance he'd rendered over the years.

He shook his head tiredly. "No. I couldn't. It became an obsession with me—that I should win her heart fully or not at all."

"What did she decide?" Shan wanted to know.

"To break with me and stay with her husband. She was with child, you see. And she thought it would be less scandal for a child than a divorce. At the time . . ." His voice trailed off, a helpless, wounded expression on his thin, pale face.

"The baby was yours?" I guessed.

"I suspect so, though in those days there was little way to be sure. The right spell might have told me, I suppose, but she wouldn't consent to it. The child was her husband's, she claimed, in the eyes of the law, and she couldn't see me anymore."

"I bet you didn't take that well," Shannon said.

A half smile quirked one corner of his mouth. "Rather the contrary. But I left her alone, as she asked, while I wallowed in wretchedness."

"That doesn't explain how you ended up stuck here."

"It doesn't. Ironically, after the child was born, she felt honor-bound to confess all to her husband. He forgave her . . . but he did not forgo vengeance."

Aha. Now everything makes sense.

"So you're stuck here because your former lover cleared her conscience at your expense," Shannon summarized.

"Not as I would have put it, perhaps, but yes."

"What are the specifics of the curse?" I turned my thoughts to practical matters, as I imagined he wanted help in destroying the spell. At this point, I wasn't sure why that would bring about his death, but I needed information.

"Yeah, what *is* this place?" Shan added.

"It is the country cottage my father purchased just before the war, where I retreated to lick my wounds after Marlena refused me. It's also where Donal Macleish confronted me for my sins against him. We . . . fought. I had some mad idea of making her a widow, claiming the child as my own."

"You lost." From the state of the house, that much was obvious.

"Yes. The result was the isolation you behold. He set the spell so I could never interfere in another marriage, never touch another woman."

"But how?" Shannon demanded.

"This place is . . . between," Booke explained. "Slightly out of step with the real world. Impossible for me to leave, impossible for anyone else to get in."

"In time or space?" I asked, trying to understand the challenge we faced.

"Both," he answered, "so far as I can tell. The spell does not respond well to any attempt to meddle with it. Or at least, it didn't for many years. In the past six months, however, I've noticed a decay in its potency."

I nodded. "No spell can remain intact forever."

"Not unless it's tied to a permanent power source." Booke gestured. "But there are no ley lines here, no pocket of crystals in the earth. Macleish was a powerful practitioner, but he has been dead and buried these many years. His casting wanes."

Shannon frowned. "But that's good, right? I mean, you'll get out soon."

His expression twisted with melancholy. "Dear Shannon, I was thirty-six when Macleish confined me here. Do the math, my girl."

I could tell Shan was crunching numbers by the way she looked upward and to the left, chewing on her lower lip. The truth dawned on her around the same time I worked it out. He *looked* sixty or sixty-five, tops. But he'd been trapped in this cottage, counting the solitary years until it was a wonder he hadn't gone mad.

"You're one hundred and two," she breathed. "How is that possible?"

Booke explained, "Time passes at a one for two ratio here. I suspect that's part of the curse, ensuring I live long enough to despise my own company."

I considered. "So one day here is two out there?"

"Did Macleish send you to fairyland or something?

This is like what happened to that Thomas the Rhymer guy."

He mustered a smile for Shan's wit. "It wouldn't surprise me if a similar spell inspired the original tale."

"So the curse is crumbling, which means you'll die when you rejoin the normal time stream. All the years will catch up to you at once." I thought I understood what he wanted of us now.

Booke shrugged. "It may not be instantaneous, but certainly my days are numbered once the magick fails."

"You want us to fix the spell?" Shannon asked.

He shook his head, fingers lacing tightly around the bone handle of his teacup. His knuckles burned white. "I want you to crack it. I've had enough waiting. I'm beyond tired, and I'm ready for it to end. I am selfish enough, however, that I do not wish to die alone. I don't want to be an undiscovered skeleton in an abandoned house. I want a proper burial . . . and I trust you to see to it."

The request hit me like a brick upside the head. His timing couldn't have been worse; I'd just lost Chance. I wasn't strong enough to do this for him. My first instinct was to run for the door, but I couldn't get out, unless I cracked the spell. He didn't seem strong enough to tweak the parameters just yet, even if I thought he would be inclined to do so.

Shannon set a hand on my arm, soothing. "This sucks," she said to him. "You've hardly lived at all, unless you count those thirty-odd years as a pleasure-seeking asshat."

"My son died," he said quietly. "He was only eighteen. His mother wasn't strong after his birth, and she wasted away. Macleish was alone within a few years of wreaking his vengeance."

I guessed he'd found out via Internet searches. At this point, I just had to ask. "How do you—"

"Acquire food and modern conveniences?"

Shan looked like she wanted to know too.

"I made a deal with a minor devil. He can't cross the spell barrier, but he can deliver items inside the house itself. It is easier for me to tweak the spell in order to permit inanimate objects to cross over."

That was rather elegant, actually.

Shan asked, "You couldn't summon anything strong enough to break the curse?"

"I have no Solomon blood. Without that surety, it's dangerous to deal with demonkind. Anything strong enough to smash the magick would also be powerful enough to destroy me or compel me to a situation more dire than this."

Her face darkened as she remembered her experiences in Sheol; then she gave a jerky nod. Things could always get worse. I respected Booke's forbearance, since I might well have summoned something just to see an end to the interminable waiting.

I wondered aloud, "Did Macleish think you would starve to death?"

"The magick is sufficient to keep me alive, but I was weak and emaciated when I stumbled over a tome that offered me the name of a bargaining devil."

"The Birsael," I supplied. "There are castes of demons."

Interesting to realize he owed his relative health and safety to a demon like Maury. But my knowledge surprised him. Booke studied me, alert for the first time since our arrival.

"You went to Sheol." Certainty rang in his plummy voice, no less beautiful for his age. "That's why I couldn't raise you in any fashion."

I nodded. My eyes burned with tears, just from that reference. For a few precious moments, I'd forgotten, absorbed in his troubles, but mine came tumbling down on me like an avalanche. The fact that he wanted me to stand his death watch and handle the funeral arrangements? Inexpressibly painful.

"She went to save me," Shan said soberly.

Booke's astute gaze flickered between us, making educated deductions about why our faces already held a funereal cast. "Chance was with you in Mexico, last I heard. Where is he now?"

My throat hurt so badly; I sipped my tea, but it didn't help. Still, anything to delay saying the words. In the end, Shan said them for me.

"Chance didn't make it."

No. He promised me. He said, Even death can't keep me from you. It was madness to believe those words, but they were all I had.

"It's late," Booke said, seeming to recognize my inability to function. "Perhaps we can continue in the morning?"

That would be four days in the real world. I couldn't bring myself to care.

He went on, "Things will look brighter then, I'm sure."

Falling Action

Sleep came in the shape of familiar nightmares.

I couldn't count the number of times I'd watched Chance die over the past week. To make matters worse, I had to live with the fact that my choices had led me to that dead-end road. I saw Chance's face; in my sleep, the knife pierced his chest again and again. His blood spilled down the stone ledge, opening a gate for us.

All along, I intended to die, if that was necessary to save Shannon. But it didn't work out that way. Sometimes no matter how hard you tried there was no good outcome. I would've paid any price to see Shannon safe . . . I just didn't realize it would come down to a choice between my best friend and the man I loved. In all likelihood, I should've seen it coming. A trip to Sheol wasn't a walk in the park—and you didn't return without dire consequences.

It was still dark when I gave up on sleep. The ticking clock hanging on the wall in the kitchen read 4:45 a.m. Soon, the dawn colors would light the sky; or at least, in the real world, they would. I didn't know how day and night worked in this tiny pocket universe Donal Macleish had created with a curse.

I wasn't entirely surprised when I found Booke already awake. He didn't bear the appearance of a well-rested man. "Are you feeling better, Corine?"

That was *so* like him. He was the one dying of a slow, evil spell . . . and yet he worried about my state of mind. I didn't see how I could fail to do as he wished, provided I possessed the means. Afterward . . . well, I couldn't consider the necessary civil responsibilities. How would I even explain his existence? As far as the authorities knew, Ian Booke vanished in 1947. It would be difficult to explain how he'd turned up seventy-some years later, looking fifty years younger than he was.

"Not really," I admitted. "But we're here to focus on your problems."

My issues weren't just emotional, however. That morning, it was all I could to do keep last night's sandwich in my stomach. The nausea I'd blamed on the train stirred again, growing sharper with each movement. I tried to cover how bad I was feeling, but Booke had sharp eyes, despite his age. He leveled a direct stare on me.

"Mine will keep," he returned quietly. "I'm not going anywhere."

Now I understood why he had been so enthralled by the idea of traveling the world via my dreams. If he hadn't gone anywhere before the curse hit, then he'd never seen anything but the U.K. I couldn't imagine being trapped in the same small house for so many years—and likely it had been at least fifty before he got on the Internet . . . and acquired a social life that way.

I covered my nausea with a question. "How long did it take you to figure out how to summon a lesser devil in order to get a few amenities?"

"Ten years."

So ten years of solitary confinement; ten years of starvation. He must have been weak and desperate when he cast the spell. Whatever his sins of hubris, whatever he had done with Macleish's wife, Booke didn't deserve this. He'd long since served his time for his crimes.

"I'm not okay with this," I said then. "There has to be a way to get you out of this spell without all those years hitting you like a truck."

He shook his head. "If there is a way, Corine, I've not found it. And it isn't as if I haven't been looking."

"Yeah, I imagine so." Curious, I went to the window, peering out into amorphous darkness. It wasn't full night, nor were there any stars. Instead it was more of a charcoal mist, swirling endlessly.

"Does this view ever change?"

Booke offered a grim, weary smile. "Unfortunately not."

"I bet those were long years between the first time you made a deal with that lesser devil and when you discovered the Internet."

"You can't imagine. I read the same books a thousand times. I paced. I talked to myself . . . and went a little mad."

"How did you discover . . ." I didn't know quite how to put it. "Modern technology, a window to the outside world."

"Anzu. That's the devil who keeps me connected. In making our deal, he agreed to keep me apprised of any changes in the modern world that could improve my standard of living."

"What did you promise him?" As I well knew, the Birsael were shrewd bargainers, ever alert for the opportunity to take advantage of a desperate human.

Booke glanced away, unwilling to disclose that information. Which meant whatever it was, it was bad. What bargaining chips did you have when you were locked away with nothing but your shadow for company?

But I let it go; there was no breaking a demon contract, once it was signed. "So he brought your first computer and you used that weakening spell to draw the gear over to your side?"

"Exactly so." He indicated the door to his office, and I followed him down the hall, studying the sigils etched into the wooden floor. "The barrier is thinnest here, which is what permits data to slip through."

"Which means emails and voice can penetrate, but not your physical form."

Sorrow lined his pale face. "Yes. It was a lifeline, often more than you know."

"I'm sorry. I had no idea." Bile rose in my throat. I wished it was directly related to how he'd suffered. This had been coming on since yesterday, however. Trust me to come down with a stomach bug at the worst possible moment.

"Why would you? I didn't want pity. Though I won't pretend to have enjoyed my imprisonment, it wasn't unjust."

"I disagree," I muttered. "It's not illegal to sleep with somebody else's wife. Immoral, yeah, bad judgment? Absolutely. But *this* is crazy."

"That's what happens when you piss off a sorcerer." For the first time, he showed a hint of the wry humor that had characterized my interactions with him.

"Well, you outlived him," I offered, like that could compensate for a lifetime trapped as he had been.

"Corine," he said gently. "I'm at peace. I don't need comfort, though I appreciate the thought. I just want an end to this. That's why I asked you to come. I thought you could unravel the spell, now that your mother's magick is functioning."

Shit. "That might be a problem."

A frown furrowed his brow. "Why?"

That was when I lost control of my stomach. Shame burned up my throat in a hot ball as I raced for the bathroom. I slammed the door behind me and hunched just in time, tears trickling from my eyes. *What the hell is wrong with me?* Comedians were always talking about how bad English food was, but this? Really? As I rose to try to patch myself together, the strange face in the mirror haunted me. This woman was thin and sickly, her skin nearly green in its pallor. By sharp contrast, my red hair seemed out of place, like a whore selling her wares on the cathedral steps.

"Corine!" Booke rapped sharply on the door.

"I'm all right," I answered.

By the time I opened the door, he was pacing. "Is this some residual sickness from your trip to Sheol? I've never known anyone who went . . . and returned."

"Gods, I never thought of that." Maybe I'd caught some demonic plague while I was there.

"How long have you been ill?"

"A day or so. I'm sure it'll pass. Touch of flu." Waving a hand, I dismissed the concern in his eyes.

He didn't like it but he let me change the subject. "You were about to tell me about your magick, I think."

Taking a breath to brace, I related the gist of events since I'd talked to him last: how demons had kidnapped Shannon to draw me into a trap, at which point I followed her to Sheol, and a latent demon queen in my bloodline woke up, controlled me, staged a coup in hell, and then it all went sideways. My throat was hoarse by the time I finished, and I was choking back tears when I concluded with what happened to Chance. Shan had mentioned as much the night before, but she hadn't provided context. I ended with, "And now my mother's magick isn't working. I think I burned it out with demon magick in Sheol. And I don't know anything about using that for anything but summonings."

While it was true that I still had Solomon blood, I wasn't sure it was a good idea to summon something to break the spell. It might have dreadful consequences, to say nothing of the cost to my soul. But if Booke asked that of me, well . . . at this point, what did it matter? He'd

helped me so often . . . and without question, that I
wanted to give back. Just . . . not like this. I had some
training from Tia in witch magick, but I couldn't use demon magick to break the curse; I could only summon.

"That's a potential solution," he said, after a long
pause. I could see he was weighing the cost to me versus
the benefit of ending his long incarceration.

But it wasn't the price. Hell, other practitioners already thought I was a black witch. What was one more
deal with a demon to help a friend?

"I have a contact, but I'd rather not call her, as she
tends to . . . well, devour people's souls."

Unfortunately, I didn't have Maury's true name, or I
could summon him to make a deal. But I didn't know if
he had the power to break the spell, and I was unclear
on what kind of energy his mate, Dumah, could consume.
I was positive she could eat human energy, but what
about spells? It seemed like a bad idea to summon her
until I did a little research. Fortunately, Booke had an
impressive, if untidy, arcane library right at my fingertips.

"Take your time. It's rather nice to have company after all these years."

"You don't mind if I do some reading?"

"Help yourself. Are you hungry?"

"Not really."

"You should eat." Now he sounded how I imagined
my dad would, if he hadn't gone to Sheol in my place.

All my life, I thought my father abandoned my
mother and me. Instead, he went to the demon realm in
my place to protect me from the demons who wanted to
use my blood. They'd tortured him in my stead, working
to make the ultimate soulstone from the Solomon line;
with it, they would've had the power to use it to open the
gate to this world repeatedly. No limitations. So Albie
Solomon bargained for my sake . . . and died in my arms
once I freed him from bondage.

That was another loss, so many—too many. I didn't

welcome this heritage. Kel—a fast-healing, super-strong Nephilim who claimed to be God's Hand—had said I was destined to be "important," and I didn't want that either. On two separate occasions, his archangel had assigned him to help or guard me, which meant the boss intended to use me in some spectacular fashion. There was only one future for me, one where Chance stood beside me again.

"Later," I promised, stepping into the office.

The room was clean, despite the clutter . . . no dust anywhere. I imagined Booke had plenty of time for household chores. You could only read, pace, sleep, and eat so often. No wonder he was on the computer at all hours, looking for a chat or chess match. *Poor Booke.* I hoped the girl had been worth it.

Hours passed while I dug through his library. He had obscure spell books, tomes about demons, summoning treatises, whole volumes dedicated to various herbs. Unfortunately, I didn't find anything helpful. According to the clock, it was late morning by the time Shannon joined me.

"My phone's not working," she said in greeting.

"Try it here by the desk. Stand on this side of the sigils. I think you should be able to call Jesse."

It made sense that Booke would've selected this spot to imprint the circle that weakened the barrier, permitting contact with the modern world. Otherwise, he would have to cast a spell each time he wanted to make a call or use the Internet.

She stepped over the symbols on the floor. "Hey, two bars. Cool! Is this crazy or what?"

"I always wondered what his deal was, but this . . . ? I didn't guess this. I thought he might be agoraphobic or something."

Shan nodded. "Me too. I always wondered if he was young or cute. I thought he might have a thing for you."

"Nah. He was just lonely. Dunno if you noticed, but

he was just as happy to talk to you or Chuch or pretty much anyone who would IM him."

"True enough. I don't know how he's not completely cracked."

"Right? Can you imagine spending ten years alone, talking to yourself?"

She shivered. "Don't even joke. Uh. We're not stuck here, are we? Jesse is gonna think this is the most elaborate breakup scenario ever."

I laughed despite myself. "No. Even if I can't shatter the spell, Booke can weaken the barrier enough to let us out, like he did so we could come in."

"I don't want to leave him like this," Shan said.

"Me either. But we'll figure something out." I closed the book on herbal remedies with a snap.

Nodding, she fell into a nearby chair with a casual grace I could never equal. "Let me ring the boyfriend, then. I can't wait to attempt to explain this. He thought I was coming home as soon as we sorted out our passports."

"We're working on it," I pointed out. "Making contacts anyway."

"Yeah, but I think he expected me to stay out of trouble during the process."

I arched a brow at her. "Does he know you at *all*?"

She grinned. "Point taken." Shan spun, kicking her legs over the side of the chair as she dialed. A few seconds later, her voice softened. "Hey, you."

Without making a conscious decision, I got up and left the office, giving them some privacy. The ache over having nobody to call throbbed like a toothache. But hell, I was still better off than Booke, who was trying to escape this noose just so he could fucking die. Under those circumstances, it seemed like I had little to complain about.

"Shannon's talking to Jesse?" Booke guessed when I joined him in the kitchen.

He had a meal on the table, and by this point I was peckish. It was just cold sliced meat, cheese, and fruit, but I was glad of it. He was toasting bread the old-fashioned way when I sat down.

"No toaster?"

"I don't like them," he admitted. "I've adapted in most respects . . . and Anzu will bring me anything I ask for, but I just prefer the way it tastes from the skillet."

"Fair enough." At his gesture of invitation, I served my plate, and he joined me a few moments later.

"I suppose it's too much to hope for that you've solved the problem."

I offered a rueful smile. "If anyone knows what's in your books, it's you. I just hoped . . ."

"Me too."

But sometimes the situation was impossible. There was only a dark night ending in the grave. Bleak thoughts filled my head as I ate in silence. Eventually it occurred to me that I hadn't tried to use the touch since returning from Sheol. Maybe it could prove helpful in this regard, assuming it still worked.

"Do you have anything that belonged to Macleish?" I asked at length.

"I do, actually."

"Let me see it?"

I was astonished when he brought me a gold tooth. Booke lifted his thin shoulders in a shrug. "I told you we fought."

Metal was generally good about capturing a charge, but this had physically been part of Donal Macleish. I had never attempted to read a glass eye or a prosthetic limb. The fact that their last encounter had been the catalyst for the tooth's removal might actually prove valuable. I braced myself when Booke dropped the chunk of gold into my palm.

After a bracing breath, I dropped the shields that kept me from indiscriminately reading everything I touched.

There came a flicker deep at the core of me, like this ability had gone dormant. At first I thought it wasn't going to work, and then the flicker became a conflagration. Pain burned through me, a fire in my palm that seared my nerves all the way up to my elbows. Sweat broke out as the vision suffused me. My eyes went blank, and then superimposed images cascaded through my head, along with lightning-fast emotional impressions. Fleeting thoughts.

Kill him. No. Make him suffer.

Two men, struggling. The punches rained between them with unskilled ferocity. One would stagger back and attempt to invoke a spell, only to be interrupted by the other in a desperate charge. Both their faces were bloody, broken noses, split lips. The room reflected the same destruction. Books were strewn about, pages torn loose, spines snapped. Crockery lay in shards, and one chair had been smashed flat, the legs surrounding it like a denuded daisy in the throes of He Loves Me Not.

Bright blue energy streamed from Booke's fingertips, but before he could complete the incantation, Donal slammed him headfirst into a wall. Which was when Booke lost the fight. I could see he was wandering in and out of consciousness, groggy as hell. Still, he lashed out with a final blow—and that was the one that knocked the tooth from Donal's mouth.

The vision dumped me on Booke's kitchen floor. Well, that was new. I didn't remember ever moving this way before, but I had been in the chair, and now I was on all fours, panting through my open mouth. And I had a new scar on my palm, the final evidence that I'd lost my mother's magick in Sheol. Her abilities made the touch easier, somewhat less damaging, but that benefit was gone now.

Booke knelt beside me, looking fearful, concerned. "Is it always like that?"

I mustered a half smile. "Sometimes it's worse."

"That's rather awful." He stroked my hair gently, a paternal gesture.

"Trust me, I know."

"Did you learn anything useful?" He couldn't help the hopeful rise in tone. It was human nature to look for the way out, even after you accepted you were fully painted into a corner.

"If I still had my mother's magick, I could use the tooth and my witch sight to unravel the spell. But since that's not an option, I need to think about it."

There might be no way out of this for Booke, apart from my summoning Dumah. And if that was the case, I'd bite the bullet for him. She could devour the spell—maybe—in lieu of our souls and should count it a worthy snack. I just hoped she didn't want additional payment, as I had shit for collateral these days. Demons didn't care for cash.

He helped me back into the chair, where we finished our lunch. Shannon joined us a few moments later, looking measurably happier.

"You got in touch with Jesse?" I asked.

"Yep. He's not thrilled, but I told him we'd be home in a week or two. That's probable, right?"

"I can't imagine it would take that long," Booke said.

The words sent a pang of grief through me. *I can't lose you too,* I thought. But I didn't say it out loud. Compared to some people, I was still rich in friends. I had Shannon and Jesse, Chuch and Eva. Even Kel counted, I supposed, provided I could find him.

You could call him, a little voice whispered.

Shit. Was that the solution? Instead of Dumah, I could call Kel. Maybe he could break the spell . . . without staining my soul in the process.

"You look like you just had an epiphany," Shan observed.

"Maybe." My tone was cautious. I needed to consider the ramifications.

An out-of-the-blue summons might get Kel in trouble with his archangel, but the alternative was dealing with a demon. Hm. He'd helped me a great deal, saving my life in the process, and there was definitely a bond between us. I didn't think he'd mind helping me, if he wasn't in the middle of some time-sensitive mission. Trouble was, I had no way to verify his status.

"I trust you'll advise us of your plan before you implement it," Booke said drily. "In case it is necessary to duck or take cover."

"Hey, my plans seldom blow up in my face."

"Seldom?" Shan eyed me.

I pushed out a sigh. "Yes, I'll let you know when I decide whether I'm taking the high or low road. I can't do this on my own, Booke, so it's going to require outsourcing. But I have some options."

He nodded. "You've no idea how grateful I am. I thought . . ." Booke trailed off, unable to articulate his fear.

You thought you'd die alone, an undiscovered corpse in a house full of rats and spiders. The possibility broke my heart. I could do this job, but I didn't want to.

Every time I ran the odds in my head, success resulted in the loss of a friend.

No More Demons

Have you ever tried dealing with a dog's bathroom needs when the outdoors isn't really the outdoors? Butch showed a marked reluctance to venture into that gray mist, even provided we could get out the front door—and we couldn't. Which left me holding him above the commode, trying to convince him this was a good plan.

To my surprise, he managed the job when I set him on the toilet seat. Then he cocked his head at me, as if to say, *Oh, you can accept me spelling with Scrabble tiles, but this is too much for you?*

Point taken, dog.

"What do you think we should do?" I asked, as I washed my hands.

He trotted off, and I followed him because he'd never steered me wrong. Oddly, the genius dog was the most normal part of my life. Ironic, when I desperately craved a white-picket-fence scenario; it didn't look like that was in the cards for me.

Butch met me in the hall, my bag clenched between his teeth. Since it was almost as heavy as he was, he was towing it with adorable Chihuahua grunts. I knelt to get out the Scrabble tiles, as I suspected that was what he wanted. Sure enough, as soon as I scattered them on the wood floor, he went to work with his little paws. When it came, his advice was succinct.

no more demons

"You're probably right," I said.

But that left only Kel as an option for breaking the spell. No matter how much information I found in Booke's library, it was useless to me. I'd had the shortest career imaginable as a witch. Still, I spent another hour among the books, looking for a way that would permit me to solve the problem. Unfortunately, I only had the touch.

By dinnertime, I had given up. As Shannon and Booke put together a meal, I withdrew to the privacy of the guest bedroom we'd shared the night before. Butch slipped in behind me, but since he wasn't whining, I couldn't be in mortal danger. I'd take that as an indication that I had made a good choice. *No more demons, indeed.*

Mentally, I braced myself. The last time I'd seen Kel, who initially scared the hell out of me, because I thought he was a murderer, he had been kissing me good-bye. Obviously, things had changed between us during our time together in Peru. But however sweet and tender those moments, I'd known from the beginning that he wasn't a viable option for a happily ever after. Most notably because he was Nephilim—half angel—and bound to serve. Unlike humans, he lacked free will.

It felt a little wrong to summon him to do my bidding, but I told myself it wasn't for me. *This is for Booke.* So I took a deep breath and spoke the words: "Kelethiel, my true friend, son of Uriel and Vashti, on the strength of your sacred vow, I call thee!"

And nothing happened.

The last time I called him, I'd pulled him out of Sheol itself, a feat that boggled the mind, now that I'd actually been there. *Maybe you got the words wrong.* I tried again, a couple of variations, but still nothing. I supposed the curse might be hindering him, but I didn't see how a decaying spell, cast by a mortal practitioner, could block an ability that had crossed dimensions before.

Confused and disappointed, I opened the bedroom door, Butch trotting at my heels. After setting out a dish of food for the dog, I ate in silence along with Shannon and Booke. At least the food stayed down, as had lunch. They could tell I wasn't in the mood to chat, so they kept the conversation alive on their own. Shannon asked a lot of questions about the war and the Blitz; it was intriguing to get a firsthand account from someone who was still coherent.

As Booke opened a tin of cookies, the air changed, gained electricity. And Kel appeared in the kitchen. He was still tall, bald, and pale; icy-eyed with impressive muscles and arcane tatts that sometimes kindled with magickal light. I stared at him, utterly confounded. That was *not* how it had worked before. Before I could frame any of the questions bubbling at the forefront of my mind, he took my arm.

"I have an urgent need to speak with you." He'd never been much on manners or pretending to be normal.

So this didn't surprise me at all. With a muttered excuse for the others, I let him tow me into the other room. "You're here."

A pang of bittersweet memory went through me, but to my astonishment, it wasn't attached to anything stronger. We'd shared a lovely interlude, but I had no desire to spin it into something else or build impossible dreams around him. The only man I wanted was beyond my reach. Kel studied my features in silence for a moment, and then he inclined his head, as if he read the truth in my face.

"I'm very relieved you called me, Corine."

"Called," I repeated. "Not summoned?"

"That's why I need to talk to you. Do you remember

in Catemaco when I said you held the potential for heaven and hell and that you had not yet chosen?"

I recalled the scene well. We had been on the lake, stranded in the *lancha*, surrounded by feral monkeys. "Yeah, why?"

"Because you *have* chosen."

"Surely I would be aware of something like that," I said skeptically.

"When you fled Sheol, you rejected the demon inherent in your line. Did you not feel it when Ninlil left you?"

There definitely had been pain when I dove through the gate, returning to the mortal realm. But Chance had just died, and I was injured. I hadn't been entirely sure whether I'd imagined that wrenching pain. To my shame, my head hadn't been clear while I was in the demon realm. I'd made an unholy bargain to save my friends, which resulted in the demon queen, Ninlil, using me as a meat puppet, doing terrible things while I watched in horror.

"I felt . . . something," I admitted.

"It's like an absence." At that, I only nodded, and he went on, "Which is why I'm glad you called me first. You no longer have the ability to summon or compel demons, Corine. At least, no more than any other practitioner. If you had called a demon without first setting all protections in place—"

"Then they would make a meal of me." I liked to think I was fairly intelligent, so I wouldn't have called a demon without all the trappings of ritual. Would I? At this juncture, distracted by the loss of Chance and worried about Booke, I had to admit it was impossible to say for sure.

Hopefully not. Probably not.

"If I didn't summon you, why are you here?"

"I felt your use of my true name," he said softly. "It was a tug on my attention, but not irresistible. I had to wrap up a few things and get permission from my arch-angel first."

"Oh. He let you come?" Bits and pieces I remem-bered through the lens of Ninlil's cruelty. She had hated the archangels with a passion—called them *ka*, which meant ancient spirits. In her reality, they had started as demons too, until being cast out of Sheol. I didn't know if that was true, but it was more information than I'd ever gotten from Kel.

"Yes, to recruit you."

I stared. "Are you *kidding*? For what?"

"Didn't you wonder why your causes received such attention?"

Obviously, I had. At first, Kel had been vague, hinting at a destiny and first claiming God had sent him to help me. Eventually, he stopped playing crazy long enough to explain how things actually worked—that his orders came through an archangel, not the high one himself.

"When we first met, you were pretending to be a lu-natic," I pointed out. "So obviously, I took your words with a grain of salt."

A whole shaker, actually.

"Why did you do that?" I added.

"What?"

"Act so . . ." There were no words for it, but I remem-bered how he had been in Texas when he escaped prison and hunted me down.

"To make myself comprehensible to you," he said gently. "You could fathom a religious fanatic. Would you have *believed* me then if I had said, 'I'm a supernatural being, impossibly ancient, and I'm here at the behest of my archangel'?"

"No. But I didn't believe you served the Lord directly either."

"Yet you've heard of people who believe the holy spirit speaks to them, impels them to do things."

"Of course. And most of them kill people." I realized I'd just made his point. "Can we talk about my destiny later? I called you to help my friend Booke."

"I'm listening," he said.

Apart from breaking this curse, the only other thing I cared about was finding a way to get Chance back. I wanted the life I had been dreaming about since I ran away from Kilmer. If I could make wishes come true, I'd have Chance and my pawnshop, and someday, down the line . . . kids. Just before he died, we'd finally gotten to a place where we trusted each other, despite the demon queen's meddling. *He* died *for me, for God's sake.* There was no matching him, now or ever.

I choose you, I told Chance silently. *Wherever you are.*

Kel read my sincerity with a glance. He knew I had accepted the end of things when he kissed me good-bye. As it turned out, I wasn't always self-destructive. Sorrow darkened his features for an instant, but only that— because he hadn't been fixed on an impossible dream either. In a life so long, he had learned the value of resignation; and without free will, he could only follow orders and obey, no matter what his heart desired. I wondered if things had ended badly for him and Asherah too, the goddess he loved so long ago. His ship did not sail toward a happy ending.

I studied him, wondering if he could be this detached. My decision meant we'd probably never see each other again. And while a long-term relationship was off the table for oh-so-many reasons, it stung for him to show so little concern over our final parting. What did I want, exactly? I had no idea. Kel pretty much wrote the book on stoic acceptance. But whatever he thought or felt, it was, frankly, irrelevant. And pursuing it wasn't fair to either of us. It served no purpose to dig into his state of mind just to sate my curiosity. He didn't owe me a damn thing.

"Will you get in trouble for helping me?"

"I'm not on the clock right now, though I have permission to be here."

In Peru, Kel had told me he could access his archangel in his head, along with a sort of divine Internet that let him find information that other members of the host knew. If I was interpreting his words correctly, he currently wasn't plugged in. Which meant we had a little time.

"Okay, here's the situation." In as few words as possible, I explained Booke's problem, and then concluded with, "That's why I called you. I wondered if you could disrupt the spell."

He had told me he couldn't interfere with most human interaction, unless specifically directed to do so, though I was starting to wonder how much of that was bullshit hand-fed to him by the archangel that Ninlil claimed had started life as a demon. I mean, if Kel found out he could do what he wanted without reprisal, it might get ugly for those who had bossed him around for eons. But then, I had no guarantee that anything Ninlil fed me in Sheol was the truth either. An old saying went: *there's his side, her side, and then there's the truth.* That adage fit this situation.

"Under ordinary circumstances, no," he answered.

"But these aren't usual?" I hoped not, anyway.

"You said the original caster is deceased?"

I nodded.

"At that juncture, his will ceased to be a factor."

"It doesn't matter anymore whether he wanted the spell to last forever," I guessed. "Since he didn't have the life expectancy to make his will reality, you can affect the outcome?"

"I can," he acknowledged.

"Will you? As a favor to me?"

"You realize it's not a solution. Dispelling the magick won't restore Booke's lost years or stop the march of time."

"I know," I said softly. "And so does he."

"There *is* a way. It requires the blood of a Luren."

That made sense, given that the Luren were a race of preternaturally beautiful, seductive demons who drank blood. So it stood to reason that their blood would possess certain rejuvenating qualities.

I cocked a brow. "I'm not sure what you're asking me."

"Whether you want to find the preservation spell, before I unlock this place."

"Oh. In that case, it's not up to me. It should be Booke's call."

I wasn't at all surprised when, ten minutes later, after having heard what was on the table, he shook his head. "No, I've had enough dark magick. There's always a cost to incantations that require a demonic touch, and I've paid as much as I care to."

Though part of me wanted to protest—we'd never gotten to travel as I had promised—I didn't say a word. Shan's brow was creased with sadness; it was different knowing your friend was living on borrowed time. Yet shouldn't Booke get to dictate when he died, as he'd had no say whatsoever in how he'd lived? Butch approved of this decision with an affirmative yap, then he trotted over to Booke to rub against his shins.

The Englishman picked the little dog up and cradled him in the crook of his arm. "Think that was a wise choice, do you? I tend to agree. Age apparently does bring wisdom."

"If you're all prepared, I'll do as Corine has asked now." Kel strode toward the front door.

I wasn't ready but five more minutes wouldn't help. So I said nothing. Instead, I followed Kel, curious as to how he would unravel the spell. His tatts glowed with arcane light, and silvery rays shone from his fingertips, gradually expanding toward the barrier that was strongest at the front door. The light brightened until it was unbearable, rippling outward over the cottage walls, then dropping away in falling sparks, as the enchantment blew apart. I narrowed my eyes, trying to track the expenditure of energy, but a low boom shook the house from the roof down.

Then I felt the heat zing through me, blinding me a second time, and when my vision cleared, everything had changed. It was twilight with a ruddy light shining through the window. All the work Booke had done on his pocket space had carried over into the real world, superimposed over the abandoned cottage. Now things were no longer dusty and abandoned. I wondered briefly what had happened to the rats and spiders displaced in the phase shift, but I was too thrilled by the view through the window to linger on the thought long; it showed wind blowing through the tall grass and whipping through the tree branches.

You did it. Thanks, Kel.

My eyes smarted a bit, tears slipping from the corners. I dashed the moisture away impatiently as I hurried toward Kel. He swayed, one hand braced on the doorjamb. His face was pale, his tattoos still glowing with a residual light, giving him an ethereal air. I touched him without thinking; my hands went to his shoulders to offer support. To my surprise, he spun away from the wall to accept my help.

He leaned into me, head bowed toward mine. "An incredible amount of rage and malice went into that working."

"How did you break the curse?"

"I drew it in and then expelled it along with enough force to shatter the curse."

No wonder he looked ill. That sounded an awful lot like how I felt after handling a particularly evil object. Because I always craved a gentle touch after a bad reading, I put my arms around him. Kel tensed, probably because people didn't comfort God's Hand.

"Easy," I whispered. "I'm not making a move, just grounding you."

I wasn't sure he knew what I meant, but after a shudder wracked him, he put his arms around me and held on tight. He probably felt sick as hell; there were limits to what a Nephilim could tolerate. I rubbed his back, trying not to remember how we had been together. Savoring that memory felt like a betrayal of Chance.

"I wish—" He broke off, leaving me to wonder.

"Better?" I asked, focusing on his welfare rather than words left unspoken.

"I need to sleep to regain my full strength. But I'm well enough, all things considered." His tone sounded strange as he stepped away from me.

"What things—" I started to ask, but Shannon and Booke joined us by the front door before I could complete the question.

"We'll talk later," Kel said, flinging the front door wide. He looked ready to collapse, but he had done what I asked.

As always.

A cool, inviting wind blew through the house, so long untouched by natural forces. Tears glinted in Booke's eyes as he turned his face toward the breeze, then he set Butch gently onto the floor. He moved with the care of a much older man; his steps were tentative, shaky, even. I took his elbow, knowing the weight of those years was already coming to bear on him. It might not show instantly like a fast-forwarded video of a decaying rose, but the pain must be phenomenal.

Worth it, I thought, *for a taste of freedom.*

"I had forgotten what the world smells like," he breathed.

Booke crooked his elbow, as if he were my escort, and not the other way around. In stately procession, we made our way to the front step of the cottage. Kel and Shannon followed. The yard was completely overgrown, the sky awash in purple, and I could tell by his expression that he had never seen anything so lovely. For me, it was a melancholy beauty; certainly there was pastoral charm, but it came knowing Booke's time to appreciate it was limited.

"I have an idea," I said then. "We'll take a trip. Our passports should be good enough to manage rail travel. Would you like to see Paris? We'll go. Italy? There too, if we can." The unspoken subtext was that I didn't know how long Booke had, but I would be damned if I didn't keep my pledge to him.

"I have no documents," Booke pointed out wryly.

That was a problem, but I'd figure out a way around it. Dreaming didn't make sense in our current situation; nor would I leave him alone. Yet I'd promised him the world, and he would have it, however much could be experienced in the short while he had left. It went without saying that he would die somewhere along the way. I didn't let myself think of that. *No more good-byes. I can't take much more.* But the universe had never listened to my pleas. If there was an intelligence running the show, as Kel's archangel claimed, then it was singularly uninterested in Corine Solomon.

"There has to be a solution," Shannon said. "We'll think of something."

Booke tilted his head, entranced by the dying rays of the sunset. "Think fast. I'm a very old man, you know."

Sands of Time

While Shannon arranged for a car to pick us up and Kel lay exhausted on the sofa, I helped Booke gather his things. He did have a birth certificate, but without a current passport he wouldn't be able to leave the country. Unfortunately, he didn't have time to apply and wait for proper channels. We had to figure this out now.

Then it hit me.

"Eva," I muttered, already dialing.

"You've thought of something?" Booke asked.

I waved him to silence, and he went back to packing, his movements slow and measured. Fortunately, the time difference worked in our favor, as it was earlier in Texas. Eva answered on the third ring.

"It's me," I said. "How are you?"

"Good. Tired. Cami keeps me hopping." Cami was Chuch and Eva's daughter. I was fuzzy on how old she was, given the time slippage in Sheol, but this didn't seem like the time to ask.

"Chuch and the baby?"

"They're both fine. Are *you* all right? Is Shannon with you?"

Dammit. I had explanations to make, so I summarized

as fast as I could, leaving out the ineffable account of Chance's death. When I finished, she said, "I get the feeling this isn't a social call."

"I'm with Booke. If you have contacts in the U.K., I could use them."

"*My* contacts," she repeated. "Not Chuch?" Obliquely, she was asking if I needed papers, not weapons.

"Yeah, do you know anyone?"

"I used to. Let me make a few calls and get back to you."

So strange, but my friends Chuch and Eva had a colorful past. Chuch had been an arms dealer before he met the love of his life, Eva, who was a talented forger. They'd left their lives of crime to settle into connubial bliss in Laredo. Now Eva was a stay-at-home mom, and Chuch restored classic cars. But they both had helpful underworld contacts at moments like this.

"Can she help?" Booke asked.

I turned to him; in the few moments I had been otherwise occupied, he'd already aged. His features reflected another five years in fine lines. His hair was a little thinner, his shoulders more stooped. At the rate the real world was catching up to him, he might not have more than a day or two. Part of me desperately wanted to find a Luren, no matter what Booke thought . . . but it would be wrong to make such an enormous choice for him. I had to respect his wishes.

Fifteen minutes later, we stood waiting outside the cottage with luggage in tow. A different driver arrived in a Range Rover, as Shannon had told him there were four of us. I suspected Kel was hanging around to have the conversation about my destiny, but I preferred to delay it as long as possible. That said, I owed him to hear him out, especially after he'd half killed himself for Booke at my behest.

I helped Booke into the back, Kel climbed in after me, and Shannon got in front with the driver, who was peering at the ghost cottage with a puzzled expression. "It looks different," he said. "Less ominous. Like any regular house."

"It's just old," Shan told him.

The guy shrugged, clearly uninterested in further debate as he maneuvered the vehicle around. "Where am I dropping you?"

It was an excellent question. I hadn't thought much past getting Booke out of the cottage where he had been trapped for so long. But before I could reply, the phone rang. Eva's number showed in the ID box, and I answered.

"Got something for me?"

She didn't protest my terse response, knowing the situation with Booke. "Yeah. The guy I know is working in London. I'm texting you his address."

That was the answer to the driver's question. I thanked her, disconnected, then said, "Take us to the train station, please."

"Very well." The driver turned to Shannon, who responded to his overture with a tired yawn.

Booke reached for Butch, who went without protest. I watched as he petted my dog with fingers that held a slight tremor. It must be overwhelming to be moving after so long. I mean, he'd been in cars before, but it had been half a century. I couldn't even imagine the isolation. He was watching the scenery with a fierce focus, even when it got too dark to see.

I turned to Kel with a questioning glance. "Do you want to have the discussion I deferred now or later? Are you on a schedule?"

"Don't worry about it. I've withstood many punishments over the years."

Guilt flared in a hard, awful twinge. "I don't want to be the reason you get hurt, Kel."

He shook his head, his smile haunting and melancholy in the dying light. "Don't concern yourself with my fate. It will not change, however much I wish it."

That sounded ominous. But he turned away, shoulders toward the door, making it clear he was uninterested in pursuing the conversation right then. It was hard to credit that we'd been close—he'd confided in me. It felt like a lifetime ago.

The ride went in silence until the driver stopped at the train station. I paid him in cash, then we unloaded. I had lost my sense of time in the real world; how long had it been exactly since Shan and I got off the train? Now we were heading back to London to look for Eva's contact. I checked the address in my phone, then bought us all tickets. It was late by the time we boarded, and Booke was looking worse. *What're you doing?* I asked myself. Maybe it would've been better to let him die in familiar surroundings, but it seemed *so wrong.* That he should pass on without ever seeing anything of the modern world firsthand. I wanted to show him everything, but there weren't sufficient moments left for that. So I had to pick and choose.

I helped Booke get settled. Then Shannon sat beside him, which left me to take a seat behind them with Kel. It was full dark by this time, no scenery to admire. But I needed to talk to him anyway. And I could tell that he was looking at my blurry face in the glass, not peering beyond the reflection at the night sky.

"Go on, then. I'm ready to listen. You've been cryptic in the past, talking about me being important, hinting I have a destiny. Now, you've said you're to recruit me?"

"Time to give the pitch," he said tiredly. "The archangel to whom I report has been building alliances, preparing to wage a war against demonkind."

"What has that got to do with me?" I asked, puzzled.

"The duality of your nature. You've tasted white magick and demon power. Ultimately, you rejected the demon queen and returned home. Thus, my archangel believes you've chosen a side."

"That seems . . . far-fetched. Just because I didn't want

to stay in Sheol, it doesn't mean I want to . . ." I trailed off, unsure what I was being asked to do.

"Fight?" he supplied.

"Would it come to that?" It didn't sound like a viable option for me. I wasn't exactly the warrior princess type.

"If Barachiel has his way, it will. He wants to conquer demonkind utterly. He's been building toward this confrontation for centuries."

"Why does he want me? What would I be doing?" Already, the rejection trembled on the tip of my tongue. I had learned the hard way that if powerful creatures sought you out, it was almost never to your benefit.

"If you agree, he'll explain everything to you personally," he answered.

I stared. "Isn't that like asking me to sign on the dotted line without reading the contract first?"

"He's not accustomed to being refused anything he wants. To his mind, you should be honored to be chosen."

"Like in the old days when an angel appeared in a halo of golden light and the peasant scrambled forth in an adoring stupor to do his bidding?"

A reluctant half smile curved Kel's mouth. "Precisely. He has not adapted well to the Information Age."

"Then . . . I have to decline. I'm sorry. But it's not fair to ask me to accept something like this without more details."

"Nobody ever said life was fair," he murmured, turning away.

"Ignoring me won't work," I whispered.

He shifted, so he was gazing at me full on again. "What is it, Corine?"

"What aren't you telling me? I know you well enough to realize something's bothering you about all this."

Surprise flickered across his impassive features. Doubtless it was my assertion that I knew him. He tried to be remote and untouchable as a mountaintop, but I had scaled his heights, breached his imperturbable silence. And now I knew how to interpret his minuscule expressions.

Kel clenched both hands into fists, balanced them upon his knees. "I'm trapped, Corine."

"I know." That wasn't news, however.

His mouth firmed into a taut, angry line. "You don't. When I report that I've failed to recruit you to our cause, my next order will be to kill you."

My blood chilled in my veins. "You wouldn't—"

"I don't want to," he said, low. "But I am incapable of rebellion."

"But . . . you were flogged in the arena." I remembered his scars, and the way he'd trembled when I ran my fingertips across them, how he flinched when I traced the place on his shoulders where his wings used to be. "What for, if not refusing to fall in line?"

"For being a half-breed. For being insolent and irreverent."

"You were whipped for . . . mouthing off?" I asked, trying to understand. "But you never actually denied a command?"

"If I could, I would have." His anguish sharpened the words, made a weapon of them, until I had to reach for him.

My palm covered his knotted fist, and I stroked his knuckles until his fingers unfurled beneath mine. Then he turned his hand slowly under mine, until our palms aligned. A small part of me still loved him. Not as you build your dreams around a man, but in the way you love the stars for shining, showering ephemeral brightness.

"What did they make you do?"

"The archangel learned I had a lover," he said quietly.

I was afraid I knew where this was going. "Asherah, the goddess of desire."

He shook his head. "Like you, she was human, though she *was* a priestess."

"He ordered you to kill her?" It seemed like the logical conclusion.

"Yes." The raw syllable told me how much the memory still hurt him, two thousand years later.

"And you couldn't refuse."

"Only humans have free will."

"But you're so strong. There must be a way to resist your orders."

"Do you think I would not walk away from endless war, endless death, if it were so simple?" Kel angled a hard look at me.

He had a point. His archangel—or whatever the hell the creature was—had a powerful hold on him. Maybe magickal compliance was in effect, making Kel think he didn't have free will, due to the bullshit mythology he had been fed since birth. Regardless, it also meant I was in a hell of a mess. If I didn't sign on with a being I wasn't convinced had humanity's best interests at heart, Kel would kill me. And then he'd spend two thousand years grieving.

Shit.

"How long do you have before he gets suspicious?"

"I'm not sure. He has many concerns, many agents. And I'm not his most important emissary."

"I don't want to fight anymore," I said tiredly.

Kel laced his fingers through mine. "Nor do I. Even before I met you, I was weary of war, sick unto death."

"But you can't die."

"No." The word carried infinite sorrow.

"I don't understand what the archangel wants from me. I'm not the Binder anymore. My mother's magick doesn't work. Which just leaves the touch. What good could that possibly do him?"

"I don't know," he answered. "But this I promise . . . I won't hurt you, Corine."

"You can't know what the future holds." If I had the option, I'd take a do-over in Sheol, find some way to save Chance. "Anyway, it's not our most pressing concern. Can you stall?"

"A few days at least. He won't expect instant capitulation from you, I think."

That sounded as if the archangel knew me. I wasn't sure how I felt about that. "What's his name, anyway?"

"Barachiel."

"Is he an utter bastard?"

The question startled a quiet chuckle out of Kel. "Yes, rather. I used to tell myself that he got his orders from a higher power. It was the only thing that made my mission bearable."

"Is the bloom off the rose?"

He inclined his head. "I am unable to grasp how it can matter to a divine being whether you work for Barachiel or not. Lately, it seems as if his will has supplanted any other . . . if there ever was anything more."

I hated to see the pain engineered by such a crisis in faith, but it might be better that he had lost his blind fanaticism. "I can't answer that. The demons said a few things that made me think maybe . . . but mostly, it seems like we're on our own."

"I thought so too, long ago. But after Asherah died . . . they broke me. Made me believe, somehow, that every horrific deed served a higher purpose."

"Maybe you had to accept that," I offered. "Or go crazy."

"You mean my belief was a form of self-preservation?"

"Possibly. I can't imagine what you've gone through."

His smile was fleeting. "You are an odd woman, Corine Solomon. I've slain many, but you're the only prospective victim who ever tried to console me."

"Is it working?" I wondered aloud.

"Somewhat."

That seemed like a good place to let the conversation rest. I left my hand in his as a comforting gesture and didn't protest when he turned his face toward the window. He closed his eyes, tilting his head against the seat; gods, I hoped we could wake him up when the train stopped.

To my relief, it wasn't a problem.

When we arrived in London, Shannon hailed us a cab, and I helped Booke climb into the back. It was late enough that we should be ashamed of turning up at Geoff Stenton's door, but I'd drag his ass out of bed if I had to. Booke needed this passport urgently.

Fortunately, the forger lived on the ground floor. Otherwise, I'm not sure whether Booke would have made it. He looked older and frailer with each passing moment. My heart broke a little as I thumped on the knocker, relentless, until I heard movement within.

The man who flung the door open was short, balding, with a pair of smudged glasses hastily perched on a broad nose. His shirt was undone and it looked as if he'd put on a pair of sweatpants that he'd grabbed from the floor. They sported a number of interesting stains, particularly around the knees. I hoped his documents were better than his hygiene.

"What the hell's wrong with you?" he demanded.

"Eva sent me," I said.

"Good for you. Come back at a decent hour."

"You don't understand, it's an emergency." I indicated Booke, holding my arm for balance. "He has to get out of the country right away."

Stenton studied my friend, frowning. "Is he a war criminal or something? Never mind," he added. "I don't want to know. Since you've gotten me out of bed, you may as well come in." I didn't know that much about British regional dialects, but when Geoff said "something" it sounded like "somefing."

We all traipsed inside. Within, the place was a typical townhome with a front room, a hallway that had a half bath on one side and ended in a small kitchen. The place was cleaner than the forger's pants. He beckoned us upstairs with an impatient wave of one hand.

"My studio's upstairs. Can you make it?" Stenton asked Booke.

"I'll manage," he answered.

With my help, he clambered up the stairs, but I could tell by his expression it was painful. How old was he now? Eighty? I wished I could calculate the rate at which the years were catching up to him. Then I might be able to predict how long he had left. My sense of urgency built even more; I had to show him something lovely before he died. I'd *promised*.

If my mother taught me anything, it was the importance of keeping my word.

Frequent Flyer

Conscious of time ticking away, I made short work of our business with Geoff Stenton, and I paid him handsomely for the interruption to his sleep. The others milled in various stages of boredom, until he needed Booke to pose for a picture. Then Stenton referred me to a local witch who could help us leave the country with our false passports.

"How long will Booke's cooked documents take?" I asked.

He considered. "Ordinarily, a couple of days, but with what you're paying, I'll get it to you within a few hours. Where should I send it?"

"Do you think the witch would mind if you sent a courier there?"

Stenton shook his head. "No, we've often dealt with gifted who have a need to leave the country in a hurry."

I didn't doubt that at all. Geoff gave off a sketchy vibe, but beggars couldn't be choosers. That concluded our business, so we caught a cab to our next destination while Booke grew frailer by the moment. At night, London radiated a much different vibe than Mexico City. Even in the evening, there were always people milling around open-air cantinas, dogs lolling on the sidewalk in hope of scraps. Police cars patrolled with their lights flashing, though you only had to worry if they turned on the sirens. The lights were just to let you know they were watching. London was quieter by comparison, less yelling in the street, certainly no mariachis, but there was plenty of traffic, even at this hour.

The cabbie dropped us at the door of a crumbling brick row house. I could tell that the neighborhood wasn't the best. If only I had my witch sight, I could check the premises for wards and see how effective her work was. Crazy, but I had gotten used to my magick, started taking it for granted. And then it was gone, leaving me to miss it. The same could be said for Chance. I banged on the door with a closed fist, angry with the awful grief that hung around my neck like an albatross. The fury accompanied the feeling because it implied I had accepted he was gone. It was a stage in the mourning process—and I *did not* concede that he was beyond my reach.

Even death cannot keep me from you.

I kept thumping on the painted red door, until it swung open to reveal a podgy little woman with her hair up in curlers; I hadn't known women still did that. At first, the witch was no happier about being awakened in the middle of the night.

"Come in, before the neighbors decide I'm running a bawdy house." She stomped inside, muttering, "At *this* hour? Can't imagine what Geoff was thinking."

"Probably that you wanted to get paid," Shan said.

"What do you need then? Spit it out." I couldn't blame her for the attitude, as being rousted from a warm bed by demanding patrons who wanted a spell right now had to suck. This never happened when you ran a store with regular hours, one of the compensations of working in retail. When she saw my cash, her mood improved dramatically.

Inside, her room was busy with arcane accoutrements paired in uneasy truce with excessive lace and hand-crafted knitted goods. I wondered if she could make an athame cozy, and then decided I was too tired to be funny. Shan helped Booke over to a chair with a kindness I found touching. She hadn't known him as long, but he was definitely part of our crew, even if he'd been a virtual member.

As my friends got comfortable, I followed the witch into the kitchen, where she had all her components — and maybe it was exhaustion, but it amused me to find esoteric ingredients neatly labeled in glass spice jars and ceramic canisters. While she put on a pair of reading glasses, I summarized our business.

As it happened, people requested this particular charm from her quite often. Once she put the kettle on and checked her stock, she found she had two of them ready, but she needed to make a third. Which worked out well, as we were waiting for a messenger anyway, and I was spared the need to ask if we could hang around her parlor until Stenton came through. She shooed me away, but I found it hard to settle, worrying about whether I was doing the right thing with Booke. Maybe she had Luren blood in stock . . . but no, I'd promised him I wouldn't. It was his choice, dammit.

Shannon curled up on one end of a sofa and went to sleep. That was a gift I shared; under normal circumstances, I could sleep anywhere, but I was too tense to be able to relax. Kel nodded off at the other end, and I didn't bother him, knowing he had depleted his resources in setting my friend free. I could see the changes in Booke's face already: more lines, faint liver spots dotting his temples. His hair seemed a little thinner, a sparse silver down.

"Are you all right?" I asked, perching on a chair near Booke.

"I'm not ill. Just old. Considering I've been alone for so very long . . . and I'm free at last, yes."

It was unlikely he would complain, regardless. But we had some important decisions to make. "Okay, so here's the deal. I have a couple of ideas. We can see as much of Europe as you can. The benefit is that it's close by, and the countries are smaller. Or we can fly across the Atlantic. I'll call Chuch and Eva, ask them to set up a kick-ass going-away party for you."

He tilted his head, much struck by that notion. "Would they do that for me?"

"You bet your ass. I just thought you might want to meet them in person, as you were friends with Chuch first. Then Eva, of course. You'd get to see Cami too."

"Then that's what I would like," he said decisively.

"To go see Chuch and Eva?" That choice would make Shannon happy, as she was dying to see Jesse. Not literally, as with Booke, thank the gods.

"I've always wanted to. I didn't dare hope . . ." He trailed off, lifting a thin shoulder in a sheepish half shrug. "Thank you."

"Then let me make the arrangements." For that, I had to borrow Shannon's smart phone. She was sound enough asleep that she didn't even twitch when I slid the cell out of her bag. A few clicks later, and we were set.

I wasn't sure if Kel would be traveling with us; as I recalled, he hated modern flight. But I booked him a seat just in case. Since it was a one-time-only occasion—and I wanted Booke to be comfortable for the transatlantic flight—I bought four first-class tickets. If Kel vanished as he had a tendency to do, then one of us would have two seats. I hated using Chance's credit card, though. I'd memorized the number due to repeated use when we were ordering furniture together in Mexico, and it wouldn't work for brick-and-mortar purchases, but it was my only option for getting plane tickets fast. Fortunately, he carried a low balance and a high limit. I'd pay the bill before anybody knew he was gone.

Still, fresh hurt lanced through me, making it difficult

to navigate the mobile travel site. When I finished, I glanced up to find Booke watching me with a concerned expression. He hesitated, natural reticence warring with sympathy.

"Does it ever get easier?" I asked.

"Sometimes days pass before I think of Marlena. But at others, it's like she's just stepped out, as if I expect, despite all this time, that she's coming back to me."

I didn't want to acclimate to his loss. Once I had Booke squared away, I meant to find some way to save Chance. The need to act on that pounded in my head, echoed in my heartbeat, but I had to take care of my friend first. *It's not a betrayal,* I told myself. *Chance will understand.*

Thinking of him in present tense helped.

An hour later, the courier arrived. I took the liberty of answering the door—and I was relieved to find Booke's documents ready to go. The passport looked fantastic for all its speed. Hard to believe Stenton had taken the picture with a digital camera just a little while ago. I tipped the messenger generously, and he saluted me before heading back down the stairs.

From the kitchen came the sounds of the witch as she worked, muttered imprecations and rattling pots. A strong medicinal smell lingered in the air; gods, I hoped we didn't have to ingest the charm for our passports to work in the scanners. That might not end well. But to my vast relief, when the woman emerged, she was carrying three sachets, which we were to wear around our necks.

"As long as the bags remain in contact with your skin," she explained, "you should have no trouble. The machines will malfunction just long enough to process your immigration."

"You make these often?" Booke inquired.

"Often enough. I'll have my cash now if you please. Then you need to quit cluttering up my front room. I'm for bed, and if Stenton sends anybody else my way in the next eight hours, I may turn him into a toad."

"The client or Geoff Stenton?" I wondered.

"Both?" The witch laughed as I paid her, counting out the cash. "Mind you, use those within forty-eight hours. The spell won't hold its charge forever."

"We're on our way to the airport," I assured her.

Shannon roused on the first try; it took longer to wake Kel, who was in his trancelike sleep. "Come on, you two. We have a plane to catch."

The earliest flight left just before five in the morning, and we were only three away from that now. In short order, I hurried them out to the taxi and gave our final destination. I wished I could've spent longer in the U.K., but there were pressing issues elsewhere. In the taxi, I borrowed Shan's phone again to email Chuch.

We're heading for Laredo. Given travel times, it will be late tomorrow or the next day. Booke's with me, long story. Tell you when I see you. Would mean a lot to him if you throw a party. Invite all your friends and relatives. Trust me when I say he has reasons to want to be surrounded by people. Including our arrival time in case you're willing to give us a ride from the airport. That was a long enough message for a tiny phone keyboard in a moving vehicle at night. Satisfied with how I'd managed things so far, I hit send and gave Shan back her phone.

She stared at me in bemusement. "You seem . . . wired. Manic, almost."

"I feel a little frantic," I confessed softly.

There was no way I could confess aloud what I truly feared—that Booke would pass away in transit. But I think she knew. She put her hand on mine and squeezed. "You're doing your best."

"Hope it's good enough," I muttered.

The rest of the journey passed in a blur of lines and waiting. For the sake of efficiency, we got Booke a chair, which he hated. But it meant slipping the main security line for one more handicap friendly. We flashed our passports multiple times, but the real test of the charm around my neck would come when we entered the U.S. He didn't need a visa, as British citizens could visit for up to ninety days on a tourist form. Given Booke would be lucky to have a month, let alone three, I didn't figure immigration would pose a problem.

By the time the pretty, polite stewardess settled us on the plane, I was running on fumes. Shan sat with Booke in the first row, still grilling him more about the war. Since he didn't appear to mind, I let it go. Maybe it was a relief for him to be able to tell his stories. I mean, if he had tried that with anyone on the Internet, they'd have been like, *sure, you were in the Blitz.* Because people that old didn't know how to work the Internet machine. Actually, there probably *were* some, but my experience with the elderly was limited; I never knew my grandparents on either side.

Kel took the window seat, leaving me on the aisle. I didn't mind. I was surprised, however, that he hadn't poofed on me. But then, if he went back to report his failure to recruit me, Barachiel would order my death. That was another complication I didn't need, amid everything else. My whole life was a wreck; gods only knew whether the workmen were still building my shop. Tia was old and frail. I had Chance's apartment to deal with too. Fortunately, he'd paid the rent several months in advance, but who knew when those payments ran out? I hoped to hell the landlord hadn't put all his things in the street. At the very least, I owed it to Min to collect them.

The thing about adventures that they never put in fairy tales? They screwed up your life in a royal fashion. Real-world business went unattended; bills didn't get paid. My freaking El Camino had been abandoned on a remote mountainside in Oaxaca. True, I didn't pay much for it, but I'd put money into repair work, and there was no way in hell I'd ever see that car again. In the first week of my sojourn in Sheol, I'd bet that my ride was jacked and possibly stripped. Or maybe, given that it was a solid car, somebody was just driving it around without the title. In a small village, nobody checked into that sort of thing.

To my left, Kel's hands were clenched on the armrests as the attendants went about their business. They handed out masks, pillows, and blankets, offered cool or hot beverages. In the back of the plane, which I dubbed steerage, they were probably deploying the cattle prods. A ten-hour flight, like the one from London to Houston, would be absolutely miserable in coach. My inner skinflint had caviled a little at the cost of four first-class tickets, but I had the money. I was just reluctant to touch it, especially for such a fleeting experience.

Seeing Kel's tension reminded me of the last time we flew together. "Let me know if there's anything I can do."

"It would help if you distracted me at least until we're in the air."

"What did you have in mind?" I asked.

He shrugged. "Talking works."

"The only thing we have to discuss is how I'm not signing on for your boss's cause. Did you tell him yet?"

"I did," he said quietly. "And he's ordered me to try to change your mind. I have clearance now to discuss your role, if you wish."

If Barachiel truly thought I'd sign on with no information, like a dazzled Joan of Arc, he'd lost touch with humanity.

But I wanted to give Kel a fair shot, so I said, "It's not at the top of my to-do list, but ignoring a problem never made it go away. So go for it."

It was unlikely in the extreme he'd change my mind, for obvious reasons—for the first time, I had a clear picture of what I wanted for my future—but if it would take his mind off his fear of flying, then I'd listen. Unlike most of my breakups, if you could even call it that after one night, this parting had been bittersweet but amicable, and I considered him a friend. Even if he might try to kill me the next time I saw him. Gods, if there wasn't even a small possibility I'd be reunited with Chance, wherever the hell he was? Then I'd let Kel do his job. But ultimately, that would be selfish, and he'd have to carry my death as he did Asherah's.

"Barachiel wants you to rally soldiers to his banner. Your lineage makes you uniquely suited to persuading the people to rise up against demonkind."

Okay, what the hell.

"You mean start a cult or something? The New Church of Solomon?"

Kel reflected visible surprise. "The archangel doesn't call it a cult, of course, but how did you know the name?"

I puffed out a breath. The plane rumbled beneath my feet, as the attendants called out completion of crosscheck. They passed multiple times, begging people to turn off their damned phones. Those things I noticed with half an eye, as I wrestled with the idea of predetermination. Kel set his hand on my forearm, and for a few terrifying seconds I glimpsed a wavering future, where I was polished and coiffed, addressing an enormous gathering of like-minded fanatics. They gazed at me with utter adoration, ready to fight or die, or donate all their worldly goods at my command. A hard shiver rolled through me. I starred in television specials, using my gift to prove that I was, indeed, touched by angels, and that I could carry their words to the masses.

No. A thousand times no.

Shaken, I jerked my arm away from him, cutting the live brain feed. I had no doubt that was exactly what Barachiel had shown Kel. If I signed on, I would have wealth, fame, and power beyond my wildest dreams. Now Ninlil had been evil, no question, but this offer reeked of infernal style, even if it came from an allegedly beatific source, so it made me wonder if maybe the demon queen had a point when she claimed the beings Kel knew as angels had started their lives in Sheol.

And I wasn't even remotely tempted. I'd ruled a city. Power wasn't all it was cracked up to be.

Safe Harbor

I slept most of the ten-hour flight to Houston. A shady past had taught me the ability to snatch rest whenever I could. When I woke, I was leaning on Kel's shoulder. He didn't seem as if he'd moved in all that time. At least he wasn't rigid with fear, as he had been the first time we took a plane together.

"We're landing soon," he said.

Sitting up, I ran a hand through my hair. If I had been thinking, I would've braided it to keep it from turning into a snarled mess. "Did I bother you?"

"Many things do. You're not one of them." There was something in his voice, a nearly imperceptible regret.

Did he wish he could've stayed? Everything would've been different if he had. But then, maybe it would've shaken out so that he died in Sheol instead, if he could even die. I thought he had when we were fighting the warlock in Laredo, so pale and still, but then he came back. The same when they'd killed him in Sheol. I gave him mouth to mouth, revived him. So maybe even if he'd sacrificed himself to open the gate, his body would still come back online. That didn't entirely make sense, however. If it required a sacrifice, it needed to be a permanent one, right? Whatever. The past was past. Dwelling served no purpose.

"Did you sleep at all?" I didn't expect trouble, but it seemed wrong for him to function at less than peak efficiency. In a world like ours, you just never knew.

"Some."

"What's going on? You're even more terse than usual."

"Barachiel contacted me, asking for a progress report. He seemed anxious to learn how you reacted to his master plan."

A chill rippled through me. The plane dipped, hitting a pocket of turbulence that unsettled my stomach to match my mental state. "What did you tell him?"

"That I was showing you the perks of cooperation."

"Did he go for that?"

Kel turned his face away. "I don't think so. From this point, we're living on borrowed time."

Just like Booke.

In my heart, it felt like Armageddon. Kel was a reminder of beauty lost as well as a looming threat. He was the Sword of Damocles. It would kill a sliver of his soul if he ended my life on Barachiel's orders. Hell, it would ruin my week too. Maybe it was wrong to make light of the situation, but I was full up on despair. If I lost humor, then I'd forfeit the ability to move forward.

"Noted. But, Kel . . . if it comes down to it, I won't fight you." There was no point. I'd seen how damned resilient he was. "Just . . . make it quick, all right?"

His words came out terse, clipped. "Stop. You've moved on. Humans do. But for me, this is a cycle repeating, a way for Barachiel to prove he owns me. Again."

"So . . . my life is a power play. I thought he wanted me for the coming war."

"It's a double-edged sword. If you accede, he gets what he wants. And if you don't, he still gets something out of it."

"A reiteration of your forced loyalty and compliance."

"Yes," he said quietly.

"Sounds like we lose, either way."

Before he could reply, the attendant interrupted with final descent announcements. We were to turn off all electronics, stow tray tables, and return seats to an upright position; oddly, the chatter sounded more courteous, delivered in a crisp British accent. While we went about disembarking, I mulled over my predicament. Talk about a rock and a hard place—this was worse than when I was caught between two rival drug lords. This time, my enemy was a powerful supernatural being, who might've started as a demon, but over the long millennia had convinced his followers—and maybe himself too—that he was an angel with divine guidance. In my experience, fanatics were more dangerous than other enemies because they believed so fervently in the cause.

I didn't see how this could end well.

Downcast, I collected my things and followed Shan and Booke off the plane. She steadied him down the aisle to the jet bridge, where an airline worker had a chair waiting for him. This time, Booke didn't protest its use. He collapsed into it gratefully; and I wondered if I was really doing the right thing. But then, this was all his choice. He could've gone to Paris, Milan, anywhere he wanted, and I'd have made it happen. For his own reasons, he had chosen people over places. He wanted to meet Chuch and Eva, so there was no way I'd deny his request. Who could blame him, really? They *were* pretty great.

Shortly after we got off the plane, Kel disappeared; he didn't need documents. When I first encountered him, Chance and I got him arrested, thinking he was a murderer, and Barachiel made him serve part of the prison sentence as a punishment for getting caught by someone like me. When the archangel deemed his mortification complete, Kel came after me . . . but not in retaliation, as

I thought at first. No, he had been serving as my guardian angel for longer than I knew. Which made me wonder . . . was he the reason nothing irredeemable happened to me during those awful months, where I had been between permanent residences? Once, I felt terrible shame with how many men I'd used for room and board, how I'd traded sex for shelter without real hope of a loving relationship. I'd since made peace with the memories, but maybe I should thank Kel because that dark time ended fairly well.

The airline employee accompanied us to immigration, where the officer at the booth was tired and bored; she asked a few rote questions about Booke. Since I was listening, I heard the faint crackle in the machine when she ran our cooked passports; traditionally speaking, magick and technology didn't play nicely together. There had been a small risk that the charm would short out the scanner, but the machine cleared us, and we caught our connection to Laredo without trouble. Kel slid on late, just before they closed the doors.

Booke and I sat together for the short commuter hop. It was a tiny plane, small enough that it freaked me out a little, and I didn't have any particular fear of flying. I wondered how Kel was doing in the row ahead of us. Shannon was talking to him, so that much was good, but I couldn't hear what they were discussing. I turned to Booke, studying his appearance. Maybe it was just wishful thinking, but he seemed to have stabilized around eighty.

"How do you feel?" I asked softly.

"I ache in a way I didn't before you broke the spell. But I'm on a plane, going to meet friends. I count that as a smashing success."

An hour and a bit later, we arrived at the Laredo airport. It was late, nudging toward midnight, but I texted Chuch as he'd instructed. He'd meet us at the curb. As we had no luggage to collect, it was a simple matter to de-

plane and make our way out. Again, we had help, but
Booke seemed resigned to it. While he could walk, he
wasn't speedy, and I knew he was ready to get shed of
airports. He wanted to hang out with friends for his last
days, not spend them trapped in a winged metal tube.

As promised, Chuch was waiting in a restored 1980s
Suburban. It had classic gold paint, trimmed in cream,
and he beeped the horn to make sure we saw him. At this
hour, the pickup lanes weren't too crowded, so I had
room to help Booke into the passenger seat. Chuch
hopped out, then raised both brows at me, inviting the
explanation I'd promised. He was a stocky fireplug, just
starting to get a belly, but he was strong as hell. His features were rugged rather than handsome, but he had the
kindest brown eyes in the world. Eva was lucky to have
him. They had been friends since we ran into them in a
wicker store while they were vacationing in Florida.
Chance stayed in touch after our breakup. I hadn't,
mostly because I was running from all things Chance-
related. Fortunately, Chuch and Eva didn't hold a grudge.

"Shan!" he called. "Jesse's gonna go postal when he
finds out you didn't tell him you're home sooner than
expected."

She flashed him an impish grin. "I want to surprise
him. Do you mind dropping me off at his apartment?"

"No prob. It's on the way. Kinda."

Actually, it wasn't, but Chuch was that kind of guy.
He'd empty his bank account for you, then claim it was
found money he wasn't using anyway. My heart lightened a little. Texas wasn't home, but it was full of people
who cared about me, and that was the next best thing.

Chance should be here. Tears threatened quite sud-
denly, the emotion a sudden and surprising rush. Through
sheer force of will I pushed them down, refusing to tar-
nish the moment. I hugged Chuch tight when he rounded
the truck.

He squeezed back, then stood back to analyze my appearance. "Damn, you're skinny. Tired too, it looks like. Bad shit went down, *prima*?"

"I'll tell you on the way to the house."

"Hecho. Eva can't wait to see you. And just wait 'til you get a load of Cami."

Mention of my goddaughter put a smile on my face. Knowing I had to explain how her godfather died took it away again. Kel and Shan climbed in the back while Chuch shook hands with Booke.

"Not gonna lie, *mano*, you're not how I pictured you."

"A bit of a story, that."

"Save it. Eva will want to hear it too." As he went back to the driver's seat, he waved a hand at me. "That goes for you too, Corine. No point in telling everything twice. She was up with Cami when I left, so I'm sure she'll be awake."

"Can't wait to see them."

The ride was quiet, though Shan's leg bounced with nervous energy. She must be excited to see Jesse, but worried too, maybe. Her boyfriend, Jesse Saldana, was an empath, and a hot one, which meant he wasn't known for constancy, as he found it hard not to respond to people's feelings. So when a woman wanted him, he tended to feel the same. In my opinion, Shannon was brave for taking a chance on him, but that was love, wasn't it? Risking it all in the hope of a happy ending. The alternative was winding up alone.

Fifteen minutes later, we pulled up outside a brick building. I hopped out so Shan could exit, and she hugged me tight. "I will never, ever be able to thank you," she said huskily. "Because of you, so many times over, I have a life to get back to. You saved me in Kilmer. Saved me in Sheol. But before I go to him, promise me we're okay. If you're not, if you have any doubt, then I'll . . ."

Break it off.

I knew what she was about to say, but I didn't let her.

I held up a hand, cutting off the thought. "Be happy, Shan. That's all I want. You're my best friend, and if you love Jesse, don't let him get away."

"I won't. It's crazy . . . because you guys thought I was a kid when we met, but I took one look at him, and well. I never wanted anybody more. I knew it wasn't likely to go anywhere. I figured I'd get over it. Called it a crush."

"But it wasn't," I said softly.

"Don't think so. It's only gotten stronger since we hooked up. You may not agree but that amnesia spell worked out awesome for me."

"It gave you a chance with him without any preconceptions," I agreed.

She ducked her head. "I chased him a bit. He was a little skeeved by the age difference at first, but I convinced him I'm not a child."

No need to ask what tactics she'd used to persuade him. Desire was a powerful aphrodisiac for Jesse Saldana, which made his constancy an issue down the line. Not my worry, fortunately.

"G'night, Shan. He's waiting."

She bounced on her heels in anticipation of the coming reunion, then went toward the building at a full run. I watched for a few seconds, smiling, imagining how Jesse would react to seeing her. And I felt not an iota of envy. Though I'd been drawn to him as I would be any attractive, personable male, we'd never had magic together. For a time, I wanted to be with him because it would be simple — and he could give me a normal life. But I feared I wasn't destined for one.

Hell, if Barachiel had his way, I wouldn't live much longer.

As I climbed back in and shut the door, Chuch asked, "All set?"

"Yep."

"Have you seen the new house?" he asked, casting a glance over his shoulder.

I shook my head. "You were staying with relatives, rebuilding, when Chance and I went back to Mexico."

"It's pretty sweet. The insurance paid off good, so we built a bigger house. I got cousins who are contractors and they cut us a deal on the labor."

That made me smile; it was kind of a running joke that Chuch had cousins for every purpose under the sun. *Need a car? Chuch has a cousin who sells them. Want somebody whacked? No problem. He's got a* primo *for that too.*

I suppressed a pang of guilt that I was the reason they lost their first house. The Montoya cartel went after them, firebombing the place in retaliation for the shit-storm I stirred up. Only the fact that they weren't hurt let me live with myself; the Ortizes didn't blame me, but *I* did. My friends, one of whom had been pregnant, became targets because of me. It was a hard thing to carry on my conscience.

"Does this mean you have room for all of us?"

"Four bedrooms," he said proudly. "Plus an office."

Which he mostly used to surf the Net. "And what's your setup outside?"

"I got a proper work space now. Four bays."

That meant a huge garage, I felt pretty sure. "Can't wait to see it."

"The Mustang still okay?"

"Yeah," I said, hoping I wasn't lying.

We had left it parked outside Chance's apartment. If he'd paid far enough in advance, then the car should be fine in the gated lot. Mexico's weather was mild enough that vehicles could sit without the battery going dead, unlike colder climes. I made a mental note to call the landlord, whose number should be in the history of my phone. Hopefully all Chance's stuff was intact. It was imperative he had everything to return to, just as he left it. Shan would call my current state of mind impressive denial.

I preferred to dub it determination.

Twenty more minutes in the car. The frantic travel was almost through. I'd kept my promise to Booke. He would be surrounded by friends, enjoy one last hurrah. I leaned forward, head against the passenger seat; I wasn't buckled in. In the past days, sometimes everything had felt like it was too much. Between Booke and Chance, the combined weight would break me.

To my surprise, a warm palm settled in the small of my back, rubbing in comforting circles. Kel cared about me. He knew we had no future, but it didn't stop the feelings. Misery overwhelmed me, and this time, the tears came. I hadn't cried since Shan and I landed in London from Sheol.

Kel pulled me to him, his big hands gentle, but he didn't try to staunch my grief. I spent most of the ride huffing quietly into his chest. Chuch and Booke didn't ask what was wrong, Booke because he knew already, and Chuch because he realized I'd tell him soon enough. God, I was dying to see Eva. I was tired of being surrounded by men. Shannon had comforted me as best she could, but she was burdened with her own guilt—at surviving where Chance had not—and at taking Jesse from me. The latter didn't matter as much, but I couldn't disregard Chance's sacrifice; that wasn't a debt I could wave away. We were still best friends, but there was a barrier between us now, partly my sorrow and her sense of culpability.

The new house was gorgeous. Built on stately lines, it still maintained a lovely Southwestern feel with the stucco and judicious use of mosaic tiles. The entry was done in terracotta and cream, warm without being busy. Chuch's personality shone in the various frogs displayed at prominent positions in the front room; he'd lost his entire collection in the fire, but he had been busy replacing them. I remembered him telling me frogs were good luck, and that was why he liked them.

Maybe that's my problem. Lack of frogs.

Eva came running down the hall, already slim again. This woman was incredibly beautiful with golden skin, shining black hair, and darkly liquid eyes. She greeted me with a huge hug, which I returned with a touch of desperation. We exchanged greetings, and then she hugged Booke too. Unlike Chuch, she didn't react to his age or his frail appearance. Kel got a friendly wave, not that I blamed her. He was rather imposing, not the sort of male you touched without an invitation. I could hardly believe I'd slept with him, in fact, or that he'd chosen to console me.

"Are you hungry?" she asked. "I have tamales in the fridge. It will only take a minute to heat them."

"Please." My stomach felt fine at the moment.

"Is Cami asleep?" Chuch wanted to know.

"Just got her down. She'll meet everyone in the morning." Eva got busy in the kitchen, dishing up green sauce and cream to go with the tamales.

I sat down on a pretty stool near the bar. "Thank you for this. You'll never know what it means to have somebody who's just always here for me, no questions asked."

"Oh, there *will* be questions," she said, aiming a wooden spoon at me. "Believe that. But food first. Then we'll talk."

Truth & Consequences

I actually told the story over our late supper, with Booke filling in where I faltered. It was a little awkward repeating his story, but by the time they had the gist, Chuch and Eva were exchanging significant glances. Then she drew me aside.

"You brought him here to *die*?"

"What else could I do?" I asked. "It was his last request."

"I don't know . . . fix it. Isn't that kind of your thing? Finding solutions when anybody else would give it up as a lost cause?"

I closed my eyes. "I don't have the fight in me anymore, Eva. Chance died. Do you get that? I just can't throw myself at monsters anymore. If"—here, my voice broke, and tears threatened—"he's really gone, then I can't make his sacrifice worth nothing. I have to live for him. He made me *promise*."

"Oh, *nena*, I'm sorry." She pulled me to her in a tight hug, and I worked not to lose it on her shoulder. After a minute, I tapped her arm to let her know I had it under control, then she stepped back.

"Don't blame Corine," Booke said then. "My hearing

is perfectly adequate. It's my joints that seem to be seizing up."

"We should all get some sleep," Chuch put in. "We won't solve this in the middle of the night."

From his expression, he still hadn't given up on the idea of saving our mutual friend . . . and that was fine with me. If Chuch could fix it, fine. Let one of his hundred cousins sort out the problem. I just . . . I couldn't. My tank was empty; I had nothing left to give.

Eva settled Booke and I in the two guest bedrooms; Kel volunteered to sleep on the couch. I couldn't think anymore about Booke's problems, or what Kel's archangel wanted from me, or what would come to pass if I held firm in my refusal. Grim, muddled thoughts occupied my mind as I brushed my teeth. Given my general misery, I expected to toss and turn, but exhaustion claimed me as soon as I hit the bed.

Overhead, the sun shone like molten gold, beaming down on a verdant field dotted with yellow flowers. Jonquils, I thought, though I lacked my mother's affinity for such things. In the distance, a smooth gray lake lapped up against a rocky shore, and across the span of the water, a trio of mountains rose in stately majesty. Pale mist wreathed their peaks, cloaking the tops from view. I spun in a slow circle, wondering where I was, but the landscape gave no clue. I had no memory of leaving the bed, no clue how I'd gotten here, but the grass felt real and crisp beneath my bare feet, lightly damp with morning dew. Despite the sweetness of the honeyed air, I had to be asleep; Booke had no reason to contact me this way anymore. Nor did I feel the familiar tingle of a lucid dream. Which meant this hyper-vivid dream was something else.

Movement through the yellow flowers caught my eye. Perhaps I should've been afraid, but I stepped forward with more curiosity than I'd felt since returning to the real world. My pace quickened until I was running, and then I saw him.

Chance.

Here, he was whole and uninjured, as he had been before the dagger, before the blood. Before he died for me. Clad in white, his black hair gleamed with a hint of blue beneath the sunlight, and his tawny skin contrasted beautifully with the loose white clothing he wore. His smile widened as he drew closer; I realized belatedly that I was wearing a T-shirt and panties, exactly what I'd had on when I fell asleep. No wonder he looked so amused.

"This isn't real," I said, expecting disbelief to pop the dream like a soap bubble.

"I've learned a great deal," he answered. "So I will simply say that reality is subjective."

It was so hard to look at him, knowing when I woke he would still be gone. I'd still be alone. We'd finally made the pieces fit in Sheol, and then I *lost* him. The hurt went through me like a barbed blade, leaving bloody rents in my heart all over again. I didn't know if I could bear waking.

"It's good to see that my subconscious manifestation of you knows enough to be annoying," I muttered.

"How can I prove to you it's me?"

"Anything you know about me, I know too."

He huffed out a sigh. "We don't have time to argue about whether I'm here or not, love. It's costing a lot for me to reach you, and there are things you need to know. Will you listen, please?"

"Fine." I couldn't resist going to him. At this point, I didn't care if he was a hallucination generated by loneliness, regret, and desire.

His arms felt deliciously real around me; he smelled of fresh green grass and sheets warmed by sunshine. And when he kissed me, it was heaven. Chance tasted of wild berries and lemon, a thirst quenched by the play of his lips on mine, the luxuriant sweep of tongues hot as a summer day. Desire cascaded through me, raw and painful, an onslaught that ended with my fingers tangled in his hair, my body flat against his. Chance tightened his arms, a low growl escaping him. He pressed me tighter, tighter, until I could hardly breathe. Then I saw the struggle in his face as he set me away.

"If we don't stop that, I'll just kiss you until the power goes out." Chance took a fortifying breath, making me wonder about the rules where he existed. "I'm working on a way back to you, but once you shuffle off the mortal coil, well, they don't mean for anyone to make a return trip."

"You weren't wholly mortal, though." I gazed up at him, then traced his cheekbones with my fingertips, wanting to memorize his features.

If nothing else, I'll have this moment, this dream.

The last time I'd seen him, he had been pale and still, face spattered with blood. *Let me remember him like this. Let me believe he went somewhere good.* Maybe that was the point of the dream . . . to offer comfort. Humans had all kinds of self-defense mechanisms that made it possible for us to survive the unthinkable.

He nodded. "That's the only reason I have a small shot. It's been interesting getting to know my dad." Chance hesitated and shook his head. "He's . . . not the usual father figure. I'm trying to cut a deal, but he seems resistant to letting me go."

That revelation gave me pause. Could he *really* be contacting me from the other side? Stranger things had happened. I mean, if he could broadcast on Shan's radio . . . hope stirred in a delicate shiver, like a dappled fawn.

"Tell me something only you and Min would know," I demanded.

His gaze sharpened with appreciation. "And you'll call her to confirm? I appreciate that, love. It will mean a lot to her to find out for sure that I'm not just gone. She's a mess right now, wondering." He said it with authority, as if he knew.

"Me too," I admitted, low.

"I'm aware. But did you have to cry all over the Nephilim?" His lovely mouth firmed into an irritated line.

"You can check up on me?" Oddly, that made me feel simultaneously better and worse.

"Not easily." Which was a yes.

"I'm sorry if you were bothered by Kel comforting me." Such a weird thing to say to your dead boyfriend.

Chance acknowledged that with a grimace, tightening his arms about me. "He still wants you. And if he makes a move, I'll find a way to kill that son of bitch."

"What he wants and what I do are two different things."

"Oh?" His eyes revealed a hint of vulnerability . . . and surely imaginary people didn't suffer from crises of confidence.

"I made up my mind before we went to Sheol, Chance. I wanted us to be together, always. I *still* want that." If only it didn't sound so crazy and impossible.

"I'll find a way, I promise. Don't give up. And try not to cry so much. It makes you fragile and irresistible."

I laughed. "Bullshit. It makes me snotty and swollen."

He dropped a kiss onto my upturned mouth. "So . . . something only Min and I would know. Ask her if my first-grade lunchbox had Archie and Jughead on it. She got it at a thrift store for a buck fifty as I recall. The thermos was cracked. We patched it with duct tape."

There was no way I knew that on any level. Chance rarely talked about his childhood. I could be inventing shit, but a phone call in the morning would verify whether I'd been with him or lost in my own crate of crazy. Gods, I hoped it was the former. After so much darkness, I desperately needed a ray of light.

"I'll ask her," I said softly.

"Good. I'm about to lose connection, so this is the important thing. I'm looking for a way to part the veil on my side, but I don't have the power to crack it all the way open. So I need you working on it too. Find a spell, an artifact, something. There are books with information on Ebisu's realm . . . some will be accurate. And that's—"

His voice faded, and his wonderful, so-tangible presence flickered. Touch went first, then sight. Soon, I could only smell him all around me, and then that dissipated too. I wanted a good-bye kiss desperately, but I was by myself in a field of yellow flowers, the sweet wind rippling over their petals. When I woke, I was alone in bed, and my pillow was damp with tears.

Checking my phone told me I had been asleep for four hours or so. Far too early to get up or call Min. There would be no more rest for me that night, however, so I got dressed and took Butch out for a walk around the property. The dog didn't seem to mind the nocturnal meanderings. A shiver ran through me as I recalled being attacked by shades on this very spot. At night, the Texas sky was huge and heavy with stars. It was chilly enough that I hunched deeper into my sweatshirt, watching the Chihuahua dance around some bushes.

When I turned, I stifled a scream because a man stood behind me. I stumbled back a couple steps as Butch lunged between us, his teeth bared. He rumbled out a warning growl, deceptively fierce for his size. In the moonlight, the stranger's features were divinely beautiful, capped with a shock of silver hair, but his eyes burned like black holes, cold and pitiless as the grave. He wore a dark trench coat, his hands tucked into the deep pockets, which should have reassured me.

It didn't.

"Can I help you?"

"You know you can." His words flowed in a silken tenor, playful, but I had never been so terrified in my life.

I had no idea why, but it was all I could do not to cower or piss my pants. "Uhm. I think I'll go in now." Stumbling back a few steps toward the house, I gauged him, wondering how fast he could move.

Other than appearing like a creeper in the dark, he hadn't actually done anything threatening, hadn't said anything scary. *So what the hell . . . ?*

"You find my aura alarming," he observed. "If you would comply with Kelethiel's request, it will cease to affect you."

Oh. Shit.

"Barachiel," I guessed.

"Clever monkey."

Blerg. Distaste for the condescension in his tone permitted me to force down some of the abject terror. In response, I picked Butch up and cradled him in one arm; the dog *did not* stand down. Without my intervention he would've chewed the archangel's ankles and pissed on his designer shoes. Barachiel seemed amused by the move, contemptuous of my pet and me.

"I'm still listening to the benefits." So far as I knew, Kel was still stalling him. "I don't make rash decisions."

"I thought it might help if you got to know me." He gazed into my eyes, apparently trying to hypnotize me.

Which might've worked if Butch hadn't been biting my forearm. *Good dog.*

"I'm willing to listen if you want to state your case." *Anything to get rid of you. This is. Not. Good.*

The only way this could be worse was if I was in my panties, like I had been when I saw Chance. I so wasn't prepared to fight an archangel or an ancient former demon—whatever the hell he was—tonight. Maybe I never would be, but it would be the apex of suckage if I got killed as Chance managed to find his way back to me. I wasn't on board with such a Romeo and Juliet ending. No damn way.

So bullshit would form my defense matrix; fortunately, I was strong in the ways of BS-fu.

"I can taste the darkness on you, even now," he whispered. "Whorls of smoke and brimstone. But it's fading. You chose the bright path. You cut the demon out. I need someone at my side, one strong enough to resist temptation. Together, we can reshape the world. No more war. No more poverty."

On the surface, it sounded great, but I remembered the vision Kel had shown me. The people who gazed up at me seemed brainwashed. Maybe the world was a shit-hole, but at least it was full of people who could call their minds their own. I didn't want to create some totalitarian regime where this creepy fucker controlled our actions and opinions. The idea of being used in that fashion made me want to barf.

"I'm unclear on what you're offering," I said softly, buying time. "I thought I'd be some kind of a religious leader. But it seems like you're inviting me to take a different role."

Before he could reply, footsteps crunched over the gravel, heavy ones. They thumped over to the lawn, coming toward us. Kel was the only person big enough to make those strides. Relief surged through me; surely he could get rid of his boss.

"What're you doing here?" Kel demanded.

"Checking up on you, Nephilim. It is my right."

"If you frighten her away, then this failure is on you," Kel said coldly.

His tats glowed with threatening power, and for a horrified moment, I wondered if they would duke it out on Chuch's lawn. I held up a hand, almost too scared to speak, but somehow I got the words out.

"Please . . . take it down the road. Find an empty field. The winner can come find me. Just . . . don't hurt my friends. Don't hurt the baby."

"There's no need for violence," Barachiel said silkily. "I always win. Isn't that right, half-breed?"

The archangel raised his arm, and Kel's body stretched taut, as if pulled on a torture rack. Then Barachiel slammed his palm downward; Kel's knees buckled, dropping him into a humble, penitent posture. I'd never imagined a force strong enough to control Kel, but Barachiel's power was undeniable. And terrible.

Kel mumbled something.

"I couldn't hear you."

"Yes, my lord."

For interminable moments, I stood holding my dog while Barachiel forced Kel to demonstrate his utter helplessness. But I didn't take the message from it he intended. Instead of seeing his potency, I saw my own death. Because now I knew for sure: Kel wouldn't be able to stop his hands from tightening on my throat or running me through with a holy blade. Though he'd hate it, as with Asherah, he was helpless before Barachiel.

"I think that is an ample demonstration." The archangel turned to me, his teeth alarmingly white in the dark. "You will find I am gentle and tender to those who please me."

I heard the unspoken message as well. *I am brutal and merciless to those who do not.* Barachiel vanished as he had come, leaving Kel to stagger to his feet. I despised seeing him so reduced; it was obvious from his expression that he felt the deepest, most piercing shame. This night he had been stripped of his pride before me, left to grovel in the dirt at Barachiel's whim. Maybe I was supposed to be impressed.

I wasn't.

"I wish I could die," he said hoarsely. "See an end to this at last. But even that, he will not allow."

"What's his hold on you? How can he—"

"If I knew, do you think I wouldn't sever the cord? Once, I believed his power must come from divine right. What else could it be? But now . . ." He trailed off, shaking his head. "I have no convictions. I am weary and alone."

Part of me ached to hold him. But his problems were too big for me, and a hug wouldn't do more than remind him things between us could never go further than that one night. In so many ways, he *was* alone. Maybe I could make it a little better, though. In some small way.

"That was awful," I said. "But you *saved* me. I was about to wet my pants before you distracted him."

That roused a reluctant smile. "Shameful cowardice."

"You didn't tell me he has that . . . death aura or whatever. It's like he radiates *I'm going to kill you and eat your liver* in gaseous form."

Butch yapped his agreement. I owed the dog too for refusing to back down, though one of these days the little goofball might get himself killed.

I went on, "So thanks. You're not assigned to protect me anymore. You could've gotten worse for interfering."

"That was nothing."

Sadly, I believed him. "Come on. I'll make you some breakfast."

His micro-expression reflected bemusement in the subtle quirk of his mouth. "I thought you never cooked."

"I can make eggs. And quesadillas. Which do you want?"

Kel looked a little less tormented already. It was good to know small pleasures like food could cheer up even a powerful Nephilim. "Can I have both?"

After the night we'd both had . . . "Why the hell not?"

I Know a Guy

I felt a little weird about rummaging in Eva's kitchen, but I was quiet, and Kel was hungry. By the time dawn lightened the sky, I had a pile of quesadillas on the table, along with a huge crock of scrambled eggs. I made them *a la Mexicana* with diced onion, tomato, and hot peppers. In her fridge, I found some leftover green sauce and I set that out too. To my relief, my stomach seemed fine, and the smell of the food didn't bother me.

Must've been a bug.

The others joined us, rubbing sandy eyes. Booke shuffled out last; I was relieved to see him. Part of me had feared he would pass away overnight before he got the party we'd promised. Eva had Cami balanced on one hip. The baby was wide-eyed and alert, and absolutely gorgeous. In the months I'd been away, her tiny face had rounded out. No longer was she a red-faced, wizened little gnome. No, now she was a doe-eyed, long-lashed cherub . . . and if she resembled her mother, she would break all the boys' hearts someday.

"Is she on table food yet?" I asked.

"She can gum a quesadilla. I already fed her, though."

Yeah, I hadn't wanted to say anything, but Eva's

boobs *did* look different. Ah, the joys of breast-feeding. The guys sat down and dug in without waiting for an invitation, even Booke. After so many years of his own cooking, it must be nice to eat something somebody else fixed, even if that person was me. Unlike my first foster mother, my kitchen prowess was limited; she'd tried to teach me, but I was too grief-stricken to do more than blindly assist.

"So I been thinking," Chuch said, piling his plate high with scrambled eggs.

I joined him, serving myself more modestly. "Oh?"

"One of my cousins is dating a witch. She might know some way to help Booke." He glanced over with an imploring air. "What could it hurt, *mano*? Nothing ventured and all that."

I already knew there was a way to help him, but Booke had vetoed the idea. So I waited to hear how he would respond.

The Englishman laid down his fork in a very precise gesture, his lined face calm but curious. "Does it mean so much to you, old friend?"

"*Sí, claro.* There's no way I can just let this shit happen."

"Then contact your cousin. Just be aware that I will not consent to any use of demon magick. If I'm to be saved, I won't invite more darkness into my soul."

I guessed if I was knocking at death's door like Booke, I'd care about my immortal spirit too. Chuch nodded, his expression brightening. As he went back to eating, he answered, "I'll get on it right after breakfast."

"I love the new place," I said to Eva. "It's beautiful."

"It only took a firebomb to get him to remodel."

I winced. "Yeah, about that—"

"Don't even," she told me. "You can't be held responsible for what crazy people do. And from what I hear, that *hijo de puta* Montoya got his."

"They both did," I said, remembering how Dumah had devoured them.

Eva grinned. "And I got a sweet new house. It worked out."

Chuch and Booke carried the conversation, talking about things unfamiliar to me. They had been friends the longest, after all. It stood to reason Chuch would take Booke's impending demise personally. He wasn't the kind of guy who stood by and let things happen either. Deep down I hoped he could find a solution. Between crazy dreams of Chance and midnight visits from terrifying supernatural beings, I had enough on my plate.

But that reminded me that I had a phone call to make. With a murmured excuse, I got my cell and went to the guest room. My hands trembled as I dialed Min's number; she might well think I was nuts to interrupt her grief with such a ridiculous question. Yet I couldn't resist the need to know if I was crazy or if I'd really seen Chance last night.

She picked up on the fourth ring. "Yi Min-chin, Magical Remedies. How can I help you?"

So the shop was open today. Life went on. I don't know why it surprised me. I mean, it had been weeks since I called her that first time, and there had been no body to bury, no arrangements to make. Work probably kept her sane.

But I was quiet a beat too long.

"Who's there?" she said.

"It's Corine." I forced the words out of a tight throat, hating what I was about to ask. "This may seem strange, but this is important. Chance said to ask you about his first-grade lunchbox."

"It had Archie and Jughead on it," she replied at once. "He hated it because it was a little rusty and so 'uncool.'" I could *hear* her quoting him. "The thermos was broken at the bottom, but I held it together with duct tape. Chance had a lot of shame that year, but I told him it would be worse if he ended up in the free lunch program."

Given his tremendous pride, I could only agree. "Then I have something crucial to tell you."

"He's not gone," she whispered. "I hoped and I tried to trust Ebisu, but it has been *so* difficult."

"Wait, did you *know* something?" I hadn't realized Min had been aware that her romance in Japan, which resulted in Chance, had transpired with a small god.

"Not at first. But when he went away, he told me everything. That our son would face great trials, and that ultimately, he would rise."

Whatever that meant.

"Not too specific."

"The spirits tend not to be." She went on, "You have no idea how this sets my mind at ease, Corine. Did you . . . hear from him?"

"I had a really vivid dream. I didn't believe it could be real, but—"

"You had to be sure."

I nodded, then realized she couldn't see it. "He said to tell you not to worry. That he'll find a way back."

"If anyone can, he will," she said with quiet assurance.

And madly, I believed her. The world had lost its luster without him. I'd managed to leave him once, but that was different; I'd known he was still out there somewhere, being Chance, doing Chance things. That made all the difference—this was stark, awful, and unbearable.

"He said he needs my help to pull it off," I told her, making a sudden decision. "And he has it. I won't stop until he's back. I can't. I love him so much."

"I know you do. You always did."

"I'll keep you posted. I have things percolating."

"Thank you, *ddal.*"

My heart twisted. Toward the end of my first relationship with Chance, Min had started calling me that, which meant "daughter" in Korean. I'd never dared to call her *Omma*, as Chance did, but this moment called for a leap of faith, a promise that we'd one day be mother and daughter, as she had expected.

"You're welcome, Omma. I'll call you soon."

As she rang off, I heard her sniffle. Hopefully it was a happy sort of crying. God knew I had done enough of that in the last few weeks. But if there was even a small possibility of a happy ending, I'd move heaven and earth for it.

Before I rejoined the others, I had one more task to complete; I scrolled through my call directory to find Chance's landlord. When he picked up, I greeted him in Spanish. "Good morning, sir. This is Corine Solomon, Chance Yi's girlfriend. I was calling to find out the status of his rent. He's . . . traveling right now, and I wondered when his rent will be due."

Señor Gomez made some noise, rummaging through his files, and then he came back on the line. "He paid in advance, so it won't be due for another month and a half. Thanks for letting me know he's not home. I'll have the guard look in on the place now and then."

"I appreciate it . . . and so does Chance." Or he would, I reasoned, if he wasn't busy trying to crack a door between the planes. "Thanks for your time, sir."

"No problem. Have a good day."

Well, at least that much went right. He'll have a home to come back to.

Feeling bolstered, I went back into the kitchen, where everyone was wrapping up their breakfast. To my surprise, Cami reached for me. I'd held her more than once before leaving for Mexico with Chance, but she didn't *know* me in the sense that most babies required before permitting cuddles.

Eva shot her daughter a bemused look. "I guess she likes you."

"The little mite has good taste," Booke said.

From any other male, I'd have taken the remark as flirtation, but he was just being courtly. In person, he had the manners of a different era, which I found fascinating, as I'd always interacted with him as if he were my age or thereabouts. I probably wouldn't have spoken as freely as I had in our shared dreams if I'd known I ought to be treating him with the respect due an elder.

I took the baby and propped her on my hip, as I'd seen Eva do. It didn't seem as awkward as it looked, particularly when Cami curled into me. She gazed up at me with impossibly big, dark eyes—and then she pulled my hair. *Aha.* So it was the braid she wanted; I moved it so she could tug to her heart's content. I might be bald by the time she finished but it was a small price to pay for a happy infant.

"You shouldn't let her do that," Eva scolded.

"Eh. Better my hair than my earrings. Did Chuch call his cousin?"

"Yep. Ramon is bringing Caridad over this afternoon to see if she can do anything for Booke."

When I glanced over at the man in question, I noticed how bright his eyes were. He flattened his hands on the table, gnarled now, as they hadn't been when Shan and I first entered his cottage a few days before. The knuckles were thick and swollen and I imagined it must be painful to hold a fork. If there was a spell that could reverse the ravages of aging, I didn't know about it, other than the ritual Kel had mentioned, which involved Luren blood.

Out of the question.

But people had been looking for the Fountain of Youth for centuries. Maybe somebody had found it. If it was as simple as ordering a potion off the Internet, I would be forever grateful. But I imagined that wasn't the case. Like Chuch, however, I understood refusing to give up; that was what I was doing with Chance, after all.

Cami gave my plait a painful tug. "Yeouch. What?" The baby offered me a stern look, as if I should know what she wanted. "Sorry, kid. I can't read minds."

Then I smelled it and gave her back to Eva. "I'll handle that when I have my own, not a minute sooner."

"Is that in the cards?" she asked over her shoulder, heading for Cami's room.

"Maybe," I murmured. "Someday."

Chuch and Booke occupied the day with a chess match, somewhat less than thrilling for the rest of us. I could tell Chuch was spending as much time as he could with his old friend, putting off the restoration work in his four-bay garage, just in case the worst came to pass. Kel disappeared, probably to take a nap. He was still sleeping off the energy he'd burned in breaking the curse that held Booke captive.

It occurred to me . . . if magick could hold Booke hostage so many years, was it possible with Kel? Maybe he *did* have free will; he just didn't realize it. If he'd been ensorcelled with obedience binding from birth, it would permit Barachiel to pretend the Nephilim were born to serve. But how would I discover the truth? There was no way to resolve the matter, so I focused on the pressing problem.

Booke. I hoped Chuch's cousin Ramon was a good lover; otherwise, with the favor we were requesting, it would take a year on the installment plan to pay for services rendered.

I'd find out when she arrived.

Ramon and Caridad were punctual, arriving at 3:00 p.m. on the dot. She was a tall, slender woman with a mass of streaked dark hair. Her highlights were done in purple and silver, lending her a dramatic, witchy look. Likewise, her style suggested her profession, as she wore a long black dress that swirled around her legs in layers of lace. Chunky silver jewelry completed the ensemble. All told, she was attractive, but she didn't look like a comfortable woman to be around. *High-maintenance,* I decided.

Ramon, on the other hand, resembled Chuch, though he was a little taller and had a slightly smaller waist. He radiated the same humor and goodwill, however. He greeted me with a kiss on the cheek and a hearty hug. I thought we'd met on several occasions, but at the mo-

ment, my head was a little foggy. So I just hugged him
back, which put a smile on his face.

"This is my girl, Caridad," he said, by way of introduc-
tion. Ramon named the rest of us for the witch's benefit,
I suspected.

"*Mucho gusto*," she said, extending her hand as if she
expected me to kiss it.

I contented myself with a polite shake, and the others
followed suit. Eva's mouth held a slight pucker, not as if
she wanted to kiss Caridad, but more like the *bruja* was a
sour taste she couldn't wash away. As hostess, she led the
way into the living room, comfortably appointed with
two couches and a love seat. I adored the angled ceilings
and the long, arched windows letting in the afternoon
light. I took a seat in the single armchair, running a hand
nervously over the pretty striped damask. It was smooth
and silken to the touch, and I wondered how this furniture would stand up to baby Cami in a few years. Still, it
was a lovely room, bright and elegant.

Once we had settled, she folded her hands in her lap,
assuming a businesslike demeanor. "Ramon tells me you
wish to hire me. Ordinarily, you understand, you would
need to make an appointment."

"Thank you for making an exception," Booke said.
"It's very kind of you, as you must see I haven't much
time."

Her brow furrowed; and for the first time, she set
aside her air of consequence. Visibly troubled, she leaned
forward. Her eyes slipped to half-mast, which I recognized as a hint of someone using witch sight rather than
normal vision. She scanned Booke top to bottom, several
times, then sat back in her chair, gnawing on her lower
lip.

"I've never seen a *maldición* like this. *Madre de Dios*,
it's strong."

"Can you fix it?" Chuch asked.

My heart fell when she shook her head. "Twila is the

only person in the entire state who could handle something like this."

The question was, could we afford her? Chance had given her something in exchange for her services, and he'd never explained to me how that went down. She always asked for something precious in payment—and I wasn't sure I was qualified to strike a deal with her, but with both Booke and Chuch staring at me, I made a quick decision.

"Fine. If you lend me a car, I'll take Booke to San Antonio."

"If this doesn't work," the older man said softly, "then we call it done, yeah? I won't have my last days ruined in a series of wild-goose chases. I wish to enjoy my freedom, such as it is."

"Be back in time for the party tomorrow," Eva reminded me.

"We will, no worries."

Chuch was muttering, "What do I got that's road-ready? Come with me, *prima*. I have a couple of options for you."

"I'm sorry I couldn't help," Caridad told Booke. "But it would've cost a great deal, if I *had* been able to."

Ramon cocked his head. "But I told you, he's like family to Chuch, *amor*. That means he's kin to me too."

Her dark eyes hardened, and she gave her hair a haughty toss. "I don't *give* my talents away. Doesn't matter who the client is."

I hurried out to the garage before I could get tangled in the argument, where I found Chuch studying two cars. One was an old Charger, and the other said it was a Maverick. Either looked okay, but the Maverick seemed more finished. The Charger still had some problems in the paint, not that cosmetic issues mattered. Finally Chuch handed me the Charger keys.

"This one's better under the hood. I want you two to get there safe."

"Thanks, *papi*," I said with just a hint of sarcasm.

"Hey, somebody's gotta look out for you."

I softened. "I know . . . and thank you. I'm glad you and Eva are all right."

"Better than ever. I never wanted to be a dad before I met Eva, but . . ." He paused, rough face charming with the goofy love he had for his wife and daughter.

"You're one of the good ones," I agreed.

He didn't ask if I meant husband or father. Clearly, it was both. And when Cami came of age, she would get the coolest, safest car ever. I envied her a little, all those father-daughter moments I had missed. It wasn't enough knowing my dad saved my life; I wished he could've shared it too.

But at least we got to say good-bye.

"I think Shannon's planning to bring Jesse over for dinner. I heard Eva talking to her on the phone earlier."

"Tell her where I went, then. And why."

"Will do." Chuch favored me with another squeeze; then he went to tell Booke we were rolling.

I climbed into the driver's seat, familiarizing myself with the setup. Good thing the car was automatic. Though I'd driven stick, I wasn't expert, and I tended to grind the gears. Chuch wouldn't thank me for burning out the clutch on a vehicle he was trying to restore to classic status and then sell at an awesome markup. Collectors paid a pretty penny for a muscle car in cherry condition.

A few minutes later, Kel helped Booke out to the car. The Englishman moved at a shuffling pace, and his balance wasn't the best. Seeing him so hurt me. In my mind's eye he was the calm, competent scholar. Not old. Not feeble. I'd imagined him as ageless, an immortal guardian of all knowledge, arcane and otherwise. This felt like learning that Athena, the goddess of wisdom, wore false teeth.

"Shotgun," Booke said, as if I'd make him ride in the back.

Then I realized Kel meant to accompany us. Well, he did have to keep up appearances. If the archangel spied on him again, it wouldn't do for him to be caught chilling in Laredo while I took a road trip to San Antone. Even an overconfident tool like Barachiel might realize he was being played, then.

So in response, I pulled up the passenger seat to let Kel climb in. "Sorry it's a little tight."

"I've had worse," he said.

Of course, he claimed that about a lot of things. It hurt a little, knowing I couldn't make it better, but I'd made my choice.

So I just nodded. "Then let's rock and roll, boys."

Bitter Bargains

Twilight hadn't changed since the last time I was there, still housed in a nondescript building with a small, unassuming neon sign marking its existence. The neighborhood was still deceptively downscale, with drunken college students roaming around the seedier clubs in the vicinity. Inside, it was a combo of brothel and roadhouse with velvet and wood accents. Per usual, the jukebox was banging away with a Dropkick Murphys tune; this time it was "Kiss Me, I'm Shitfaced."

Damn, I wish. I wished I had nothing to regret other than going home with a smooth-talking stranger.

Jeannie, a pretty woman in her forties who sported a ponytail, was tending bar tonight. She narrowed her eyes on me, as if she recognized me but couldn't place me. Then a smile split her cheeks. "Corine! It's been a coon's age. Bucky was just asking me about you the other day. What've you been up to?"

"It's a long story," I said.

And one I'd had enough of telling.

I went on, "We need to see Twila, if she can squeeze us in."

Her expression immediately sobered; then her eyes

went to Booke. In his old-fashioned slacks and sweater vest, he stuck out like a sore thumb. "I'll see if she can make time for you. Have a drink on the house." Jeannie waved the assistant 'tender over to take our orders.

"Do you have lager?" Booke asked.

"Keith's Pale Ale work for you?" the man asked.

Booke looked blank. "Why not?"

It took only a few seconds for him to open the bottle. It wasn't every day you saw a man this old out for a night on the town, so his quiet, respectful tone obviously stemmed from Booke's age. "Would you like an iced glass, sir?"

"No, thank you. I'll be Bohemian tonight."

The bartender flashed an appreciative smile at Booke's wit, then he turned to me. "For you, miss?"

"Mix me an Agave Kiss." I felt the need for a happy drink.

As I watched, he expertly combined tequila, white creme de cacao, double cream, and Chambord, then rimmed the glass with white chocolate flakes. For the final touch, he garnished the beautiful creamy cocktail with a skewer of fresh raspberries. I took it, thanked him, and tasted the delightful concoction.

"Mmmm. Fantastic."

Booke was watching with both brows arched. "Drinks have certainly gotten complex, haven't they? Martinis used to be the height of sophistication."

"I don't think this drink is particularly sophisticated," I said, sipping it. "It's more like dessert in a glass. But I could use something sweet."

"You certainly could. I regret dumping my problems in your lap. You have enough to—"

"Don't. If I minded, I'd have declined. I'm not *that* selfless."

"I don't want to be selfish, but I'd give nearly anything to live a bit. See the world. I've glimpsed it through the Internet, but to experience it?" Booke's tone was both desperate and hopeful.

Before I could caution him not to offer such generous terms to Twila, the bartender cut in, "And for your tall, quiet friend?"

I glanced at Kel, who shook his head. "Apparently he's not drinking tonight."

"Designated driver, huh? Tough break, pal."

That made me laugh because I couldn't imagine Kel getting hammered and blowing off steam. He was so rigidly controlled all the time, all but the smallest emotions ruthlessly locked down. Doubtless that restraint made a life of servitude more bearable . . . and my amusement died. *Poor Kel.* I wanted to free him. Well, why not add it to my list of three impossible things to do before going home? It didn't seem any more unattainable than bringing Chance back from Ebisu's realm or saving Booke from the old curse that was killing him.

As I downed more of my drink, Jeannie came out of the back. I remembered the way to Twila's office. The other woman nodded in response to my inquiring look. "She says she'll see you." Her voice lowered. "She said she was *expecting* you."

I wasn't surprised. "Come on, guys. The queen awaits."

That was neither an exaggeration nor sarcasm. If anyone could be said to rule the state of Texas, all the supernatural events and portents, it was Twila, a voodoun priestess of incredible power. She kept tabs on all the witches, warlocks, wizards, and sorcerers, all the gifted parties in her demesne. For the right price, she could be convinced to help as well, but often what she wanted cost such dear coin that only the desperate were willing to pay it. That summed up our circumstances too.

Twila was a tall, dark-skinned woman with beautiful brown eyes, lined in kohl. She wore her hair in a mass of braids, caught together in a golden snood. It should have looked old-fashioned, but on her it was incredibly elegant, as she had an aura of majesty and command. Three rings adorned her slender fingers: one of onyx, one of jade, and the other ivory. I imagined there must be some ritual significance, but that wasn't why we were here.

Her office was a treasure trove of the arcane. On my first visit, I hadn't known much about the magickal world, but through my studies with Tia, I could sense the artifacts. Though I'd lost my ability to cast, I still felt the faint thrum through the soles of my shoes, an infinitesimal hum disparate from the bass thrum in the bar beyond. The whole room radiated power, a good portion of which came from Twila herself.

"Corine," she said in her melodic accent. "It's been a long time."

She sat down at the massive cherry desk and indicated with a gesture that we should avail ourselves of the two leather chairs opposite. Kel shook his head once more, declining a seat. He was visibly uncomfortable in her presence; with him, that meant he wore a faint frown. I helped Booke into a chair before taking my own.

"I guess you're wondering why I'm here."

Her half smile alarmed me. "You're a supplicant. The only question is what you seek."

Straight to the point.

"Booke, will you do the honors?" Since it was his problem, it made sense for him to do the talking.

Which he did, in his plummy English accent. Twila seemed to enjoy his recounting of the tale, probably more than she would've in my drawl. Booke's courtly manner didn't hurt either. Though he was an elderly gentleman, he knew how to charm a lady. She was smiling when he finished, and not the hungry, eager one that made me think of sharks.

"Let me see if I understand correctly. You wish to be free of this curse . . . for me to undo the years you spent confined in Macleish's prison."

"You probably *can't* banish so much time," Booke said humbly. "I'm not asking the impossible. But yes, I'd like to live a little longer, so long as it doesn't involve demon magick."

Twila pushed to her feet in a graceful motion. "The loa have much strength, so I could do this, but I will require a great deal in payment as well. Are you willing to pay my price, Ian Booke?"

"Could do what?" Kel asked, the first time he'd spoken since we entered.

She cut her eyes sharply to Kel. "This is not your affair, fallen one. Twilight may be neutral ground, but you'll start a war if you interfere with my work."

His broad shoulders tightened, as if she'd injured him. He said nothing more. I chewed on the implication in her words. Did that mean Barachiel couldn't touch us in here? I wondered if Twila was powerful enough to defeat him.

Using her desk for balance, Booke pulled himself to his feet, and for the first time I noticed he was her height, though his stooped shoulders made him seem smaller. "Before I answer, I must know what I'm bargaining for."

"I'll spell it out, *monsieur*. I can wipe away those years. You will be thirty-six years old with your life before you. The loa can do this, yes, without demons."

"And your terms?" Booke asked.

"What will you offer me?" Her tone was amused. I felt extraneous, but when I shifted, her look sharpened on me. "Don't run away, Corine Solomon. Your friend requires your support. Will you leave him when he needs you most?"

"Of course not," I muttered.

I didn't necessarily want to learn what Booke would give up to keep from shuffling off to oblivion. Under the weight of her eyes, I kept my seat, but Kel came up behind me. His hands lit on my shoulders, giving me courage. Foreboding rolled through me, like the heaviness in the air before a thunderous storm.

"Give me one year of freedom," Booke said, after a moment's consideration. "A chance to see the world. At the end of those days, I will return to serve you in any capacity you desire for as long as you mandate."

What the hell, no. It was too much, too open-ended. *Such an* awful *contract.* I had to get him better terms. As I opened my mouth to protest, Kel's hands tightened; I glanced over my shoulder to see a forbidding expression in his pale eyes. Then his voice rang in my head. *We must not interfere, dādu. You owe him the honor of forging his own fate.*

Apart from those words, his mind didn't intrude on mine. With a pang, I remembered that *dādu* meant "beloved." *You shouldn't call me that. It's done.*

Your heart may have changed. Mine has not.

I decided not to argue with him. *How are you doing this?*

We have joined, Corine. For the first time, I noticed he wasn't calling me Binder anymore. *The connection lingers, permits such intimate communication.*

Is it because you're touching me?

Clever.

Deliberately, I covered his hand with one of mine, and then I pulled his palms away from me. It hurt a little, knowing he would take it as a rejection, but I couldn't encourage him when he was trapped by Barachiel and might have to kill me, and when I meant to do my damnedest to get Chance back, so we could have the life I'd glimpsed just before we went to Sheol to save Shannon. I didn't want to serve a maniacal archangel or worry that my lover would live ten thousand years without me. I wanted normal. That was all I *ever* craved.

The rest of this bullshit? No more.

Kel stepped back.

And in the moments I had been occupied with Kel, Booke had apparently struck a deal with the priestess. *Dammit. He wasn't kidding when he told me he'd give nearly anything.* His hand clasped hers, sealing the bargain, and then she turned to us. "You two are welcome to wait in the bar. As you know, I prefer that certain transactions take place in private."

Which meant she wouldn't show the loa—or her powers—to anyone but her contracted client. I understood that, even as I worried about Booke. But I had my own business with Twila, first. "I'd like to swear to you."

Twila's elegant brows shot up. For the first time in our acquaintance, I'd surprised her. "Do you mean to move to Texas, then?"

"I'm already living here. I don't know when, if ever, that I'm going back to Mexico. I have so many things to wrap up."

"And you have powerful enemies." The queen of San Antonio smiled, showing lovely white teeth. "You understand the terms?"

"I think so, but I'd appreciate it if you laid them out for clarity."

"In becoming one of my vassals, you pledge yourself to my cause. My enemies become yours, and you offer to fight willingly in my service at any time for any reason. In return, I will do battle on your behalf as well and I guarantee your safety while you remain within my demesne. Should my protection falter for any reason, I will exact a most harrowing revenge upon your foes."

To be honest, I didn't care a whole lot about vengeance. If I died to demons or Barachiel, Twila could cut off all their heads, but it wouldn't change anything. Still, it seemed like a good idea to join her team with the opposition I had lined up.

"It sounds like I get the better of that bargain," I said quietly.

"You say that until I ask you to fight for me. You have not seen how demanding I can be. Do you still wish to swear to my service, handler?"

That was better than Binder. I nodded. "Is there a blood oath or—"

"Put your hand on this and repeat after me." "This" was the bone ring she wore. I rested my hand on hers, fingers on the ivory. My gift stirred, begging to read her secrets, but I locked it down. Curiosity killed the cat, and I wasn't sure I could trust the additional adage "satisfaction brought it back." The touch settled into a burn that came from Twila, not me.

"Kneel," she said softly. My knees obeyed before my brain decided to comply. She cupped her other hand around mine, completing the circle, and then she murmured, "I, Corine Solomon, promise to be faithful in all things required of a vassal, to love whatever the lady cherishes, and hate when she hates."

I repeated the words; and the pain in my fingers grew stronger. Magick kindled between us, solemnizing the vow.

Twila spoke on, "I will go to war on her word and cry peace when she calls for it. I will serve until death, so long as I remain within her demesne."

Those words came harder, but I spoke them too. Then the lady of San Antonio made her own promises. "I accept you as vassal. Your enemies are mine, your life in my hands. I will warrant it to the full extent of my power." She bussed my brow to seal the compact, then she raised me to my feet. "It is done, Corine Solomon. You are now one of my children."

"Thank you," I said.

"Now I must see to your friend. Go."

As I passed Booke, I kissed him on the cheek, hoping we had both made the right decisions. Back in the bar, they had Shania Twain crooning and a few couples were dancing on the crowded floor. Crazy, but this place was the supernatural hangout; if I looked hard, I'd probably find some demons grinding up on the gifted. I just didn't care to peer below the façade of normalcy. I took a seat at the bar, which left Kel to hover or cop a squat beside me. I was a little surprised when he did the customary thing and perched.

"I'm sorry if I intruded," he said quietly.

"I appreciate your advice about Booke. I do tend to be overprotective . . . and I believe it's my job to fix everything. That comes from foster care. You think if you're good enough, if you don't make trouble, if you do more than you're supposed to, then everything will be okay, and they'll let you stay."

I had no idea why I'd told him that. He was the last person who wanted my confidence at this point. But he looked surprisingly intrigued.

"I suppose that is true. The world you grew to maturity in is very different than the one I knew."

I couldn't even imagine. "I know you were born to Uriel and Vashti, but did they raise you? How did that work?"

He shook his head, an old sorrow weighing on him. "Barachiel took me to oversee my upbringing. My birth was a sin. The archangels were forbidden to consort with mortal females. That my father could not resist the temptation was his shame . . . and mine."

An old Bible quote surfaced, probably due to one of the foster parents who had dragged me to Christian church. "'Yet he does not leave the guilty unpunished; he punishes the children and their children for the sin of the parents to the third and fourth generation.'"

Kel nodded. "So it's just as well I cannot reproduce."

"Cannot?" That one night we shared in Peru, I hadn't asked about contraception or STDs. Which was actually kind of irresponsible of me.

"Like many hybrid creatures," he said quietly. "I am sterile. But it is not a bad thing. My children would be cursed as well."

"Provided it's true. That you're Nephilim . . . and not half demon, as the demon queen, Ninlil, believed." I wasn't sure what the rules were on half demons, whether a half demon could reproduce with a human. *Maybe not.* But the Old Testament curse was probably bullshit.

He jerked upright, eyes locked on my face. I realized it was the first time I'd spoken of it to him. "What did you say?"

Uneasily, I gave him her version of history—how there was a war in Sheol and his team lost, thereby being banished to the human world; I finished with my theory about magickal compulsion. Back in Booke's cottage, it had occurred to me that if he could be trapped by a curse, so could Kel. Who was pale as I've ever seen him by the time I stopped talking. His knuckles burned white on the edge of the bar, the wood groaning, bowing inward. I grabbed his hand, trying to calm him down, as Jeannie was giving us the stink-eye.

"I must go," he said dazedly. "I . . . have to think."

"Kel, wait. Don't do anything stupid. Don't confront Barachiel until we have a chance to—" But dammit, I was talking to air.

He must be upset as hell because he poofed right in the middle of the bar, leaving me talking to an empty stool. Even in an establishment like this one, that display of power drew some looks. In twos and threes, they glanced away and went back to talking and dancing, once it became clear there was no brawl brewing.

Jeannie slid me another Agave Kiss. "You look like you could use one. He's an intense drink of water, huh? What is he, a tetchy warlock?"

"I wish I knew," I said.

And so does Kel.

Worry knotted my stomach into badge-worthy tangles. While waiting for Booke, I shut down two guys who tried their luck, both decent looking. Once, I'd have given anything to draw attention like this. Now I just wanted Chance . . . and for my friends to be all right.

Which included Booke and Kel. Maybe this was a bad idea, but I couldn't sit here, not knowing what Twila was doing to my friend. When Jeannie turned to help another customer, I slid off my stool and crept down the corridor that led to her private rooms. Her office door was wide open, which meant she had taken him to the apartment upstairs, where I had once spent the night with Jesse. Shannon didn't know that, but we'd only made out a little, no sex, which was just as well. It could only make things weird. Weirder.

I might end up fried for this, but so be it. The door to the stairwell swung open; no preventative spell exploded as I put my weight on the first step. As I climbed, a sound reached me, like ten souls moaning in harmony, but it wasn't pain, more an inexorable pleasure. When I peered over the top step, the scene hit me in a rush: the dark and shifting spirits writhing around Booke, who was completely naked. Twila governed the moment like the priestess she was, arms upraised to press the loas on. I couldn't tell exactly what they were doing to him, but he didn't seem to mind.

That was when I lost my nerve, and the fear of getting caught outweighed my curiosity. As quietly as I could manage, I slipped back down the stairs. Jeannie cut me a look when I reclaimed my bar stool, but I wasn't talking. I'd never tell a soul what I saw up there. Shaken, I nursed my second Agave Kiss.

An hour later, I almost didn't recognize Booke when he strode out of Twila's office, but the chunky sweater vest and the seventy-year-old slacks gave him away. He looked *exactly* as he always did in my dreams—nut brown hair with a gentle wave, soft gray eyes, lean, acetic face. Despite the indenture that bought him those additional years, I couldn't stifle the happy squeal as I bounded toward him. He caught me in his arms and lifted me, not a romantic gesture, but more of a demonstrative one: *Look how healthy and strong I am.*

Tears leaked out the corners of my eyes, until I didn't know why I was weeping, really. It was so good to see him hale and whole, but I hated the bargain he'd made, as if he'd traded one prison for another. But it was unlikely Twila would chain him to the bar, so however she used him, it would still be better than that damned cottage in Stoke.

"Was it bad?" I whispered, hugging him hard around the neck.

"Dodgy enough," he answered, "and a bit humbling, but she kept her word. No demons. I shouldn't like to meet those loa in a dark alley, however."

"What now? Where will you go?"

"Are you cracked? I'll stay and help you bring our lad back, of course."

I shook my head. "Don't be stupid. You only have a year, Booke. You've got to make the most of it. If you need money—"

"Tosh. I had a bank account in 1947. I've no doubt it's quite healthy by now, though I may have some difficulty obtaining access, or retrieving the funds, if the account was closed due to inactivity." He shrugged. "But I shall fret about that later. I propose a deal then. I'll grant you two weeks. If we haven't solved the problem by then, I'll go about my business. Will you accede to those terms?"

"Sounds good," I managed.

"Where's Kel got to, then?"

"I don't know. But we should get back to relieve Chuch's mind. He's going to be *so happy.*"

Until he finds out the terms of the deal. But I didn't say so aloud.

"Indeed. I'm quite looking forward to the party, as it won't be the depressing farewell I feared. But I do have one request," Booke added.

"Shoot." I was already headed for the door, lifting a hand to Jeannie.

"Let me drive."

What the hell. If Booke wrecked the Charger, he could make it right with Chuch. He had the time, after all, and it appeared he was moving to Texas.

In reply, I tossed him the keys.

Amends

Booke drove like a bat out of hell—or to coin a specific metaphor, a recently released Englishman. He made the trip back at speeds Chance would've envied. I didn't talk, fretting about Chance and Kel by turns. Fortunately Booke was too enthralled with the Charger to notice. He only turned to me if he had questions about the route, and those were few, as he'd been paying attention on the way.

After we arrived at the Ortiz place, he parked in the garage with a flourish and then leaped out on legs that were much stronger than the ones he'd left with. Chuch and Eva hurried out to see the results of our trip. Both froze in the doorway, hovering between delight and disbelief. I understood the reaction; part of me thought it was too good to be true. The aspect that understood how Twila worked worried about how things would turn out for him. He might have a long indenture ahead of him.

Then Eva clapped. "Look at you! It's fantastic."

Booke had the cheek to do a slow spin like a showgirl. It was absurdly charming. "Look at me indeed. I'm fantastic."

"*Si*, no doubt," Chuch said, grinning.

Booke flashed the other man a grin. "I wasn't asking you, mate."

"Are you hitting on my Eva?" The mechanic raised both brows, pretending to bristle. Or maybe, knowing Chuch, it wasn't wholly pretense. In most situations he was pretty easygoing, but when it came to his wife and daughter, he was a rabid dog.

"No. Well, maybe a little. I'm out of practice, I fear." Being a smart man, Booke changed the subject. "This automatic gearbox is rather spectacular, is it not?"

Dismissing the minor flirtation, the stocky mechanic headed over to his old friend to wrap him in a bruising, rib-crushing bear hug. Booke bore the embrace, at first with customary reserve, and then he returned it. They slapped backs for a good minute, and when they broke apart, they were both misty, which caused much throat clearing and them turning away to study random walls in the garage.

Eva and I exchanged amused glances, but she seemed touched too, as well as impressed by the change wrought by our trip to San Antonio. "So Twila solved his problem?"

"Yep. He cut a deal." In a low voice, as we went back into the house to check on Cami, busy with blocks in her playpen, I explained the terms.

She shook her head. "That's terrible. Chuch will hit the roof when he finds out. But servitude's better than dying in a few days . . . or staying stuck in that house."

"If she's clever, she won't make his employment unbearable. Then she will have gained a loyal, resourceful wizard for life."

"He does know more about the arcane arts than anybody I ever met."

I nodded. "After he completes his world tour, I'm sure he'll want to ship his library over for use in any of Twila's special projects."

Eva gave an exaggerated shudder. "I'm scared to think about it."

"Too bad Caridad couldn't help him."

She nodded. "She pointed us in the right direction at least, but Ramon can do better."

"You think it's serious?" I hadn't gotten that vibe from the couple; they weren't like Chuch and Eva, communicating with a look or completing each other's sentences. But others didn't hit that level of synchronicity, even after years together.

"Who knows? Ramon wants to settle down. Trouble is, he keeps hooking up with these difficult women who I can't imagine making good mothers."

Yeah, I didn't see Caridad with babies clinging to her lace skirts either. Without her, however, Booke wouldn't have a second chance. As I'd lost my powers, it required a real witch to judge how powerful the curse was—and to advise us as to who could break it. I didn't think he regretted his deal with Twila; gods willing, he never would.

Shortly thereafter, Eva went into the kitchen to begin cooking. People would arrive late tomorrow afternoon, so she needed to get a head start on party food. Booke came into the kitchen in an easy, loping stride. He was at least two inches taller, lean as a blade, and bristling with nervous energy. His gray gaze sought and found me by the patio doors, where I had been gazing out into the backyard, where Chuch intended to build a play area for Cami but hadn't gotten around to it yet.

"I'd forgotten how good I could feel," Booke admitted in an abashed tone. "I'd gotten accustomed to all the aches."

"I can't tell you how relieved I am. It was killing me to think—"

"Then don't." He cut me off before I could complete the sentence. "I'm already making a list of all the places I intend to visit . . . if I can resolve the logistics."

"I'm not sure how well your fake passport will serve

without a charm, but I have an idea as to how you can get a real one."

"Tell me?" He propped himself against the French doors, expression eager.

"You know how there's this mystery in Stoke as to what became of you?"

"I've read accounts on the Internet," he said drily, as if aware of the irony.

"Here's my plan. You apply for identification as your own son. It sounds crazy at first, but hear me out. If the original Ian Booke moved quietly to some remote village in South Africa, there's no reason anyone would've known. They assumed he died and his house was sold, but in fact, no body was ever found. He married late in life to a much younger woman. If you're willing to add four or five years to your actual age, on paper, it will make even more sense. I've done the math in my head. You were born in 1910. If you married at fifty-five and your new bride came up pregnant, say five years later, when you were sixty, your son, Ian Booke, Jr., would now be around forty years old."

"It's a plausible tale," he admitted, "but I don't see how that gets me documents."

"Don't you see? In most third world countries, they only require a minister or another official to sign an affidavit, saying you were born there, on that date."

His clever face lit with an appreciative expression. "And in such places, they're always in dire need of coin. You suggest I should bribe someone to sign the necessary paperwork, which would get me a South African birth certificate along with a credible identity that allows me to keep my own name."

"Exactly."

"Corine," he said softly. "Why were you *thinking* about this? Didn't you expect me to die?"

I ducked my head. "I was braced for the worst, but I hadn't given up hope."

He surprised me by tilting my chin up and planting a firm kiss on my mouth. It wasn't at all sexual or romantic; it was a fierce thank-you of a kiss, one you would receive from the dearest of friends. Whatever else life had in store for Ian Booke, I hoped it would be wonderful. He turned shy then, and soon fled to the garage to assist Chuch. Those modern gearboxes didn't repair themselves. I imagined after such a long confinement, the freedom was intoxicating. In the morning, we'd probably find him running down the road at top speed, simply because he could.

That night, dinner was a simple affair, as Eva was saving all her culinary creations for the fiesta. Chuch was downcast over that, but he soon cheered up over board games, where he and Eva kicked our asses. Booke and I just weren't on the same page for Pictionary. Kel didn't return before I went to sleep, and I worried about him until I drifted off.

No Chance that night. I was a little disappointed.

In the morning, I cleaned alongside Eva, making the house shine for guests. It was exhausting, but it took my mind off my worries. Hopefully, we'd finish in time for me to shower and get ready. Around two, Shannon showed up with boyfriend in tow.

Jesse Saldana was a tall, lean drink of water with a shock of sun-streaked brown hair and bitter chocolate eyes. He had a permanent tan, courtesy of his Mexican heritage, and he was an all-around good guy. I had semi-dated him a while back, but courtesy of a forget spell that went massively awry, both he and my best friend forgot all about me, just long enough to get together. Looking at them now, I couldn't doubt it had been for the best. She radiated adoration and joy in equal measures, and he looked just about as gone on her. I caught them in a tender, unguarded moment as we prepared for the other guests. As they paused in the foyer, he leaned his head down to hers, just content to touch, and she reached up for a kiss that literally curled her toes, visible through the peep-toe of her platform Lolita Mary Janes. When Jesse saw me, his hands tightened briefly on Shan's shoulders. I glimpsed unease as she turned—and as she spotted me, she lost a little of her radiance, like it wasn't okay to kiss her man in front of me.

Yeah, this has to stop.

"Can you give me a minute?" Jesse asked Shan.

"Yeah, no prob. I'll just, uh, help Eva in the kitchen. I guess."

"Come on." Jesse beckoned me out to the back patio, which was presently deserted.

I took one of the rattan chairs, waiting to hear what he had to say. While he collected his thoughts, I admired the tropical feel Eva had managed out here, making the most of the new terracotta tile with rectangular planters accented with round ones. All the blooms were lush and green, spiky fronds, flowing leaves, peppered with vibrant blooms. A few hanging baskets framed the space beautifully, making me want something like this back home in Mexico.

"I feel like I need to explain," he began.

"You really don't. No promises were broken. It's just one of those things."

"Well, you started it," he muttered. "With your damned spell."

I lifted a brow at his tone. "I'm aware. I haven't bitched at you."

"Maybe it'd be better if you did. Then I wouldn't feel so guilty."

"About what? Being with Shan or disappointing me?"

"A little of both."

I laughed. "Jesse, forget about the latter. You and me, we weren't meant to be. The spell proved that. I honestly believe that if you'd loved me, you wouldn't have hooked up with Shan. Some part of you would've realized it was wrong—that something was missing."

He gazed at me somberly with the clear sunlight finding toffee flecks in his dark cocoa eyes. "I hope you're right about that. You know I worry—"

"About being inconstant, too easily influenced by other people's emotions," I supplied. This wasn't the first time we'd discussed that particular fear. "So let me ask you this. When Shan was missing, there were probably other women who were attracted to you, who gave signals. How did that go?"

"You mean did I *cheat*?" His mouth drew taut, likely restraining a stream of angry words.

"Not even that. How did you respond to them? Did they have a shot?"

"No way. I love her. *Nobody* can replace her." The reply came in a blazing rush, seeming to surprise Jesse with its fervor.

But it made me really glad to hear. "See? We never had that."

He considered for a moment, pensive rather than regretful, which made for a nice alternative. "I think . . . you just had too many reservations about us. I couldn't help but sense that. It really wouldn't have lasted, would it?"

I shook my head. "It looked great on paper, but no."

"Whereas with Shan, there are none. I never had *anybody* go after me so all-in from the jump. There's no doubt in her whatsoever."

"You're her lobster," I said, wondering if he'd get the reference.

"Okay, Phoebe," he mumbled, but I could tell by his expression that he liked the comparison. "With Shan, she loves and wants me so fiercely, so unconditionally, that it's like a perfect broadcast that blocks out all other signals. There's no room for anyone but her. And it's so . . . restful. So perfect."

"Her intensity might scare somebody else," I pointed out. "Somebody who doesn't need it like you do. Which makes you two a perfect match."

"So you really don't mind? Shan is a little worried."

"I've told her repeatedly that it's fine. Somehow I'll make it sink in."

"She tells me you got back with Chance, anyway." Neutral tone there, carefully nonjudgmental.

"Working on that. But yes. I'm very happy for you two." I pushed out of my chair and met him in the middle of the patio, where he had been pacing nervously. Reaching up, I hugged him tight around the neck, then whispered into his ear, "If you hurt her, I'll cut off your balls and make you eat them."

He didn't take offense. "I won't. The whole time she was gone, I was just . . . empty. I hardly ate. Didn't sleep much. I could only think how hellish it would be if she never came back, if I never saw her again. I lay in bed at night, just wanting to hear her laugh one more time."

Tears started in my eyes because I could so fully relate to his suffering. That was how I felt about Chance at any given moment. But if Shan could come back from Sheol and make Jesse a happy man, I didn't see why I couldn't retrieve my lover from his father's realm. But first, we had a party to attend—in honor of Booke's lost birthdays. Hell of a thing to celebrate.

I stepped away from him to find Shan standing in the doorway; and from her expression, she'd heard everything. Her blue eyes simply glowed. "You're so getting lucky tonight, Saldana."

Pointing at Jesse, I made a shooing motion toward the house. "Go. I'll deal with her now."

"Uh-oh," she said. "Am I in trouble?"

"Only for thinking I'm not glad you're happy and in a healthy relationship. My only reservation would be his age, but you're not a kid, and he's not a creeper."

She laughed. "He sure felt like one at first."

"But he got over it . . . and everything is fine between the two of you. I care about him as a friend, that's all. I'm not harboring any hidden longings. An idiot could see

that you're right together. Hopefully I don't fit that cri-
teria."

She nudged me. "No way. All right, consider me ab-
solved of the heinous crime of boyfriend stealing, 'kay?"

"Deal. Now let's help Eva finish up the appetizers before she kills Chuch."

As expected, I found Señor Ortiz in the kitchen, pick-
ing at the pretty plates his wife was creating. I chased
him out to the garage. Not being a fool, Jesse soon followed, leaving us to finish the preparations. It was com-
panionable, working with two other women. Though I
wasn't much of a cook, I was good at chopping. In our
new relationship, barely begun, Chance had done most
of the actual food making. I served best as sous chef.

And you will again, I promised myself.

While she put together an enchilada casserole, Eva
teased Shannon about her relationship with Jesse, but
for the first time, Shan didn't react with guilt. She flipped
Eva double birds before she went back to sautéing on-
ions. "Whatever, I'm happy."

"I hear you're thinking of moving in together," Eva
pried.

"Not for a while," Shan answered. "I signed a lease
with Maria, and I won't leave her hanging like her last
roomie did."

"I'm sure she appreciates that."

Thinking hard, I remembered reading some emails on
Shan's laptop. Maria must be Shan's roommate, another
of Chuch's cousins. After the forget spell, I'd had no
choice but to vanish, giving Jess and Shan a chance to
remember naturally to avoid further harm. So that
meant Shan had been a regular part of Chuch and Eva's
life for months, so they knew people that were only
names to me.

I listened as they chatted, contemplating my options.
Who could I turn to for help with Chance? Twila was
out, as I had nothing valuable to offer her, and I wasn't

willing to present an open-ended bargain as Booke had done. So I put the matter aside for the time being; it wasn't like giving up. I was still focused on the problem, but it wouldn't be solved before the barbecue.

At three, Eva pronounced the house ready and the food sufficient for the guests she'd invited. With a sigh of relief, I escaped to the guest room to shower. Once I was clean, I poked through my backpack. What I'd bought in London didn't provide much choice, but as I stood in my T-shirt, Eva came in with an armful of clothes. She laid them on the bed with a smile.

"My stuff should work for you. I figured you might want to dress up."

"Thanks. That should cheer me up a little." It was the first time I'd referred to the emotional devastation I carried, hung around my neck like prison chains.

She hugged me. "Don't give up, *chiquita*. We're all here for you."

"That's the only thing keeping me going."

Party Hearty

In the end, I wore my own jeans, paired with a silver sparkly top that belonged to Eva. I left my hair down and put on minimal makeup, as I didn't feel like celebrating, but for Booke, I'd put on a good show. I came out of the guest room in time to act as hostess alongside Eva, who was run ragged between the food and a clingy Cami. My goddaughter liked people, but not in these quantities. I wished I could take her to her room and hide, but nobody was letting that happen. Various aunts and cousins whisked her away, handing her off like a beloved parcel, until all the attention cheered Cami up.

Which freed me to mingle. *Awesome.*

The musicians were setting up out back, a four-piece roughneck crew who looked like they laid pavement for a living, but after they started tuning their instruments, I changed my mind. Amazing how fast Chuch and Eva had put this together, never imagining it would be a congratulations party and not a farewell. Rich melody poured out of the guitar, sultry and danceable. Apparently others had the same idea, as couples formed up on the patio and spilled over into the yard, Shan and Jesse among them. I was glad to see they didn't seem self-conscious around me anymore; that was one loose end tied off.

Booke was dancing with one of Chuch's cousins, the thin and bedazzled Dolores, who had participated in a séance with us a while back. We had been seeking answers from Jesse's deceased ex, but she didn't respond well to the fact that he brought a diaphragm as the focus object . . . that belonged to some other woman. That didn't end well. After the garbage disposal exploded all over the kitchen, I was a little startled to see her, but she seemed to be having a good time with Booke, laughing at his jokes. For my part, I was glad to see him manage a spirited Texas two-step.

A few minutes later, Ramon came up to me, sans Caridad. "Wanna dance?"

The band was just striking up a new tune. "What happened to—"

"Eh, she didn't pass the family test. Chuch told his mom that she refused to help out, and Tia Elena burned up the phone lines. An hour later, I had my mother on the phone, yelling at me."

"Not worth the grief?" I wondered aloud.

"Hey, I'd only been out with her four times. I'd have to be nuts to piss off my entire family unless I was crazy in love."

"Then, sure," I said. "I'll dance, as long as there's not a vicious witch of an ex waiting to hex me over it."

"Nah." He wheeled me into the grass, as all the patio space was taken. "I'm pretty irresistible and all, but it takes more than four dates to work the Ortiz magic."

"You mean that in the figurative sense, right?"

Ramon laughed. "*Si,* I didn't get the gift, but my sister did. She throws some mean bones."

"How does that work?" Though I wasn't sure, I had the impression Jesse Saldana's mother didn't know about his father's ability to grow gigantic vegetables or her son's empathy.

Chuch's cousin raised a brow at me. "You don't know?"

"I didn't have a gifted support network growing up, so I missed a lot of things, including the forum where you outsource work, and the ins and outs of—"

"I understand." He cut me off politely, which I appreciated. Rambling explanations while trying to follow his enthusiastic turns hadn't been easy. "If you marry into a gifted family, it's pretty much common knowledge. If you marry a normal, then you keep it quiet, even from your spouse."

"So Jesse's mother doesn't come from a gifted background," I guessed.

"Probably not. My family, on the other hand, tends to seek mates in the life, so to speak. So even those of us born without any abilities still know the score."

"That makes sense. Thanks for the tip." It also explained why Chuch and Eva remained unfazed by the strangeness that I routinely sprang on them.

Based on what I knew of Jesse's romantic past, he was trying not to follow in his father's footsteps. He must've seen how hard it was to keep a crucial secret, so he started looking at gifted girls when he was ready to settle down. I hadn't been the one, but maybe Shannon was; given how crazy she was about him, I hoped so.

"You look thoughtful," Ramon said.

"Is that bad?"

"You're supposed to be having fun."

"I'll do better." With some effort, I got into the party spirit. "I've been meaning to thank you."

"For what?"

"Hooking me up with the trailer . . . and the Chevelle. I still need to repay you for losing it."

He shrugged. "It was a lemon anyway. Chuch told me about your problem keeping cars."

"He makes it sound worse than it is," I protested.

"Really?" Ramon cocked a skeptical brow, and I fell quiet.

After him, I danced with a number of other cousins. Most of them had wives who didn't mind parting with them for five minutes, and I put a good face on for the occasion. It wasn't that I didn't like Chuch's *primos*, just that they were the wrong men. An hour into the dancing, I begged off and went to look for something to eat.

Eva's food was a big hit; I loaded up my plate more than once. Since I'd helped make everything on the buffet table, I felt justified in savoring it. There were homemade chips and fresh salsa, guacamole and empanadas, plus more American standards, like deviled eggs and a cheese and fruit plate. There were multiple salads other women had brought in—my favorite was one with marshmallows, mandarin oranges, and plenty of whipped cream. It looked more like a dessert to me but I didn't argue its placement in the food pyramid.

Once it got dark, Chuch fired up the barbecue, and Ramon kindled the strands of twinkle lights, which gave the yard a festive air. Booke came up beside me, as I was having seconds on the fruit and whipped cream salad. He had been dancing nonstop, enjoying his newfound vitality. His moves were a little old-fashioned, but the ladies seemed to find him charming.

"Having fun?" I asked.

"It's fantastic. American women are astonishingly susceptible to the accent," he told me. "If I'd known that in 1947, I'd have done a number of things differently."

"I imagine," I said drily.

He laughed, then his clever face fell into somber lines. "I don't know that I deserve a second chance, but I intend to make the most of this one."

"Where are you going first?"

He thought about that. "Shanghai, I think. I've always fancied a tour of the Orient. For a while, I thought our dreams were the closest I'd ever come to seeing the real world again."

Yeah, about the dreams . . . "If you ever need me, don't

hesitate to contact me that way. But maybe . . ." I didn't know how to put it.

It's time to impose some boundaries . . . I don't think you should be in my head anymore when I'm helplessly, impossibly in love with somebody else.

Fortunately, Booke was every bit as smart as he looked. "I understand. Emergencies only. I won't wander into your dreams on a whim. I've other things to do now anyway."

"You'll be busy seducing susceptible American women," I teased.

He colored, but didn't deny the allegation. After all, he had been celibate a long time. Which was when it occurred to me . . .

"Um . . . okay, so I know you had Internet access—" Oh, God, why was I broaching this subject and not Chuch . . . ? *Don't be a wuss. He's your friend.* Yet my tongue cleaved to the roof of my mouth, and for the life of me, I couldn't get the safe sex lecture off the ground.

Booke interrupted my fumbling. "I've seen my share of pornography over the years, and I'm familiar, at least in the abstract, with the perils of modern courtship."

By which I guessed he meant STDs and the like. I just nodded and mumbled, "That's good. Wear a jimmy hat."

He eyed me oddly. "Jimmy hat. Must Google that later." Before he could say more, Dolores waved at him from across the yard, her face alight.

She had a prominent nose and receding chin, but nice eyes. And her style drew attention anyway, as she was draped with a load of flowing scarves and bangles, plus twelve rings on ten fingers, along with three ankle bracelets, one of which had bells on it, and a glimmering toe ring that complemented a pretty French pedicure.

Booke responded to her hail with a lifted hand, indicating he was almost through. "I expect this will be a lively overnight visit."

Oh, man. He was going home with her later? *Go, Do-*

lores. For her sake, I hoped Booke remembered what to do with his equipment, but that wasn't my problem. Inwardly masking my impatience, as I longed to apply myself to Chance's return, I joined a group of wives who were chatting at the edge of the patio, children playing—or napping—at their feet, Eva among them. I listened to their jokes and stories, feeling more alone than I did in bed in the dark. Something about being surrounded by happy people made grief worse.

Still, the party was a success. Though it had started early, people kept arriving late, until the Ortiz house and yard was overflowing. The music got louder and more boisterous, until I thought it was a good thing they didn't have close neighbors. I knew from personal experience that these shindigs could run until three in the morning. *At least we don't have a full mariachi band.*

"You look tired," Jesse said, plopping down in a chair beside me.

He had been dancing with Shannon all night, so tender and sweet that it made me glad to see them together, even if things were a mess for me. I wasn't such a selfish person that I couldn't stand for others to be happy, even when I wasn't. But apparently he didn't feel like he needed to be tactful anymore either. No woman wanted to hear she looked like a train wreck, even at her worst.

"That's not the right word," I answered.

"What is?"

Part of me wasn't sure if I was ready to confide in him as I had during the early days of our uncertain relationship. Once, it had been really easy to talk to him, but so much had changed. Everything, in fact. Before, I had been a roiling ball of doubt, unsure of what I wanted. Not anymore. But if I didn't try, there would always be this awkwardness between us, and Jesse might always wonder if, no matter my claims otherwise, I harbored a smidgeon of resentment toward him.

"I'm just . . . tired of waiting. I'm glad for Booke, but

for me, this party is something I have to endure before I apply myself to getting Chance back."

From his expression, I could see I'd shocked him. "Corine . . . from what Shan said, he *died*. People don't come back from that. He's gone, sugar. I'm sorry, but he is, and you have to—"

"Normal people don't," I cut in. "But Chance wasn't and neither am I. If she told you everything, then you know I had a demon queen running amok in my head. I ruled *hell* for a while. Didn't do a particularly good job of it but that's not the point."

"What is?"

"That if I could go to Sheol and come back, Chance can cross back from wherever he is. His mortal body died, but he's still out there. I talked to him."

"Through Shan's radio."

Which only reached dead people. Yes, I knew that. Anger suffused me, and I opened my mouth to yell at him. Who knew what I might've said . . . because at that point, the demons arrived, and the party I wasn't enjoying went from bad to worse.

Three extraordinarily handsome men strode around the side of the house, chiseled features, well dressed, and impeccably coiffed. One was blond, the second brunette, and the other one had a remarkable shock of white hair, though his face looked young. As one, the women sighed and mentally offered up their ovaries. I might've reacted the same way if I hadn't recognized the stink of brimstone and sulfur on them—and if they didn't move with a hint of awkwardness in their newly acquired bodies.

These weren't just any old demons. They were Luren, drawn to beautiful victims and summoned in the most intricate of sex rites. God only knew what they were doing at Chuch's backyard barbecue, but I couldn't imagine it meant anything good. I headed them off before they could start an estrogen riot, as the female guests were staring like they couldn't wait to get to know the new guests better, preferably topless. Maybe I was reading into the situation, but it seemed likely that this visit related to my recent sojourn in Sheol.

"What're you doing here?" I demanded.

"We've come for reparations, Corine Solomon." The taller one with the white hair did the talking for the diabolically sexy trio.

"What the hell—" Chuch started.

The demon ignored him. "You made a bargain with our knight, Sibella. Those terms were not met."

"Because the Hazo staged a *coup*," I said incredulously. "Not through any contractual failure of mine."

He was right; I'd made a deal with Sibella. I was supposed to take seven days to learn the lay of the land in Sheol and then return to come to terms with whatever it was Sibella had wanted of me. Instead, the demon queen living in my head broke the terms. It appeared it was time for me to pay her bill.

Fantastic.

"You did not return to our stronghold in seven days, as promised. Instead you attempted to claim the city for your own. The original bargain was not met."

"Good luck enforcing that."

"That's why we're here. Unless you're prepared to meet Sibella's champion, you will deal with us, here and now."

Uh-oh. It sounded an awful lot like they intended to wreck up the place. But how much damage could sex demons do? Some of Chuch and Eva's family were gifted, but would they fight? I didn't like my odds, three on one, and though Butch had the heart of a lion, he still had the teeth of a Chihuahua. Still, I had to try to minimize the collateral damage. I'd cost the Ortizes enough over the course of our friendship.

"Come with me," I invited, "and we'll have it out."

Mostly I wanted to get them away from the rest of the guests. Fortunately, most women had downed enough booze to react with less intensity to the Luren appeal as they would otherwise. Still, some of them were looking for their husbands, initiating long, intimate kisses without understanding why. It helped that the Luren weren't here incarnate; the draw was lessened in possession. Still, their human hosts radiated a raw lust that unsettled me. Jesse and Shannon had stopped dancing, and were mostly just grinding on each other. His face was a taut, erotic portrait, and she looked like she wanted to climb him. In two minutes, we'd be in the middle of an orgy, or somebody would be dead.

Tense, I waited to see if the demons would take the bait. Namely me.

No such luck.

The dark-haired one was becoming alert to the potential in the situation, both for feeding and chaos. He smiled with beautiful white teeth. "I think not. Perhaps we'll take payment from your friends and loved ones instead."

"I'm pretty sure that's illegal," I said. "Sibella made the deal with me. Any breach—and I am not admitting there was one—must be addressed with me."

"She's right," a silky voice said.

Oh, gods, it only needs this.

I turned slowly, hoping I hadn't identified the speaker correctly. Barachiel stood at my shoulder, cloaked in radiance from head to toe. No lie, he was actually glowing a little bit, and the light show hinted at great white feathery wings unfurling at his back. Then I blinked and the suggested shape blurred into the line of his jacket, but I knew better than to believe it was a trick of my tired eyes. Barachiel did everything for a reason.

"Corine has aligned herself with the host," he told the Luren. "Should you choose to pursue this debt, it will be tantamount to an act of war. Are you content to begin the battle tonight?" He tilted his head, visibly charmed by the idea. "I am."

"No. This is *not* happening. I'm not the catalyst for the end of days or whatever."

"Are you sure?" Barachiel asked.

I wasn't.

Inwardly, I quaked in terror. This was too much, yet another choice being forced on me. I could see if I permitted Barachiel to protect me now, he would call the balance due later. I wanted to cut free of all supernatural things and just live my life, but I had long since lost any ability to chart that course. Yet I was weary of bouncing from one catastrophe to the next, living on borrowed karma.

The blond one cocked his head, as if listening to unheard voices. "Yes. We are content to fire the opening salvo, Barachiel."

Uh-oh. That had to mean they had some trick up their sleeves. I feared Barachiel, and I didn't want to work for him. That didn't mean I wanted him to end up in a cage match at my friend's barbecue. Sometimes my life sucked so much, there were no words. *So. Not. Good.* I had to stop this, somehow, but my mind was an utter blank; I had no cards left to play.

The archangel whipped out a gleaming silver sword, forged of a metal sharp and preternaturally strong, like the knife Kel carried. Moonlight ran like water down the blade. In response, the three demons drew their own weapons, black as night, barbed and serrated like hungry teeth.

And that was when the screaming started.

Battle Royale

The party guests weren't prepared for Armageddon to break out amid cheese rolls and onion dip, so I didn't blame them for panicking.

Half of them dialed 911, but since Jesse was already here, I guessed the police were already on the way. Unfortunately, it would be too late by the time the authorities arrived, and Jesse would have some hard-core 'splaining to do. As Barachiel lunged at the white-haired Luren, I wondered if this attack would be written off as cartel-driven, ascribed to Chuch's past unsavory associates. That being said, I understood the need for damage control. Otherwise the paranormal world would come out in a big way, as a result of a Texas BBQ. Talk about bizarre cause and effect.

For once, I wasn't in the middle of the fight. These four were trying to kill each other, not me, but it didn't make it better. I didn't like being the juicy bone between four hungry dogs; things almost never worked out well for the bone. And if the Luren won, they wouldn't wait to drag me back to Sheol for a final accounting. As if he read my thought—could alleged archangels *do* that?— Barachiel cut me a mordant look, laced with warning. I took it to mean he wouldn't be distracted long . . . because these demons didn't pose a serious threat, no matter what they thought. He also seemed a little insulted that I'd even considered the possibility he could lose.

Either way, it was no comfort. No matter who won, I lost.

The Luren were fast for all their feral beauty; they encircled Barachiel. His broad sweeps with the sword kept them back, but everywhere he turned, there was a demon, waiting for him to weaken. He didn't seem to tire, however. They exchanged a flurry of feints and parries while people ran for their cars, yelling incomprehensibly at Chuch.

The motion of their blades made me dizzy. I couldn't track Barachiel's movements; he wasn't even pretending to be human. It was like a movie fight, sped up with special effects, only the slashes and blocks were real. Barachiel slammed his sword so hard into the tall Luren's that the demon's blade broke, splintering into a dozen shards. The archangel didn't pull his next blow either. He took off the creature's head, and it bounced in a spray of blood. Demon blood was a little thicker, a little darker, and the smell was unmistakable. The stench of sulfur and brimstone permeated the air, dominating the gentler aromas of mesquite and good food.

At that, the last remaining guests who had been frozen with shock and disbelief sprang into motion. I had no idea how we would keep something like this quiet. Surely everyone on the guest list couldn't be in on the secret, so what the hell . . . ? But that was way low on my priority list at the moment. I had so many emergencies to tackle that I didn't even know where to start.

"My odds just got better," Barachiel observed, holding his swordsman's stance.

"If I die here or in Sheol, it makes no difference," the demon responded. "You remember the price of failing the knight who commands you." The Luren paused, smiling. "No, perhaps you don't. You've rewritten your own history, after all."

So maybe what Ninlil said was true. There were no angels or demons. Just other sentient beings, who lived in an alternate realm, and whose division gave rise to alternate mythos. Both sides had been playing with humanity for eons, though. Neither could claim benevolence or altruism. To my mind, both factions wanted something, whether it was as simple as entertainment or as ominous as power.

"Lies," Barachiel returned. "Designed to seed doubt from one who has already lost. Don't grant them even that small victory." So saying, he wheeled into the fight once more, his sword a blur of light slashing at his foes.

Where the hell is Kel?

At that point, Eva shouted something about getting the guns, which would've been reassuring if she hadn't been talking to a woman who looked eighty years old. But when Eva came back with a couple of shotguns, she handed one to Chuch's *abuela*, and the old lady cocked it like she knew which way to point it.

The crowd thinned as the two remaining demons lashed at Barachiel. They hadn't landed a single hit when I heard sirens in the distance.

Jesse strode forward. "You're all out of your jurisdiction. I already texted Twila, and she's got people on the way. You don't do business in the state of Texas without her express approval. Y'all will clear out if you know what's good for you."

"Yep," Chuch said. "Plus, you went and pissed my *abuela* off. That's not a good idea."

The old woman fired a warning shot, but not into the air. Her round ate a divot in the yard, right near where the three were fighting. To my surprise, they froze. Why wasn't Barachiel owning them with some impressive archangel magick anyway? The ready answer seemed to be that he wasn't as powerful as he projected or that he was weakened somehow. I wondered if that had something to do with Kel. A fight with an angry Nephilim could really take it out of you, I guessed.

Which meant Kel might not have come back because he couldn't. *Dammit*. Now I had two men to save.

Eva cocked her weapon as well, stepping up beside Chuch's grandmother. Shannon had a kitchen knife in her hand, and while it wasn't a sword, she could do some damage with it. Unfortunately, I was unarmed; I didn't even have my athame on me, as I'd stopped carrying it when my magick stopped working. So I didn't have its psychological reassurance while we faced down Barachiel and the two strongest Luren I'd ever encountered. But I had faith in my friends, which was better than any blade.

After a short pause, the two Luren stepped back. The blond one pointed his weapon at me. "This isn't over, Corine Solomon. You owe Sibella a debt, and one way or another, it will be paid. You cannot hide forever."

"As long as she's in Texas, however, you can't have her," Jesse said flatly.

So if I go home, I'm screwed. Awesome.

Maybe Tia knew who ran Mexico City, however. Possibly I could apply for protection, swear fealty, something that would make it worth his or her while to keep the Luren away from me. But I wouldn't be going home without Chance . . . and I needed to find out what had happened to Kel. The demons strode away, around the side of the house, but before they left my sight, a cloud of darkness swathed them, and when it dissipated they were gone.

"We'll finish this dance another time." Barachiel sheathed his sword. Then he turned to me. "I have shed blood on your behalf. That constitutes an agreement."

Shannon glared at him. "My ass, it does. She didn't ask for your help . . . you assumed she wanted it. Looked to me like you picked a fight with those assholes on your own."

"I agree," Chuch's grandmother said in Spanish. "No compacts were made, spirit. You did not await her answer."

Saved by a technicality. I might've asked Barachiel to step in, but we'd never know, now. His countenance darkened with fury, mouth pulling taut. For a few seconds, he couldn't find the words. Then he spat, "In this war, you cannot sit on the sidelines. You must choose, and if you're not my ally, you are my enemy."

I thought, *Bullshit,* but had the good sense not to say it out loud. He was still laboring under the presumption that I couldn't find a plan C. I had gotten pretty good at spotting unlikely solutions. His agenda wasn't mine, but I needed to stall him a little longer while I figured out what happened to Kel.

Unlike the demons, Barachiel vanished in a shimmer of silver light. Chuch's grandmother lowered her shotgun. After her prior moxie, I expected her to offer up a one-liner like, *I'm getting too old for this shit,* but she just sighed, rolled her shoulders, and shuffled over to a patio chair.

Eva collected the guns, presumably to hide them again before the cops arrived. Of the huge crowd, only Booke, Dolores, Chuch's immediate family, Jesse and Shannon remained. It would help that Saldana was here to run interference, but I didn't envy him and Chuch the task of making this attack sound remotely sensible.

Leaving them to manage damage control, I went into the house on a mission. Once I was sure I had sufficient privacy, I called Kel. With a capital C. He had said I didn't have the power to compel him anymore, but if he was able, he would surely respond. Moments passed in tense silence. I hoped he would appear in the room, mildly annoyed at my presumption.

He didn't.

Barachiel was here, I thought. *He's getting impatient. I need you, Kel.*

I didn't want to, but I did.

A prickle stirred at the back of my mind. It wasn't strong, like it had been when I heard his thoughts. This was like sitting on a hairbrush . . . in my brain—obviously uncomfortable, but nonspecific. *Help me out here. Give me something.*

I suspected just this much contact was draining him; a full connection might kill him, if Nephilim *could* die. Fear spiked through me like a gladiator's gauntlet. Closing my eyes, I willed my energy through that tenuous connection, knowing that was more wishful thinking than true magick.

But maybe, maybe it was enough. Because a place popped into my head, or rather, the image of one. Unfortunately, I had no idea where it was. From the surrounding countryside, it was probably on the Tex-Mex border, scrubland full of broken mesas and dry as dust.

Then even the prickle left me.

I got a piece of paper before the image left my mind's eye. Though I wasn't much of an artist, I captured the shape of the rock. I hurried out to the patio, where Jesse and Chuch were talking to some uniformed officers. Three squad cars had turned up, and since there was a dead body on the premises, they'd call the crime scene unit out too.

". . . dunno who they were," Chuch was saying. "Never saw 'em before."

"You had trouble with the Montoya cartel, correct?" At Chuch's nod, the officer made a note.

I could already see who would get the blame for this. It would probably be the first severed head in Texas that the Montoyas could honestly say they had nothing to do with. The two surviving brothers weren't running the op anyway. A second in command had stepped up, from what I heard, and eventually it would be known as the Ramirez cartel, once he consolidated power. Not my business. I was finished with the cartels. I wanted to be done with angels, demons, and decapitations as well.

It took hours for them to gather all the witness state-
ments and wrap up the scene. Since the criminals never
entered the house, it minimized the inconvenience to the
Ortizes, at least. Jesse stayed, overseeing the process, and
offering plausible theories whenever another officer
picked a hole in Chuch's story. I was grateful to have him
here.

At two a.m., the last of the city officials finally left. I
touched Eva on the arm. After all the drama, I hated to
bother her, but I intended to get moving as soon as I had
enough information. "Who would know the famous rock
formations nearby?" I asked.

Her jaw dropped. "You want to go sightseeing? Tonight?"

"No." I hastened to explain, then showed her the drawing I had done.

"Oh. So you're looking for Kel. You think he's
trapped?"

"I'm afraid he is."

"Honestly, my mind's a blank. Let me sleep on it. I'm
sure I can come up with a local expert in the morning."

That was frustrating, but it wasn't like I could do anything about it. If I'd known where to look on my own, I'd
already be asking to borrow the Charger. In their shoes,
I didn't know whether I'd loan me a ride, as I had a history of losing them. Over the past few years, I had gone
through three vehicles; only the Mustang had withstood
my reign of terror, and technically speaking, that belonged to Chance. Which was probably why it had survived.

So many problems to solve and I had so few resources.
I closed my eyes on a sigh, resting my head on the back
of the couch.

"That was more excitement than I'm used to," Booke
said, breaking my reverie. "Well, in person at least."

Dolores laughed. "Stick around, you'll get used to it."

"If you get the chance, bid the others *bonne nuit* for

me, will you?" He offered a cheery salute. "Oh, and don't wait up."

The slender woman blushed a little, and swatted at him with one of her myriad scarves. But she didn't dispute his assessment of the situation. The two strode out to her car, entirely in charity with one another. Apparently Dolores only cut and ran if the spatter got on her outfit, which was a pretty impressive line in the sand. Otherwise, like most of Chuch's relatives, she was rock solid. Of course, maybe she'd be more upset if the deceased had been fully human.

"We ID'd the host," Jesse said, coming to the doorway a few minutes later. "Gigolo out of Vegas who went missing a few months back."

"Is it possible for the Luren to take an unwilling host?" I asked.

"I'm not the expert, but I don't think so. I'm pretty sure they can only be summoned into a willing body via sex magick."

That sounded right, based on what I remembered from Sheol, but my time there was becoming vague and fragmented. Since I hadn't been driving most of the time, that made sense. And sometimes the memories sneaked up on me like a sudden kick in the face. Then horror suffused me, and I worked to bury it all over again. Some of those things I said and did . . . how did I handle it? Denial wasn't a solution, but I just couldn't deal with everything at once.

One step at a time, right?

"I'm guessing the guy didn't imagine the demon would use his body to go up against Barachiel, though."

"Probably not." Jesse didn't sound sympathetic, though.

I figured he thought the dude should've known better than to rent his body out to a Luren. All kinds of things might've been promised in payment, none of which the guy would ever enjoy. No matter how foolish he'd been,

I couldn't be utterly unmoved by his fate. I hadn't wanted to think about it until now, but that was a human being who lost his life in Chuch's backyard.

Dammit.

"I don't envy the detective working the case," I said then.

He shook his head ruefully. "Me either. He'll be looking for normal connections between the vic and killer, but there won't be any. He'll spin his wheels for a week and get nothing, even with our descriptions of the attackers. That'll really stick in his craw."

"You sound like you've been there."

"Not under these circumstances, but yeah. And sometimes I wonder if a crime is demon-touched, if that's why I'm coming up empty."

A sudden thought struck me. "Is there an underground gifted network within law enforcement? To keep things hushed up?"

He smiled down at me. "Good question. It's kinda nice to get back to the old footing, Corine. I'd almost forgotten I'm supposed to be mentoring you."

"That's not an answer."

"Yes. Weird tales would be in all the papers, not just the tabloids, if we didn't do our part."

"It must be pretty hard sometimes. Do you ever wish the gifted could come out to the world?"

He shook his head. "We tried that. It didn't end well."

"The witch hunts?" It was incredible to realize that for every name on the rolls of the dead, it had probably been a woman like me. Not evil. Not possessed by the devil, just a person with a strange gift and no ability to blend in.

"Yep."

"Listen, Corine, if you have more questions, text me. I have work in the morning, so I need to get to bed."

"That's my cue," Shan said.

She leaned down to give me a hug, and I squeezed

back. Gods, I was so freakin' proud of her. *Two girls from Kilmer got out,* I thought. *And we're both doing all right.* Frankly, her success ratio was higher than mine. Despite the whole talks-to-dead-people thing, she didn't seem to attract trouble the way I did. And I was incredibly tired of it.

I said my good nights. Then I checked on Butch. When the fighting started, he'd hidden and hadn't come out since. He was cowering behind a flowerpot on the patio when I found him, ears down, paws over his face.

"It's going to be fine," I promised him. "Things are a mess right now, but I'll figure it out."

Butch whined at me; then he offered two yaps. *No.* Whether he doubted my promise or the likelihood of my finding a workable solution, I wasn't sure. Bending down, I picked him up and cuddled him to my cheek, whispering reassurances. I only wished I believed them.

The dog didn't even pretend; he knew bad things were coming, and as usual, they had my name written all over them.

Dream Lover

This time, there was no period of disorientation, no confusion when the dream came. I recognized the field of jonquils and the perpetually sunny day immediately, and I ran through the flowers in the direction Chance had come last time. But instead of Chance, I met an unfamiliar man by the river. The water was clear and fast-moving, rippling over the pretty polished stones lining its bed. As for the man, he was middle-aged, Japanese, with a softly rounded belly and a balding pate. His dark eyes held a merry twinkle, and when I met his warm look, I understood why Min had succumbed to his charms.

"Ebisu," I whispered.

I had *no* freakin' idea how one greeted a god, even one present in dreams. Should I drop to one knee, curtsy, genuflect . . . ? While I agonized over what gesture of respect to offer, he held up a hand, smiling.

"Today, I greet you as my son's father, though I would not mind if you wished to pay proper respect at a shrine after we conclude our discussion."

"I will," I managed. "Sir, I'm sorry—"

He held up a hand. "No apologies. I have wanted to

meet my son, and he chose his manner of ascension in the style of a true hero."

"Ascension?"

"That's why I wished to speak with you." His friendly face took on a rather forbidding air. "I am not sure how familiar you are with my story."

"Not very," I admitted.

"In the scrolls, I am paired with Daikokuten, the god of wealth, and in some variations, we are father and son."

Uh-oh. I had a feeling I knew where this conversation was headed. I only offered a nod, encouraging him to go on, when I feared the conclusion of his revelation.

"Chance has shed his mortal skin and dwells among the gods now. He will assume the mantle of Daikokuten, as he was always meant to do."

"I'm sensing a 'but.' "

"You're a clever woman," he said approvingly. "He refuses to drink from the fountain of renewal and claim his godhood. He thinks of nothing but getting back to you, of keeping his promise. So I've come to appeal to your conscience. Do what's best . . . and let him go."

The request hit me like a blackjack in the back of the head, and the pain came as a shock in contrast to the sunny splendor of the meadow. For a few seconds, I couldn't get my breath; the idea of never seeing him again felt like it might kill me.

Then I realized I didn't *care* what Ebisu wanted. He'd let Min raise Chance alone all these years. If I could bring him back to her, I would. But I wasn't that unselfish because I wanted him back for me too, for the life he'd promised me.

Yet it didn't seem like a good idea to defy a god, even a small one, on his home turf. If I declined, maybe he wouldn't let me go. So I prevaricated.

"Will I have the opportunity to say good-bye?"

"One last meeting, I can permit," he said quietly. "But

then, Daikokuten must accept his destiny. One cannot fight fate . . . and he is not meant for you."

"So you had a son, knowing he would die?" That sounded so horrible, so calculating. And it reinforced my decision not to fall in with his plan.

"Everyone dies, Corine Solomon. I did not know the manner of his passing. It is not given to me to see the future, but I did know he would come to me in time."

That was a little better than the Christian version of this story, anyway. At least he hadn't known what would happen to Chance, when he lay down with Min in the orchard all those years ago. I offered a watery smile, trying to seem resigned.

Instead of dead stubborn, which was what I'd always been.

"It must've been hard to leave them," I said softly.

"Yes," he admitted. "But all great deeds are done with purpose. I will summon Daikokuten. Please keep your conversation short, as my power is limited." His friendly, open face grew wistful. "People do not visit the shrines as they once did."

"I understand. I'll be brief."

What do I even say, I wondered. *I can't let on, even to Chance.* No answers came to me; then my love was striding along the river, his steps quickening as he glimpsed me. He pushed into a run, and I met him. His arms came around me, and he buried his face in my hair. The wind blew, carrying the sweetness of blooming flowers and the gentle hint of mist from the river. It would've been perfect if I hadn't known how the interlude ended. I breathed him in, trying to store up the memories for when he was lost to me for good, even in dreams.

You have to do this, I told myself. *Otherwise, he'll give the ruse away and Ebisu may keep you here, keep you from saving him.*

"I missed you," he whispered. "But I've got a lock on a solution. There's a weak spot between the realms. I found out how my father passed into our world. There's a particular festival when—"

I couldn't let him continue. So I kissed him. He'd shut me up that way before, but it wasn't a strategy I employed often. Fortunately, he fell into the kiss with a fierce hunger, tasting me as if I were a delectable treat he hadn't enjoyed in months. I ran my fingers through his hair, traced down his neck and shoulders. My arms tightened around him compulsively; letting go might prove more than I could bear.

Then I said the words, praying he believed them, hoping he didn't. "You can't go down this road."

He reacted as if I'd punched him. "Are you kidding? We can do this, I swear. I don't have the same juice my father has because he's stored it up from the years of reverences, but I have a little residual power from the shrines. I just need some help from your side, and I can come through. And unlike my father, I won't leave again."

Ebisu appeared beside us then, his face stern. "What he is not telling you, Corine Solomon, is that if he does this foolish thing, he yields all claim to immortality. He will be stripped of his power and become nothing more than a mortal man. No luck. No magick. No future."

"No future, except the one I choose . . . with *her*," Chance bit out, his eyes livid with rage. "I already told you once, I'm *not staying*. I don't want to be a god. I don't want to be worshipped. The whispers from the shrines are fucking creepy."

"So you hear them." Ebisu seemed pleased. "Good. Very good. Now then." He turned to me. "It's time for you to go . . . and you will not be welcome here again."

I opened my mouth to convince Ebisu I'd lost my resolve, but somehow, what came out was: "I love you, Chance."

Please let that be enough. Let him know I won't stop until he's back with me.

When I woke, I had tears streaming down my cheeks,

burning salt in the corners of my eyes. I swiped my hands across my cheeks and rolled out of bed. It was ridiculously early, considering what time I'd gotten to sleep, but four-hour bursts had been the norm since I got back from Sheol. If I wasn't dreaming of Chance, I had nightmares about what happened in the demon realm. Gods, I was a fucking mess.

Butch roused when I went into the kitchen to put on some coffee, so I let him out and he did his business in the backyard. His nails clicked on the patio as he came back inside to investigate his dish, which I took the hint and filled, then freshened up his water. I knelt to pet him.

I wondered if I was being selfish, so single-minded in my intentions. Ebisu had seemed so positive it was Chance's destiny. Would he be better off becoming a god? Such an odd question. But then Barachiel was certain I was destined to help him rewrite the world, and he couldn't be more wrong.

Maybe the dog has an opinion.

"What do you think? Should I let Chance go?" I asked Butch.

Obviously, I didn't mean it. There wasn't a force on earth that could get me to deviate from this goal. But he took me seriously. Instead of eating his breakfast, he trotted into the living room to nudge my purse. I took that to mean he wanted the Scrabble tiles, so I got them out, then plopped on the floor to watch him sort them with his paws. After a few minutes of arranging them, the message emerged:

chance doesnt want to be a god

"How do you know that?" I demanded. "You don't see my dreams, do you?"

The dog huffed out a disgusted sigh, as if he couldn't believe I'd ask that. "How am I supposed to know what you can do?" I muttered. "How, then?"

chance is dead i see ghosts

Aha. I did remember that Butch had warned us once via that same skill. So that meant . . . "You see Chance sometimes? He's here. I just can't see or hear him."

That earned me the affirmative yap. "Do you talk to him much?" He cocked his head, and I rephrased. "Fine, do you *hear* him much?"

Affirmative yap. "Oh, wow. Can you pass his messages along to me?"

thats why im doing this

"Okay, go for it."

he says please dont give up

That meant he hadn't been sure what to make of my mixed messages. So he was reduced to begging the dog to keep me on track. Regardless of Ebisu's convictions, only what Chance wanted mattered to me. I'd push on, no matter what.

"Is he here now?" I glanced around, wishing I could see the world through Butch's eyes.

But I got the negatory yaps. Then Butch trotted off to eat his breakfast, which I took to mean the conversation was over, so I scooped up the Scrabble tiles and put them away. My head ached from the interrupted sleep. The dreams, possibly because they were incredibly vivid, didn't offer the same restorative quality as REM ones. I suspected energy might literally be drawn from me to make such communication possible. Certainly I felt more exhausted than before I went to bed, and that wasn't a good sign, given everything I needed to accomplish today.

I made scrambled eggs since I was already up and had the coffee brewing. By the time I put bread in the toaster, Chuch came into the kitchen, rumpled and in need of a shave. He looked tired too, no surprise there. Once again, I had dropped my problems in his lap and interrupted his peaceful life.

"Some night," I said, serving him a plate.

"Thanks, *prima.* And yes, that was some crazy shit.

Never had a dead demon in my yard before. That Barachiel, he's got some moves."

"Yeah, he's gonna be a problem," I predicted glumly.

"Eva said you're looking for somebody who knows the land around here."

"Let me guess, you have a cousin."

Chuch laughed. "No. But there's an old guy who likes to drink at La Rosa Negra. If he doesn't know the rock formation in the picture, he'll be able to tell you who does."

"Do you mind if I take the Charger again?"

He narrowed dark eyes on me. "Don't hit anything with it. No high-speed chases. Avoid bullets. And *no* explosions."

Despite the lingering sorrow that tightened my chest, I mustered a smile threaded with genuine amusement. "I dunno if I can promise all that. You know how it goes."

He leveled a stern look on me. "Then no Charger for you. I got a Pinto out back that runs."

"You're restoring a Pinto?" Incredulity sent my voice up an octave.

"Not so much. It was too good a deal to pass up, four hundred bucks." His posture became defensive, and I wondered how Eva felt about his propensity for collecting crappy cars.

I muttered, "Yeah, but it's a Pinto."

Nonetheless, I took the keys when he tossed them to me from the peg on the kitchen wall. There were so many, it looked like a valet parking board. I nibbled a little breakfast with him; my stomach churned, not quite nausea, but a lurch. With some deep breathing, I kept my eggs down. I switched to dry toast while listening to the comforting morning noises: Eva was stirring down the hall, taking care of Cami. The baby giggled at something her mama did, and a warm, soft feeling permeated me. *This,* I thought. *I want this.*

A home was more than a place. It meant security, certainly, but it was also about the people who loved you. Without that, a house was only a building. Their love cemented my resolve. Maybe it would be better for him—better for the world—but I still wanted Chance back, no matter what his father said. He'd promised to build a life with me. I intended to hold him to it.

"You're so lucky," I told Chuch quietly.

He glanced up from his breakfast. "I know."

"How did you meet Eva anyway? And did you know right away . . . ?" I wondered if the question was too personal.

The mechanic's rough face softened. "I was on a job, years ago, in Nicaragua. She was hooked up with one of the lesser bosses."

"She was a gun moll?" I asked, delighted.

Chuch flashed me a sour look. "I don't think they still call them that. And yeah, I knew as soon as I saw her. She was wearing the hell out of this red dress, and I thought, 'I'm gonna marry her.' Two weeks later, I killed the guy she was dating, screwed over the Bolivar cartel, and we ran like hell."

I had the feeling there was a whole lot of story he wasn't telling me. "It was that easy?"

"That's all you're getting today. Don't you have a mission to accomplish?"

"I'm taking the Pinto to the cantina, then. What time do they open?" See, I could take a hint.

Chuch grinned. "I don't think they ever close."

"Then what time does the old man start drinking? What's his name anyway? And what does he look like?"

"People call him Beto, real name's Roberto . . . something. He's shorter than me. Less hair. More wrinkles. He always wears a straw cowboy hat."

"That should be enough for me to spot him. Thanks."

Before he could reply, Eva joined us with Cami on her hip. As she usually did, the baby clapped her hands when she saw me and then reached out. I took her gladly. "I'll watch her for a few hours, if you have other things to do."

The way Eva looked at me, you'd think I had offered to clean her whole house. "*Thank* you."

"Uhm. No problem," I said.

"You'll understand when you have your own kids." She made herself a plate and ate it uninterrupted while Cami pulled my hair and tried to steal my jewelry.

Flailing baby hands made it pretty hard for me to get bites of cereal into her mouth. By the time the bowl was empty, I was wearing a good portion of her oatmeal, and she was covered in it. Chuch smirked at me over the edge of his paper.

"You should have like five," he said.

I nodded. "At least. I'm thinking we'll just hose off in the backyard."

"Watch the crime scene tape."

A cold chill washed over me. For a few moments, playing with Cami, I had forgotten everything. Kel, missing. Chance, trapped between his desire and his destiny. The demons who wanted me to pay my debt and the archangel who wanted my help in changing the world. What amazing power in a child's laughter—that it could carry me away even for a heartbeat. I wanted to go back to that mental quietus, but it was impossible. The real world had intruded.

But I'd promised Eva I would watch the baby for a while, so I bathed her. By the time I finished, I needed another shower, but there was no time. Cami wanted to play, and it was more exhausting than I would've imagined. I was ready for a nap by the time she started fussing and rubbing her eyes.

"That means she's done," Chuch said helpfully. "Lay her down. She may complain for a little while but she'll go to sleep."

He was right. After five minutes of grumbling, Cami passed out, freeing me to clean up for the second time. I put on jeans, a white lace-trimmed tank top and a long, belted charcoal cardigan. The plain colors fit my mood. I left my hair loose, mostly because I didn't feel like fooling with it, and I was putting on my shoes when Booke came back.

He was whistling. Which I took to mean that Dolores had lived up to expectations. "Fun night?"

"Better than yours from the looks of it."

First Jesse, now Booke? What the hell was wrong with these two? "It's rude to insinuate that a woman looks less than her best."

He flashed me a charming grin. "And I'm sure I'd care greatly if I were trying to sleep with you."

I eyed him. "Thanks, I'm sure."

His good mood dimmed a little; I could see the self-consciousness kick in, as if he was trying to guess whether he'd insulted me. Sometimes British people were incredibly cute. "It's not personal," he hastened to assure me. "I do like you. Just—"

"You don't have to make excuses for not being attracted to me." I grinned at him. "You made it clear in our dreams that you go for the tall, leggy type. Dolores has far more of that going on than I do."

"You were having me on then."

"A little, maybe. Don't tell me how terrible I look, even when it's true, and we're good."

"Done. Are you off somewhere?"

"Yeah, I'm trying to find Kel."

"Is he lost?" Alarm flickered across his face, dispelling the satisfied glow.

"I'm afraid he's trapped."

Booke appeared to make a quick decision. "Give me a moment and I'll come with you."

"You don't have to." I was touched, but part of me wished he'd get on with his life. I felt guilty that he wasn't already on the road, seeing the beauties he had missed while trapped in Stoke. The idea of being an obligation made me feel queasy.

"I want to," he promised.

I studied his face, and eventually I believed his sincerity. Since it made no sense to argue, I jingled the Pinto keys in my palm. True to his word, Booke was fast in the bathroom, returning with damp hair and fresh clothes five minutes later. On the way to the car, I teased him about making the walk of shame, but since I had to explain what I was talking about, it killed some of the humor. Still, he seemed amused when he got the gist.

"Yes," he said drily. "It's very humiliating for the world to know I had intercourse last night. I don't know how I'll bear it."

"Smart ass."

I got into the Pinto and stuck the key in the ignition. Like most of Chuch's cars, this one ran well. Not perfectly, but the engine sounded smooth enough, though the exterior looked like crap. The Pinto had patchy paint, bits of primer showing through, two doors didn't match the sides, and the hood was a different color entirely, making the car resemble a quilt.

"Are we going to that seedy cantina I've heard so much about?"

I nodded, putting the car in drive to pull around the garage and onto the street. Without GPS, we'd have to rely on my memory, so this should be fun. However, as I'd been there more than once, maybe I wouldn't get lost. *Maybe.*

"Oh, that's splendid. I can't express how delighted I am to be having adventures of my own, rather than hearing about them."

"Stick with me," I muttered, "and you'll get more excitement than you really want."

Booke leveled a sober gaze on me. "Somehow I doubt that."

Finding Kel

A quick call to Ramon netted me an address for his ex-girlfriend, Caridad. Since I would be arriving today with cash in hand, I didn't imagine she'd mind seeing me during business hours. Booke, Butch, and I drove downtown, which was a little run-down, populated with Popeyes and cheap clothing stores, along with a shop that sold various designer knockoffs. I got lucky with a parking space, and we only had to walk a block down to the small storefront where Caridad had her shop.

Orange neon rimmed the window and a small palm glowed red at the center. The frosted letters read FORTUNES BY CARIDAD; and the sign with the hours on it had been flipped to OPEN, so I pushed through the door, jangling a bell tied to the top. Booke came up behind me to stand at my shoulder while I took stock of the room; it was decorated like an old-fashioned parlor with velvet and damask furniture in hues of wine and saffron. In the middle sat a table with a black fringed cloth. Handwoven tapestries covered the walls, presumably to make potential patrons forget they were five minutes away from chicken being sold by the bucket.

"The only thing missing is the crystal ball," Booke said.

I nodded as Caridad came out of the back.

"I suspect you don't want your palm read," she said, after she placed me. Booke, she seemed not to recognize at all, which was probably for the best. "So I won't give you my usual patter about palmistry. What do you need?"

"My friend's gone missing, and I have reason to believe he may be in trouble. I wondered if there was a way you could scry for him."

Once, I could've cast this spell myself. Now, I'd only be able to do it via demon magick, and I was resolved not to use it, unless it was a matter of life and death. I didn't know how bad things were for Kel at the moment, so I needed to find out. If it required deploying Dumah to save him, I would . . . but *not* without further intel. I hoped Caridad wouldn't check me out with witch sight, then she did.

Her gaze narrowed. "Why should I help you?"

"Because I'm paying cash."

"Do you have any of his personal effects?" That was the magic word apparently. Caridad cared more about the state of my wallet than for my morality.

I cast a look at Booke and then answered softly, "No. But he and I were lovers once. He said that means we still have a . . . connection."

"Does your friend have any unusual qualities?"

"Yes, definitely." If I understood the question correctly, she was asking if he was gifted, or could use magick. Since I wasn't about to tell her he was Nephilim—or half demon, whatever—that was the most I could reveal.

"Then it's possible I can scry for him using your blood. Unless this connection he mentioned is strong, however, the results will probably be weak and limited, provided it works at all. The cost for the spell is five hundred dollars, payable up front and regardless of results."

Without haggling I counted out the bills. "I assume you don't do your real workings in the front?"

She shook her head. "Let me flip the sign and lock the door. Go on back."

We passed through a black velvet curtain into a more utilitarian space. Caridad had a stove for cooking potions and salves, a plain wood table, and four rows of shelves filled with various components neatly labeled in glass canisters. Booke took a seat as Caridad joined us. Muttering, the witch set the ingredients she needed on the counter, then she turned to me with a sharp silver athame.

"I need seven drops of your blood in the chalice, please." Now that she had my money, she was polite and professional, no hint of the arrogance that had colored our interaction at Chuch's place.

After pricking my finger, I squeezed out the requested amount; then she gave me a gauze pad. "This will take a few moments."

I nodded. "Anything else?"

"No. Just permit me to focus."

The hair rose on my arms as she summoned her power. Caridad mixed the herbs along with oil, water, and my blood, which gave it an oddly prismatic effect. As she whispered to the mixture, images resolved in the shimmering liquid, but they were vague and weak; I could only make out what looked like the thrashing of limbs—

But she was frowning. "It looks as if he's confined. Chained. I can't make out more, unfortunately. If you had something that belonged to him, I might be able to pinpoint his precise location. But this is the best I can do. I'm sorry."

I pushed out a slow breath. "It's fine. I'll track him down another way. It's enough to receive confirmation that he needs my help."

"Was that all?" she asked.

"Yes, thanks for your time."

Caridad escorted us to the door, unlocked it, and turned the sign back to OPEN. "Please consider me if you need more assistance. Have a good day."

I supposed there were worse things a witch could be, other than mercenary. Before we set out for La Rosa Negra, I gave Butch a drink and let him stretch his legs on the sidewalk. He promptly found a strip of grass and anointed it. Then he trotted back to me with a cocky Chihuahua strut.

"Done?" I asked.

Affirmative yap.

The trip wasn't bad if you stuck to the highways.

Driving in Texas was always a bit of a crap shoot, as sometimes there were great ruts in the roads, but not this time. Highway repair crews had been out recently, so the Pinto putted along, reliable if not desirable. Sadly, the route didn't offer much in the way of scenery—dry scrubland interspersed with rest areas and the occasional overpass oasis. Summer had fried the grass to a fire-hazard brown, and I imagined I could hear it crackling like tinfoil in the breeze as we blew past.

Booke was quiet as we drove, then he seemed to make a decision to exist in the present with me. I could only imagine what memories had been haunting him. He'd lost the woman he loved, a son he hardly knew, and his whole life. This had to feel like a dream to him sometimes, where he feared wakening with all his muscles clenched and in a cold sweat only to find he'd never left the ghost cottage after all.

"Tell me about this cantina." In his quiet voice I heard the unspoken plea.

Help me forget.

Because I wished somebody would do that for me, I regaled him with stories about La Rosa Negra, though I don't think he believed me about the cherry classic cars surrounding the dive. I told him about my first visit there,

Esteban, whose sister's body I helped to find, and the killer we brought to light years later through the tattoos on his knuckles. Without meaning to, I told him about dancing with Chance—the first time he ever broke his long-held reserve with me. In that moment, my hands clenched on the wheel. I could feel him moving behind me, his arms around me, his scent wrapping me up. With every fiber in my being, I ached.

When I paused, Booke said gently, "You love him so."

There were no words, so I just nodded. The conversation stalled after that. Just as well. I needed full attention to navigate the busier streets of San Antonio. Laredo wasn't a Podunk town, but there was more traffic here, more people too. After a series of wrong turns, I located the right street. In daytime, the area was on the seedy side. Darkness cloaked the peeling paint on the surrounding houses, the sun-faded pavement and cracked sidewalks with scraggly grass forcing its way up through the cement. A few kids were sitting on cars half a block up, likely lookouts for whoever ran the business in the neighborhood. I ignored them, knowing they wouldn't pay any attention to the Pinto. A major player wouldn't be caught dead in this ride.

La Rosa Negra was a lime green one-story building in crumbling stucco. It needed a coat of paint; hell, it could've used one the first time I visited. Inside, the bar was quiet, no waitress, just the guy behind the bar. He had long dark hair pulled into a sleek ponytail, and he chin-checked me in greeting, as I came out of the sun into the shady interior. Behind the counter, the picture of the maiden with the black rose clenched in her teeth still hung in its place of honor. The ceilings were low, beams and plaster giving the place a rustic air reinforced by the mismatched furniture and the scarred dance floor, empty at the moment. Ranchera music played quietly on an old radio, not a song I recognized, though. I scanned the room for potential troublemakers, but there were only a couple of drinkers . . . and one matched the description Chuch had given me, including the straw cowboy hat.

"That's our guy," I told Booke, who followed me to the old-timer's table.

"Mind if I join you?" I asked in English, then repeated in Spanish to be polite.

Beto offered a smile in reply, showing a couple of missing teeth. His sclera were faintly yellowed, his nose red, but he seemed happy to have company. With a broad, sweeping gesture, he indicated the seats opposite. "Not at all."

Booke and I settled. Then I said, "I heard you used to do some border work."

"I'm no coyote." He narrowed his eyes. "And even if I did help some people out back in the day, I'm retired now."

"That's not why we're asking," Booke put in. His accent surprised the old man, defusing some of his righteous indignation.

Beto cut an uncertain look at me. "What then?"

"I need to find someone, but I only have a vague idea where to start. A friend said you might be able to identify a sketch of a rock formation."

"Maybe. Buy me a drink, tell me a story, and I'll have a look." He waved the 'tender over without awaiting my response. "The good tequila, make it a double. She's paying my shot."

I nodded; as I put my money on the table, Booke said, "I'll have a bourbon, neat. Please."

At the barman's inquiring look, I added, "Nothing for me. I'm driving."

And trying to find a chained Nephilim. But I didn't figure the 'tender cared, though he might've heard weirder stories in his day. He served us quickly, then returned to his semi-doze behind the bar. To Beto I gave a condensed version of the situation: my friend was missing, but he'd managed to describe what he'd seen before we were cut off. That version of events had the benefit of not making me sound like a total headcase, even to a drunk.

Beto knocked his booze back without waiting for salt or lime. He swiped the back of his hand across his mouth, and then said, "Show me what you have."

I pushed the sketch across to him. "It's not much, I know."

He perused it with a faint frown. "I feel like I should know this place, but I can't place it. The formation is unique."

"That's what I thought too." Booke killed his bourbon with a pleased expression.

The cool thing about rolling with Booke was that for him, everything was an adventure. For the longest time, the modern world had just been a fable, though technology trickled into his prison via demon magick. Still, it must be hard to envision the changes until you saw them with your own eyes. Harder still to accept that you'd never see anything firsthand; instead you'd live out your unnaturally long life alone. Macleish had planned his punishment well.

"Any suggestions?" It had been a long shot that this former coyote would be able to place the locale at a glance. My luck just didn't run that way.

"Hire a witch to dowse?" Beto offered.

"That won't work," I murmured. "We already tried. Well, thanks anyway."

As I pushed to my feet, the old man snapped his fingers. "Must be your lucky day, señorita. I just remembered where I've seen that place. Back in the bad old days, it was used as a temporary holding pen for girls—"

"Who had been kidnapped and enslaved?" I'd stumbled into a human trafficking ring back when I was trying to locate Chance's mother, kidnapped by a cartel she crossed years ago. Ambivalence stirred in reaction to Beto's revelation. On one hand, I was glad the op had been shut down for good when we took out their chief warlock . . . but so many girls had died.

But the idea of driving out to a remote hidey-hole associated with cartel business? It didn't seem like the sanest thing I'd ever done. *But what the hell.*

"Can you give me directions?"

"I think so. Let me make a call. I was only out that way once, and I wasn't driving." He gazed at me expectantly, so I handed him my phone.

The subsequent conversation passed in rapid-fire Spanish; I caught bits and pieces, but some of it was too fast for me to translate. By the time he hung up, Beto looked pasty, and when he flattened his hands on the table, they were trembling.

"They're not using it anymore, but I just talked to an *amigo.* Said he knows a guy who went out there recently, but . . . he never came back."

So there's something guarding Kel. Makes sense.

"You feel like battling some demons?" I whispered to Booke.

He flashed me a wide smile. "I feel as if I've waited my whole life for someone to ask me that."

"Two lives, even. Brush up on some combat spells on the way, okay? I'm not gonna be much use out there."

"Don't sell yourself short."

Beto cleared his throat. "If you need some weapons, I know a guy."

Of course he did. I smothered a smile. "I'm not a very good shot, but if he sells Tasers and knives, I might survive long enough for Booke to do his thing."

"*Si*, he's got anything you could want."

"Not in a store?" I guessed.

"He sells out of his trunk."

That sounded familiar. Chuch had gotten me an emergency cell phone from a market that consisted of parked cars. "Let me guess . . ." I described the location.

"That's the place. Look for a tan Malibu, early eighties."

"Thanks. Can you write down the directions to the cartel hideout?"

"No problem." He borrowed a scrap of paper from the bartender, and I handed him a pen.

Booke leaned over. "Is this likely to get dicey?"

"Probably."

The Englishman smiled. "Finally."

I was less sanguine about facing monsters and death, but it was good he wasn't whining, like the dog in my handbag. Butch had been emitting a high-frequency moan ever since he heard about the unknown beast that killed the last dude who went out there. Like me, he was ready to settle down to a normal life.

After taking the directions, I dropped a couple of twenties on the table. "For your time."

"Don't die," the old man advised.

I offered a wry smile. "Will do my best."

Butch was still whimpering, so I set him on the scraggly grass, where he peed again out of sheer nerves. Booke picked him up to comfort him as we returned to the Pinto. He was smiling as he slid into the car, face upturned to bask in the sunlight. He had the pallor of a long-term invalid, like he'd just woken from a ten-year coma. Maybe it felt that way to him too.

"First, the street market?" Booke asked.

"Yeah, but it doesn't open until dusk. In daylight, it would draw too much attention."

"That makes sense. I suppose the area clears out when all the businesses close."

"Exactly."

We ended up killing time over lunch, and then I took him shopping. Impossible to believe, but the guy had never been to a mall. By the time we came out, he was loaded down with purchases, mostly tech toys he was dying to try. Since it was expensive, energy-wise, he'd only had the Birsael demon deliver the most essential items required to keep him healthy and sane.

"Ready to rock?" I asked, as we locked his new gear in the trunk. Gods help me if he ever discovered the Sharper Image.

"Indisputably."

The street market was much as I remembered it, hidden behind an abandoned warehouse. There was an unused parking lot, but the cars parked in the alley behind the building. There were a few merchants already doing business. To my surprise, the cell phone guy remembered me. "Need a hookup?" he yelled, making the universal "call me" sign with his thumb and forefinger.

Smiling, I shook my head, skimming the vehicles for a tan Malibu. Then I sighed. "Not here yet."

"What if he doesn't come?" Booke asked.

"Then I guess we wade in unprepared."

"There's a difference between 'yen for adventure' and 'death wish,'" he observed.

I shrugged. "I can't leave Kel hanging. Though I'm not the witch I used to be, and the touch won't do me much good in a fight, I have to try."

"That's what makes you such a good friend."

He put an arm around me and squeezed my shoulders in a friendly fashion. Though he looked younger, he felt like a favorite uncle. We didn't wait long for Tan Malibu. Part of me wondered if he knew Chuch, but I didn't want to drag the Ortizes further into this mess. Bad enough they had a crime scene in their yard. I watched as the dealer settled onto the hood, then I made my way over to his car.

"Can I help you?" he asked.

"Beto sent me."

"Yeah, he gave me the heads-up that you're okay. Otherwise I'd have to ask you to show me your belly."

In case I was wearing a wire. Just to settle the issue for his peace of mind, I flashed some skin and raised each of my pant legs. "I'll tell my friend to wait over there with my bag, if you're really worried."

At this suggestion, Butch popped his head out of my purse and growled. He didn't like being banished from the action.

The guy laughed. "Nah, it's cool. I see you got a guard dog. My auntie raises Chihuahuas . . . yappy little ankle biters."

Butch's growl went lower. I tapped him gently on the skull. "Pipe down, you know I love you."

He shut up.

"Whatcha need?"

"A Taser and a good knife, for sure."

He seemed a little disappointed. "You could buy that anywhere. I got some serious hardware up in here."

"I know, but I'm not the best shot."

"I'll take a piece," Booke said in his plummy accent.

The dealer's face was priceless. "Really?"

I stifled a smile, letting Booke take the lead. "It's been some years—" Massive understatement. "But I used to be quite a good shot. Let me see your hardware."

"With pleasure." The guy popped the trunk, revealing a dazzling array of weapons.

Some had obviously seen hard street use; others looked pristine, as if they'd just come off the factory floor. I didn't ask questions, as that tended to piss off entrepreneurs like Tan Malibu. Booke leaned over for a better look and then he indicated what I thought was a Glock.

"May I?"

The merchant nodded. "Sure, it's not loaded."

Though I wasn't the best judge of such things, Booke seemed to know what he was doing when he handled the gun. He held it two-handed with his fingers curled around for support, and it looked to me like he wasn't exaggerating his experience. I'd love to know more about his past, but it wasn't the time. I could hardly ask in front of GM when the story was so implausible.

"How's the recoil?" Booke asked, along with a number of technical questions, before nodding. "I'll take the nine millimeter."

"I only have one type of Taser in stock," GM told me. "But I don't think you'll be disappointed. And if you're looking for a quick kill after you incapacitate someone, then this is the blade for you." He demonstrated a few moves and explained where I should be stabbing.

That alarmed me, as he looked so *normal*, but it wasn't like killers went around with signs around their necks, or tattoos on their foreheads. That would make life so much simpler. In the end, I bought all three, plus some ammo for Booke's gun, and a shoulder harness that he slipped on under his jacket.

"Remember," GM called as we headed out. "If you're caught, it's illegal to carry concealed and I never met you."

I assured him, "We won't flip."

"Heard that before," he muttered.

Butch yapped at him in disapproval, as a Chihuahua's word was his bond. Funny, but even a gangly Englishman gained some swagger with a gun hidden beneath his coat. I teased him about it as I swung back into the car.

"Now you've got a total James Bond thing going on, only you're cooler because you do magick. You'll have to beat the ladies off with a stick."

He colored, cutting his eyes to the stained floor mat in the Pinto. Lord, it was a good thing our outcome didn't depend on image. The engine purred to life, however, a testament to Chuch's good work. Someday, I'd love to have him restore a car for me, totally custom from bumper to bumper.

Then Booke changed the subject; clearly he didn't want to talk about his own charms. "Speaking of magick, if you know of a shop, I need to get a few things. I'm not sure if you're familiar with how hermetic tradition works—"

"No clue." I figured I'd save him a few words. "Tell me how I can help."

He nodded as I pulled onto the street. "I'm not as versatile as a witch. I need more preparation, and to use my spells in combat, I must store them in a focus object, which is destroyed in the process."

"Gotcha. Yeah, I know a place. Shannon and I found it a while back when I was squaring off against the Montoyas."

Caridad didn't sell supplies; there was more profit to be made in offering spells only. But after this last stop, we should be ready to head into the wilderness to find Kel. *Hopefully it won't take forty days and nights.*

Then it occurred to me to ask, "How did you learn to shoot? I thought the U.K. had much stricter gun laws than the U.S."

"Not for soldiers," Booke said quietly.

Mentally, I did some math. He had been thirty-six in 1947, which meant he could've fought in World War II, but he'd said he had been with his lover for eight years, which would've taken place during wartime. But maybe they were separated until it ended . . . ? As I pulled into traffic, I decided to find out.

"Did you fight?"

"Yes. Perhaps that's why the romance seemed so much more desperate, more doomed . . . and therefore, more important. Ironically, by the time she told her husband everything, I was a different man. War changes you."

It had started as an indulgence of his ego, ended in tragedy. "So those eight years, it was off and on . . . all the stolen moments you could snatch."

"Precisely. I lived for those hours when she could sneak away . . . or I was on leave. Though toward the end . . ." He lifted a shoulder in a weary, self-deprecating shrug. "I loved her, but she wasn't the woman I wanted her to be."

I made a left turn, heading toward the highway. The directions fluttered on the scrap of paper on the dash, lifted by the vent, while Butch paced in the backseat. If he had his Scrabble tiles, he'd be Han Soloing all over the place, with a bad feeling about this. He wasn't the only one, but Kel was my friend. I never left people behind if I had a choice. Just one more errand, and then we'd see how bad the opposition was.

"I get it. Love is worth fighting for."

His face went pensive. "Sometimes I think it's the only thing that is. That's why you mustn't give up on your young man, no matter what."

The lump in my throat surprised me. "I won't. I'm facing some pretty steep opposition, maybe even going up against nature itself, but if hell didn't stop me, death won't either."

Booke gave a half smile. "Remind me never to cross you."

Unlikely Heroes

The arcane shop where Booke bought his supplies was housed in an Oriental Home Furnishings shop. Or that was the front. If you had the fortitude to shake off the aversion spell, you progressed to the real goods in the back. This time, I couldn't see the runes pulsing, but I felt them; and without my mother's magick, I had a strong inclination to get out before we ran into the creepy old woman again.

Booke grabbed my arm, forceful when he had to be. "None of that," he cautioned me in an undertone. "We've a job to do."

"Yes, sir."

He cut me a chiding look for the sarcasm and led the way toward the private sales floor. Though he'd never been to this shop before, apparently he was familiar with the premise. The room was filled with short shelves covered in esoteric supplies: wands, chalices, athames, and spell components, cunningly arrayed. There was a young woman at the counter this time, and I let out a small sigh of relief. Not subtle, it seemed, as the clerk focused on me.

"You're glad not to see my great-aunt." She had

strawberry blond curls, blue eyes, and she hardly looked old enough to be out of high school, but something told me her baby face was deceptive.

So I didn't bother to dissemble. "Maybe a little."

"She's retired now. In recent years she'd gotten a bit . . . odd, which makes for poor customer service."

Too many demons wandering in and out of her head, I thought, but didn't say so out loud.

The girl went on, "I'm Karen. If you need anything specific, have questions, or can't find what you're looking for, let me know. If we don't stock it, I'm sure I can special order what you need." There was a reassuring solidity behind her prettiness, making me think I wouldn't converse with any demons through her anytime soon.

"I have a list," Booke cut in.

His accent made Karen take notice, as did most Texan females. She brought him colorful powders, stored in glass vials, small ceramic figures, various herbs and liquids. It was like watching an alchemist prepare to transmute lead into gold—while carrying on a courtly flirtation. At the end of the transaction, she slipped him a business card, and I didn't think it was for special orders. I grinned at him as we went out to the Pinto, parked at a meter a block away. We passed Popeyes on the way, so the air smelled like fried chicken and biscuits. He didn't notice, too busy smirking.

I teased gently, "You should be ashamed, the way they tumble for you. What about Dolores?"

"She and I shared an amicable, somewhat calisthenic evening, not to be repeated." He held up a hand as I swung into the car, forestalling my commentary. "At her request, not mine. She knows I'm leaving and isn't interested in playing at a long-distance romance."

"I'm glad you were up front with her."

"I don't lie to women to get what I want. I'm not a scoundrel," he said in an aggrieved tone, but his word choice made me laugh.

"I think you mean 'dog' or 'player.'"

"My original point stands." He changed the subject, becoming brisk. "Is there a safe place where I can craft my foci?"

Starting the Pinto, I thought about that. There was no way I'd condone any magickal shenanigans where I was staying; no more complications for the Ortiz family. At one point, I'd used an Escobar safe house, but I wouldn't go there without the boss's sanction. My options in Texas were limited . . . and then I had it.

"If you're not picky, yes."

"I just need quiet and room to work," he said.

"Then this will suffice."

Making a decision, I put the car in gear, backed out of the parking space, and drove toward Ramon's trailer, where Chuch had stashed me when I was laying low after a long day of driving the Montoya cartel crazy. Hopefully, nobody had rented the place. If so, I'd claim to be lost, and try to find an alternative. But from what I remembered, it was more of a crash pad than a home.

Booke and I bickered amicably as we rolled toward our penultimate destination. I teased him about his lady-killer moves and he gave as good as he got. It was good to see him acting normal, a man with a future instead of one who had given up on happiness. When I found him at the ghost cottage, he'd seemed so beaten, so hopeless. I never wanted to see him that way again.

The Pinto rode like a horse wagon, no shocks to speak of, but at least if I lost this ride or it got blown up, Chuch wouldn't stroke out over it. Given how things were shaping up, either possibility seemed plausible. I was lucky I remembered the route Chuch had taken when he delivered me here, past the highway, past town, past everything worth seeing.

This RV park was a little slice of hell. Trash lay in moldering heaps, rusted carburetors and engines up on blocks. As I recalled from my last visit, one trailer nearby had license plates all over it, and the diagonal neighbor collected hubcaps. Stolen, I was sure. Trees featured sparsely in the landscaping, but on the plus side, if you were looking for broken glass to do an abstract mosaic, you only had to look down. Plastic bags blew in the wind, tangling in the scrubby bushes. As I parked in front of a run-down single-wide, Booke stared.

"Do they even have trailer parks in the U.K.?" I wondered aloud.

"Yes, but they're called caravans . . . and they're nothing like this."

I imagined not. The cracks in the underpinning had gotten worse, so that the vinyl hung completely askew on one side. For obvious reasons, the door wasn't locked. Since I'd been inside once, I thought I was prepared; only I wasn't—but not for the reasons I expected. Someone had hauled off the plaid purple couch, and the stained brown carpet had been removed too. The subfloor had been covered in new vinyl, and it wasn't catastrophically ugly. Nobody would ever mistake it for real Italian tile, but it was a big improvement. All of the rubbish had been hauled away, and it now smelled of orange cleaner. Judging by his remodeling efforts, Ramon was seriously trying to rent the place out; the area was undesirable, but price it low and somebody would jump at it. This wasn't a large trailer, but it had a kitchenette, along with some typical mobile features like a table and dinette, a small living area, minuscule bath, and a bedroom large enough to house a queen-sized bed.

Booke surveyed the space, then gave an approving nod. "I can work at the pull-down table."

"Go for it."

I went into the bedroom to find the stained mattress had been removed and the walls scrubbed down. It smelled clean in here too. Strange to think while I had been in Sheol, people I knew had been going about their ordinary lives. Yet that didn't sound boring to me at *all*.

I longed for the day when work and paying the bills constituted my biggest problem.

Since there was nowhere else to wait, I returned to the main room and sat down on the dining bench, careful not to disrupt Booke. His hands were quick and elegant as he laid the sigils that would protect his work. Not that it was demon magick, but you could never be sure what spells would attract attention. Best not to put all that shimmering energy out as a lure.

I'd worked as a witch and witnessed Tia crafting some impressive charms, but it was nothing like the hermetic tradition. Often our magick was sympathetic, invoked with one thing that represented something else. There was a precision to this; and I wished I could see how he was channeling the energy. Unfortunately, witch sight was closed to me, so I could only feel a faint, residual tingle as he poured power into his focus objects, storing them for future use. His items of choice were ceramic figurines, which would shatter on impact, unleashing the spell. Each statuette correlated with the chosen effect, though sometimes in ways I didn't understand.

"What does the mouse do?" I asked, after he finished.

"Increases stealth."

"Really?"

"How often do you see them?" he pointed out. "But they're everywhere."

"Fair enough. Are you set?"

He looked tired, but not as drained as he had been from the working that let me into the ghost cottage, and he still had the Glock. There was no question Booke would be the heavy hitter on this run while I provided backup as best I could with touch, Taser, and blade. That had to make him happy, as he'd spent so many years playing a support role. It was past time for this guy to be an action hero.

"Yes, let's go for a drive, Corine."

"We need to work on your heroic verbiage," I told him.

"Not fierce enough? Shall I try again?"

Laughing, I shook my head and led the way out of the trailer. I'd remember this place, if I needed to lay low again. The Pinto blended right in, so none of the neighbors would pay any attention. Even Barachiel might lose track of me here.

Okay, probably not. He probably has a magickal Lo-Jack on my soul.

The mood darkened as I drove out of the trailer park and cut toward the highway. Booke read the directions to me as a better-than-automated form of GPS, and bonus, his voice didn't go all demonic in pronouncing street names. By this time, it was getting late, the sky heavy with sunset, and I clicked on the lights. Other cars passed while I searched for the turnoff.

"Here," Booke said at last, but the road was so close by then that the car fishtailed when I slammed on the brakes.

I checked the rearview, found no traffic behind me, so I reversed twenty feet and hung right. This reminded me a little of the final battle between the Montoyas and me, but I wasn't alone this time, and I wouldn't solve my problems by calling Dumah to eat anybody's soul. Expedience had driven that decision but I wouldn't repeat it.

"How far do we have to go?"

"Five miles. We're heading north, parallel to the border."

Nodding, I drove on, my stomach tight with fear. Crazy as it seemed, I had a wizardly World War II veteran as my point man on this operation. Sometimes my life was just too weird for belief. Worried thoughts carried me to our destination; the gravel road had ended long before, making it tough going for the Pinto. This was 4WD territory, but the car had heart, and the suspension was already shot. Chuch wouldn't care much. I hoped.

I parked, climbed out of the vehicle to survey what lay ahead. By this point, the moon was high, throwing a

silver sheen over the remote landscape. The rock formation matched the one I'd glimpsed in the vision Kel
shared—moreover, I recognized the honeycomb nature
of the site. People had lived here, ages before; folks still
lived in the quarries in France, tunneling into the soft
limestone cliffs. Here, the rock had a forbidding, desolate
air, as if blood had been spilled, and then soaked into the
stones themselves.

His door slammed; then Booke joined me. "It's quite
dreadful, isn't it?"

"We shouldn't waste time. It's taken too long already
to get to Kel."

He nodded. "I can imagine few things more horrible
than being trapped, unless it's being imprisoned and at
someone else's mercy."

Yeah, you didn't have that, at least. To my mind, loneliness was almost as bad. I put aside my fear and jerked
my head toward the stairs cut into the side of the mesa.
They were so old that they looked like they might only
be safe for mountain goats, but I had to try. With every
fiber of me, I wanted to call out to Kel, give him some
warning we were close, but I was afraid that might tip off
his captors. He'd said the host punished him for inso-
lence, including a stint in prison, but this . . . well, the
dead man's hands running up and down my spine had
little to do with the weather.

I strode forward, shoes crunching over loose gravel
that created a makeshift parking lot, perfect for loading
shipments. Nothing I saw here made me think the cartel
was still using this place as a staging ground; it simply felt
abandoned, not even a lingering hint of old gas or machinery. Instead, I could only smell sage and saguaro, the
crisp nip of air sweeping down from the mountains.

Using my hands for purchase, I scrambled up the
weathered stairs, as erosion had left them crumbling beneath my feet. Booke swore behind me, his hand on my
shoulder to steady me when I slipped backward. My

heart thudded in my ears. I hated heights, hated closed spaces. In saving Kel, I would face both.

This is too much, I thought. *I never wanted this.*

But maybe if I didn't think about it, I could do it. Heroes never went around in capes; they just did what they had to. And so would I.

Above us, the first entrance loomed, dark and narrow, like a slit of a mouth in the rock. I clicked on my flashlight and slipped inside. Once, I wouldn't have needed it, but my light spell didn't work anymore. It was dark here, quiet, no hint of occupancy. This was just a shallow room with a shelf cut from the wall, and it reminded me of Greydusk's home in Sheol.

He died for you. Like Chance. Like your father.

The wave of pain swamped me, crippling in its intensity. I hadn't wanted that, never asked for it. Sometimes the worst fate was being left behind, being asked to deal with what other people had given up for you. In this case, everything. I wasn't so special that I deserved any of this; and so I was a mess, crawling from one catastrophe to another.

"This was somebody's home," Booke said quietly. He was holding a shard of pottery in his hand, the paint faded but still perceptible.

"That makes it even worse, what the cartel did here . . . and what's being done to Kel now. Let's move." I forced myself to sound fierce and determined when my knees wanted to buckle.

Fake it 'til you make it. One of these days that strategy would fail me in spectacular, horrifying ways. Until then, it was all I had.

Killing Ground

Booke and I explored a number of similar spaces before locating a natural room that had an opening at the back of the wall, a natural cavern connected to the man-made spaces. From deeper within, I heard movement. When I glanced at Booke, he wore an intent look.

"Thoughts?" I asked in a whisper.

"It's time to break out the mouse."

Incredibly, I knew what he meant. He retreated far enough that crushing the statuette shouldn't alert anyone deeper within, and as he did so, the magick swept over us at once. It was subtler than witch workings, but the first step I took into the tunnel made no sound at all. I crept over loose stones, expecting to turn the corner at any moment and run into something horrible. As I went deeper, the smell increased: not the sulfur and brimstone stench that marked demonic presence, but something sharper and sweeter, like old blood mixed with burnt sugar.

A rasp in repetitive cadence echoed softly against the stone to the point that I couldn't place where the sound was coming from. The tunnel sloped down, and I had the terrifying thought that Kel could be in Sheol. What if this led to a natural gate? Greydusk—the demon who helped me save Shannon and died in the attempt—had said that there were places where the barrier between the planes was thin, but to open the way, I would need a sacrifice in order to save Kel. My inchoate fear slid away when I realized I could see the back of the cave ahead. It was fairly deep in the mesa, but it didn't look to be so far underground as to lead to hell. And the panting noises were punctuated by groans of pain.

Kel was here—and they were torturing him.

I crept forward, Booke at my side, to get a better view of the scene. In order to plan a strategy, we had to see what we were dealing with. Kel lay on a natural stone table, shimmering bonds of energy holding him in place. An unfamiliar male whom I took to be another member of the host stood over him with a shining silver knife, similar to the one Kel used. So I guessed the torturer was Nephilim as well; otherwise, he'd have a bigger blade, à la Barachiel. The huffing sounds came from the creatures pacing around his feet. They bore a rudimentary resemblance to Rottweilers yet they were so dark that their fur seemed to drink the light, with coils of plumed smoke swirling about their legs, and when they turned their massive heads to scan for intruders, their eyes glinted bloodred.

"What the hell are those?" I whispered to Booke, so soft that he could scarcely hear me inches away—and yet that noise made one of the animals prick up his ears.

He put his lips near my ear to make his reply. "Legend would call them hellhounds, but they're ordinary animals possessed and corrupted by the Klothod."

That made sense. I had some experience with that phenomenon, as demonic monkeys had tried to kill me in Catemaco. They hadn't been easy to destroy either, as I recalled. During that fight, I used my inherent Solomon power for the first time. Unfortunately, I could no longer bind or banish demons through the might of a demon queen chained to my DNA. *Dammit.*

But that brought up a more salient point. "If this colleague of Kel's is using bound Klothod, doesn't that substantiate the claim that they were all demons at one point and that the 'host' has simply changed its backstory?"

Booke nodded. "This doesn't look particularly angelic, does it?"

A hellhound broke away from the other two, its nails clicking on the stone as it sniffed in our general direction. I froze, willing it not to find us, willing Butch not to make a sound. Sometimes my dog could be inappropriately confrontational, barking when he had no hope of winning a fight. This time, however, he cowered like a pro at the bottom of my purse, so I guessed he knew how high the stakes were. We'd get only one chance to take these guys out.

"What's our play?"

Booke was searching silently through his pockets, seeking a spell. Gods, I wished I could be more useful in a fight. Though I didn't miss the incredible power for myself, magick would come in handy at times like this. No use in wishing for the moon, however; I could only use the skills the trip to Sheol had left me. At best, we faced two-to-one odds—three ferocious hellhounds, plus a Nephilim, wielding a knife that would kill anything, from what I'd seen. He probably had Kel's fast healing abilities too, but there had to be some way to incapacitate him.

"No creature, however powerful, can function without its head."

"Cockroaches can live for weeks without their heads," I pointed out.

Booke aimed a sober look at me. "These aren't cold-blooded creatures, except in the moral sense. Which means my strategy is sound."

But before we could tackle the Nephilim, we had to take out the Klothod-powered dogs. The one sniffing toward us decided there was something hiding in the shadows, breaking away from the others to investigate. I didn't have the ability to destroy the hosts by banishing the demons, but there were fewer Rottweilers than there had been monkeys, so maybe if we killed the animals one by one, it would have the same effect. I backed away from the main chamber, letting the natural shadows of the tunnel swallow me. The spell Booke had used earlier helped in that regard, but the hellhound knew we were there. It could smell us; the creature just couldn't see or hear us, which might permit my impromptu plan to work. I tightened my grip on the Taser, signaling that I had this.

I hope.

Booke crab-walked back behind me, not bad for a guy who could barely move, period, a few days ago. He was ready with a spell just in case, but the premise was sound. As soon as the dog rounded the corner, I pressed the button and the sparking filament leapt between us. I poured full voltage into the animal—and as I'd hoped, its host body couldn't handle so much electricity. It dropped in spasms, rendering the demon temporarily helpless. At best, we had seconds.

I sprang forward with the knife and opened its throat. The stink of sulfur and brimstone boiled out. This animal had been possessed a long time, as it reeked of death and decay—and even in this faint light, I could see the blood wasn't red anymore; it looked more like tar, black as pitch and just as sticky. Booke motioned at me to be careful as midnight smoke rose up from the corpse. Instead of dissipating, as I'd hoped, it sped off toward the other dogs.

"Run," Booke whispered.

He didn't need to tell me. As soon as the Klothod joined its brethren, they'd know we were here, and then the next dog we faced would be twice as strong. As I ran, I fumbled in my bag, fingers brushing Butch's shivering body, while I searched for a fresh cartridge. The Taser only offered one shot as a distance weapon. Though I could still use it as a stun gun otherwise, I didn't like my odds of survival if these two monsters got close enough to bite me.

An awful, blood-curdling howl echoed through the caverns behind us. I stumbled as I ran, scraping my palms on the rock; fresh blood prickled my hands. Booke scrambled out ahead of me and spun in search of better ground. Outside, there were only rocks, dirt, and darkness, no staging ground for a fight of this magnitude.

Please let the Nephilim think these demon dogs are chasing squirrels. Give us time to deal with them, before we have to fight him.

"Take the left," Booke ordered.

I hoped he had a plan for the one on the right. At his command, I planted my feet, aimed the Taser . . . and missed, as the monstrous Rottweiler leapt at me. Impact rocked me back, and the thing sank its slavering fangs into my upper thigh. Its jaws clamped down, savaging the muscle, and my leg buckled. I went down as Booke threw something at the other monster. The statuette shattered, freezing the creature in place. I slammed the Taser against the hellhound's throat and stunned the shit out of it, probably more volts than it needed—but no. It still didn't let go. Shocks ran through the animal's body, but it must have twice the demon-enhanced power, so it only bit down harder. I swallowed a scream, determined not to be the weak link. Some dogs wouldn't let go until their prey was dead or they were. My leg hurt too much for me to remember if Rottweilers were among them.

"Your blade, Corine! The spell won't hold forever."

I tossed the knife at Booke—or tried to, but it dropped from my trembling fingers. Now I could feel the Klothod draining me through the host animal. My life essence trickled away like the blood running down my thigh. My vision went gray and sparky, and I couldn't feel my fingers anymore. With my last burst of strength, I rammed the Taser against the hellhound one last time. The resultant shock finally dropped it, but it still didn't let go. Booke came in with my dagger in hand, and he stabbed it repeatedly in the neck. At first, through dizziness and pain, I thought he was in a rage, but when he kicked it hard in the skull and the monstrous head popped off, I realized he had been perforating the thing. With gentle hands, he opened the inert jaws and removed the teeth from my leg. I fell back onto the rocks, sick and woozy with shock.

"We don't have long," he said. "Soon the Nephilim will notice that its guardians have gone missing and come to investigate."

"I know," I managed to say.

My jeans were shredded and sticky with blood; he cut part of the material away from my thigh, and I bit down on my lower lip to keep from screaming. His hands were gentle, and I imagined him in a trench during the Second World War, tending to his comrades. Clearly he had some first aid experience, but Booke wore a ferocious frown.

"I brought a couple of healing spells, but if I use them on you, we won't have any left for Kel, and I don't know whether he'll be able to walk out of here without them."

"Don't worry about me, just wrap it up."

"I could numb it for you."

"Then do it. Fast."

This wasn't a spell, apparently, as he drew out a stoppered vial full of white powder. He poured some into his palm and blew it against the wound. Immediately it stopped hurting, though I could tell it wasn't any better. The flesh was still torn; blood still oozed sluggishly from the punctures. I took Booke's hand, allowing him to pull me upright. Yeah, this would do for a stopgap measure.

"I hope I haven't crippled you," he said worriedly. "That's not meant as a first aid treatment."

"What is it, then?"

"A spell component from the binding spell I used on the third dog."

Seemed logical. At last the animal didn't feel any pain when Booke cut its throat. I took an experimental step, found that my leg would bear weight. I'd deal with potential muscle and nerve damage later. For now, I had to focus on getting Kel out of here.

I'll just go kill a Nephilim now, no problem. After nearly getting my ass kicked by a demon-enhanced Rottie.

That was kind of sad, actually. In Sheol, I had thrown down with the best of them, spells flying fast and furious. But then, that wasn't really me either. Sometimes those memories got tangled in my head, until I couldn't remember what had been Ninlil and what had been me. There was still a huge hole inside me where she had been. Barachiel had told me that feeling came from paring the demonic taint from the Solomon line. What that meant for future offspring, I had no idea.

With grim determination, I got the last cartridge out of my purse and loaded the Taser. It was unlikely this would work on an opponent of the Nephilim's caliber, but maybe keeping Kel on the torture table had weakened him, and that was why he had guard dogs to watch his back in the first place. I could dream anyway. I didn't know if I had the stamina for a knock-down, drag-out fight.

"Keep your head down," I told Butch, who didn't look interested in doing anything else. Then I fell behind Booke. "I think we have to use his own knife on him. Kel can heal from anything else almost immediately."

He caught on at once. "But the damage the other Nephilim is inflicting isn't going away as fast."

"Yeah, exactly. Is the mouse spell still in effect?"

Belatedly I realized I could find out by stepping on some loose gravel. When my footfall came whisper soft, I had my answer. I was too drained to devise a plan, so I just trudged after Booke. At the moment I didn't know what spells he had left in his arsenal, but as we drew closer, I tapped him on the shoulder.

"Strategy? You've got the damage portfolio."

"See if you can free Kel while I deal with the Nephilim. We can't risk him killing your friend. He may have orders to that effect."

Given what I knew of Barachiel, that seemed likely. I wished I could fuel up on magick as I had done in Sheol, but here and now I was weak, wounded, and . . . human. So I had to solve this problem with my brain; too bad it was muzzy and felt like a melon atop my shoulders. Still, I applied myself to the problem. Coming around the last curve in the tunnel, I searched my memory for any useful details about the setup; there had been magickal restraints on Kel—

When I hit the kill site, my feet skidded in the smoldering blood still oozing from the first hellhound. The soles of my shoes smoked, and Booke lifted me away. I was surprised at his strength, though maybe I shouldn't be. Trapped in the ghost cottage, he must've done a basic workout in order to keep fit and sane. I clutched his shoulder as he set me on my feet on the other side of the corpse, wishing I could just dump this problem on his shoulders while I passed out. But that had never been my style, plus this was a two-person job.

Kill the Nephilim. Rescue Kel. Not necessarily in that order.

Free at Last

The Nephilim didn't look like Kel. I didn't know why I expected he would, but when I crept around to the side, I saw that he looked more like a normal human male, except for the gleaming silver blade in his hand. His expression, however, said he reveled in the cruelties he inflicted on his victim. There was nothing angelic about his demeanor at all. Privately I marveled that Barachiel—and others—had managed to construct this elaborate fiction, maintain it over eons.

When I got into position, I signaled Booke. Worry bubbled in my stomach, making me feel nauseous, or maybe it was a resurgence of the illness that had plagued me earlier. It wouldn't shock me to learn I'd developed an ulcer. I wished I could be the one taking on the enemy, but between the Glock and his foci, the Englishman was far better suited to the task, especially since I was injured and still bleeding. Fortunately, the torturer didn't possess the same sense of smell as the Rottweilers.

"You look bored," Booke said, and the half demon spun. I wouldn't call them Nephilim anymore, now that I knew the truth.

That was my cue. I crawled forward, using the edge of

the stone table as cover. With preternatural speed, the demon lunged at Booke, who fired off a round. It pinged into the rock and ricocheted; I couldn't watch the fight any longer. I had to find some way to free Kel. Bonds of shimmering energy coiled around his wrists and ankles, but I couldn't find a genesis point on top of the table. From what I knew, all energy required a source, or continuous concentration. Since the half demon was trying to choke Booke at the moment, he couldn't be the source. Which meant something near the table was keeping Kel in check.

Booke slammed a statuette to the ground and a riot of dark energy blossomed up. It wrapped around him like a cloak, lending him a terrifying aspect, as if he'd become death itself. Even the half demon paused his assault. Then he pressed, only to find that the black-violet tendrils lashed at him like snakes, and when they struck, they pulsed with a paler power, as if siphoning out his life force. The torturer scrambled back, seeing that he couldn't complete a direct attack.

"You cannot defeat me," he told Booke. "I am Nephilim. I am Ahadiel, enforcer of divine will."

By his tone, he actually believed that. *Poor bastard.* They'd told Kel that he was God's Hand, and that all the bad shit they made him do was ordered by a higher power. Now I knew that wasn't true. And when he realized that, I didn't know how he could live with it. He didn't kill easily or lightly; each death weighed on him, but at least before he had the comfort of believing it was for the greater good.

"Your handlers had a sense of humor," Booke responded, his tone gentle.

"You mock heaven itself."

"No, I don't." He raised the Glock and fired, the dark energy still whirling about him. "And you've weakened. The reason that's so interesting? The spell I used is a demon drain."

"That's not true." Shock and horror colored the words. "I am *Nephilim*."

"So they've told you." Booke sounded sympathetic.

I dropped to my knees, knowing how much my thigh would hurt if the numbing powder wore off. Possibly my movements were damaging my leg even more, but I had to get Kel off this table, and if the torturer noticed somebody coming in the back way, no telling what he'd do. Right now, Booke had him off guard, and that was the best-case scenario. The wizard was smart as hell; maybe *only* he could provoke an enemy to chat during a fight.

Angling my head, I peered beneath the table. *Bingo.* There were four gems inset into the stone, reminiscent of the soulstones that powered the gate between earth and Sheol. Hoping they weren't full of somebody's spirit, I took a deep breath and grabbed the one closest to me. Pain howled through me like a banshee's wail, hot and cold at once, so my palm felt as if it was simultaneously smoldering and flash freezing. My nerve endings couldn't process the overwhelming stimuli, so they shut down, leaving me with a numb right hand—and the jewel didn't budge. I pulled with dead fingers, agony driving up my forearm toward my elbow. Only death and demon magick tended to be that strong. *Please don't let these be soulstones.* If the paralysis reached my lungs, my heart, my brain, well, it was over. But I'd already started, so there was no way out but through. I wouldn't let Kel down.

Maybe there's a trick to it. I pushed and pulled, twisted, until I heard a click, and the crystal dropped into my hand. Inert. With trembling fingers, I set it down. *Three more to go.* Maybe setting a circle for protection would've helped, but I didn't have witch magick, and the touch hadn't responded; there was no emotional charge in these gems, just pure, crackling power. *It's too late to draw a demon magick circle.*

I knee-walked to the second spot. Booke was cursing,

so I guessed the fight was back on; Ahadiel had chosen to disbelieve the truth, but the demon-drain spell was making it hard for him to melee. And that gave Booke a fighting chance—strategy, not brute strength, would carry the day.

This time, I knew how to remove the gem, and my hand was already dead, so I didn't feel much new pain, though the old anguish was busy chewing my biceps, up toward my shoulder. It felt as if there were tiny teeth savaging their way through tendon and muscle. Pretty soon, my arm would hang limp at my side, and I'd be unable to use it, except as a club.

Two more.

I couldn't manipulate my right hand well enough to remove the jewel so I used my left, and the pain came at me fresh. This time, I wasn't strong enough to stop the scream. It bubbled up from my throat, past my lips, into a pathetic sound that roused an answering howl from Butch, who was still cowering in my bag. The sounds echoed in the chamber, ringing off the walls. *No hope he didn't hear.*

"Is someone else here?" Ahadiel demanded.

"No," Booke said quickly. "Let's finish this."

"I heard a woman. Where is she?" He didn't wait for a reply.

Instead I heard footsteps cracking closer and closer to where I fumbled with the third stone. As Ahadiel peered under the table, it dropped into my hand, and a shot rang out. The half demon toppled forward, cracking his head on the rock. The back of his head oozed blood, then Booke limped into sight. His cheekbone was bruised, his lip split and puffy, and I could see the marks from where he'd been throttled. The demon-drain spell must've worn off, giving Ahadiel the opportunity to fight.

"Are you all right?" I asked.

"He very nearly stabbed me in the kidney. Bloody fast, that one. But I dropped a spell just in time. Are you almost done?"

"Almost," I said.

Only one left.

Booke bent to investigate the body. "He's not dead, just incapacitated."

"I'll hurry."

My left hand was clumsy, fingers numb, but I forced them to fasten around the final gem. It took me four tries to manage the special push and twist to disengage the connection. The pain in my right side had reached the juncture between neck and shoulder; on my left, it was at my elbow. I didn't have long left. Moments, maybe just seconds. Breath felt more labored each time I pulled it into my sluggish lungs.

"The bindings have dissipated. He's not responding, though. We'll have to—" His words choked off, presumably because Kel had his hands on Booke's throat.

Crawling out from under the stone table took all my coordination, given that I could hardly feel my arms, and I had pain shooting into my spine. My voice came out hoarse. "Kel, we're here to help. Let go."

His icy eyes opened and cut to me. On waking to find himself freed, he'd lashed out at his tormenters instinctively; I had some experience with his tendency to do that. He breathed once, twice, and then opened his hands. I put my dead fingers over his, hoping it was a comforting touch, as I couldn't feel it. *So much* of my body was numb at the moment. That couldn't be good.

Booke staggered back a few steps. Another wave of agony pulsed through me, and my vision darkened at the edges. It was all I could do to gasp, "Can you remove a . . . curse? If not . . . I think I might . . . die."

His mouth dropped open, but he didn't ask questions. Booke dug into his coat as I reeled backward. Kel's hands steadied me against the stone table. He was horribly wounded yet he could still manage to be gentle; I felt it in the careful press of his palms to the small of my back, one of the few spots on my body that retained any feeling. Booke crushed the statuette at my feet, and I received immediate relief. As the attacking magick drained away, I regained more motor control.

"What happened?" he demanded, once he could see I was breathing easier.

"I think it was some kind of magickal trap. Like a poison, kind of. There's one that shuts down your bodily systems one by one, inducing paralysis until your lungs don't work anymore." I shrugged. "That's what it felt like anyway."

Booke glared at me with startling ferocity, the first time I'd ever seen him angry. "Corine, that's absurd. You shouldn't have continued. I could've — "

"How many curse removals did you have in your bag?"

He paused. "Just the one."

"Exactly. So once I started, if I didn't finish, we couldn't have freed Kel without one of us dying. I had to gamble."

"You should not have taken such a risk for me," Kel said softly.

He wore his sorrow and disillusionment nakedly, as visible as his tattoos. Though he was still big and powerful-looking, he also carried despair with him, worn like a dark cloak. His eyes gleamed with powerful regret, a millennia of misdeeds weighing on him like gravestones. Now he must live with the knowledge that he'd done everything for Barachiel's agenda, not a higher power.

"You're my friend. Of course I should."

He shook his head. "When I confronted Barachiel with the truth, he laughed, Corine. He *laughed*. I tried to fight him . . . and could not. I am bound to serve him, bound to suffer his punishments, for no purpose greater than his whim. And I begin to think he is truly mad."

"It wouldn't surprise me," I said.

Barachiel hadn't struck me as possessing an excess of sanity anyway. Plus, power had a track record of sending people around the bend. The more they had, the more they wanted, until they reached critical mass, where nothing in the world could content them. I feared Barachiel had long since reached that tipping point.

The half demon stirred at our feet. A bullet in the brain had only slowed him down, not neutralized him. Given what I'd seen my friend endure, I had no idea how to take this monster out. To make matters worse, I felt sorry for Ahadiel, as he was trapped, just like Kel. *If only there was some way to break Barachiel's hold . . .*

Kel's features hardened. "Take his head. It's the only way."

I didn't blame him for that response. The wounds Ahadiel had inflicted were still raw and numerous, and since they had been carved with one of those special silver knives, they took longer to heal. The agony must be excruciating.

But Booke paled, his face going green at the prospect of decapitating a humanoid. I guessed it was different with hellhounds. And I didn't look forward to doing that job either. Kel seemed to read our reluctance.

"Help me up. If you cannot, I will. It must be done."

I offered him my hand, as did Booke, and together we towed him to his feet. He rocked a little but got his balance, and then he took the knife from the other half demon. I could see it required all his energy, but he bent to do the job. He sawed through the neck while the half demon squirmed on the ground, moaning. Butch whimpered inside my bag. *Poor dog. I know just how you feel.*

When I realized how Kel intended to finish the job, I grimaced and turned my face away. But I still heard the wet, squelching pop of a head being torn away via brute strength. Some horrific part of me had to see, had to know, so I glanced back, to find Kel standing with bloody hands, a hopeless expression on his face. His tatts glimmered with faint, arcane light, a sign of magick being expended, or strong emotion. In this case, I suspected it was both.

The dead half demon on the ground crumbled from fresh corpse to dry remains and then down into dust. I figured once the magick keeping him alive went away, age and physics took over. Kel raked his boot through the ashes, head bowed. I could only imagine what must be running through his mind.

"Are you good to go?" I asked.

That wasn't what I wanted to know. I wanted to ask if he was all right—and yet I already knew the answer. He wasn't—not even close—and his problems weren't physical. Kel had just discovered that his whole life was a lie, and that those he trusted had used him for evil. I stumbled away from the table, hating the pain I saw in him, but unable to impact it.

"I can walk," Kel said.

As for me, I needed Booke's shoulder because the charm he'd used to remove all magickal effects from me also negated the numbing powder he'd used on my thigh. So while my arms and shoulders were all right again, my leg hurt like a bitch. He guided me carefully out through the tunnels, though I rested periodically, fighting the urge to pain-vomit. Eventually we made it to the car, so I handed him the keys.

"I can't. I think we need to find a hospital."

"I could not agree more," Booke said.

He held the seat so I could tumble into the back of the Pinto. Kel offered, but he was hurt worse than me; I feared the wrong angle would make his intestines fall out. He just needed a place to sleep for three days. My leg would grow putrid if I tried the same treatment. I angled to the side to stretch my thigh, but it hurt so much, a fierce throbbing deep in the muscle.

"I'll probably be unconscious by the time we get to the hospital," Kel said softly. "So I'll say it now. Thank you. Nobody's ever come for me before."

Gods, that just broke my heart. By the way he cleared his throat and murmured a choked *You're welcome*,

Booke felt the same way. To cover his reaction, he started the car, then belted in.

I dug into my bag to get my phone. A few clicks and then: "This is the nearest hospital, and I've mapped the route for you." I handed it to Booke.

"Hang on, Corine. Everything will be all right."

Emergency Services

That was all I knew for a little while. I blacked out in the car and woke to Booke dragging me out of the Pinto. He'd parked the car askew at the Emergency entrance. I didn't blame him, as two of his passengers had passed out.

As I pulled myself onto the pavement, I said, "Go park the car. We can't let them see Kel. They'll want to admit him too, and we're gonna have a hard enough time explaining my wounds. Let's not add his fast healing to the mix."

"Are you sure?"

I nodded, limping toward the doors, which slid open at my approach. Fortunately, an orderly was passing with a wheelchair when I stumbled in, and he rushed forward to help me. I sank down into the seat, huffing out a pained sigh. He pushed me toward the front desk.

"Animal attack?" he asked.

"Yes, a big dog."

"Surely you didn't drive yourself to the ER? Why didn't you call 911?"

Here we go, I thought. *Now I get to tell the story in a way that makes sense . . . and doesn't include demons.*

"No. I was out hiking with a friend, no emergency response where we were. We paused to eat, and some wild dogs came after us. They must've been hungry."

"Probably. How many were there?"

"Three. All Rottweilers." That much was true.

"Jesus. Somebody running a fight ring probably. How many of them got at you?"

"Just one. My friend managed to kill the others."

"Shit, did the biter get away?"

I had no idea why that mattered. "No, we got that one too, eventually. But not before it chewed the hell out of my thigh."

"Did you bring the body with you?"

"Uh, what? No."

"Your friend will need to go back out there. We can't be sure if you need the rabies vaccine until we test the animal."

Oh, crap. I never even thought of that. "Isn't that like sixteen horrible shots in the stomach?"

He laughed. "These days, it's like a flu shot, and you get it in the arm. But you'll need multiple vaccines over a few weeks to complete the course."

That was better than a needle in the gut. "When Booke gets in here, I'll tell him to drive back out there. Hopefully the carcasses are still there."

"Don't leave it long, or other predators may carry off the remains."

"I'll take care of it."

He signaled to the woman behind the desk, conveying my story in far fewer words than I'd used. Then he concluded, "I'll park her until you get the paperwork done and you're ready to send her back."

There were others ahead of me, of course. A gunshot wound, a stabbing, a little boy with a burned hand. His eyes were red and puffy with crying, his mother stroking his head worriedly. What a crappy place to end the day. Besides the antiseptic smell, hospitals radiated despair, as if the walls absorbed all the illness until it radiated on an emotional level. Probably that was just my personal distaste showing through. Probably. But I was careful not to touch anything, not to let my gift break free in these environs.

I'd filled out one form by the time Booke joined me, wearing a worried look. He knelt beside the chair. "Do you want me to take over?"

"My hands are fine. If you really want to help, apparently they need the dead dog for testing."

"Rabies," he guessed. The guy was smarter and more strategic than me.

"Exactly. I hate to send you back out there, but—"

"It's not a problem. I'd rather stay with you, but if it needs done, I'm happy to help. But I insist on ringing Chuch or Shannon. You shouldn't be here alone."

Since I really hated hospitals, I didn't argue. "Call Shan."

Booke did as I asked, and the conversation was brief. Then he reported, "She'll be here in half an hour."

"Thanks, B."

"I've never had a sporty nickname before. I rather like it." Smiling, he kissed my cheek and then he strode toward the sliding doors.

The room didn't get less depressing after he departed. In fact it was worse. At first I had the paperwork to occupy me, but that went pretty fast. The receptionist gave me a look when I presented my insurance card; I guessed I didn't look like the sort who had any, but I paid the premiums knowing I was prone to trouble. Until now, I had been fairly lucky—I hadn't been in the hospital as a patient since I fell through the floor of a burning building, years back.

The reason you finally left Chance.

Once I filled out all the forms and the receptionist copied my information, I wheeled myself away from the desk and found a place to park out of the way of hall traffic. The other patients went before me. I was still waiting when Shannon arrived, breathless and pale. I mean, she was always pale, but this time she didn't have on any makeup to brighten her up.

She hugged me hard, brushing the hair out of my face. "You look like shit."

"Right back at you."

"Had a fight with Jesse," she muttered.

"What about?"

"Please. I didn't come to the ER to dump my probs on you. What the hell happened . . . and *why* didn't you take me with you? I could've brought the undead, you know, dropped the unholy might of ghost-fu on their demon asses."

It hadn't even occurred to me. "I just got you home and safe. You're crazy if you think I'm putting you at risk again."

Saving you once cost too much already.

"Bullshit." Her blue eyes snapped anger at me. "Don't put that on me. We already went one round on this, and this is the last time I'll say it. If we're friends, we're equals. You can't protect me, can't decide what I get to do . . . and I don't want you around if you try."

That was pure Shannon, bitching me out when I had a hole in my thigh. To be fair, maybe I wouldn't *be* in this situation if I'd let her guard my back. She commanded the dead, plus some pretty impressive expertise with a sword these days, a skill she'd learned in Sheol. I still wasn't clear on how long we'd been there. I only knew that time ran differently, so I suspected it was like a reversal of fairy legends, where it seemed like forever in hell, but on earth it had only been a few weeks.

"Fair enough," I said quietly. "I should've brought you in when we went after Kel. I wasn't thinking."

"You've got too much on your plate," she told me.

I sighed. "No argument from me."

"You promise no more of this? I'm not a kid. You accept this?"

"I do." Still, when you cared, it was second nature to try to protect them, even if they were old enough—and fierce enough—to do their own ass-kicking. "And when I figure out what I need to do to bring Chance back, you'll be there. Promise."

"That's what I fought with Jesse about, actually."

I raised a brow. "Really? Why?"

"He thinks I'm enabling you, encouraging your delusions." Her mouth tightened. "But he wasn't there. He didn't hear what Chance said . . . and *how* he said it. If anybody can come back from the other side—"

"It's him," I finished.

"Yeah. I mean, he's got the godling thing going on. That's not normal either. So I told Jesse to STFU and butt out, unless there's some reason he doesn't want you back with Chance."

"I'm guessing that pissed him off."

Shan grinned. "Hells to the yeah. He accused me of not trusting him. I'm pretty sure he's heard that shit before, but I was just ringing his bell."

A belly laugh escaped me, startling the guy who had shot his own foot while cleaning his gun. "He's gonna be even madder when he realizes you were just distracting him from the real issue. But I swear I'm not crazy." I started to tell her about the dreams, but at that moment the receptionist called me to the back.

Shannon wouldn't give way to the orderly; she pushed my wheelchair toward the door that led through into a kind of holding pen separated by cloth screens, metal framework and what looked like curtain rods holding everything together. She helped me from the chair onto the bed, and the medical equipment surrounding me gave me an unpleasant flashback to the last time I was admitted.

Please just fix me and release me.

The orderly—the same one who had helped me at the start—gave us a few instructions, which included me putting on a stupid gown. With Shan's help, I managed it after he left. By the time I got settled I was winded . . . and my thigh was on fire. A few moments later, a doctor pushed through the curtain with my new chart in hand, looking too young to be done with medical school. But I didn't care about her age, only her qualifications, and she looked professional with her dark hair caught up in a neat ponytail and a pair of rectangular glasses perched on her nose. Her name tag read DOCTOR ROSALES.

"I see you ran into some wild dogs while you were hiking. Let's have a look." She folded my gown back to reveal the wound, and my stomach churned.

By closing my eyes, I tolerated her examination, which seemed to take forever. So much poking and prodding while Shan stroked my head in a comforting fashion. Gods, I was lucky to have her.

Then the doc said, "I saw on your chart that you didn't know your blood type. Have you never been treated before?"

"I just don't remember what it is," I admitted. "You can send to the hospital in Tampa for my records if you like."

"Which one?"

I told her.

"We'll do that, but I'm going to order a full panel of routine blood work just to be safe before we operate."

"Why?"

"Just as a precaution. I need to make sure there's nothing else going on before we put you under. If you have high blood pressure, we need to know in order to decide what kind of anesthetic to use."

Put me under . . . ?

Shan put in, "You should tell her about the vomiting."

I cut her a sharp look. "It's eased off in the last week. I think the food in the U.K. just didn't agree with me."

Dr. Rosales studied me, made a note on my chart. "Have you experienced light-headedness, vertigo, stomach pain or dizziness, along with the vomiting?"

"A little dizziness or light-headedness, I guess. What does that have to do with my leg?"

"Nothing immediately, but we need a full picture of your current health, Ms. Solomon. It all factors into the ultimate treatment plan. I'll clean and dress the wound, order your admission—"

"What? I thought I'd just get some stitches." Panic set in. I looked to Shannon for support, and her eyes were sympathetic, but she wasn't going to argue against me getting necessary medical care.

Dammit.

"Unfortunately, you have some structural damage. The torn muscles require a suture, and you may need some physical therapy to restore full strength to your thigh. In fact, given the location of the wound, it's a miracle the animal didn't open your femoral artery. If it had, we wouldn't be having this conversation."

If that was meant to make me feel better about surgery, well, it was working. I'd be a huge baby to complain about my lot when I could be dead in the wilderness right now. So I sucked it up.

"Okay, let's get this over with."

Dr. Rosales offered me a half smile. "I know you want to get in and out, but hospitals don't always work that way. There are tests to run, lab work. I understand you have a friend delivering the animal's body?"

"Yeah. Where should he bring it? Here?"

"No, it goes to Laboratory Services, run by the state. If you give me his cell number, I can text him the address."

"Shan?"

In reply, she got out my cell and showed the number to Dr. Rosales, who quickly copied it to her phone.

"I know it's been a terrible day, but you're alive, and that's what counts. We'll do everything we can to make things better." She had a nice bedside manner for an ER doc.

Shannon didn't leave my side at any part of the process, even when they asked her to step outside. But her angry face was intimidating, so they let her carry my purse with hidden dog, and my other personal effects, up to the room for me. It wasn't long before I was settled into a bed every bit as uncomfortable as I remembered. Hospital rooms and cheap motel rooms had a few things in common: TVs bolted down and a weary procession of people in and out who didn't really want to be there.

"Be careful," Shan cautioned me. "There's probably some bad shit stored up."

"Yeah, I already thought of that. I'll focus on keeping the evil memories out." Gods knew, I had enough of my own.

In a little while, a nurse came in with a bunch of supplies on a tray, vials for blood, and needles, I hoped for pain relief. Fortunately, that was the first thing she did. The shot stung a little, but nothing compared to the agony in my thigh. It was like the hellhound was still chewing on me. I knew that was psychological—if there had been anything magickal about the bite, Booke's statuette neutralized it. The medicine worked fast, which meant it was the good stuff. By the time Nurse Judy drew my blood, I didn't even care. Of course, Butch got worried when she stole my life fluids and growled at her. That prompted a whole lot of drama and an angry diatribe about how I should know better than to bring that filthy animal into a hospital room. Shannon apologized on my behalf, as I thought the woman's face was funny when she yelled and I couldn't stop giggling.

Shannon finished with, "I'm really sorry. I didn't think. I'll take the dog home. I was just worried about my girl. You get that, right?"

The nurse softened. "I understand. And he's a little guy. He didn't run around in here, did he?"

"No," I managed.

Soon after, Shan left with a promise to return as soon as she could, leaving me alone with beeping monitors and my fear.

Dude, This Is Huge

Over the next few days, my life dwindled to what other people were doing to me. I ate when someone told me, slept, woke for various tests, and then went back to sleep. I barely remembered the corrective surgery where they sutured the tears in my thigh, but I sure felt the stitches. Visitors came and went, though they couldn't bring Butch, much to my dismay. But the nurse was canny after that first time; she insisted on checking purses thereafter.

It was the third day after my arrival at the ER when Dr. Rosales came into the room. I was itching to be released, but from the look on her face she had news for me. Hopefully it wasn't something dire, like I'd never again walk without a limp. She'd mentioned PT, of course, but not permanent disability. Still, I clicked the mute button on the remote and let her determine her approach.

"From our prior discussion, I'm positive you don't know . . . but I wanted to be the one to tell you."

"What?"

"You're approximately six weeks pregnant. Congratulations."

I stared, unable to process this newest crisis. Me? A mother? Good gods. Though I managed well enough with Cami, any time I spent with her was influenced by the awareness it would end. My own kid wouldn't be like that at all, no giving the baby back when it started driving me crazy. Maybe I should've been excited, ecstatic even, that part of Chance would live on through me, but cold terror coiled in my stomach instead.

Somehow I managed not to babble the usual denials and incoherent questions, but I think my silence alarmed her. The doctor studied me. "This was an unplanned pregnancy, I take it? I can't make any recommendations, of course, but just remember that you have a number of options."

"I know," I whispered.

But no matter how scared I might be, that wasn't an option. I ached, thinking about the life Chance and I had created. Gods, I hoped I hadn't hurt it with all the crazy shit I'd done in the last six weeks. The poison magick spell I'd set off, *oh, baby, I'm so sorry*. But maybe the amniotic fluid filtered such effects. That wasn't the kind of question a doctor could answer, but Eva might know.

"Is the peanut okay? I mean, I've had pain meds and there was anesthetic . . ."

"Yes, all your treatments are known to be safe for expectant mothers. No worries on that front, though you do need to take better care of yourself. Rest more, drink plenty of fluids, eat well, take prenatal vitamins, and see your regular practitioner for regular checks."

"Yes, I will."

A horrifying thought occurred to me. Not long ago, I'd been in La Rosa Negra with Booke—I searched my brain frantically—but I'd refused alcohol that day because I was driving. *Oh, gods.* At Twilight, I'd had one full Agave Kiss and part of a second one, comped by Jeannie the bartender, who thought I looked like I was having a rough night.

My panic must've shown because Dr. Rosales asked, "What's wrong?"

"I had a few cocktails. Before I knew. Will it hurt the baby? I'm not normally a big drinker—"

"How many is a few?"

"One . . . and part of a second." I told her what was in the Agave Kiss. Hopefully, I hadn't hurt the peanut.

"That's not heavy or binge drinking. Alcohol can lead to fetal cell death, but thousands of women have a few drinks before they realize they're pregnant. Just . . . take care of yourself from this point. Your body will do its best to protect your child. It's your job to make it easy."

"I'm on the wagon from this point on," I promised. "I just . . . I had no idea."

She laughed. "You'd be surprised how often I hear that, sometimes from women who come in with severe abdominal pain and have no clue they're about to deliver."

"Really? I think the barfing might've clued me in eventually. The nausea hit hard for a few days, then it tapered off. Now it's mostly triggered by certain smells. Is that normal?"

Dr. Rosales answered, "To be honest, every woman and every pregnancy is different. I've treated women who were so sick, the whole time, that they were malnourished by the time they delivered. And I've admitted those who never had a moment of discomfort."

"I think I'm jealous. Do you have kids?"

She shook her head. "Too busy."

We shared a smile. Then I said, "Not that I'm ungrateful, but when will you spring me?"

Her smile widened, telling me she had good news. "That's why I'm here. I've already signed your paperwork, so if you want to call a friend to come get you, you're ready for discharge."

"Thanks. I appreciate everything you've done."

With a few words in parting, the doctor went on her

way. I crawled out of the hospital bed and rang Shannon's cell. "I'm out of here. Can you pick me up?"

"I'd be mad if you *didn't* call. I'll borrow Maria's car and be right there."

She didn't have a job at the moment, as she had been gone a while, and retail managers didn't waver when employees stopped coming in. People quit mall jobs just like that all the time; it was a simple matter to replace a clerk. If Shan had a vehicle of her own to drive, it would be easier. I resolved to do something about that, but it couldn't be my top priority. Once everything else was squared away, I'd help her out.

After hanging up, I got dressed, which took me ten minutes. I was tired and shaky by the time I got my skirt on, and I was grateful someone had thought to bring me one with an elastic waist and flowing lines. The T-shirt wasn't elegant, but it covered me. At this point, I only cared about the latter, not the former. I shoved my feet into some sandals and waited for Shan, all my other possessions in a plastic bag beside me.

It was half past the hour when Shannon arrived and another fifteen minutes to find an orderly to wheel me down. This was for insurance reasons, but honestly, I wasn't sure if I had the fortitude to make it to the car on my own anyway. Things felt like they were such a mess, important matters unresolved, and I was in no condition to fix them—now more than ever.

When Shannon had to repeat herself for the fourth time, as she drove me to Chuch and Eva's place, she finally asked, "What is *with you* today? Are you stoned?"

"Not anymore. But there's something major on my mind."

"Chance," she guessed.

"For once, no."

"Kel?"

"Colder." I wasn't trying to be annoying; I just didn't

know if I was ready to share such fresh, earthshaking news.

"Just tell me already. *What?*"

I pressed both hands to my abdomen. "Baby."

The car slung sideways as she slammed on the brakes, as she'd nearly run a red light in gawking at me. "No way. You're knocked up?"

"Yep. Apparently."

"Dude, this is huge."

She wasn't telling me anything I didn't know; my skull still felt too small for my baffled brain. I mean, I could ask Eva for practical advice, but down the line? All of this rested squarely on me. If I had eaten more of the gross hospital food, just the worry could make me up-chuck, forget about morning sickness.

"I know."

"Is it . . . does it change your plans any?"

I understood what she was asking; maybe it was too risky to keep trying to bring Chance back — and I'd wres-tled with the question as I sat on the hospital bed. "I'm still considering," I said softly. "This is . . . there's no road map for where I am, you know?"

Shan nodded. "Yeah, it's not like there's a self-help book for this."

"Common sense says I should stop. Take this no fur-ther and start making plans for the baby. But . . ." I shook my head. "I don't think I can live with myself if I do that. He gave up everything for me. I'll be careful, play it safer than I have been, but . . . I think I have to try. No matter what."

"I'll back you up . . . but trust I'm not letting you take stupid risks anymore. That's my future niece growing in your belly."

"Niece? You're sure of that, are you?" Inwardly I smiled over her assumption of an auntie's role, but it was true. Shan was the closest I'd ever get to a sister.

"I can hope, anyway. A boy would be cool, but less fun for shopping."

A few minutes later, we pulled up at the Ortiz house. I was thinking about how to break the news, but Shannon saved me the trouble. The girl could run like the wind, even in platform Mary Janes. By the time I hobbled out of the car and into the front room, she'd already told everyone. So it was just as well I hadn't planned to keep it secret. Eva and Chuch hugged me while Booke studied me with equal measures of awe and a single man's terror of reproduction.

They were all asking questions faster than I could process them. I swayed on my sore leg, and Kel scooped me up, carried me toward his favorite armchair. Weird that a half demon would have such strong preferences in furniture, but there you go. Oddly it made him seem more human to me; that he enjoyed small comforts and watching TV Azteca while curled up with my dog. But even though his wounds had healed, the sorrow hadn't left his icy eyes. I wasn't sure it ever would.

"I think she's feeling a bit overwhelmed," Booke observed. "Let's give her some space, shall we?"

To my relief, the others took him at his word. Kel knelt beside me, offering Butch like a gift, and I huffed out a choky breath. Gods, pregnancy hormones—no wonder I was tearing up over the smallest thing. But it felt like a century since I'd cuddled my dog. The Chihuahua settled into the crook of my arm after spinning around multiple times. Good to see some things didn't change.

Kel asked, "Are you well, Corine?"

"Mostly. Are you hiding from Barachiel?" I didn't ask if he had been crashing at the Ortiz house this whole time.

"Not hiding. Planning. This can only end in his death . . . or mine. I can't think of any other way I'll ever be free."

"Kel," I started to say, but he held up a hand.

"This isn't your concern any longer. I'll handle it."

"Like you handled him before?" As soon as the words came out, I wished I could swallow them.

Kel flinched, dropping back onto his haunches as if I'd kicked him. "You're right to remark upon my weakness."

"No. I didn't mean it like that. Look, Shannon just bitched me out for taking too much on myself . . . for forgetting I have friends to help me out. That's all I'm saying to you in turn. There's no need for you to be a lone wolf. Maybe we can figure something out together."

"After all the harm I've caused," he said humbly, "I don't deserve your friendship. But I treasure it."

"Bullshit." I tried on a *do not argue with me* look, and it worked.

Kel didn't say any more about his inadequacies, which was just as well. I didn't feel emotionally equipped to reassure anyone else; at the moment, my psyche was held together with duct tape and baling wire. But I did give him a hug, as those I could offer freely. He returned it fiercely, burying his head in the crook between my neck and shoulder. I stroked his back, feeling maternal toward him, possibly because he was so very broken.

Eventually, he whispered, "I can't fight him and win . . . but I think I can grant you time to do what's needed."

Though I had no idea what that meant, Eva interrupted the conversation by asking how I felt. The others tiptoed around me that night, though Chuch was adorable, bringing me food and beverages, standing in for Chance, as he put it. I kinda loved him in a nonsexual, utterly platonic fashion.

That night, I called Tia to check in, and she seemed delighted to hear my voice. *"Hola, mija."*

Until this moment, I hadn't realized how much I missed her . . . and Mexico. We chatted a little about how she was doing, she promised to wire me some more money in the morning, and then she said, "Are you coming home soon?"

Five words, but they broke my heart, because I had to answer, "I don't know when. I'm still following some leads here, looking for Chance."

Feels like I'm totally Cat-in-the-Cradle-ing her. I hadn't told her exactly what happened or how I ended up stranded in the U.K., but her tone became sympathetic. "You don't come home without that boy, okay? He's the one for you."

"Si, claro," I promised, hoping I could make the words true.

Once we hung up, I struggled with the pit opening in my stomach, sadness wrapped around despair. I beat them both down because that couldn't be good for the baby. Oh, gods, from this point on, that refrain would haunt my every moment. Part of me wondered if it was okay to be this conflicted, so ambivalent about bringing a life into this world. It wasn't that I didn't want Chance's baby, more that I doubted my ability to raise a kid properly. Shit, what did I know about *anything*?

The next day, Kel disappeared. He didn't say good-bye, and I hoped like hell he had sense enough not to go after Barachiel a second time on his own. There was no way I could cut him free again. Not now. Between a bun in the oven, a bum leg, and an impossible quest, I had too many other chainsaws to juggle.

That night, I found a note from him in my purse. *Corine,* he wrote in perfectly elegant calligraphy. *Where I've gone, you must not follow. For while Barachiel chases me, he cannot hunt you. The time I can grant you is limited; eventually, he will find me, and I do not know if we will meet again. Yours always, Kelethiel.*

I pressed the note to my heart, trying to stem a pang of pain. Fear for my friend tightened my chest. And so I brooded while my other loved ones gave me a wide berth. Though it hurt, I couldn't go after him this time; my priorities had changed forever.

For the next week, my life consisted of sleep and food. It couldn't go on in that fashion, however. Once I started physical therapy, the crew had to admit I was well enough to get on with my mission, regardless of how crazy it sounded. To their credit, my friends didn't argue with me, and I half suspected it was out of a desire not to enrage the pregnant lady. They'd learned that lesson with Eva.

Booke approached me when the others didn't dare. "Are you recovered enough to get on with saving Chance?"

I stared, astonished that he seemed to understand how driven I was. Physical pain didn't matter. Nor did obstacles. If there was a brick wall between Chance and me, I'd demolish it. "Where do we start?"

"I've been reading on Area 51 . . . and it seems that there's one place we can start looking."

"Oh?" I hauled myself out of the chair. The stitches pulled, but I could walk if I took it slow. I wobbled a bit, despite the tight wrap on my upper thigh. This was both to protect the surgical work and to provide extra support. If Eva caught me, this mission would end in an argument.

He answered, "It's an arcane library in San Antonio, and like most gifted places, the actual purpose is concealed from the public."

"So where is it exactly?" I asked, pushing to my feet.

"You'll see." Booke could be annoyingly mysterious. "First, we need to see about a home base while we're in San Antonio."

I nodded. "It's too far to drive back and forth."

While Eva and Shannon were occupied with the baby and Chuch was in the enormous garage, showing Jesse the rebuilt 440 Magnum engine he'd dropped into the car recently, I limped back to the guest room to gather up my stuff. I hoped to sneak out without it becoming a big deal. Which would mean stealing a car from my friends.

Dammit.

I had just realized my getaway plan had a fatal flaw when Eva said, "Just *where* do you think you're going?"

Every Dog Has His Day

"To San Antonio," I murmured.

"Are you coming back? What's our plan?" Eva was already summoning everybody back into the house for an impromptu meeting.

While I appreciated the support, it just wasn't feasible for them to put their lives on pause, especially when I didn't know what I was doing. What I needed. Sighing, I sat down at the kitchen table and perused some listings on Booke's phone, which we'd purchased at the mall the other day. Within minutes, I found a furnished apartment for five hundred bucks a month, and it made sense to get my own place, as it was hard to say when I would be up to the task of finishing what I'd started. Physical therapy would go slower than I preferred—not that I expected an insta-fix—and I couldn't impose on Chuch and Eva forever. An argument ensued, wherein they all talked about me as if I wasn't present.

"She can't be on her own," Eva protested. "Corine needs support."

"Yeah, we can't be sure she's sleeping right or eating enough," Chuch agreed.

Shannon and Jesse both had opinions; he said I could

stay with him, but that would be super awkward, and
Shannon had a roomie who might object to a long-term
houseguest. Finally, Booke cleared his throat—and it actually worked. In a quiet, understated way, he had quite
a commanding presence. The others fell quiet.

"I think it's best if Corine rents the flat. It's likely to
be small, but I'll happily sleep on the couch. That way,
she has company . . . and backup, should she require it."

Booke . . . I could stand rooming with him. And hopefully, as he noted, it wouldn't be too long. Time felt like a
ticking bomb, as if my relationship with Chance had an
expiration date—and that was to say nothing of other
dangers: an open dispute with demons, plus an insane
"archangel" who intended to recruit me . . . or murder
me. *Either way.* Ferocious certainty hardened my spine.
There was *no way* that crazy bastard would ever hurt my
baby.

"That's fine," I said into the silence.

Before they could pose objections, I got on the phone,
reached the owner on the first try. "I'm interested in the
apartment you have for rent."

The woman sounded husky, as if she smoked, or did a
lot of yelling. "Did you want to see it? I'll need a month's
rent, plus half for damages."

"To be honest, I just need a place for a little while. So
I don't really care what it looks like, as long as it's clean."

"It is that." From her less than ringing endorse-
ment, I figured it was a dump, but at this point, I didn't
care. She gave me the address over the phone, and I
turned to Chuch with an inquiring look. "Can I buy
the Pinto?"

"Three hundred bucks," he said.

Eva swatted him on the arm. "You're *not* charging her
for that piece of shit."

Oh, gods. Another argument.

"But she'll get mad if she thinks we're offering charity," he protested.

"He's right," I said. "And stop talking about me as if I'm not *right here.*"

Getting away from my friends was paramount; they might smother me with good intentions, plus I needed space—and time—to plan my next move. Getting maimed by a hellhound hadn't been in my playbook, and it definitely set me back in terms of progress. But I'd handle this, as I'd navigated every other obstacle.

I always knew a relationship with Chance wouldn't be easy. But even I didn't guess it would end up being this hard.

The drive to San Antonio felt like it got longer each time, though I was becoming very familiar with the highway in between. At the midway point, we stopped at a gas station to fill up, get snacks, and use the restroom. Inside the store, I spotted a rack of canes of all things. After pricing them, I decided I needed one, and added that to the fuel and food. I paid our shot, then used the walking stick to make my way back to the car, where Booke was giving Butch a drink. For somebody who had spent so much time alone, he sure knew how to look after a dog. I slid into the front seat again and nodded off before I realized what had happened.

When I woke, Booke had turned down a side street. I couldn't tell what side of San Antone we were in, but it appeared to be inner city, near to the jail, judging from the bars on the windows and the number of bail bondsmen doing business in the neighborhood. Our building was a run-down adobe duplex, divided neatly in the middle. We were in the B unit, so I figured the landlady lived next door.

With a whispered admonition for Butch, I knocked on her door with cash in hand. The woman who answered wore a green sweat suit and a tired look. She didn't ask questions, just took my money and handed over the keys.

"If you plan to stay over," she told me, "then I need another five hundred this time next month."

"I'll let you know."

"And keep it down over there. I don't like a noisy neighbor."

"We'll be model tenants," Booke promised.

As usual, his accent got a second look. Then she smiled. "A pleasure doing business with you."

I limped over to our side of the house and unlocked the front door. The apartment *was* a dump. But then, what did I expect for five hundred a month, furnished? It looked like a crash pad for a desperate college kid whose roommate situation fell through at the last minute, but as the landlady had promised, the place was clean, albeit furnished in mid-century rummage sale. The couch sagged in the middle and the brown fabric was worn nearly through in places. Each end table came from a different set, and the coffee table had an odd leg; someone had hammered a different one into place so it sat faintly lopsided. There were no paintings on the walls, and no TV, not even an old one. The bedroom looked like a monk's cell with a single mattress on a metal frame and an ornate crucifix on the wall. A battered chest of drawers sat to one side of the narrow window.

None of those things bothered me. Gods willing, I wouldn't be here long. To my relief, the rental was on the ground floor; otherwise I might've had some trouble, as my leg still hurt like a bitch. My phone rang as I was putting my stuff away.

"Corine Solomon."

"This is Sarah Messner calling from Our Lady. I'm pleased to report that the test came back negative on the animal that attacked you. There's no need for the rabies vaccine."

My knees went weak, dropping me onto the narrow bed. Best news I'd had all day. Maybe demonic possession rendered an animal immune to viruses. I pressed both palms to my belly and managed to say, "Thanks for letting me know."

"You've made an appointment for your first physical therapy?"

"Yes, ma'am."

I went to tell Booke the good news. He hugged me, then said, "You realize I won't let you shirk your medical obligations."

"I know. Single-minded pursuit of Chance is off the table." I collapsed on the couch more than sat. Gods, was it the injury or the baby sapping my energy this way? I didn't know how women survived nine months of this, and from what I'd seen with Eva, it would only get worse.

"Home sweet home," Booke said as he settled beside me.

I glanced at the tired furnishings and the scarred veneer on the shelves. It was, unquestionably, a depressing base of operations. *But not for long,* I promised myself. *You'll get this sorted. Then Booke can travel . . . and you can go back to Mexico.*

"You didn't have to come with me."

"I know. I chose to."

Butch wandered around the apartment, smelling everything. I wondered how many different tenants he could still detect. Now and then he paused to growl. Booke watched in apparent fascination as the dog asserted his dominance over his new surroundings. I struggled to my feet to show him where I'd put his food and water dish in the kitchen. He licked my fingers as I jiggled the bowl, so I stroked his head. Poor little dude had really gone through a lot in the past months.

So have I.

After Butch ate, he trotted to me and pawed my leg, but when I went to pick him up, he gave two negative yaps. Which meant I got to play the guessing game.

"Something on your mind?"

One yap. *Yes.*

"Should I get the Scrabble tiles?"

Again, yes.

"Would you mind?" I asked Booke. "They're in my purse."

"Your dog *really* talks."

I raised a brow, wondering if I hadn't mentioned that to Booke. No, I was sure I'd regaled him with stories prior, and I wouldn't have omitted such a pertinent detail. "This is not news."

"But . . . I thought it was colorful embellishment for the sake of the story. Scrabble tiles! How marvelous." Smiling, he went to the small table where I'd dumped my bag earlier.

The tiles were still in their Ziploc baggie from the last use. Butch pranced at my feet, his body shaking so hard that I'd think he needed to go outside if we hadn't paused on the way in. By the time Booke put the letters on the floor, he was whining.

"We get it, this is important." Deep down I hoped it was another message from Chance.

Butch had told me that he visited sometimes—and only the dog could see him. That must be incredibly lonely. Chilled, I glanced around the apartment, wondering if Chance was standing at my shoulder. I wished I could sense him—I *wanted* to—but nothing supernatural communicated with me. Butch pawed at the tiles, frantic in his haste. This was obviously important.

youre running out of time

"For what? Chance?"

Butch gave an affirmative yap. Then he went back to work. This time the letters shaped into:

if you dont open the way during the festival of the dead it will be too late

I glanced at Booke, who got out his phone. He Googled, then said, "It's in October. You have a few weeks yet."

But given the complications so far, I could understand why Chance was worried. I still hadn't figured out a way to handle things on my end. The only thing I knew about opening gates between realms involved sacrificing a soul, and I damn sure wasn't doing that. But there must be a solution, somewhere.

"Why? I don't want to wait another year, but—"

By the way that Butch went after the tiles, Chance had an urgent message to convey. I stopped, waiting for the letters to fall into shape. Booke patted my hand as if he could make things better with a touch. And it helped a little.

next year i wont remember you

Shit. "Is that your father's solution to your unwillingness to assume Daikokuten's mantle?"

this realm strips you of mortal ties

That made sense. Otherwise people who crossed over would constantly be trying to get back, like Chance. I guessed only his divine heritage made it possible for him to hold on to us—me—for this long. But time was running out. No wonder Butch had been so agitated. I felt that way myself.

"What can I do?"

open the way

i love you

Feeling stupid, I said to open space, "Chance, don't give up. I'll find a way. See, you have more reason than ever to get back here." I drew in a hard, hurting breath, wondering if I should tell him like this. "We're having a baby."

Silence. The Chihuahua eyed me, but didn't respond. Instead, Butch sat back on his haunches, studying me with liquid, sympathetic eyes. By his current demeanor, I guessed Chance had gone, but I needed to confirm. "It's just us now?"

Affirmative yap.

"Did he hear me?"

I got the dog equivalent of a shrug. It was possible

Chance had heard me as he was slipping away, but Butch couldn't guarantee that. *Dammit. You should've said something sooner, given him a reason to fight harder.*

Still, I owed appreciation where it was due. "Thank you, buddy. You gave me a much-needed heads-up."

If I didn't solve this problem in fourteen days, Chance would be lost to me forever. That *could not* happen. In my head, I heard that stupid song from *Jeopardy!* I blocked out the nerves that were surely creating that distraction, then turned to Booke.

"You're the resident genius. You said you want to repay me. This is the time. I'm . . ." My voice broke. "I'm at my wit's end. I don't have anything left to give, and yet it's more critical than ever—"

"Hush, sweetheart." His tone was endearingly avuncular as he drew me against him, and I ugly-cried all over his gray sweater. "You didn't just let me die . . . and I'm not going to let you lose the man you love either."

"Okay." Booke's unconditional support gave me the strength to clamber to my feet. "Let's check out this arcane library."

My backpack was already in the bedroom, courtesy of Booke, and he'd staked his claim on the couch. He gave me his arm like a proper gentleman, though I think it was more out of concern for my balance than out of good manners. Together, we headed out to the car, and Butch trotted at my heels with a faintly aggrieved doggy sigh. Without urging, he hopped into the back of the Pinto. Booke still had the keys, so when he swung into the driver's seat, I didn't protest. My right leg was iffy anyway, and it made sense to rest it as much as I could, as much as the mission allowed.

"This is a terrible car," he observed, starting it.

"At least it runs. And I have a propensity for misplacing my rides, so I understand why Chuch didn't want to sell me anything he could make real money off restoring."

"I can't imagine there's much demand for a classic Pinto."

"Exactly. That's why I don't have the Charger or the Maverick. And he took a loss on this." It was all I could do to get him to accept a measly three hundred, when I knew he'd paid four, then bought some parts and spent some time on the engine, if he hadn't gotten around to the body yet.

"It can be hard to let friends help when you're in a bind, but they have the comfort of knowing they did right by you. And you can offer the same support when their backs are to the wall."

"You just need to call, any of you," I said huskily.

"I know," Booke said. "I did. And you came."

His obvious gratitude and affection warmed me. I patted his leg because it would be a bad idea to strangle-hug the driver while the vehicle was in motion. Our journey ended at a large tan brick building with a giant red and yellow sign that proclaimed WONDER LANES on it. If that hadn't clued me in, the black ball and white pins depicted below would've done the trick.

Staring incredulously, I asked, "The arcane library is in a bowling alley?"

"Would you come here to learn the secrets of the universe?" He raised a brow.

"You've got a point." The people I'd known who bowled certainly weren't on quests for enlightenment. They were there to hang out, have fun, drink some beer, maybe eat a pizza, no chance of them stumbling through a hidden door, unless they were drunk and looking for the bathroom.

I figured gifted secrets were concealed better than that. "Does Twila run this place?"

"She runs the whole state of Texas. So the short answer is yes. But she doesn't manage the library personally."

"She must have her fingers in a lot of pies," I said.

"You've no idea." He paused, as if wondering whether he should tell me something. Then he came to a decision. "I suppose there's no harm. I know you've been worried about me, but you truly shouldn't be. You see, I've agreed to step in as the curator at the library here . . . when my sabbatical ends."

"That's the deal you made with her?" Learning the truth was a big load off my mind. But I had questions. "You won't be forced to live there, will you? I mean, it's not like exchanging one magickal prison for another?"

"No," he answered, laughing softly. "It's an employment contract. While it's true that it doesn't end until Twila deems my debt repaid, this will be a job, not an incarceration. I'm free to live as I choose when I'm not on duty. Obviously, that necessitates my relocation to San Antonio, but I don't mind. I'm quite weary of Stoke."

"Then you must be pretty excited, getting to see the place for the first time."

"I am, rather. The librarian who's been running the place for the last twenty years has nearly squared her account with Twila, so I'm queued up to take her place."

"You don't draw a salary, I guess?"

"Of course not. But once I resolve my identity crisis and claim my inheritance, I'll be fine. And I have some other irons in the fire, financially speaking."

I studied him, impressed with his fortitude and resilience. "You're amazing. Not many could endure what you have."

"Loneliness and introspection made me a better man," he admitted. "I had no choice but to own my role in the mess my life had become. Of course, after that I went a bit mad for ten years or so . . . but I got better."

I grinned as I climbed from the car and opened my arms to Butch. "*Monty Python*."

"Yes, I caught sketches on the Web. By the time they were new to me, they were old to the world. So odd, that.

I had such a limited window to learn and experience *anything*."

"It'll be different from now on."

Working in the library didn't sound like a bad job, especially for an intellectual like Booke. He might even find it fascinating, and on the plus side, he got to go home at the end of the day. Presumably, there would be weekends off, a chance to travel around Texas, see the sights, and have sex with lots of women who couldn't resist the accent. That picture of his prospects made me smile.

"Let's go see what my future holds, shall we?"

Yet knowing Kel was out there, buying time, at such personal cost, knowing that the punishment for his escape might be death this time, it was all I could do to put one foot in front of the other. I felt as though in pursuing a ritual to bring Chance back, I was abandoning Kel. Regardless, I had made my decision in Sheol. No matter how much it hurt, this time, it wouldn't change.

Squaring my shoulders, I stowed Butch in my bag, shouldered it, and followed Booke. My stick made no sound against the pavement due to the rubber tips on the bottom, but it steadied me. Eventually the Englishman noticed I couldn't keep up with his long strides and he slowed his pace to match mine. I had constant pain in my leg; part of me wondered if it was permanent, and if the injury would end up being for nothing if Kel got himself killed playing bait. But that was dark and desperate thinking. I couldn't permit such ideas to take root. Without hope, I had nothing.

Booke strode confidently toward the building and pushed open the doors, which took us into a real bowling alley. This time of day, there were a few people using the lanes, some bored waitresses filling plastic cups of beer. The place smelled simultaneously dusty and alcoholic with a soupçon of sweaty feet and oregano. He led the way past the shoe rental and the snack counter; nobody was interested in our business. When he opened a maintenance closet door, I thought he had to be kidding.

But nope, he pushed it open, stepped in, and beckoned to me to follow. Shrugging, I closed the door behind me, which prompted him to jiggle one of the shelves, and a secret door opened; the whole unit moved to reveal cement steps leading down.

"Is this safe?" I asked. "Couldn't the janitor find that by mistake?"

"Not unless he has one of these." Booke showed me a token with Twila's personal insignia branded on it.

"Ah, so this is magickally secured as well as hidden."

"Yes. Come along."

Marveling at how weird reality could be, I followed him.

Mystifying Secrets of Mystery

No lie, the library had been built beneath a bowling alley. But it had the charm of a historical building, despite the subterranean locale. The shelves were burnished mahogany, filled with books that looked incredibly old. Overhead, the noise from the bowling alley wasn't audible, which meant the walls were extremely thick . . . or that the spell securing the place also incorporated some soundproofing.

There were a few other patrons paging through tomes at a couple of tables nearby. Booke spared them no attention; instead he made straight for the desk he would presumably occupy in just under a year's time. His predecessor was a slim woman in her early fifties with retro tortoiseshell glasses and smooth silver hair, styled in an elegant bob. She wore a good gray suit and a string of quality pearls. The pawnshop owner in me immediately appraised them. Yeah, they'd fetch a nice price.

"Twila didn't mention you'd be stopping by today," the woman said coolly. Her accent was hard to place at first, and then it came to me—Boston. Not Southie, but subtler, the vowels not quite as sharp. Between her appearance and her cultured tones, her whole presence spoke of moneyed antecedents.

"This is personal business," he told her. "But it's good to meet you, Ms. Devlin. I expect we'll have a number of details to cover . . . another time. Are we free to access library resources?"

"Certainly. The books are available to all in good standing within Twila's demesne." Her eyes held a warning light, however.

Booke ignored the subtext. "Could you acquaint me with the filing system?"

While he handled our business with the curator, I wandered off to peruse the stacks. The tomes in here were impressive; some looked comical, as if they had been printed in someone's garage as a joke. But I knew better than to dismiss something based on appearances. After all, you'd never guess by looking that my dog could talk.

I had read a few pages of *The Baroness's Cure for Intimate Ailments* by the time Booke joined me. "She gave me a few leads, though she wants you to know she doesn't approve of our endeavor."

"I don't care," I said honestly. "I have one shot at this. One. If we don't have the right ritual, or if something goes wrong? I'll never see Chance again . . . and this kid won't ever meet his dad."

"I understand. Just be warned that such powerful spells always exact a price. You may not like the cost of what you want."

"That's not news." After the trip to Sheol, I understood better than anyone how much could be taken in recompense.

"Then let's move forward. As you said, time's running out."

He settled me at a table, then went off to collect a vast number of books, based on recommendations from Ms. Devlin. We split them down the middle, and that was a long damn day, punctuated by page turning and ponderous silence. Followed by another one just like it. All the while, I was aware of the clock ticking down. After the second day, I got smart and packed us a lunch. On the fourth day, I had a doctor's appointment in the morning, so we got a late start. Booke went with me, which was odd, but cool. At least I didn't endure everything alone.

The doctor was aware I'd seek out another physician once I returned home, so he didn't ask a lot of questions. He just gave me a general OB tune-up and assured me that the baby was fine, despite the damage to my leg. Then he put a gizmo on my stomach, so we could listen to the heartbeat, and that was when I fell in love. I pressed both hands to my stomach, unable to believe there was really somebody in there. I mean, I had known, but until this moment it wasn't 100 percent real to me. Now I had this other person, somebody to love and protect, and everything I did going forward would be for him or her.

The doctor pronounced me sound, but cautioned, "Make sure to take your prenatal vitamins daily and get plenty of rest."

"I'll make sure she does," Booke promised.

I shot him a dirty look for making it sound like I couldn't care for myself, but I knew he meant well, so I kept quiet. At the front desk, I paid for the office visit, then we walked out to the Pinto.

"Do you mind if we stop by a pharmacy before going to Wonder Lanes?"

"I intended to insist, if you didn't mention it."

"You're a sneaky alpha male, you know that?"

"It often works to my advantage. Dress a man in wool cardigans and women simply don't expect him to be domineering."

"That was pretty amazing, right?" I touched my belly.

His expression softened, his gray eyes warm and friendly. "It was. I'm honored I got to be there." He paused as we got into the car, and he didn't speak until we were almost at the drugstore. "They didn't have any-

thing like that when Marlena was pregnant. I never
heard my son's heartbeat like that . . . and after he was
born, I saw him very little. I don't think he ever knew—"

Oh, man.

"I'm sorry."

"I think of them as belonging to another life," he said
quietly. "It's the only way to manage it. Since escaping
Stoke, I'm a new man. I have to be. I won't make the
same mistakes."

"No question of that. From what you told me you
weren't at all responsible or controlling back then, more
of a hedonistic devil." I grinned to show I was teasing.

"I still have those tendencies, but I'm doing my best
to quell them."

Booke waited in the car while I ran into the drugstore.
As mine wasn't a complicated scrip, it only took a few
moments to get what I needed. Then I hurried back out.
There wasn't nearly enough time to do everything. With
the baby to think about and Chance, whom I loved and
might never see again, I felt like I was drowning; each
breath was a gasp, pulled into tight, burning lungs.

As if he shared my dark mood, Booke fell silent as we
drove back to Wonder Lanes. This afternoon, it was
packed—jumping even—due to league activity. Men in
bowling shirts high-fived each other over pitchers of
beer. The high population made it easier to slip into the
maintenance closet and then venture downstairs. I supposed if the foot traffic were higher, people might eventually notice, but there had never been more than four
other patrons downstairs, no matter how often we came.
The gifted didn't often need to do extensive research in
San Antonio, it seemed.

Another fruitless day dragged on. By the end of it, my
eyes hurt, my back hurt, I was cranky, and I wanted a
nap. Plus, I had a sick suspicion that I'd waited too long.
Spent too much time on Booke and Kel—and that there
was no way to find out what I needed to know before the

deadline. Panic clutched at my throat with cold, clawing hands, until I had to put my head on the table to meter my breaths.

Booke's hand rested on the back of my head. "Calm down. Nobody said this search would be easy. We have a little time yet."

"I'm gonna fail. And then he'll lose all desire to be human again—"

"Shh, sweetheart, don't cry."

Somehow I restrained my overactive pregnancy hormones; surely that was the reason I kept melting down. I'd been in some tough spots and rarely yielded to the urge to bawl about it. But lately, I couldn't seem to help myself. The other night at Eva's, I was watching a commercial about a woman who couldn't get ahold of her mother due to a bad long-distance plan, and I nearly burst into tears.

Gods, I don't think I can stand nine months, being this emotional.

Then I wanted to cry because that sounded like I didn't want the baby—and that wasn't true. In a long history of untenable situations and being an emotional mess, I had never been *this* mercurial or unstable. The inside of my head was a train wreck, teeming with dark thoughts and irrational fears.

"Smack me or something. I'm *crazy.*" I sat up, striving for control.

"In my day, it wasn't remotely appropriate to manhandle expectant ladies."

"Yeah, they frown on it today too." I paused. "Do you seriously think—"

"I don't know. But it's certain he'll never return if you give up. But that's your call to make. I understand if it's too much, especially right now."

An exhausted sigh pushed out of me. "No. We'll keep at it, right up until the wire. If I fail, it won't be because I stopped trying."

"We'll start back in the morning. There are still twenty more books to examine, some of which might actually be relevant. Perhaps one full week will mark lucky seven indeed."

I could only hope.

That night, I didn't sleep much. I tossed and turned, and when I did finally drift off my dreams were haunted by images of failure. First, it was Chance, stranded in his father's realm and forgetting all about his human life, and then it was my child's accusing eyes every time some other kid mentioned his dad. From that point, the dreams morphed into nightmares, becoming odd and disjointed, and incorporated events from Sheol that still haunted me. I woke bathed in sweat that I'd thought was blood, and my heart was going like a trip-hammer. Taking a few bolstering breaths, I got up and padded barefoot to the bathroom. The fixtures were dull and water-stained, and the whole place needed to be regrouted, but for five hundred bucks a month, it was the best I could hope for. I tried not to wake Booke, but he was used to being alone so my footfalls roused him as I crept back toward the bedroom.

"Bad dreams?" he asked.

"That obvious?"

Booke shrugged. "I've had a few in my time."

"I'd imagine so."

"The worst one used to be dying alone and undiscovered."

I came toward him, then perched on the edge of the couch, which was covered in rumpled bedding. "At least you don't have to worry about that anymore."

He smiled at me. "See, things do get better."

At that point, I really didn't want to talk about it. "What time does the library open?" It made sense that it could only be accessible to the public during bowling alley operating hours, but I waited for confirmation.

"Not until ten."

I smiled. "You'll get to sleep in once you start this new gig."

"It works out beautifully for all my anticipated carousing. You should try to get a bit more rest, Corine. For the baby, if not yourself."

"That's a low blow." I *was* still tired, but I couldn't face going back to bed. "Tell me something about your life."

"Are you asking for a bedtime story?" His tone was amused.

Closing my eyes, I leaned my head against the back of the sofa. "Maybe."

"I've already told you the worst, but there are some amusing anecdotes along the way. You know that my father was an influential man among his peers. His spells were powerful and highly sought-after. Which meant we lived well."

I didn't ask what he meant by that, but I figured people hired his dad as a kind of magickal merc. Though not everyone did that, there were a number of practitioners who found it to be the most practical way to make ends meet. Some would cast any spell for the right coin; others had a code that prevented inflicting harm.

"Go on," I prompted.

"I grew spoiled. Self-indulgent. As you already know from my behavior with Marlena. So when I chose to enlist, my father was surprised. And resistant. He couldn't have his only son and heir at risk with common barbarians."

"This was the Second World War?" I felt reasonably confident on that, based on what I knew of his life and my history classes, but it couldn't hurt to confirm.

"Yes. My reasons for joining up were complicated. Part of it was hoping to impress Marlena, make her love me. But some small aspect of me wanted to do something important—fight the good fight. The propaganda films in those days were incredibly effective."

"That was before the Internet."

Ignoring me, he went on at length, describing the German countryside and the people he met. His voice took on a suspicious lull, but before I could protest, Booke did the job, and I passed out. It was daylight when I woke next; my sleep was dreamless. I didn't know if he'd slept any more, but he'd clearly showered and was fiddling in the kitchen with an old toaster.

"What a dirty trick," I muttered. "Was there ever a point to any of it?"

"Of course. And that point was to get you some rest. Mission accomplished."

"One of these days, I want a real story out of you. I'm sure you have one."

"I do," he said, smiling. "Peanut butter toast and fruit sound all right for breakfast? Is your stomach sound today?"

I shifted in an experimental fashion. *No nausea.* I was a little queasy, but unless somebody started cooking pork roast, I should be fine.

"Got a crick in my neck, and I think I drooled in my sleep, but otherwise I'm well enough."

Deadpan, he offered, "That is, obviously, your most charming quality."

"Whatever. I'm taking a shower."

Because I actually was hungry, I hurried through my daily routine—scrubbing up, washing my hair, and then moisturizing in the steamy bathroom. The niceties didn't run to an air extractor, which meant by the time I finished, it was hard to see for all the steam. In the misty whorls and the fog covering the glass, I imagined I glimpsed Chance peering at me through the mirror, his expression anxious and imploring. But when I stepped forward to get a clearer look, the picture vanished, leaving me with a tightness in my stomach comprised entirely of fear. At that moment, I desperately wanted to hear his voice, a reiteration of his promise: *Even death will not keep me from you.* But there was only the sad drip-drip from the showerhead. Chance's vow could only go so far; I had to do my part or there could be no happy ending.

A little voice whispered, *Maybe his father's right. He's not meant for you.*

With great fortitude, I shut the doubts down. I couldn't afford them. After wrapping in a rough towel, I went to the bedroom to dress and braid my hair. All signs indicated it would be another long, fruitless day at the arcane library, poring over our last few possible tomes. If we didn't find the spell soon—well.

I took care of Butch's needs and then headed grimly out to the car. Though we had a week left, it felt as though time had already run out.

Against All Odds

At four that afternoon, I gave up hope.

It might be hormones, but I had spent so many days belowground that I was probably suffering from SAD, as well as feeling sad, but when I laid my head down on the library table, I didn't have the heart to read on. This was just wasting my time when I should be planning for my baby's future, not spinning my wheels. The tears I expected didn't come, though. Instead I had this awful, creeping numbness.

I'm sorry, Chance. I left it too long—

"Corine! Wake up." Booke's excited voice attracted the attention of the two elderly women who had been paging through resource materials with us all week. For them, I suspected it was a hobby more than life and death; everyone knew how elderly witches could be after retirement.

"Did you find something?" I asked without raising my head.

Gods, I was so tired. Surely this wasn't normal. Otherwise, how did women manage to hold down a job? All I wanted to do was sleep, even with so much resting on my shoulders. He yanked me upright, not particularly delicate in his excitement. Booke didn't notice my dirty look, as he was reading aloud in what sounded like Old German. Not that I was an expert. I'd barely made it through *The Miller's Tale* during the brief portion of my high school career when we studied Chaucer.

When he paused, I put in testily, "Translation, please?"

"Right, sorry. Basically, the text references the ritual we're looking for, naming another tome. It wasn't on the list Ms. Devlin gave us, most probably because there's no existing translation. The volume we need is *that* old, probably written in Sumerian or Babylonian."

"And there happens to be a copy of it here in San Antonio?"

He bit his lip. "Unfortunately, no. It's not a book at all, in fact. More a set of scrolls. And I'm not sure whether I can run down a surviving copy in time. There weren't many . . . and only the most prestigious private collectors would own such a rare treasure."

"So . . . we have six days to track down the rarest of rare ancient scrolls, get a translation, and flawlessly perform an unknown ritual?"

Booke sighed. "When you put it that way, it sounds rather daunting."

"At least we have a lead now. Do you know any top-tier collectors?"

"I can put out a few feelers," he said. "And I'm sure the curator could give me some names."

"There's no point in hanging out here, though. We're not finding what we need on these shelves."

"Yes, at least we've hurdled this particular obstacle."

"Is that how you see this venture? Like a course laid out with hoops for us to jump through and barricades to clamber over?"

"Perhaps," he admitted sheepishly.

"No wonder I've been so miserable. My coordination sucks."

"But your determination is top-notch."

"Smooth talker. Save it for Dolores."

"Speaking of which . . ." He winked. "I've got an engagement tonight. Will you be all right at the flat on your own?"

"You're seeing her again?" My eyes widened.

"Not Dolores. Ms. Devlin."

"You're incorrigible. So I'm taking the car and the dog, and you'll make your way home when you're good and ready?"

"That's the size of it. May I have the spare key? And I trust you don't mind?"

"Not at all. Here you go."

Amusement at Booke's ability to find the bright side of any situation carried me all the way back to the dismal apartment. Where I had my mood ruined by the demon laying in wait. Sick terror roiled in my stomach, knotting the bread from the sandwich into a heavy lump of dough that I might launch at the impossibly handsome male lounging on my couch. At a glance, I ID'd him as White Hair, who had crashed Chuch's backyard BBQ. His insouciance on Twila's turf made me nervous, as Jesse had been clear about what would happen if the demons pressed their claim; and since I was under Twila's protection, her retaliation would be even worse. From his expression, the Luren no longer cared.

But he was alone, another matter of concern. I froze by the door while Butch snapped and snarled from my purse. Somehow I managed to set him gently on the floor, afraid of him getting hurt in the cross fire. Moreover, I was terrified the Luren would harm the baby. *Gods, no.* In this fight, I was completely alone, no hope of rescue, and with far too much at stake.

"It's polite to call before you drop by," I said, as if I wasn't scared to death.

"I thought it best to have this conversation in private. You've accumulated quite an entourage . . . and their company can be tiresome."

"Say your piece and get out." There was no hope in hell that this encounter would end peacefully, but I'd offer bravado until the end.

Is the Taser still in my purse? Will it work on a demon?

"Come, there's no need to be hostile. Not when I know so very much about you."

My blood chilled. "Am I supposed to be impressed? Anyone over the age of eight can master the art of innuendo."

The Luren frowned, his expression playful, but his dark eyes remained dead and dark in contrast to his shining hair. "Do you remember an encounter you had with an exceedingly helpful orderly? He was so solicitous, so knowledgeable . . ."

Actually, I'd been in such a bad way that I hadn't noticed much about the admission process. My hospital stay was a blur, apart from learning I was pregnant. So I shook my head reflexively, knowing I wouldn't like what was coming.

"Come now. He gave you all the necessary information about animal bites. Do you think that's customary?"

"I have no idea," I said honestly.

"Well, it's not. He was one of ours, once-Binder. Not handsome enough to host, but fair enough to serve. He watched you. Reported on you." He paused delicately, his smile sharpening until I had chills. "We know about the whelp."

It's worse than I thought.

"I never promised Sibella my unborn child," I said quietly.

"But you are in arrears. Leaving Sheol is not an acceptable dispensation of your debt."

"I take it you have a plan?" If I could keep him talking, it might give me time to figure out how to kill him. I inched my fingers into my purse while Butch growled from behind my legs. My fingers brushed up against wallet, brush, phone, crumpled tissues . . . *aha. Taser.* "I'm sure I won't like it, but go ahead."

"With its unique heritage, your child is exceedingly valuable to the Luren. Not only did your consort possess supernal beauty, but he also sprang from divinity. Your antecedents are exceptional as well. And the conception itself? Fascinating. For obvious reasons, we intend to make use of this hybrid."

Over my dead body, I thought.

Rage crashed over me in a massive wave, so fierce I was surprised it didn't slay the demon where it sat, sprawled with lazy grace on my sofa. In my head, I saw mass destruction: tsunamis destroyed villages, mushroom clouds detonated, and fires raged until the land was nothing but a blackened husk. With incredible focus, I honed that anger as my fingers curled around the Taser's handle.

"What do you have in mind?" I asked. Neutral tone.

Yeah, I should win an Oscar for this performance.

Especially because I wanted to fly at him and kill him with my bare hands. Until this moment, I was a mess, coping with the unexpected, but it was like some switch flipped in my head, and I was a mother. Not just expecting; I would do anything—*anything*—to keep this child safe.

"You will pledge the child to our service. Should you make this bargain, Sibella reckons it sufficient recompense for the deal that was broken."

Gods, the Luren didn't know shit about human beings. First the lady knight put a whammy on my pet, thinking I intended to eat it later. Now, she honestly believed I would agree to this insane deal to save my own skin? If the situation wasn't heart-attack serious, I'd laugh at how misguided they were.

"Do I get a grace period to think about it?"

"The last time Sibella extended you such a courtesy, you staged a coup and then fled the realm when it failed."

"So that's a no, then."

By its expression, the demon wasn't amused. "It irritates me that you don't seem to be giving this offer the requisite amount of consideration."

That's because it's not happening, asshole.

"I'm sorry. Have you prepared documents for me to sign?" My tone was snide, but the Luren didn't seem to notice.

"In blood."

"Really?" Belatedly I remembered how the contracts that my fallen friend Greydusk—the demon who had helped me in Sheol—signed had not only been in blood, but with an arcane compulsion as well, so if he failed to fulfill it, he died. "I'm fixing a cup of tea. Then I'll take a look at the papers. Want anything?"

"You'd serve me hemlock," the demon observed.

"Unfortunately, my canisters don't run to exotic poisons."

"Indeed. I'm glad you're being reasonable about this. The chances are excellent that service to the Luren will come with incomparable rewards."

"Oh yeah?" I didn't care, but I had to keep him talking.

My brain wasn't working nearly as fast as it should. While the Taser should render his host helpless temporarily, how the hell could I kill a demon? I wished I had one of those shining silver blades that Kel used. In Barachiel's hand, it took out the Luren leader just fine. Unfortunately, I had dull kitchen knives and the one I'd bought from Gold Malibu's trunk. Probably not demonworthy.

"Those who rule the cult of personality . . . haven't you ever wondered why people who do nothing other than exist—and look attractive—should become so absurdly famous?"

Well, now that you mention it . . .

"Yeah. So the pretty people and certain reality stars are Luren?"

"Often, they're hosts. Being famous makes for an irresistible sexual draw to a certain psyche, which offers us a rich feeding ground. Is your tea done yet?"

"Steeping now." I dunked the tea bag a few times to show I meant business with the drink. Then I carried it over to the table. I set my purse carefully beside me on the floor within easy reach. "Let's see the contract."

The document he brought out of an expensive brief-case had to be fifty pages long. Reading that—and I actually was a slow reader—would take me a while. By the time I flipped the last page, I'd have a plan, or I was dead. It was that simple.

"You might want to find a book," I suggested. "I'm not signing anything without reading the fine print. I learned that lesson on my last cell phone plan."

To my surprise, the Luren laughed. He seemed at ease, now that he imagined we'd come to amicable terms. Which substantiated my long-held belief that the Luren tended toward the stupid end of the demon spectrum. Not that I was complaining; a smarter demon like a Birsael would've long since copped to my ruse and be devouring my soul in retaliation for my bullshit.

The Luren got a magazine off the side table. Since it wasn't mine, it must belong to Booke—and gods only knew what he was reading. Instead of the contract, I peered at the cover. A travel zine. That made sense. Maybe the demon had vacation time coming . . . pity he wouldn't live to see it. Then I remembered what he planned for my unborn child.

Okay, not really.

I paged through the contract while pretending to read, frantically racking my brain. *Taser, then what . . . ?* Searching for inspiration, I skimmed the room, taking in the paltry furnishings as if a solution would jump out at me. And then it did, at least figuratively. On the far shelf, Booke had left a couple of foci left over from our rescue run. I couldn't remember what the tiny horse did, but the ceramic knot? I absolutely recognized that one.

To keep from letting on, I skimmed through the rest of the papers. Then I took a sip of my tea. "It looks reasonable," I said at last.

"Finally," the Luren muttered.

"Bring your implements, your bloodletting knife, et cetera. Let's get this done." I hoped I sounded the right amount of resigned—and not eager to get him within striking distance.

My tone must've struck the proper note—or the demon was just stupid as a stump—because he withdrew the items from his ubiquitous briefcase and came toward me. I leaned down to take a drink of tea, covering my reach. My fingers closed on the Taser, and as he bent to deposit the accoutrements on the table, I slammed it into his side, stun-gunning him for all I was worth. He lashed out, but I was already scrambling away; his human host had a limited nervous system. Regardless of how robust the Luren was, he couldn't force an immediate recovery. But I had less than thirty seconds to execute the second half of my plan. Bounding from the table, I stumbled toward the shelving unit and grabbed the Celtic knot. Unless I recalled wrong—well, no time to second-guess. I slammed the statuette to the ground above my target's head. His writhing wouldn't impact the magick.

My breath and heartbeat stalled until I saw the dark coils of energy twining around his body. *Thank the gods. It* is *a binding spell.* Since I wasn't sure how long it would last, I had to get backup over here pronto. Since I was in San Antonio, there was only one call to make, though she scared the hell out of me; she'd promised to help in these situations, though. I was her vassal, after all.

With shaking hands, I dialed Twila's number. "This is Corine Solomon. I feel like you should know . . . there's a Luren incapacitated on my kitchen floor."

Her cursing response was both colorful and impressive. "Bind him, hand, foot, and mouth, in addition to any magick you may have used. Once you do that, cast a circle. Can you do that?"

"I can't pull anymore." There was demon magick, of course, but I'd vowed not to use it if there was an alternative. "I only have the touch left."

More swearing. "Then just confine him. I'll be there in person in ten minutes."

"But I haven't told you—"

"Do you really think there's anything I don't know within my own demesne?"

Actually, I hadn't thought about it, one way or another. But the implications of that were terrifying. "All right. I used a binding spell on him, cast by a powerful wizard. Not sure how long that will last—"

"You should've led with that. He'll be out of commission for at least an hour, depending on how well fed he is. See you soon." She cut the connection.

Just to be safe, I found some extension cords in a cupboard and tied his wrists and ankles as tight as I could manage. He glared at me with hate-filled eyes, but he couldn't even blink as yet. Even his respiration was pared down, just enough to sustain the human brain. I wasn't dumb enough to linger nearby, however, in case the spell wore off sooner than Twila guessed. When she arrived, I was waiting for her on the front step, listening anxiously for the sound of a demon on a rampage inside.

Each time, her majesty struck me anew. With her midnight skin and impressive corona of braids, she looked like she ruled the city—and she did. Her white dress was lovely and expensive; I'd seen one like it retail for three hundred dollars. I loved the simple elegance of the lines, the way it flowed from her strong shoulders to nip in at her waist, and then the skirt belled around her ankles, tastefully adorned with glimmering gems on a silver chain. On a good day, I didn't have half her style or presence.

"Shall we?" she asked, but it was clearly a rhetorical

question, as she brushed past me and went into the apartment.

The Luren lay where I'd left him, still tied like a hog about to be butchered. From the way he blinked at us, the feeling had returned in his eyelids but that was it. He couldn't fight or flee Twila's judgment—and by her expression, it wouldn't be gentle or merciful. She stared down at him with eyes that burned like twin coals, ferocity and vengeance in equal measure.

"Come to me," she whispered. "Come, brothers and sisters."

The power in the room rose tangibly, a crackling electricity that stirred the hair on my arms. I wasn't clear on what exactly the loas were, but the juice they gave her made her a force to be reckoned with; she was the queen of San Antonio, and you *did not* screw with her. In a few seconds, she proved why.

My shabby apartment filled with smoky figures, not ghosts, at least none like I'd ever seen before. They were more . . . animal creatures, but not real ones. They came from the darkest depths of the imagination—terrifying, furious, and burning with hunger. The loa descended on the demon, much as Dumah had done, only they dove beneath the skin. White Hair couldn't flinch, couldn't cry out, but his eyes revealed his utter horror at the feast beneath the skin, which writhed and boiled as if maggots flowed in human veins.

When the loa finished their meal, they came to Twila like favored pets, twining around her arms and legs, nesting in her hair as if their pulsing energies constituted a crown. The fact that I could see them with the naked eye . . . I had no idea what that meant. My witch sight was gone, so these things were . . . what? A shudder worked through me as I stared at the corpse on my floor. The creature looked scarcely human anymore, the skin waxy and pallid, limbs stiff as stone.

"The remains are your problem," Twila said coolly.

"Our compact has been honored, but *do* try not to get in any more trouble, Ms. Solomon. A woman in your condition can't be too careful." On that exit line, she departed, leaving me gaping.

Am I wearing a KNOCKED UP sign in the astral? But that knowledge supported her claim to knowing everything that happened in her territory. If my landlady decided on a spot inspection right now, I was so screwed. The residual stress and fear sent me into the bathroom, where I lost my last meal. Eventually I gathered the presence of mind to call the one person who wouldn't bat an eye at this mess.

"Chuch," I said when he picked up. "I need you. Bring a tarp and a shovel."

Buried Treasure

Sometimes it sucked being my friend.

At least, I imagined that's what Chuch was thinking as he stared at the corpse on my kitchen floor. Like any good partner in crime, he'd left the supplies in the car, instead choosing to assess the situation before making any decisions. Glancing out the window, I saw he'd driven a car with a sizable trunk. This wasn't his first time.

Chuch studied the apartment and its limited contents with an air of intense concentration. "There's no rug. Once it gets dark, that's my first choice for moving him." Then he flashed me a grin. "Good thing I could tell what we'd be doing by what you said on the phone."

I stared. "You brought your own?"

"Plus the tarp and shovel. Eva wants to know what the hell you're doing killing people in your condition."

"I only bound him. I didn't know how to finish the job, so I called Twila."

Some of his agitation faded. "Smart move. I guess you pledged to her, huh? So what happened here, *prima*?"

"She fed him to her loas." I shivered. "One of the worst things I've ever seen." And I wasn't a sheltered, hothouse flower. In my time I had witnessed some shit.

Nothing like that, though. As deaths went, this one was memorable.

"I'll go get the tarp. It's in my duffel bag so the neighbors won't see it."

"You talk like you've gotten away with murder," I whispered.

Chuch flashed me a look that told me I didn't want the answer and went out to the car. When he returned, he had a gray vinyl bag in hand. After drawing on some latex gloves, he went to work efficiently, making me wonder how much of his history as an arms dealer I knew. I mean, it was a dangerous profession; and to earn enough to afford retirement, he must've been good at it. He made sufficient money restoring cars to support his family, but I suspected the Ortizes had hidden resources.

I felt a little better once the body was hidden from view. It didn't change the reality—and maybe the human host had been a shallow, venal human being—but it didn't lessen my sorrow. It was possible the guy just made a few really bad calls and didn't deserve to go out like that. But given the choice between a physical fight that could've hurt my baby or signing away his or her future? *No.* I'd make the same play again, even knowing how it shook out.

Afterward, Chuch used the extension cords I'd wrapped around the demon's wrists to tie up the tarp. Then he dragged the package over near the door and washed up in the bathroom. Shaky, I sat down at the kitchen table, buried my head in my hands. I only roused when he set a gentle hand on my shoulder, sans gloves.

"Hey, you outsmarted that *cabron*. Did what you had to do. I promise you, there's nothing Eva wouldn't do to keep Cami safe. And that goes for me too."

"Thanks." Because I couldn't let myself fall apart, I said, "I don't have much around here, but I could make you a sandwich. Some tea?"

"Both sound good. Can I get the tea iced?"

"I can steep a cup, and then pour it over some cubes for you."

"Sounds fine. I was actually about to sit down to dinner when you called." He sounded sheepish, like he wasn't allowed to have a life outside of my dramas.

That bothered me. I was tired of drawing my friends away from their own business, tired of being the needy one who couldn't go a day without stumbling into trouble. "Gods, I'm sorry. I'll be out of your hair soon."

One way or another. Six more days of this. If I haven't gotten Chance back, then it's time to call it. The awful truth hit me like an anvil. That might be my future, trying to be everything to a kid for the next twenty years. *How the hell did my mom do it?* She had six years of help, true, but watching the man she adored sacrifice himself for the child they both loved—for *me*—I didn't know how she'd done it. Any of it. Deep down I hoped that since I'd freed her power from Maury in Kilmer that her spirit was likewise free; and I'd liberated my father from Sheol, so maybe they were together now, somewhere. I'd keep that hope close because I needed the promise of happy endings now more than ever. I needed to believe.

This time, Chuch didn't contradict me. He wasn't rude enough to say, *Dios mio, get your shit in order and go home already,* but I felt keenly that I had taken advantage of them. The debt might never be adequately repaid. Silently, I put together ham and cheese sandwiches with a side of chips and pickle, a new and clichéd craving. At least I didn't want them dipped in ice cream yet. We ate without addressing my most pressing questions: When the hell were we burying the body . . . and where?

"Thanks for dinner," Chuch said, once we finished.

"It's not much. If I'd known I was hosting a dinner party, I'd have had the fancy meatballs in spicy grape jelly." It was a lame joke, but he smiled, probably appreciating how hard it was for me to pretend I was calm.

"No worries, *prima.*"

By this time, it was full dark. *Time to go.*

"Stay," I told Butch, who whined at me.

At Chuch's request, I took the bottom, though I suspected he was doing most of the lifting. Chuch backed down the steps and we had the dead demon in the trunk before I saw a curtain twitch. This wasn't the kind of neighborhood where people stared out their windows in search of trouble. Around here, most were just trying to make ends meet and keep their own problems at bay.

I climbed in the car, belted in. My body functioned on automatic, as I had come so far past shock that I didn't know what to call it. Chuch cut me a sympathetic look as he backed the car onto the street, but when he spoke, it wasn't about the mission at all. "You still have the Pinto, I see. I should've sold you a POS before."

"Yep. It's like the cheap sunglasses you never lose."

He laughed, angling our route toward the desolate country out near the border. He didn't volunteer information. In his line of work, that was smart, but it also worked my already frazzled nerves. His driving was competent, confident, right at the speed limit. Chuch obeyed all traffic laws to the letter; no way he was giving a cop the chance to pull us over. The *he was a demon, trying to steal my unborn child* defense would probably only qualify me for an insanity plea.

We had been on the road for ten minutes when I couldn't take it anymore. "You know a place, I guess?"

"Don't ask me any questions or I'll have to blindfold you." Though Chuch was one of my closest friends, I wasn't 100 percent sure he was joking until he laughed and added, "Relax, *peke*. You're wound so tight, it can't be good for the baby."

"Wouldn't you be in my shoes?"

"Well, since I'd be a woman, pregnant, and trying to get my lost man back, *si*. Even one of those things would pose a huge problem for me." Chuch's grin widened, making it impossible for me not to share his amusement.

The laughter boiled out of me until I felt near hysterical, but it was such a welcome change from hovering on the verge of tears that I didn't try to stop it, even when it came in noisy, giggly spurts. Chuch just kept driving. Eva had really trained him well; he was equipped to deal with any emergency a woman could have.

Eventually we got off the highway, but drove away from the rock formation where I'd found Kel. Once, Chuch checked the coordinates in his GPS, made another turn. Then he said, "We're almost there."

"There" turned out to be a rocky stretch of nowhere, kind of the point, I supposed. Once more, I helped move the body. Not something I ever thought I'd do. I felt guilty that this guy's family would never know what happened to him, but most likely he was lost to them by the time he ended up as a Luren host. Drugs, maybe, or a permissive lifestyle took the blame, and his family had already written him off.

I'd tell myself that anyway.

Chuch got the shovel.

"Can I help—" I started to ask, but he cut me off with a curt gesture.

"I'll take care of it. Get back in the car, please."

I'd never heard quite that tone from him before. Gone was the laughing, gentle man who adored his family. This was the guy who took care of business, who could smuggle any weapon you wanted and not get caught. In response, I slid back into my seat, quietly closed my door, and watched the proceedings in the side mirror.

He dug a shallow trench, unwound the tarp, then rolled the body into the furrow. With quick capable rakes of the shovel, he smoothed sandy soil over the top and then he tossed a number of rocks to cover the signs of recent digging, not that I expected anyone to stumble across the grave site. To my surprise, he put all the supplies back in the trunk.

As he got in, he read my look. "I'll sterilize everything

and put it away. Since there's no connection between me and the vic, the stuff's safer in my garage."

That made sense. If he left the tarp here and somebody found the body, there might be trace evidence left behind. Since neither of us had handled the corpse with our bare skin, there shouldn't be anything left to find. I'd bet there were all kinds of people buried out here in shallow graves.

"Thank you. It's not enough, but—"

"You'd come if I needed you, right?"

"Of course." So far, I was the troublesome friend, however, and the uneven balance bothered me. My friendship had cost the Ortizes so much while giving back relatively little.

Chuch went on, "And you promised to look after Cami, if somebody ever comes gunning for me."

"That's not gonna happen," I whispered.

Even if it did, he had a huge extended family. I suspected he and Eva had chosen Chance and me for the honor of godparents just to prevent infighting between their massive respective clans. But if the worst came to pass, yeah, I'd take Cami. Get her out of the country and keep her safe, no matter what. Just like I would for the peanut growing in my belly.

His expression grew stern in the starlight. "Friends don't keep a score sheet. You should know that."

"Yeah, but they don't take advantage either."

"It's been a rough few years for you, granted. But things will level out . . . and then it'll be time for you to pay up in free babysitting when Eva and I desperately need to go on a cruise to remember what it's like to sleep past five a.m."

"Deal," I said. "Anytime you want."

Chuch grinned. "You say that now. It'll be a different story in a year when I call and you've got one of your own."

"I'll still help you out. Promise."

"Don't think I won't hold you to it either." By his tone, he was dead serious.

On the way back to the apartment, I fell asleep. Chuch woke me as he pulled into the drive, a gentle touch to my arm that left me feeling like a narcoleptic. I was eating as well as I could manage, but stress and worry took their toll, and I didn't do well alone in a strange bed at night. That was when all my fears played knick-knack on my head.

"Is Booke coming back tonight?"

I shook my head. "But I'll be fine."

There was still one Luren in the wind, but I had my Taser and a watchdog. It was unlikely I'd sleep anyway. All factors suggested that I wouldn't get much rest until this thing played out. Even if the ritual didn't end as I wanted it to, at least I'd have my answer: Chance or no Chance. Either way, I had to get back to my life.

"I don't like leaving you alone. Eva would be pissed." From his expression, though, he was ready to get home.

So I offered a small lie with a clear conscience. "I'll call Booke. Get him to wrap his evening up early. I'm sure he won't mind."

"Thanks, *prima*. Now I can tell Eva I left you in good hands."

Chuch came to the door and walked through to make sure I had no more unwanted visitors. I hoped the Luren intelligence network, which included the damned hospital orderly, took a while to notice White Hair's failure and send the last Luren to handle me. No question they wouldn't be social this time around. Barachiel killed the first emissary in a throwdown, and I offed another—well, nearly, anyway. I served him up for Twila, so I was an accomplice for sure. The gloves would come off in the final round, and I had no clue how to fight back.

Butch had been penned up, so I took him for a short walk around the neighborhood after Chuch left. It was dark enough to be creepy with a few broken streetlights, and I felt like somebody was watching me the whole time. The atmosphere got to the dog as well. He peed really fast and whined to go inside. He didn't have to tell me twice.

The constant napping had screwed with my schedule, so I couldn't get to sleep. I puttered in the apartment, vaguely creeped out by the memory of the dead thing on my kitchen floor. *Dammit. At this rate, I won't doze off until dawn.* Eventually I laid on the couch and listened to the radio. There was no TV or stereo, and the analog music solution was so old that Shannon might be able to use it to talk to the dead. More to the point, it still worked, so I played it softly, so it wouldn't drown out an intruder. Butch curled up on my stomach, keeping the baby company. My ears strained for footfalls, and around two a.m., I heard someone creeping toward the front door. Butch froze too, his ears cocked. He couldn't seem to make up his mind if we needed to panic or not. Such indecision was unlike him. After rolling off the couch, I ran for my Taser. Gods, this was getting old. I missed safety and the right arms to hold me, having someone to lean on when I needed them most. Right then, I felt incredibly alone. But I was poised to strike, do what I had to do, as Chuch put it. Then I heard the jingle of keys.

Booke. It must be Booke.

As he stepped into the apartment, I wilted with relief, lowering the stun gun. He moved closer and I smelled a hint of alcohol. *Is that why Butch didn't greet him with excited tail wagging?* In his defense, the Englishman wasn't unsteady on his feet, but I could see he'd enjoyed a wild night.

"I thought you weren't coming back until the morning," I said quietly.

"Was worried about you. Also, Ms. Devlin's not keen on sleepovers." A faint softening of his vowels was the only sign he'd been drinking, nothing to worry about.

His motion didn't seem impaired, and he hadn't

driven home, so no trouble in that regard. So why was Butch staring at him so intently, ears back, tail still?

My dog seemed suspicious—and if he was, then I took him seriously. He'd saved me too often for it to be otherwise. I took a cautious step out of Booke's reach.

"There's something wrong." It wasn't a question.

"I wish you hadn't noticed," Barachiel said.

Booke opened his mouth. Blood poured out. He managed one word. "Run."

I woke in a cold sweat.

Butch was at my feet, snoozing away. Sunlight streamed into my face from the spotty windows. Though my neck was stiff and I'd had nightmares, that was actually the best sleep I'd had in weeks. These I could shrug off as mere bad dreams, not omens. Given the mess my life was in, it was understandable that I was scared. I'd have to be an idiot not to be. Mostly I tried not to think about everything that could go wrong, how many factors needed to align in only a few days.

Booke came home for real as I was eating breakfast. Crackers and tea first to make sure I kept my food down. Then half an hour later, I had yogurt and frozen berries. To make my doctor happy, I ate a spoonful of peanut butter for protein and took my vitamin. He looked content and exhausted, glowing with the enjoyment of personal freedom. *I had a hand in that,* I thought.

"Good night?" I asked.

"The best. She's a wildcat."

"Eh, you can stop there. Really."

He grinned, pouring himself a cup of tea from the pot I'd steeped earlier. "And what did you do last night, Ms. Solomon?"

"Killed a demon, buried the body. The usual."

His first sip choked him. "*Tell* me you're joking."

Licking my peanut butter spoon, I shook my head and then explained in detail what had gone down. His expression darkened as he listened, and by the time I finished my account, his gray eyes were lightning fierce with outrage. This was the second time I'd pissed him off; and he had a pretty even temper. If we hung around much longer, he might throttle me.

"You should have *called me.* I wasn't performing open-heart surgery . . . I was just having a bit of fun."

"But you haven't had any in a long time. At least not like that. I didn't want to interrupt—"

"Shut. Up," he bit off. "Your other friends seem unwilling to speak, but I am not. You have all the common sense and self-preservation of a tinned ham. Furthermore, you place your pride ahead of your own well-being, and that simply will not do. Not anymore. Your child *must* come first, now and always. You can't fret about being a burden or any such rubbish. You've been alone for so long that you can't imagine you can truly trust anyone and that, too, is bollocks. Unless you really mean to die alone, then *stop it.* Immediately." He ranted longer, leaving me speechless. Not because the things he was saying shocked or hurt me. More that it had been ages since I had a friend who cared enough to yell at me.

Even Shan doesn't go off on me like this. Ian Booke loves me.

I must've had a goofy, ridiculous smile on my face because he paused in the tirade to demand, "What?!"

"I'm sorry," I said meekly. "You're right. About everything. I need to stop feeling like I'm a pain in the ass when people want to help me. It's just . . . hard. When you grow up the way I did, you have issues."

His tone gentled. "Believe me, I understand, Corine. I was alone longer than anyone should be. But I'm letting the world in now. You should try it."

"I will," I promised. "I am."

Starting with you.

And I truly hoped the nightmare had been only that, not a portent of dire misfortune to come.

Last Call

Three days left. By this point, I was a total knot of anxiety, but when Booke's phone rang, I froze. Hope stirred, but it was faint and unfamiliar, a tremulous shadow on the wall cast by someone else. He moved off down the hall toward the bedroom, speaking in low tones. I strained to overhear, but he was a master at turning his body so the sound didn't carry.

What the hell, Booke.

Of course, maybe it was one of his lady friends. At this point, he was one of San Antonio's most eligible gifted bachelors between his courtly, old school manners, his giant throbbing brain, and the accent. He probably had other assets as well, but I wasn't placed to appreciate them. Pushing off the couch, I edged closer. He caught me trying to eavesdrop, as he was already off the phone . . . and vibrating with excitement.

"Good news?" I asked.

"I didn't want to get your hopes up, should this last effort prove fruitless, but that was Ms. Devlin."

I raised a brow. "You still call her Ms., after . . ." At his pointed look, I shook my head. "Never mind. Go on."

"She found a copy of the scroll and someone who might be able to translate the text for us."

"Fast enough?" I demanded.

There, he paused. "It'll be a near thing, Corine. It's a rare language . . . and we can't pay the fees that would cause a professor to put aside his other responsibilities. We can certainly offer an honorarium that makes it worth his time, but the sort of people who go into dead languages don't tend to be motivated by money anyway."

"You mean there's not huge profit in ancient Babylonian? Huh. Never would've guessed." Kel could read and translate this ritual, but he was busy protecting me from Barachiel.

As a last resort, I'll call him.

"May I borrow the car?"

"I dunno, it's a pretty sweet ride. Can I trust you not to do doughnuts in it?"

"I don't even like doughnuts," Booke said.

Right, though he's kept up with some of the world via the Internet, he's still not 100 percent current. So then I had to explain the joke, which eliminated all humor. But he promised me soberly not to do anything that would impact the life of the tires, so I agreed. I stayed behind, cuddling Butch and fretting more.

When he returned, he said, "Ms. Devlin has called in a few favors for us. The collector agreed to send copies of the scroll to the university in Cairo."

"I wish we knew enough to start gathering supplies." I didn't mean to sound snippy, but his face fell.

"As do I. I feel as though I haven't been nearly useful enough, particularly since you delayed your quest to help *me*."

"I delayed it for Kel too. Those were my decisions, nobody else's. And I don't regret either of them."

I might, if we ran out of time, and I lost Chance forever, if my kid grew up never knowing his father because of choices I'd made. But I hadn't realized that the ritual had an expiration date or that the other realm would strip away his ties to the mortal coil. It made sense, but there was no way I could've acted based on information I didn't have at the time. In that case, it would've been a tough call, as I had never been one to walk away from a friend in need. I remembered too clearly how it felt to have your back to the wall and nobody in your corner.

"Anyway," I went on, "we're not down to the wire yet."

Two days later, we were.

It had to be tonight . . . or I lost everything. And we still didn't have a translation of the ritual. Booke had been on the phone, bitching at the professor in Cairo, who was sorry, but he didn't have the fluency necessary for a detailed translation such as we required, plus the pages from the scroll appeared to be in dialect. While he might be able to work out an approximate meaning, that would take months, not days.

A voice in my head said, *That's it, then. It's over.* I screamed silently to drown it out. Even if it controverted all logic, I wouldn't give up one second before time ran out and the buzzer went off. After all, love itself was a defiant shout in the face of a bleak world. It was saying, *I know things are terrible, but I believe this person will always be there for me. I believe I have a chance to be happy.*

I believe.

Maybe it was just too Tinker Bell of me, but I clung to the faith that on the other side, Chance was working just as hard, pushing to be ready when the veil thinned enough for this to be feasible. He wouldn't let his father convince him there was no point in trying. If we failed, it would be because I couldn't open the way on my end. I imagined Chance gathering his strength, gaining power from Daikokuten's worshippers, not to rise as the new incarnation of a god but to use in returning to me.

"Okay," I said. "Plan B."

Booke gazed at me, astonished. "There's a plan B?"

"Do you have a copy of the scroll pages?"

"Yes. Ms. Devlin asked the collector to CC me."

"Then I need you to craft a spell that'll hide our location for a while. Can you do that?" I knew less than shit about the sorts of spells he could create.

"I'll need to pop by the shop, but yes. It's of limited duration, and it applies only to magickal tracking and scrying. I take it that's what you're after?"

I nodded. "We don't need to be invisible. I'll find us a place to perform the ritual while you're gone."

"But we don't have a translation."

"Just get the stuff for the hide-and-seek spell. Leave the rest to me."

He scowled at me. "I rather hate being treated like a minion."

"There's *no time*," I snapped.

That ship had sailed. This was my last Hail Mary play, and if we dropped the ball here, well . . . As Booke left, I dug out my phone and dialed Jesse. He seemed surprised to hear from me, but not tense or awkward, which made me happy. Maybe one day, we'd get back to our old footing.

"What's up?" he asked.

"I need a quiet place with little opportunity for collateral damage, if something goes wrong. You can find out what buildings have been seized."

"Shit. You're asking me to use police resources for personal reasons. I could get fired."

"This is the last favor I'll ever ask of you. Promise." Then I played the blackmail card without blinking; he had to know I wasn't fucking around. "Frankly, I figure you owe me. You'd be in mourning if it wasn't for me. I brought the woman you love back to you. Help me do the same for my man."

"Goddammit." That was the sound of him giving in. "Ten minutes. I'll find you something. I don't know what you've got planned, understand? Don't tell me. Especially if it's illegal."

"I don't think it is," I said.

But likely there weren't any statutes on the books about opening portals between worlds. I suspected Congress wouldn't like it, but I didn't plan to put the matter to a vote, so it was all good. It actually took Jesse twenty minutes, and he didn't call back. Instead, he texted me an address. I borrowed Booke's computer and looked at it on Google maps; the street view was incredibly helpful—disturbingly so, in fact. He'd found me a warehouse in the industrial district. By the graffiti tags and the broken windows, the buildings on each side looked to be abandoned.

"Perfect," I said.

Butch sighed at me.

"You don't approve?"

Negative yaps.

"You think I should play it safe?"

More negative yaps.

"What's wrong, then?"

He stared at me pointedly. Right. I forgot that he couldn't talk unless I got the tiles. So I fetched them, spread them out for him, and he told me:

ready to go home i miss tia

"Me too, pal. Me too."

By the time Booke got back, I had packed our stuff. One way or another, I wasn't coming back. This apartment had served its purpose, but I was ready to move on. The leg wrap made it possible for me to move without limping much, but the pain was constant. Hopefully my muscle strength would return after I completed the PT, but the injury wouldn't keep me from doing what I had to tonight.

"You got everything for the spell?"

"Yes, and I've the focus object right here."

"Wrap it all up. You can work it when we get to the warehouse."

Frustration etched into his features, but we didn't have time for me to lay everything out for him. I texted Shannon the address and let her know the shit was going down tonight. After the talk we had in the hospital, it couldn't be otherwise. She'd never forgive me if I did this without her. Then, I remembered Booke's lecture on asking for help. I didn't think I needed backup, but who knew what, exactly, would happen tonight? If Ebisu sent enforcers through the gate to try and bring Chance back, well, I wasn't in any shape to fight, between my bum leg and the bun in the oven.

So I sent the details and the time to Chuch and Eva as well. Eva pinged back with confirmation. *I'll be there, chica, dressed to the nines.* Which I took to mean she would bring heavy weapons, just in case. I had Booke for magickal defense, Chuch and Eva for an old school throwdown. Ten minutes later, Shan got back to me.

Wouldn't miss it for the world. I'll bring the silverware.

She had a sword? During our lifetime in Sheol, she'd become accomplished with a blade, and she had mentioned that she intended to continue fencing to keep her skills sharp. There was no doubt she'd keep Jesse jumping. He knew where we'd be, but there was no way he'd show, unless something horrible happened. He had to steer clear of breaking and entering; and that, I was sure, along with trespassing, would be the least of my crimes tonight.

"This is a bit absurd," Booke said, as he drove toward the warehouse. "You're setting up to cast a spell we don't have."

"We'll have it."

"How?" he demanded.

"Kel."

A frown creased his brow. "Why didn't you contact him in the first place?"

"He's already playing bait to keep Barachiel off me long enough to do this. Problem is, I can't do it without him. We tried."

"And you were afraid if he stopped running, Barachiel would track Kel down and kill him."

"Pretty much."

"That's why you asked for the spell to hide our whereabouts. It's a gamble."

I nodded.

"Corine, I don't know whether my magick is strong enough to block a demon of his strength. He may have resources of which I'm unaware."

"Then you see why I didn't want to call Kel until it became unavoidable."

"He was always your ace in the hole," Booke realized aloud.

"Yep. I didn't want to put him at risk more than he's already offered, but there's no choice now."

"Needs must, devil drives."

There was nothing more to say. The final minutes were up on the scoreboard, game winding down. When we arrived at the warehouse, it looked even worse than it had on Google. Easy to imagine shady doings here. Booke took the tire iron out of the trunk and whacked the rusty padlock on the back door until it gave. Inside, it was dark, dank, reeking of pigeon shit and the acrid tang of urine. Not a romantic locale for a long-anticipated reunion. I wandered around until I found a janitor's closet; fortunately, there was a dirty broom amid the other abandoned supplies, so I swept a portion of the cement floor clear. There only needed to be room to cast a circle, but my mother's power was gone.

You have to use the demon magick.

Though the thought revolted me, I'd do it. My vow limited its practice to life and death, and this qualified. So one last stain to serve my purposes, and then I would turn my back on that world forever. *But what if it hurts the baby?* Was demon magick like drinking, drugs, or too much caffeine? *Shit. Who would I even ask?* No doubt I had made some impossible choices in my life, but father of child versus child? Much as I hated it, I'd have to pick our baby over Chance.

But maybe there's a solution. You haven't even gotten the translation yet.

I dialed the panic down to DefCon 4.

While I'd been tidying, Booke had cast his spell. He brought me the statuette, placing it in my hand with a sober look. "If everything goes to hell tonight, it's been an honor."

"Seriously? That's your pep talk?"

"I *am* British, you know."

That was a joke. I thought. So I laughed, but the sound resonated with nervous tension. Booke rubbed my shoulder with gentle affection, evidently over his prior aggravation. It hit me then that he'd be leaving soon. Regardless of how this ended he'd be in the wind, living out his dream of seeing the world before he replaced Ms. Devlin at the arcane library beneath Wonder Lanes.

Gods, I'll miss him.

I checked the time. "I'm calling Kel. Get ready."

Booke knew without being told that he had only seconds to keep us from ending up with Barachiel right on top of us. Hopefully his blocker would last long enough to bring Chance back, and then I'd help Kel fight the crazy-ass demon that had him on a magickal leash. We all would. The whole crew would be assembled at that point and ready for a fight.

Bring it on.

I whispered the summons soft enough that Booke couldn't make out Kel's true name, and this time, I put a little demon magick in the call. Using it in this realm stung, like pushing up too fast through the ocean and taking a load of salt water up the nose. But it didn't hurt like using my mother's magick had—and that worried me. I noticed no response from the baby, no pain, no nausea.

Kel appeared before me a few seconds later, battered,

bewildered. He was also filthy, exhausted, covered in half-healed wounds. Gods, what had he been doing for the past two weeks? Booke smashed the statuette at our feet, bringing up a cloud of dust that shimmered, settling gently on my skin. The blocker was on the job. We'd see how well it worked.

"What have you done?" Kel demanded. "I warned you, this is madness."

"We have a little time at least. Booke's got us covered. Literally." I paused for Kel to sense the truth, and some of his tension and rage diffused. "I need your help. You're the only one who can do this for me. Believe me, if there was any other way . . ." I shook my head. "We tried. This is it."

Anyone else would've persisted in the questions, but he read my desperation. Kel ran a hand down my cheek, left the stickiness of his blood behind. Fortunately, I had no open wounds on my face, or I'd be high as a kite right now. Last time, I went tripping balls after a hit of his blood. That made me wonder if all demon blood had healing properties, or only the ones who had been magickally fooled into believing they came from angelic origins. Not a critical question right now, though.

"What do you need?" he asked.

Ritual of Doom

Booke handed Kel his phone. "A precise translation, if possible."

Kel skimmed the pages with quick cognition. Then he handed the cell back. "It's a spell to part the veil. Not to Sheol. Elsewhere. But it won't work unless you have help from the other side."

"I do," I said. "Can you lay it out for me? What do we need to cast it?"

Without protest, Kel made a shopping list for Booke, who took the keys to the Pinto and hurried off, muttering, "They're going to love us at the shop."

"You don't have to stay," I said to Kel. "Just write down what I need to do. I'll take it from there."

"Barachiel will find me," he replied wearily. "The wizard's spell will slow him, but the ending is inevitable. Knowing the truth, I cannot swerve. We've played cat and mouse for days."

Judging from his injuries, Kel had been the mouse. "I'm sorry."

"Don't be. Everything ends, *dādu*."

This time, I didn't forbid the endearment. While he was constant, he was also an immortal half-demon, bound to a maniacal creature that believed it was an archangel destined to rewrite the world. It had been working toward that until I stumbled into the mix. With a combination of Chance's backlash luck and my own stubbornness, I fucked up Barachiel's life; he didn't take rejection well either.

"Seriously, I don't want you here if Barachiel shows up. I'll have backup." Whether Booke, Shannon, Chuch, Eva and I could take out an ancient demon, I had no idea. But Kel would die if we didn't. "Just write the spell down."

I handed him a notebook from my purse, along with a pen. Kel heaved a sigh, but he wrote in his lovely, old-fashioned hand. A few minutes later, I took the pad from him, scanned the steps.

"That doesn't look too bad."

"What you're not seeing is that all great workings require a sacrifice."

"Shit. Like a life? If I cast this spell, it might kill my baby?"

Oh, gods, no. No. Fate couldn't be so cruel. I'd gladly die to give Chance the life he wanted in this world, but I couldn't kill our child for him. He wouldn't want me to if he knew that was the price.

"You choose the sacrifice before you cast."

"So it wouldn't just randomly take my kid?"

Kel shook his head. "Generally, it's a magickal sacrifice, an artifact or a foci brimming with power."

"It's not death magick, then."

"Not usually, though death magick would serve as a workable substitute."

"Dammit. I don't have any—oh. I could give the spell the touch . . . and what's left of my demon magick." I gazed up at him, anxious. "Would that be enough?"

"I don't know. It depends how much power your partner brings to bear on the other side."

"It's all I have to offer," I whispered. "I'll try."

The ritual would leave me a normal human. That wasn't a deterrent, however, as that was all I'd ever wanted, my whole life. If this didn't work, I'd end up a single mom, just like my mother. *It has to work.* I was in no way strong enough to follow the example set by Cherie Solomon. All those years, she knew where my father had gone—and that he was never coming home.

Chance is. *He promised.*

Kel went over the ritual with me with tireless patience, drilling until I felt sure I had memorized all of the steps. By the time the others started arriving, I'd recited the incantation eighteen times. Shan got there first, sword in hand. Tonight, she eschewed her usual Lolita-goth gear; she was practically garbed in black leggings and a fitted black tee, no loose fabric to interfere with her movements or allow an opponent to grab hold of her. Likewise, she'd bound her black hair back into a tight French braid. Her makeup was still Shan: eyes heavily lined in kohl, ivory pale cheeks, and a blood-red mouth. She looked like a poster of a vampire I'd seen once; I didn't say that, as she was so over the undead.

"You nervous?" she asked, giving me a one-armed hug.

"Kinda. If I let myself think about what I'm doing for more than two seconds."

"Semper fi." She threw some complicated hand gestures at me, which could've been military, or they might've been gang signs.

I ignored them. "Isn't that the Marine Corps motto?"

"That's not the point. What does it mean?"

Though I didn't speak Latin, I actually knew this. "Always faithful?"

"Yep." She flashed me a triumphant grin. "And that's you."

My heart gave a little squeeze. "Thanks."

"Don't mention it. Where's the dog?"

"Cowering in my purse. I'm thinking of charging him rent."

Butch gave an indignant yap and trotted out to greet her. He wagged his tail hard enough to shake his whole body when she rubbed him just the way he liked. Sadly for the dog, it couldn't last. She moved off for some practice swings, and her arcs with her sword were beautiful to behold.

Next, Chuch and Eva rolled up, looking like they could star in an action movie. Both had dressed in dark, nondescript clothing. Eva was strapped with a 12-gauge shotgun and a handgun in a thigh holster. Chuch had automatics, plus a duffle bag bulging with other goodies. If shit went down, he'd make it real. I squinted, realizing that was the same bag he'd carried the tarp in the other night.

Night had fallen while I memorized the ritual, a dark and starless night earmarked for Chance's return. Inside the warehouse, it was gloomier still, but Eva had foreseen that eventuality. "Storm lamps," she said, setting them around the circle I was drawing in chalk. She activated the batteries one by one, so the squalor was more evident. In the far corner, three rats skittered toward a crack in the wall.

Eva made a face. "Not exactly pretty, is it?"

"No, but if things go hideously wrong, we won't take out a city block either."

"There is that," Chuch said, joining us.

I smiled, but didn't pause in sketching the circle. My thigh hurt, the way I was crouched on the cement, but I ignored the pain. "Thanks for coming, all of you."

"It wouldn't be a welcome back party if the gang wasn't all here," Chuch said.

Well, everyone except Jesse. And he wouldn't show unless things went catastrophically wrong. *Here's hoping I don't see Jesse Saldana tonight.*

Booke returned last, but he had everything I needed. And he wore a harried look. "I may have scraped another car getting out of downtown."

"I'm not worried about it," I told him frankly.

"But I'm an outlaw now. A felon."

"You didn't mind leaving the country on a fake passport and a charm," I pointed out.

"That was before I realized I'd be here to face the consequences."

I laughed. "Quit fretting, granddad, and show me what you got."

With a grumble, Booke handed me various dried herbs and powders while Kel reminded me when to use each one. *Soon this will be over.* That became my mantra as I prepared the site with the spell components. From that point, I ignored the others; my focus had to be complete, the ritual flawless. The susurration of their voices rolled over me in waves, but the snippets didn't penetrate. Finally, I had everything in place, and I was ready to begin.

"I need you all to step off. I'm not exactly sure how big the gate will be —"

"Then shouldn't you back up as well?" Chuch wondered.

"I have to stay close to the circle. Theoretically, it should contain the energies and keep the portal from spreading to alarming proportions, but . . ." I shrugged. "Just move, okay? And keep a sharp eye out for trouble." Demon magick was notorious for rebounding in powerful, unexpected ways.

"On it," Shan said.

Since I would be using the touch — and sacrificing it, plus the remainder of my demon magick — I got out the athame I had carried with me from Sheol. In this realm, it didn't look as ominous, so possibly the trip back had stripped it of some of its power. But it still didn't look harmless. I whispered the words in ancient Babylonian as I drew the blade across my palm. My blood welled up ruby red and ready to work. The crimson fluid dripped down the blade; then the warehouse seemed oddly, ominously quiet, as if there were a barrier between the others and me. When my blood trickled onto the chalk, I released the concentration that kept me from reading random objects and murmured the words of gifting—of sacrifice—and then the circle shimmered.

I hadn't been positive this would work, but I gained confidence as my remaining abilities went into the protective ring. If this worked as a power exchange, the circle would be drained when the way opened. The ritual would take my magick and give me back Chance. *Easy, right?*

Not so much.

The demon magick clawed on the way out, raking like barbed wire in my veins as blood spilled from my palm. It stuck to me like tar, unwilling to be sacrificed. With pure will, I forced it out until I had nothing left. Then I closed my fingers to get the bleeding to taper off. Booke was there with a roll of gauze; I hadn't asked him to buy it, but he wrapped my palm without comment.

"I never saw anything like that," Chuch murmured with a hint of awe.

I surveyed my work, and it was a pretty damn fine circle. Now, for the fun part. Chanting for gods knew how long, pushing at the way between worlds, until it thinned enough to permit passage. The ritual didn't say how long it would take.

Eva cocked her gun. "It smells like trouble in here."

Now that she mentioned it, I *did* smell something burning; maybe it was just the storm lamps heating up. The Babylonian words sounded strange rolling off my tongue, but they had a hypnotic quality, making it easier to focus. After a few repetitions, all distractions faded. I poured myself into the spell, all I was, all my will, until I was focused only on the circle.

How will I know if it's working—

Before I finished the mental question, a massive boom behind me tempted me to look, but I couldn't stop chanting, no matter what had happened.

Chuch was shouting, "Incoming! Take cover."

"I count eight," Eva called back.

"Fuckin' demons," Shan muttered.

Awesome. So the last Luren in the trifecta of Sexy Evil had come gunning for me—and he was smarter than the others. He'd brought backup . . . but this time, so had I. I didn't let my concentration lapse; if I did, even for a second, then the spell failed, and there would be no second chances.

"What the hell *is* that?" Eva asked.

Her shotgun went off. I desperately wished I could see the action, and then some of it spilled onto the other side of the circle. *Eight shades. Shit.* The demon must've hired a contractor. Since shades couldn't be harmed by mundane weapons, Eva, Chuch, and Shan needed to get away from them. But I couldn't shout the warning, couldn't pause in my chant, even though my thigh felt like it was on fire and my throat was raw, my lips parched, and my voice had dwindled to a husky croak.

How long have I been casting?

"We can't hurt these," Shan called. "Back off. Leave it to Kel and Booke."

Thank God for Shan.

I heard Kel fighting. Despite his wounds, he wouldn't let these monsters get me or my friends. He shouted, "Show yourself, demon!"

"Look in the mirror," the Luren said slyly.

Its voice carried in the sprawling warehouse. The thing could be hiding anywhere . . . and it was clearly smarter than its predecessors. If I knew demons, this one hadn't limited itself to shades . . . because it wasn't just trying to return me to Sheol to pay my debt to Sibella; it was also fighting for its life. And nothing was stronger than self-preservation . . . except for love.

Chance . . .

Booke smashed one of his statuettes and the powerful pop of strong magick filled the air, raising the hair on my arms. A shade hissed as it winked out of existence. The Englishman laughed, triumph in the sound, but then I heard his footsteps as he scrambled away . . . from something.

"Run." Shan's calm tone terrified me.

"Kelethiel!" The shout boomed like thunder, shaking the walls around me. Even the concrete floor trembled beneath my aching knees.

Barachiel. Oh, shit.

I tried to break off then—to end the spell. My friends would need all the help they could get—and even knowing it meant I'd never see Chance again, I tried to stop. But I *couldn't*. I was trapped in the loop and the chanting continued, ancient words spilling out of my raw throat like the girl with the cursed dancing slippers. I was past the point of turning back; I would cast until I died, the ritual drawing energy out of me until I was a withered husk.

Had my sacrifice been insufficient to open the way?

I'm so sorry.

"Eva!" Chuch's weapon went full auto, but I didn't know what he was shooting. Maybe Barachiel.

Not Eva. Oh, gods, no.

The words hurt now, drawn out of me like blood. My eyes filled with tears, so a watery veil blurred the world. In that mist, I glimpsed a swirl of something—maybe—a hint of Chance's face, but it was too far away, thin and warped. Something . . . something was wrong.

This isn't working.

Shannon called out a challenge. *Don't piss off Barachiel,* I thought. *Leave him to Kel.* But even Kel couldn't kill him. *Maybe they can tag team him . . . but there's the Luren . . . and his shades . . .*

The ritual took more, pulling my life force like silken threads in a skilled weaver's loom. I tasted bitter ashes on my tongue. *I should never have done this. Oh, gods, baby, I'm sorry. I thought it was safe.*

I thought—

Nothing.

There were only the words. They became reality. Owned me. They were thunder and the smell of fire in a pine forest. My friends receded. Their struggles seemed dim and faint, awful but inevitable. The mist rolled closer. A hand stretched toward me, but it was ghostly and ephemeral.

Not enough.

Not—

Kel and Barachiel stumbled toward the circle, locked in a death grip. My friend had his arm around the demon's neck, his silver knife in its side, and he was using it like a handle. Kel bled from so many wounds that it was impossible he could still be on his feet. I didn't know why Barachiel wasn't using the compulsion; maybe knowing the truth gave Kel some limited ability to resist it . . . or maybe it required concentration like the spell that was killing me by inches. Pain broke focus.

If only I could get someone to hurt me . . .

My vision sparked black and white. Even the pain in my body felt distant. And then Kel heaved them both forward, breaking the circle, still full of my power. The explosion rocked me backward, out of the trance, but I was stunned, barely conscious, when I pushed to my hands and knees. The ritual swelled with the added power, incredible energy, and both Kel and Barachiel arched into postures that bespoke impossible pain. I sensed the river of life funneling from the two of them, quickening the ancient spell; it became a black and red tornado swirling around them.

"This is not how it ends," Barachiel screamed.

The sound went on and on, until it fused with the chant I still could not stop, even now, though my lips were trickling blood. Another explosion rocked the warehouse and the mist caught fire, blasting a tunnel of hell toward us. I lacked the energy to move, but Shan pulled me away from the flames. I expected a horde of

demons or angry divine enforcers, but Chance strode
from the fires untouched. With every step, he became
more real until at last he stood on the other side. From
behind him came a quiet voice that was so beautiful it
hurt my ears, echoing with bells, wind chimes, and laughing children.

Farewell, my son.

A shiver rolled through me. *No wonder Min slept with
you, Ebisu.*

Shan kept me upright, as I had no ability to balance.
Booke was cleaning up the last of the shades. I still had
no idea where the last Luren was. If it was smart, it would
forget about Sheol and live out its human life here.
Chance shook his head once, twice, as if to clear it. He
moved his fingers, as if testing his own solidity.

Chuch knelt beside Eva, and when he caught my eye,
he circled his thumb and forefinger. "She's okay, just
knocked out."

Thank the gods.

The moment I could, I pulled away from Shan,
crawled across the filthy floor toward Kel. Surely, he was
all right. He opened his eyes when I fell beside him. His
fingers flexed; and I wrapped mine around his, slick with
blood. He labored to breathe, his chest rent, his body
charred. I sensed Chance coming toward me, but it
wasn't quite time for a joyful reunion. *Not yet.* Not until
I knew the cost. Tears fell, dripping hot down my cheeks.

"You'll be fine," I whispered. "You just need to sleep."

"No. The future lies before you, *dādu*, but I have outlived my purpose. I choose to die a free man. Everything
ends." Light flared in his tats, a final brightness before
the dark. Kel closed his lovely, icy eyes and breathed,
"Asherah."

Then he was gone.

I knelt beside his body, his charred fingers in mine.
When the last of the magick crumbled away, he was ash
in my fingers. More tears slipped down my cheeks; a

scream built in my chest, but my throat was too raw to bear it. So I held it in my head, echoing endlessly, while I rocked, a ball of white-hot pain. I hadn't wanted happiness built on top of death, but Booke had warned there would be a cost.

I just hadn't expected Kel to pay it in my stead.

Why didn't you go when I told you? It appeared my dream had been prophetic in a sense; one life was lost in bringing Chance back, an even exchange to keep the universe in balance. The others stood away from me while I grieved; I heard them whispering, but . . . there was no one else to mourn him.

"Not like this," I whispered. "Not like this."

Future Perfect

Eventually Chance pulled me to my feet . . . into his arms. I rocked on shaky legs, but he held me so tight. He shouldn't be here. This shouldn't be possible . . . and it only was because I'd fed the ritual enough raw power to open the gate. I never meant to, but Kel made the choice, dragging the ancient demon into the circle with him. By doing so, he'd saved the world from the war Barachiel planned to wage.

And he brought love back to me.

Oh, Kel. Thank you. And I'm sorry.

Chance kissed me endlessly, his hands in my tangled hair. It was better than anything I'd ever known yet the kiss tasted of smoke and tears. Nothing beautiful came without pain, and our love had been fireproofed. Chance felt exactly as I remembered, his hands possessive and warm on my back.

"Welcome home," I whispered when we finally came up for air.

"We need to get you to a doctor. Make sure the baby's all right."

I swallowed hard. "You heard."

"Barely. I wondered if I had imagined it, but that kernel of possibility let me cling to you when the other realm started working on me."

"Cleansing you of ties?" I guessed.

He nodded. "Sometimes this life felt like a dream, you know?"

"So do you have all kinds of secrets to share?" I smiled through the pain, conscious of how high the price had been to bring him home.

"No. They keep you . . . quarantined until you've made the transition."

"You were in solitary the whole time?" I stroked his cheek, unable to believe he thought I was worth this.

"Apart from my dad, yeah."

"I hate to ruin the moment," Booke cut in, "but the demon wants to parlay."

Chance kept his arm around me, helping me toward the others. My knees still felt weak and shaky, but at least I wasn't bleeding anywhere. I tested my abdomen for pain, but there was none. Now only my throat and thigh hurt.

The beautiful demon stood apart from my friends, wearing a terrified look. "Your crew took out Barachiel."

More accurately, a rogue ritual had—with Kel's assistance—but I didn't see any point in disillusioning him. We had dispatched all the shades he'd contracted, and that was plenty intimidating. I raised a brow, trying to look menacing, when I felt as scary as day-old tuna salad. "Still want to fight?"

Gods, I hope not.

"I propose a truce. I'll tell Sibella that you slew our ancient enemy in her name. Unless she's mad, she will reckon your debt paid."

"If I see you near my family," Chance said coldly, "then I'll take your head. No warnings, no questions."

"Understood." The Luren hurried away, seeming desperate to escape.

By this point, Eva had woken in a rage. "Find me

something to shoot! There's *no way* I end this fight on the ground like a punk."

Chuch kissed her on the lips. "I'm sorry, *amor*. It's over. If you like, we'll go down to La Rosa Negra tomorrow night, and you can punch some dudes."

"Sounds good," she muttered, accepting Chuch's hand.

Before we could leave this place, I needed to do one more thing. I walked over to the ashes that had been my friend Kelethiel. Chance wound his arm around my shoulder, a quiet tension in him. I knew how he felt about my bond with Kel, the fact that I'd slept with him while we were apart. But he couldn't doubt my commitment; it would've been much simpler to write him off, find a replacement. But I would never, ever do that.

"We need to honor him somehow," I said softly. My cheeks felt tight and hot, a residual effect from such fierce weeping.

"I'll fill one of my empty vials," Booke offered. "Unless that would be too macabre . . ."

I thought about it. "I'd like that. Maybe . . . I could have a statue built, include his ashes in the cement or something. Would that be weird?"

"A little," Shan said. "But cool. Better than burying a whole body in the dirt."

Booke did as he'd suggested. Then Chuch and Eva came over to wrap their arms around Chance and me, both emotional nearly to the point of tears. Shan and Booke joined the group hug, which lasted a while. All of us were exhausted past the point of bearing. Part of me felt like we should be more exultant, but it was all . . . too much. So much had happened that I couldn't process everything.

Eventually, Chance said, "While I appreciate what you've done tonight, more than words can say, I need to get Corine to a doctor. Then, if it's all the same to you—and after she's pronounced sound—I need some time alone with my girl."

Chuch grinned, slapping him on the back. "I missed you, *mano*. And I'd have been pissed if you got out of buying my little girl presents so easily."

"It's good to finally meet you in person," Booke said, offering his hand.

"You too. Thanks for taking care of her while I was gone." Chance made it sound like he had been on a business trip. They shook firmly, then he hugged Shan around the neck. "Looks like you turned into a badass."

Shannon hefted her sword. "This trims peen, you know. Hurt her and I'll make you wish for demons. And welcome back." She kissed his cheek.

After Eva hugged him again, we turned toward the exit. The warehouse looked like hell, but it had been almost this bad before we invited Armageddon out to play. No collateral damage, so Twila wouldn't come gunning for me. Chance matched his steps to mine, his arm tight about me. He'd hardly let go of me since Kel died. At the Pinto, Booke tossed me the keys, and Shannon handed me the bag. My dog popped out, safe and sound. He had had the brains to hide while the worst shit was going down. To my amusement, he lunged from the purse toward Chance, who caught him, accepting the Chihuahua kisses as his due.

"I'll give Booke and Shannon a ride," Chuch said. "We can catch up tomorrow. I figure you're all heading out soon?"

Booke nodded. In the starlight, his gaze was already far away as he planned his world tour.

Shan said, "No way. You're stuck with me."

"We'll go as soon as she's ready," Chance murmured.

He guided me into the passenger seat, then ran around the car to drive. Anxious nausea rose in my throat. *Please let the baby be all right. Please.* If it turned out that I had chosen Chance over our child—I cut the terrified thought, but I felt sure he knew my worry as he pulled away from the warehouse. First, we stopped at a gas station so I could clean up a little. The way I looked,

I was afraid I'd be admitted whether I needed it or not. Then Chance found a twenty-four-hour clinic.

There were a hundred questions, but with his natural charm, he came up with a story that satisfied the doctor on duty at this hour. The lateness made it so we didn't have to wait. They ran a few tests, listened to the baby's heartbeat, which Chance heard for the first time. His expression melted, tiger's eyes liquid with love and wonder. He pressed a palm to my belly, his gaze locked on my face. At his request, they also checked my thigh beneath the wrap.

"You're a lucky woman," the doctor told me, warming up to a lecture. "No more hiking in dangerous areas. I understand how you daredevil types are, but you'll have to put off the adrenaline rushes until after the baby's born. Is that clear?"

"Yes, sir," I said meekly, amused at the cover story Chance had devised.

"Take her home. See that she rests and drinks plenty of fluids. Her throat will heal in a few days."

He thought I'd strained it screaming for help after a fall. Of course, the doc also thought I was an idiot for hiking and climbing on a bum leg while pregnant. But I was sure there were people that stupid in the world. It was definitely more plausible than the truth. In short order, we were back in the Pinto and heading to a hotel.

Any will do. The closest one.

Maybe it was an incomprehensible, unforgivable reaction, maybe it was hormones or a need to affirm the fact that we were alive and together, but I wanted to get naked with Chance. He rushed through check-in, and then he carried me through the lobby. He had no luggage. I had a few things in a backpack and a dog in a purse; that didn't deter us. The elevator moved like a snail up to the third floor. This wasn't a posh place, but the relentlessly airport lodge décor in the room couldn't distract me from my need to touch him.

Evidently he felt the same way. As I was unbuttoning his shirt, he pulled mine over my head. With shaking, eager hands, we undressed each other. I led him toward the bathroom because after everything that had happened tonight, there would be no sex without a shower. Well, I needed one anyway . . . and I never turned down a chance to see him with water glistening on his tawny skin.

With tender hands, he unwrapped the bandage on my palm, then the one on my thigh. "I hate how much it hurt you, bringing me back."

"Living without you would've hurt more," I whispered.

He went for me with a growl, his mouth ravenous. His body felt incredibly good against mine, hard and hot, throbbing with need. Chance lifted me into the warm spray, then stepped in behind me. I went for a washcloth but he plucked it from my fingers with a laden look.

"Let me."

"I could be persuaded . . ."

With deliberate care, he washed me all over, lingering on my breasts and between my legs. I moved against his fingers, maddened by the teasing, but he shook his head. "You need a bed, not shower sex."

"But I like shower sex."

He groaned. "I *want* to. But your leg."

Yeah, the muscles in my thigh probably weren't up to that level of acrobatics, however hot it sounded. A flash of a memory heated me all over. He'd taken me in Sheol like an animal—on desks, against walls—even when it was Ninlil, it was still me. Maybe I should be jealous of her, but she was gone, and I was here. He'd come back for *me*. And *I'd* enjoyed the rough sex every bit as much as she did. Talk about weird, orgasms in stereo.

He swept me into his arms, wrapped me in a towel. I submitted to the caretaking because I knew he needed to assert himself, put his stamp on me. As he dried me, I warned, "I won't put up with this forever."

"Until the baby's born?"

"Maybe. It depends on how crazy and/or cranky I get. And right now, I want you so bad, I can't stand it."

"God, me too." He shook with it. "Ever since I came through, it's all I can think about. You. Mine. Baby. I think my brain's short-circuited."

"Too much testosterone. You weren't used to it over there?"

"Don't know. Don't care." Yeah, he was out of patience.

Thank God.

No foreplay. There would be years and years for slow, seductive sex. This, this was raw and primal when he came down on me, taking me in one powerful stroke. He cupped my hip, drawing my good leg around his. I left the other straight, as it hurt enough already. The pain added a layer of spice to the pleasure as he pushed. His thrusts lost their cadence, going ragged and fast straightaway. I matched him as best I could, pushing hard, my fingers digging into his shoulders.

Chance kissed me as the intensity ramped up. His tongue moved in my mouth as he did within me. The hint of passivity of my straight leg and his wildness drove me higher. It had never, ever felt this good—and we'd had some amazing sex. He sensed he was outpacing me and he reached between us, strumming so I arched, working against him with agonized, delighted gasps. He broke the kiss when he lost control completely, but he didn't avert his eyes or hide his face. As he came, he stared down into my eyes, giving me everything.

No barriers. No doubts.

My whole body clenched, rocked in gradually diminishing waves. He didn't let go of me, even afterward. He eased off me, on my good side, and wrapped me up in his arms, hands gentle on my back. I peppered his face with kisses, unable to stop, as if we broke physical contact for even a second, then this reality would dissolve.

"I'm not going away again," he promised.

"Me either."

For just a moment, I closed my eyes, head on his chest listening to his heartbeat. *This man gave up godhood for you. He died for you.* Part of me still felt I didn't deserve him, but that girl was mostly gone. I *did* deserve to be loved; I wasn't a cipher, insignificant and unworthy of joy. Contentment laced with sorrow swelled in me—I'd always grieve quietly for Kel.

I didn't mean to sleep, but the day's events overwhelmed me. The next thing I knew, it was late morning . . . and I was alone. Panic spiked, but there was definitely an indent on the pillow beside me to promise I wasn't crazy. Then I heard the shower running.

He's still here. This is real. This is my life.

I pushed out a long breath, then joined him. The shower was long and messy, and the housekeeper probably wouldn't thank us later. But I managed shower sex. Afterward, I dressed in clean clothes while Chance put on what he'd been wearing the day before. I gave Butch his breakfast and a drink in his collapsible travel dishes. Then we took him out for his morning business.

Just in time, it seemed.

Once the dog was settled, Chance said, "Let's swing by Chuch and Eva's. Then I'm ready to go home if you are."

"One stop before that."

"Oh?" He cocked his head in a heartbreakingly familiar gesture.

I know him, I thought. *I love him. Always.*

With some effort, I roused myself to answer. "Twila."

"You have business with her?"

"I swore to her. It's polite to let her know I'm leaving her demesne."

"Okay." I could tell he was eager to get out of Texas—to get back to the life we had been building together before the demons ruined everything.

Talk about unusual relationship obstacles.

"This won't take long."

Twilight was closed when we arrived, but Bucky, Jeannie's husband, was cleaning the place and stocking the bar. He smiled at me, likely remembering the time he helped me with some remote viewing. Good to see him one last time. If I could help it, I wouldn't be back in Texas for a while. Our friends could visit *us* for a change, and the baby gave me a great excuse to make them.

"Twila in?" I asked.

"Go on back. She's expecting you."

"Of course," I murmured.

Chance cut me a grin. He knew firsthand how knowing and powerful Twila was. One of these days, I'd get the truth of what went down between them. She was working on account books when I walked in, Chance behind me, and her brows shot up. To be honest, I think she expected this quest to kill me.

If not for Kel, it would have.

"Well, I'll be damned. The loas gave you low odds for success," she said in lieu of greeting.

"I had an ace in the hole."

Not really. I had friends who loved me beyond reason.

"Smart girl." Twila skimmed me head to toe, then smiled. "Looks like smooth sailing ahead, Ms. Solomon. The darkness I saw before has fallen away."

"I just stopped by to tell you I'm on my way out of San Antonio. I'll be in Laredo for a little while. Then I'm gone from Texas entirely. You still have my pledge, if you ever need—"

"Oh, child," she said, shaking her head. "That vow doesn't bind you now."

"Why not?" Astonishment radiated through me, like the spinning colors of a kaleidoscope, until I couldn't process a rational thought.

Twila sighed; clearly my ignorance was a great trial to her. "Because you're *human*. I govern only the gifted."

Holy shit.

Just in case I didn't get it, she elaborated, "Your concerns are mortal now. None of my business."

That was unexpected good news. If Twila had washed her hands of me, the rest of the supernatural world should follow suit. "I made peace with the Luren, so hopefully I'm done with demons. And the rest of them should be busy fighting for power in Sheol."

The tall, majestic woman came around the desk to kiss Chance on the cheek. "You have a tiger's eyes but a lion's heart. Guard your family well."

"I will," he said firmly.

I fixed a stern look on her. "Look after Booke for me. He's the best . . . and I don't know if you appreciate how amazing he is."

"Oh, child. I have *such* plans for that man." Her tone was positively lascivious, her smile greedy with anticipation.

Twila and Booke? Well, why not? Texas could do worse than a man like Ian Booke as their king. I wondered if he had an inkling of her attraction. Theirs would be an interesting courtship and I looked forward to hearing about it secondhand. They could have the adventures from this point; I was done.

Then Twila offered me her hand. Since I had no gifts, only a pentacle scar on my palm, I didn't expect the flash between us. She pulled me into a vision so fast that I couldn't fight it, like the riptide of rushing rapids. Images flickered before my eyes, faster than I could process them. A party with all our friends, Chance laughing forty years from now, a baby dressed in a blue onesy, a little boy with black hair and amber eyes, running toward me. I saw Jesse and Shannon, ten years down the road, and Twila, holding hands with Ian Booke. The images sped up until they were a blur of color, and they flung me back out into the real world when she let me go.

"What the hell," I panted.

Chance wrapped an arm around me, his expression worried. "What did you do to her? I might not have the power I once had, but—"

"A parting gift." Twila ignored my furious lover. Her smile was gentle, almost tender, as if she knew how disorienting the exchange had been.

Damned freakin' loas. It would serve her right if I barfed on her carpet.

But there was a more important matter to hand. So I asked, "You're saying that's what lies ahead?"

"Possibly. Such things are never certain. Witness love's triumphant return." She tipped her head at Chance. "There are no destinies now. Life will be what you make of it, whatever you choose."

"Thank you," I said softly. "Freedom is a priceless gift."

I remembered Kel. I ached. And yet I didn't see how it could've ended otherwise. He had given up all hope.

"You earned it, not me. Farewell, Corine Solomon." That was a dismissal, and one didn't waste Twila's time, so I backed out of the room like she was an empress, a courtesy I'd learned in Sheol. Her smile flashed wide and white; she understood.

Then she went back to work. Texas didn't run itself.

The drive to Laredo went in a wink. At least, it seemed fast with all the talking. We both had so much to say, so many questions.

"I hated seeing how broken you were," Chance said softly. "But . . . I loved it too. Since you left, I've felt like I was fighting to gain equal ground."

"I was afraid. Of so many things. And then the worst came to pass. I lost you. If I could do it all over, forgive you sooner—"

But he was already shaking his head. "I wasn't ready in Kilmer. You were right to call me on my bullshit. I

needed you, but I didn't want to open up. I was still clinging to the old double standard that had already failed
once."

"So you're saying if I'd taken you back in Georgia, it
wouldn't have lasted."

He lifted a shoulder in a graceful shrug. "I suspect not.
You needed more from me than I was willing to give
then. It took some straight talk from both you and my
mom to wake me up."

"Not many couples can say they've literally been to
hell and back."

His smile melted me from the inside out, and when he
reached out to caress my stomach through my thin T-
shirt, the tingles increased. I'd heard that sex drive spiked
during pregnancy, but I could totally drag him into the
backseat right now. From the way his eyes heated and his
breath caught, he read my desire.

"Keep looking at me like that and we won't make it
to Laredo today."

Butch yapped, keeping us on task. I fixed my gaze on
the road and changed the subject. Already, Chance didn't
remember much about his time in his father's realm. It
was a protective measure, preventing humans from
learning too much, coveting power they shouldn't possess. But Ebisu didn't need to worry about that with his
son. Maybe, in time, he would be comforted to know he
had a grandchild on the way—that his line would continue in the human fashion.

Then it occurred to me.

"Oh, my God," I said.

"What?" Chance cut me a worried look.

"Pull over. *Right now.*"

His worry escalated to fear. "What's wrong? Is it the
baby? Oh, God, are you bleeding?" He was shaking
when he pulled onto the highway shoulder, eyes frantic.

To shut him up, I kissed him as he'd done me in Sheol.
That took longer than I expected, as he responded with

full ferocity and desire. Only the honking of an eighteen-wheeler reminded me why we'd stopped in the first place. Otherwise, we might've tried to see if we could have sex in a Pinto.

Breathless, I handed him my phone. "Call your mother."

Fond Farewells

Min was incoherent when she heard Chance's voice. For the first ten minutes of the conversation, it was just her sobbing and him reassuring her. Eventually, she said, "I love you. I love you. Tell me where you are."

I said quickly, "Have her meet us in Mexico. Give her Tia's address."

Chance complied. Then he added, "I'll see you soon. It's all right, I promise."

More joyful tears, and I joined in, while the big trucks rolling by shook the Pinto's windows. "Put Corine on the phone," she eventually demanded.

With a surprised look, Chance gave back my cell. "Here."

"Yeah, Omma?"

That surprised him again. He laced our fingers and brought my hand to his lips, thanking me silently for honoring his mother. But I'd *always* loved Min, even when he and I were apart. But from his expression, you'd think I had given her a chalice of solid gold. Since they'd had only each other for so long, in a way, I had.

"Thank you," she whispered. "Thank you, *ddal*."

"I have even better news for you," I said then.

"Impossible. Nothing could be better than this. Nothing." Her voice was strong, certain, but also shaky with repressed tears.

"Not even your first grandchild?"

The silence held for almost thirty seconds, and then she deafened me with incoherent, joyous shrieks. When she found the words at last, she said, "I was wrong."

As she rang off, Min was mumbling about buying plane tickets. It seemed we would see her soon. Chance didn't let go of my hand as he pulled back onto the highway. Our fingers clung for the remainder of the drive, and he didn't release me until he had to in order to open my door at the Ortiz place. Inside the house, I got hugs from Chuch and Eva, but Booke wasn't in the front room to greet us. I caught him packing. When I came into the bedroom, he folded the shirt in his hands meticulously and then faced me. As soon as Barachiel's body hit the ground, he must've been booking travel arrangements. I didn't blame him. He had only eleven months of freedom left. I hoped Twila treated him well upon his return, but that was his issue to deal with; he'd made the bargain freely, after all.

"I'm sorry about Kel," he said softly.

"He chose his fate. Not everyone is so fortunate." But it still hurt.

In my mind's eye, I saw him fighting Barachiel, fierce and magnificent. I remembered what he'd said in his last moments. *The future lies before you, dādu, but I have outlived my purpose. I choose to die a free man.* Tears welled up in my eyes. Loss was inevitable; I couldn't have saved everyone, no matter how I wanted to. I'd freed Booke, rescued Kel once, but his ultimate fate wasn't mine to decide. At least I had given him that much. The wound in my thigh burned like righteous fire, a reminder of what my fate would have been without the half demon who had *not* been ordered to protect me, that last time. That ritual would've killed me.

He chose his path.

"Speaking as one with experience in adaptation, I think he never quite got over the shock of learning his whole existence had been constructed on a lie. He couldn't adjust . . . and so, in those final moments, he thought only of surcease."

"He seemed to be at peace." But those were only words, what people said in order to comfort each other. Yet I hoped Booke's interpretation was accurate.

And I hoped, unlike the full-blood demons in Sheol, that Kel hadn't simply ceased to be. Perhaps his human half meant he had a soul, so there was an afterlife or reincarnation waiting for him. Those were the most cheerful thoughts I could muster, and they didn't stem the tears. Booke hugged me, his hands gentle on my back. Soon, I got myself under control and stepped away.

"That wasn't what I came to talk to you about, actually." I put on a cheerful expression, as I had so many reasons to be happy . . . and grateful.

"Sorry I saddened you."

"It was the circumstances, not you. The edge will dull in time."

He nodded. "All things do."

"I came to find out when you're leaving. Have you made arrangements yet?"

"I've arranged a flight to South Africa, as you suggested. I'm taking steps to secure a legal identity."

I grinned. "As your own son. How very Connor MacLeod of you."

"In my case, there can be only one as well, I think. It's best for the world."

"So you don't plan to get married and settle down?" I teased.

"Not for years, if ever. I was forcibly tied to one spot for so long that I can't imagine anything more heavenly than being a nomad."

"For eleven months. Then you have to come back to

work for Twila." I wondered if I should give him a heads-up about her romantic inclinations, but no. She wouldn't thank me for it, and I was sure she would take no for an answer, should Booke be disinclined to her pursuit. Personally, I thought they would make an awesome couple, once he got done sowing his wild oats.

"Don't fret. It won't be as onerous as you seem to fear."

That wasn't my concern at all. I'd seen the library and it would be a good fit for his abilities and interests. "So when are you leaving?"

"On the red-eye."

"We'll take you to the airport." This was kind of a delicate question, but . . . "How are you fixed for money?"

"I have an account that's been untouched, earning interest, for some years. If I can get them to release the funds, I'll be set. That will probably require a forged will."

"But until then . . . ?" I didn't know how he'd afforded the fare to South Africa.

"I crafted some spells and sold them. Apparently hermetic tradition is rather rare here in the Southwest. They fetched an excellent price. I expect I shall have no trouble moving more arcane accoutrements to fund my travels." He patted the smart phone in his pocket. "I can always ask on Area 51 for prospective buyers if there are no shops handy."

"I had no idea there was so much money in what you do."

"Nor did I, but it stands to reason. The spells can be used by anyone, which makes them invaluable, once I imbue a focus object with the power."

"Oh, wow." Such things would be priceless to the right parties.

"I can take things from here, my darling girl. Don't trouble yourself further."

"By which you mean, leave me alone already." I smiled to show I was joking.

"Never that," he said soberly. "I've been alone far too long ever to take good friends for granted. I'll email when I can, but don't look for me on chat."

"Duh. I expect you to have awesome adventures. I'll tell the baby all about you." Unable to believe I'd spoken those words in that context, I pressed a palm against my belly, but I wasn't showing yet. In three months or so, I'd have a bump, and a bit after that, I should be able to feel movement.

Silently, I worried; I mean, this kid had been conceived in Sheol while his father was a demon queen's consort, and I wrestled with Ninlil, trying to keep her from doing crazy evil shit twenty-four seven. Moreover, my full-on Solomon Binder heritage had been in play, and Chance had still been a godling. There was no telling what I was incubating, though all early tests showed a healthy pregnancy against all odds. Which meant this peanut was a fighter. With Chance and me as parents, he or she would need to be.

"I'll come when the baby's born. Promise."

"Twila might not let you. You'll be starting your indenture around that time."

"I'll find a way. I know you said emergencies only, but . . . could we dream walk under those circumstances?"

I smiled up at him. "Absolutely."

"What can you absolutely do?" Chance joined us in the bedroom, wrapping an arm around my shoulder.

In the past day, I hadn't gotten many moments alone. He was a bit reluctant to let me out of his sight and I didn't blame him. Things still felt fragile, like we needed to touch each other to remain grounded. No matter what, I'd never accepted that his last words to me in Sheol weren't the literal truth. *Even death can't keep me from you.* And here he was; he'd given up godhood for my sake. I nestled against him, marveling that he was *here*; he'd chosen me against his father's wishes.

"Meet Booke in a dream to show off the baby."

His arm tightened on me, a reflexive reaction to the crazy fact that we'd made a new life in hell. "That presumes he can't come in person? I'm inviting everyone we know when the little guy is born."

"You know something I don't?" I raised a brow.

Chance shook his head. "I couldn't see the future, even from the other side. And now . . . I'm just an average guy."

My gaze swept him from head to toe, then I laughed. "You'll never be that."

He kissed me as if he couldn't help himself and didn't stop until Booke cleared his throat. "Far be it for me to stop a PDA, but I need to finish packing."

"Sorry," I said, but I was too happy to be embarrassed.

Chance accompanied me to the living room, where Chuch was holding Cami. Eva was in the kitchen, putting the final touches on dinner. Jesse and Shannon would be here soon; this was a farewell party for Booke, but unlike the other one, it would be small and intimate. Hopefully, it wouldn't be crashed by demons either.

We'd all gone through so many changes over the years. I was no longer a solitary creature, desperately longing for acceptance and a sense of belonging. Instead, I had friends, a man who loved me, and a family on the way. The latter sent a pang of pure visceral terror through me, but I reined it in with the surety that I had a great example of how to love a kid from my own parents. And our little one would have Min as a loving grandma. Not to mention we had the entire Ortiz clan at our backs; Chuch had claimed me long ago as an honorary cousin, which meant I had an extended family the like of which I'd never known.

"We'll figure it out," Chance whispered as he drew me down beside him on the couch.

I believed him.

Dinner was a lively affair. For old times' sake, Eva made her famous tamales. I served them up with green sauce, cream, and grated cheese. That night, we talked and laughed with our friends, knowing it was the last time for a while. After this, there would be no more insane adventures. When you had a kid to protect, you got serious about staying out of trouble. I planned to post charms all over our residence in Mexico, paying Tia handsomely for protection. No matter what, our child *would* be safe. I could tell Chance felt the same way; his expression revealed the awareness that our lives were about to change irrevocably.

After the meal, we sat in groups of two. Chance kept me close while Jesse snuggled with Shannon. By the time Eva got Cami down for the night, nobody really felt like playing party games. I just wanted to chill and enjoy their company. I listened to the guys talking about sports for a little while, until Shannon pulled away from Jesse, beckoning me into the other room.

Butch followed us, so I figured I might as well kill two birds with one stone. I said, "Let's take him out."

I had the feeling she wanted to talk about something, but I hoped it wasn't more guilt over hooking up with Jesse. I was having another guy's baby, for fuck's sake; if that wasn't the definition of *I've moved on*, then I had no idea what would convince her. Over the past months, I'd done my best to convey that I was cool with the way things went down. Plus, I was totally, absurdly in love with Chance—to the point that Jesse had thought, at one point, that I was in serious denial and in danger of needing mental health care.

She read my look as Butch trotted into the grass, and laughed. "It's not what you think."

"No?"

"I just want to make sure we're okay. Before the

whole amnesia thing, we talked about going into business together—"

Yeah, I remembered. We'd discussed running a consignment shop together, what seemed like ages ago. But circumstances changed. She had new dreams now, and I understood. So did I, actually.

She went on, "Now, I'm putting together a business plan for my own deal. I just don't want you to think that—"

"Shan, you're *always* going to be my best friend." I put an end to her verbal stumbling. "It doesn't matter if we live together . . . or work together. As for your idea, I think Zombye Gear will be epic."

"It'll hit the goth market anyway."

"All I've ever wanted was for you to be safe and happy. I know that sounds super motherly, but I don't care, and you have to deal." More tears prickled at my eyes. "Gods, these hormones. I don't even know how Eva survived it."

Shan laughed. "I won't say you're glowing, but I *am* relieved to have an explanation for all the barfing."

"Me too," I muttered.

"That was trippy, right? You go in with a demon dog bite and come out with, 'Surprise, in seven months, you're having a baby.'"

"It was terrifying," I confessed.

"Yeah, and with Chance—"

"Dead. It's fine, you can say it. I know what happened in Sheol . . . and normally, that would be an impediment to a life together."

"Little bit."

Butch trotted over to me, his job done, and I picked him up. When I straightened, I wore a smirk. "Anyway, I'm happy for you on all counts. I do, however, expect free clothing and cosmetics as you're perfecting the prototypes."

"Deal. But I have years of school ahead of me before then."

"You'll be famous by the time Cami is old enough to think your products are cool," I predicted.

Shan waved a hand in dismissal but I could tell she was pleased. "Maybe. It'll take some start-up money. I have some ideas on that."

"Oh?"

"Well, I was thinking I might do séances. Talk to dead people?"

"Be careful. You might cause trouble for Jesse if you get a reputation as a charlatan. And if people think you're legit, that's a whole different set of problems."

She grinned. "I didn't say it was a perfect plan."

I hugged her with a squirming dog between us. "I was wondering . . . would you and Jesse be willing to serve as godparents?"

It was a huge thing to ask, considering her age, but she was my closest friend. If all went well, it'd just be a titular role that involved spoiling the baby rotten; so far, it hadn't been hard with Cami. There were more overtones, like religious training and raising the kid if something happened to Chance and me, but I wasn't asking with those things in mind. This was a gesture that proved things were—and would always be—good between two Kilmer girls who made it out despite the odds.

Her arms tightened around my shoulders. "God, yes. I mean, I have to ask Jesse, but I don't think he'll mind." Shan's voice thickened, and I could tell she was on the verge of tears. "I have . . . *so much* now, Corine— family . . ." I suspected she meant the Ortiz clan and Jesse's folks, plus all his other relatives. From what she'd said, they had welcomed her with open arms, even though she was young for him and didn't dress like a nice girl.

She took a breath, continuing, "Friends, a future. I can't tell you—"

"Then don't. I get it."

"Okay." Shan pushed out a shuddering breath, hugged me hard, then let go. That felt a little symbolic.

At the beginning, she was a lost kid, but she'd turned into a strong woman who could meet me as an equal. She had her own plans and dreams . . . her own life—and that was as it should be. Maybe if I hadn't cast that forget spell, she wouldn't have figured out what she wanted from life so soon. I hated to think I could've limited her by being overprotective; damn, I had to watch that with my own kid.

"There's one thing I want to give you," I said.

"I've taken enough from you," she protested, but I was having none of it.

I put the Pinto keys in her palm. "Chuch can work with you on the title, make it official. It's a hell of an ugly car, but you need one, and it's served me well."

Shan paused, like she might argue. Then she tucked the keys into her pocket. "Thank you." She'd evidently decided to be gracious. "Now let's get back in there," she said. "And party like it's 1999."

I nodded. "Yep. We're taking Booke to the airport late tonight, and then we're heading out too."

"God, it hurts to think of saying good-bye to you," she choked out.

"Don't make the pregnant lady cry again. And it's not a good-bye, Shan, *never* a good-bye between you and me. This is only sayonara."

Home at Last

It was tough leaving everyone in Texas, knowing it would be months before we got together again. Chance and I intended to catch a midnight bus, so we could sleep on the way home. Airports had better security, and he didn't have any ID on him. His passport was back in Mexico City at the apartment, along with everything else he owned. I knew from experience that they didn't care about illegal entry into Mexico. It was only tough getting back into the States.

That night at the bus terminal, I gave hugs and kisses multiple times, nuzzled Cami's soft baby cheeks until she chortled. Booke was already gone, of course. We'd dropped him off at the airport first. He'd kissed me on the tip of the nose and asked, "How would you like a postcard from Shanghai?"

"I'd love one," I'd said.

Shan hugged me hardest of all. "I expect regular Skype calls."

"Every night if you want, at least for a few minutes."

"Deal."

Jesse stepped up beside her, letting me know he had her back. She wasn't sketchy like some gifted girls he'd dated. Maybe she was a little off-kilter to be a cop's girl, but like complex puzzle pieces, they fit perfectly, creating a larger design. She teared up when Chuch walked Chance and me to the front doors of the station, and I waved until she turned a tearful face into Jesse's shoulder.

For once at a loss for words, Chuch shifted back and forth on his heels. "I could totally drive you to Monterrey. It'd be no trouble. Eva said—"

I held up a hand, stemming his protest. "And *I* said you should get home to your family. We'll be seeing you soon."

"You better invite us over." Chuch cleared his throat, hard.

I choked up in turn. "As soon as possible. Please don't make me bawl at the bus station, *primo*."

At that he managed a smile, then hugged us both, hard. Other people surged around us while Chuch clutched us around the neck; he smelled of cologne and motor oil. Eventually Chance brought the tableaux to a close with a murmur that our bus was leaving in fifteen minutes.

It wasn't a dramatic exit, more a quiet setting to rights. Chuch, Jesse, and Shan stayed to watch us pull out of the terminal. Though I hadn't realized it, I was crying silently. Too much had happened, too much change, and my world would never be the same. It wasn't bad, but it was different; and I'd never been one to adapt too fast.

"We could move to Texas," Chance said quietly. "All our friends are there."

"Not Booke."

"True. But he will be in a year."

I smiled. "Let's talk about it then."

The truth was, even though so many of my loved ones made their homes in Texas, it didn't feel like home to me. Since leaving Chance, I'd only ever been content in Mexico . . . and I wanted to see how much better it could be with him at my side, building our lives together. If he hated it, then we'd revisit the question.

"I just want to be with *you*," he said then. "I don't care where."

I melted.

"Twila showed me a glimpse of things to come, you know."

He smiled at me. "Anything good waiting down the line?"

"The vision was kind of a mess, but we might be having a boy. If what she showed me is true."

"Really?" The lights from the parking lot outside illuminated his face well enough that I saw his brows arch. "I guess we should talk about names, then."

"I was hoping to convince you to name him after Kel."

His fingers tensed in mine. I knew he had mixed feelings about the guy, but since he was gone, I wanted to do something to honor his life . . . and his sacrifice. So I tried to explain.

"Not Kelethiel. That's too weird to hang on a kid. But something that could shorten to Kel as a nickname. Kelvin, Kelton, Kel—"

"Kellen," he cut in. "I could live with Kellen."

"Wow. You've been thinking about this already."

He nodded, bringing my hand to his lips. The kiss to my palm roused tingles up and down my whole arm. "I have, actually. I'll never like the fact that you cared about him . . . or that he wanted you for himself. But I'm here with you, and he died to make that happen. I feel like I need to repay the debt somehow."

"Me too," I admitted.

"Kellen means mighty warrior," Chance said as the bus pulled away from the terminal. Chuch's car drove out after us, and they turned the other way to take Shannon home.

"That sure fits, considering what this kid has already been through."

"He's a fighter, like you. I'm sure, down the line, he'll make our lives hell."

"In the best possible way."

A family, I thought. *That's what we are—with shared dreams, a promise of forever.* It had been so long that I didn't remember how I should feel about that, and I strangled more tears. Men didn't usually understand that they could come from a place of joy too, and I didn't want to worry Chance.

He held my hand the entire trip. Not because he was afraid, but because he wanted to. He laced our fingers together after we talked about baby names and only relinquished me in Monterrey. No hitches prevented us from catching the next bus, a twelve-hour trip that ended with us exhausted in Mexico City. I fell asleep on Chance's shoulder; he only woke me when we pulled into the final station. Then he collected our bags and hailed a cab in halting Spanish. I glowed a little that he was trying so hard. As we got in the taxi, I rang Tia to let her know we'd be there soon.

Though it was early, traffic was heavy, and it took forty-five minutes to reach my mentor's house. She opened the door before I'd hardly rung the bell and hugged me hard. As usual, she wore a loose housedress and an apron in competing floral patterns. Her gray hair was braided neatly; her lined face revealed nothing but pleasure in my arrival.

"It's so good to see you," she said in Spanish.

"Likewise." I kissed her cheek.

She gave me a serious look. "I wondered if I had to die to get you to come home."

"No, I just had some business to take care of first."

"I know, *nena.* Looks like you tracked Chance down too. I told you to keep this one. You'll make beautiful babies."

A blush heated my cheeks, but I didn't dispute her words. "I hope so. We'll find out in seven months or so."

Her eyes dropped to my belly; then she pressed gnarled fingers to my abdomen. *"Felicidades!* Do you want to know if it's a boy or a girl?"

"You can tell?" Chance asked in surprise. "Just from a touch?"

Tia cackled. "Of course not. I'm a witch, not a gypsy. But if I guess, I have a fifty percent chance of being right. I used a little of your money," she went on, as she ushered me into the house for warm gorditas and cold horchata.

Once she settled us at the kitchen table, I waved her statement away. "I intend to settle some money on you, so you don't have to work so hard."

"I appreciate that, *mija.*" The diminutive endearment meant she looked on me as a daughter, or more likely, granddaughter.

Touched, I ate the snack she had prepared, and we chatted about how life had treated her in our absence. She complained about a rival named Juanita and the witch who was undercutting her at the market stalls. Comforting that some things never changed . . . that I had a place where somebody always welcomed me.

After we finished, Chance kissed Tia's hand and said, "I trust you have no objection to my attentions to Corine, especially in light of her interesting condition."

"You're a good boy," she said. "But cheeky!" She turned to me with a playful scowl. "Didn't I tell you not to let him have his fun without a ring on your finger? And look where it got you."

"I had fun too," I pointed out, and she swatted me with a striped dish towel.

Chance was grinning, delighted with our exchange, which I assumed meant he had translated it correctly. He dropped a hot kiss on my smiling mouth. I tangled my fingers in his hair and forgot about Tia, until she splashed some water on us.

"Dios mio, you're like a pair of shameless dogs. Out!"

"Wait! We need some protective charms," I told her.

That appeased her sense of the proprieties. *"Claro.*
With a baby on the way, it's only prudent. I'll get to work
on them right away."

Thus shooed from Tia's kitchen, I went with Chance
into the front room, where we killed two hours kissing
and whispering. If I'd been watching us, I suspect I'd
have hated every minute of it. But I didn't move away
until the bell rang. Chance went with me to answer it,
hoping it was his mother. Min stood with a pile of bags
at her feet, a taxi pulling away into the cool twilight. She
went into her son's arms in a puddle of tears; I retreated
into the house so they could have some time alone. Their
voices rose and fell in the courtyard garden, a lovely
place for such a reunion. *Better than a filthy warehouse,
for sure.* But it didn't matter where Chance came back to
us, only that he was here.

And he's not going away again.

Slowly, surely, I was accepting this as truth. My life's
path had been rewritten, and I couldn't wait to see where
it led. Twila's words rang in my head, and this time they
sounded like a benediction: *There are no destinies now.
Life will be what you make of it, whatever you choose.*

Half an hour later, Min accompanied Chance into the
house; he hauled her bags into the living room, then
looked bemused as to where to put them. An idea struck
me, so I hurried into the kitchen to check with Tia.

"Chance's mother is here. We don't have room for her
at the apartment, and I was wondering if you would
mind if she took my room for a little while. I'll cover
room and board—"

"She's family," the old woman cut in. "You're family.
And you take care of me very well, *mija.* Of course your
suegra can stay."

Suegra meant mother-in-law in Spanish. Though
Chance and I weren't married, it was close enough to the
truth that I just hugged Tia and thanked her. If I stepped

on her pride, she would make my life difficult in count-
less ways. She squeezed me back, ending with a firm pat.

"You just keep giving me reasons not to die. I think
I'll stay another year. I want to see the baby."

Tia talked about death like it was a decision to be
made; and maybe it was. You heard stories about people
who lived to be eighty-seven and only passed on after
they had no work to do, no useful purpose. If my baby
gave her a reason to stick around, I was glad. I went to
the bedroom I had used once, collected the remainder of
my things. Whether Tia wanted the money or not, I left
her three thousand dollars in the treasure box. So long
as she lived, she would want for nothing. I'd stand as
family for her, as she'd done for me.

I came out with my bags packed. Chance and Min
were sitting together on the couch, his mother tucked
beneath his arm. I didn't intrude, knowing he was her
whole world, but not in a way that made her dependent
or clipped his wings. Min was one of the strongest women
I knew, apart from my other mother; but then I had an
abundance of powerful ladies in my life. Between Shannon, Eva, Tia, and Twila, I would be hard-pressed to find
one who didn't totally kick ass and take names.

"Tia says she'll put you up, however long you want to
stay."

Min leveled a quiet look on me. "I mentioned this to
Chance, but I wasn't sure how you'd feel."

"What?" I settled on the chair across from them.

"I might sell the business in Tampa, relocate. If that
wouldn't bother you."

I beamed at her. "I'd love that. You could go into business with Tia, maybe. Open a storefront selling her
charms and your salves and potions?"

"Is she any good?" Min hadn't made a living in home-
opathy without examining the bottom line.

"The best. I owe her my life," I said honestly, remembering the charm that saved me in Sheol.

"It doesn't have to be decided right now," Chance pointed out. "I'm just so glad to see you, Omma."

"Me too," Min whispered.

Their tenderness touched me, and because I was still wrestling the hormones, I went into the kitchen to help Tia to keep from crying. I couldn't pull power anymore, but I could measure supplies and mix things as ordered. Her eyes weren't as sharp as they had been, so she didn't object to my presence while she crafted the charms. She didn't comment on my lack of magick; and I wasn't sure if she knew that I'd lost the touch too.

I'm human, I thought in wonder. *With all implicit benefits and limitations.*

An hour later, Min and Chance joined us. We ate dinner together, food that Tia had cooked the day before, and which I heated without mishap. By ten o'clock, I was dying of exhaustion between the month I'd had, the peanut, and the long bus ride with its inherent broken sleep. My thigh was hurting too, but I didn't feel like I had any right to complain. Not when I had my family all together and the man I loved in my life again.

But Chance noticed. "It's time to get you home. I'll see you in the morning," he added to Min.

She hugged him so tight around the neck that I could tell she was reluctant to let him out of her sight, and I so understood that feeling. He gently disengaged. "I'll be back tomorrow. Promise."

Min managed a shaky smile, wiping away a joyful tear. "Part of me can't believe you're here. I was so afraid you would choose greatness instead."

"Omma," he said softly, "I *did*."

Then he took my hand and led me home.

Happy Endings

Not surprisingly, Chance had no keys, so I used the spare set I kept at Tia's place. By the time we climbed the last step to his apartment, my leg was on fire. I could tell I had a long road of physical therapy ahead of me, but the pain was worth it. Everything had been. That night, I slept in Chance's arms, and it was perfect. The next day, we went over to join Tia and Min for lunch, mostly to reassure Chance's mother that he hadn't disappeared again. She should acclimate to his return soon, lose some of her clutching fear. It had taken me a few days to accept the new reality.

I was so happy it hurt.

Much later, after unpacking my things, I went out to the balcony to admire the sunset. Chance came up behind me, wrapping his arms about me. I finally had everything I had ever wanted. There were questions to be answered in the future: how many more children, and where we'd buy our home so our friends could visit. Chuch and Eva would bring Cami. Booke, too, might find his way here eventually, on his way back from the world tour. Someday, Jesse and Shan might have kids, and hopefully they'd bring the whole family.

I wouldn't be opening a consignment shop with Shan, but that was fine. She had her own dream to pursue, a bigger one than she'd dared entertain before. I didn't doubt that she could achieve it either. Someday, she'd have her own clothing line, her own cosmetics, and she was going to school to make it happen. I believed in her; and Jesse would support her all the way.

"Do you ever regret giving up—"

Chance stopped me with a kiss, which answered all my questions and then some. *No.* He wanted this life . . . and me. "The apartment's fine for now, but I'd like to buy a house within the next six months. We need to put down roots."

How well he knew me. The shop had been my first attempt to do exactly that, but the bond had been damaged. Now I needed more to make Mexico wholly my home. The baby had changed everything in a beautiful, shattering, unexpected way. Chance and I planned to take classes together, so we could both become entirely fluent in the language, which would help in forming relationships. Since I had a jump on him and could speak functional Spanish, I'd help him along, and in return, he intended to teach me to speak Korean, which would make Min happy. I wanted our child to speak all three languages—to have a better start in life than I had. Chance would help make it possible. He'd built an empire from nothing. He was fierce and savage and determined . . . and mine.

Mine.

The sunset was gorgeous, a fierce and furious dying of the light over the distant mountains. I loved the crisp night weather and the sunny days, the cheerful people at the local farmer's market, and the tourists who used to wander into my shop. With Chance beside me, *this* Chance, devoid of inhuman luck, life could be whatever we made of it. No hidden curses, no secret pitfalls. Just him and me, together.

"It's hard to believe it's finally over," I whispered into his shoulders.

"Sometimes I wake up . . . and I think I'm dreaming. That I'm still there, and you're still here, and I'm so afraid you won't wait that I can't breathe."

My heart twisted as I reached up to cup his cheek. "I made up my mind in Sheol. It's you or nobody. Always. I don't want anyone else."

His lovely mouth quirked at one corner. "Yeah, well, that Nephilim demon, or whatever he was, sure made it clear you had options."

"In dying, Kel brought you back to me. So I can't blame him for wishing. And without his help, there's no way I could've ever beaten Barachiel."

He nodded at that indisputable fact. "From the glimpses I got from my father's realm, you were steadfast. It was . . . heartening when I felt like giving up hope."

"If I had to, I would've undone my work on the loom every night for twenty years, waiting for you."

"Thank you, love." He squeezed his arms about me, and then let go. "Would you go for a drive with me?"

I thought about that. My stomach was steady, and I wasn't hungry. I had no immediate needs. But I feared surprises instead of longing for them, as in my life they'd often brought bad mojo. "Do I get to know where we're going?"

Chance shook his head, smiling. "I'd prefer to show you."

"Then c'mon." I decided not to argue.

Thanks to gated parking and a warm climate, the Mustang started with a purr when Chance turned the key in the ignition, even after long absence. He ran his hands happily over the wheel, so human and *here* that my whole body panged with gratitude and longing. Some folks said people couldn't change, but both of us had, just enough. He was still the man I'd always loved, even after

I left him, but without the icy control and endless distance. He'd learned to share himself and I'd learned to trust us both.

The gate attendant waved as we eased out into traffic and down the mountain. Chance took the road that led toward Atizapan and the *cuota*—toll road—which could take you either to Queretaro or Toluca, depending. He went west, toward Toluca, which would also take us past Interlomas, an upscale development, and eventually Santa Fe, another fashionable suburb popular with American expats. But he surprised me by exiting at Huixquilucan; though I wracked my brain for anything at this stop, I couldn't imagine where we were headed. The mystery deepened, but Chance didn't volunteer any info. In fact, when I tried to ask, he deliberately turned the volume up on the radio. I shot him a look, but he ignored that too.

Which clearly meant he had something up his sleeve.

I sat back and watched the darkness. He chose roads seemingly at random, worrying me further. We weren't headed toward town at all; Chance was driving us out into the wilderness. I hoped his phone had reliable GPS in case he got turned around. The way became precarious, littered with stones, and an unpleasant recollection flared—last time we'd gone somewhere like this together—and the loss it presaged. Mostly, I tried to keep a lid on the horror of Sheol and Greydusk's sacrifice, but sometimes the memories couldn't be quelled. I regulated my breathing, telling myself it would be all right. Chance wouldn't bring me out here to torment me.

He stopped the car at the edge of a jutting promontory, overlooking a valley below. It was bathed in moonlight, heavily forested. All around us, cacti bloomed in the rocky soil, agave blossoms so fiercely yellow even in the dark. It was a remote and wild place, but in some ways it perfectly represented my kinship with this country. Like Mexico, I was not easy to love.

"Do you know why I brought you here?"

I shook my head, gazing up at the massive twinkle of the stars. Within the city proper, you lost sight of these. Instead you saw planes and other lights; the sky never seemed to darken entirely. Here, the stars acquired a religious significance, as if we were standing in a holy place, lifted toward heaven. This was a mountaintop where monks might feel at home.

Then he went to one knee, drawing my attention down. My breath caught, and I just . . . I couldn't believe it. Intellectually, I knew what came next, but my brain was frozen, looping incredulity that overlaid my delight. He flipped open a small box, but instead of a ring, it contained his silver coin, the one he used to roll along his knuckles. Chance presented it to me with a flourish.

"I don't understand," I said.

"You're my luck now, love. I want you to have the formal keeping of it."

Tears welled up in my eyes because this felt like he was handing me his soul. With trembling fingers, I plucked the coin out and curled my fingers around the smooth, cool metal. "I'll keep it safe," I promised.

Yet he still didn't rise, which meant he wasn't finished. A second box, this one blue velvet, came out of his pocket. When he snapped it open, I already knew what it contained, but the beauty of the ring astonished me. It shouldn't have, I supposed, because Chance always had exquisite taste. He'd judged my preferences perfectly from the platinum shine to the princess-cut diamond, surrounded by sapphires.

"Corine, you were my love first . . . and then my lifeline. You didn't abandon hope that we could be together—that we *should* be—even when it must've seemed impossible. For those reasons . . . and many others, I'm begging you to be my wife. Become Corine Yi and start a new adventure with me."

"Yes, please," I whispered, afraid to reach for him, because it seemed likely I might wake alone and in tears.

As if he sensed my trepidation, he took my hand and slid the engagement ring onto the fourth finger of my left hand. To my delight, it fit perfectly. Chance folded to his feet then and pressed a kiss against my knuckles.

Oh, gods, he loves me so much. He does. And there was no question how I felt about him. I didn't feel unworthy. Yes, I'd done terrible things, and the stains would never wash off my soul, but I had done them for the best of reasons. Maybe friendship and affection didn't excuse bad deeds, but for Shannon Cheney and Ian Booke, I'd do them again. My chief regret was that I hadn't been able to save Kel, but he made his choice to die a free man. After such a long life, maybe it had been time.

I'd tell myself that anyway.

"How?" I demanded.

He understood what I was asking. "I measured your finger while you were asleep, before we left Texas."

I was a little amazed I hadn't woken up. But then, if it had been after rousing reunion sex, maybe it wasn't so shocking after all. Holding my finger up to the moon, I admired the gleam of the stones . . . but also what it meant. Home. Belonging. A future. These were the things I'd wanted when I ran away from Kilmer's cursed ground. People might never understand how a Southern girl like me ended up living in Mexico, but that didn't matter. It was far enough away to be a fresh start.

"Why here?" I asked.

It was a lovely spot, but rather untraditional. Old Chance would've proposed over a romantic dinner in a trendy restaurant, maybe had the waiter deliver the ring on a silver platter. This was simple, heartfelt, and I preferred it, truth be told, but I wanted to understand his motivations. I needed to understand *everything* about him.

"Do you see the spot below us?" He pointed down the mountain, toward the lush valley below.

I nodded.

"You remember how I said I wanted to buy a house soon? That wasn't exactly true."

"You didn't. Did you?" I craned my neck, wondering if there was a house I hadn't seen. Surely Chance wouldn't revert to his high-handed ways and purchase a home without letting me look the place over first. I bristled a little.

"Relax," he said, smiling. "I *did* buy some land, outside the city. The property's big enough to build whatever you'd like. There's room for a pool and for Butch to roam. We can get more dogs. Maybe breed Chihuahuas." He was kidding about the last thing. I hoped.

"Building is a huge undertaking. It just about drove me crazy putting the pawnshop back together."

"That's part of why I'm working so hard in my Spanish classes. I want to be able to help you deal with the workmen." *Help me, not control everything.* "I figure we can find an architect, show him some styles we like, and choose from a couple different designs."

This would end in my dream home, and this wasn't so far from the pawnshop that it would make an awful commute. I could still do what I loved, then come home to a beautiful house and my handsome husband. "I can see if Armando is willing to take on the job as foreman."

That was the same as saying yes. Chance brightened, as if he'd been a bit nervous about my reaction to the surprise. Then he kissed me. "I'll bring you back during the day to walk the land with me. I know you'll appreciate it as much as I do."

"I'm sure. It will be nice to get out of the city. The noise is the only thing I don't love."

"I just want you to know . . . I can afford to look after you." He held up a hand, forestalling my protest. "I realize you're not looking for that, but if you ever decide you've had enough of the shop, we'll do all right."

"Well, I earned you a great deal of that seed money," I reminded him.

"But the clever investments were all mine."

"True." Still, he was right; it felt good to know that I didn't live on the ragged edge of disaster anymore. I had a safety net now—one I could trust—and Chance wanted me to marry him.

The wind swept over the agave blossoms, rippling the petals. Musky sweetness filled the air as Chance bent his head to kiss me. He tasted of sangria and summer, of past and future intertwined. I responded with all the love, all the passion in my soul. Maybe the future Twila had shown me would come to pass. Maybe not. Foretellings were mutable, written in water.

Life lay before us like the valley below—indistinct, wreathed in shadow, but dreamy with promise.

ABOUT THE AUTHOR

Ann Aguirre is a national bestselling author with a degree in English Literature; before she began writing full time, she was a clown, a clerk, a voice actress, and a savior of stray kittens, not necessarily in that order. She grew up in a yellow house across from a cornfield, but now she lives in sunny Mexico with her husband, children, two cats, and one lazy dog.

CONNECT ONLINE

www.annaguirre.com

Read on for an exciting excerpt from a new
science fiction series, set in a world
where only the strong survive

PERDITION

by Ann Aguirre

Coming in September 2013 from Ace Books.

Pain was a flower.

It began with crimson petals, threaded white, and ended with a black, black heart. *Like mine.*

Dred watched as her men carved lines into the intruder's skin. "It doesn't have to go down like this, Eli. Tell me why you're really here. Then defect from Grigor and swear to me, and I'll let you serve."

That was a lie. Since they were all liars, murderers, and thieves, it wasn't as if she could trust Eli's word, should he give it. She might convince him of her sincerity, however, and learn something about her enemies' intentions. The deception didn't trouble her. For all she knew, this man's mission was to stick a silent knife in her kidney.

"Never," Eli gasped, red-tinged sweat dripping down his arms. "You don't understand. Grigor will kill me. He'll hunt me down."

Fear wins over self-preservation.

"Not inside my territory," Dred said.

She leaped down from the throne cobbled together from scrap metal and rusty chains. It was an affectation, but one that amused her. Between the braids, the tattoos, and the leather rumored to be human skin, men found it hard to meet her gaze. Eli was no exception; Tameron had sold her legend completely. Some of it was bullshit, of course.

"You can't keep me safe," he whispered. "Grigor has eyes everywhere."

"That's impressive cowardice." When she got within kicking distance, Eli flinched and shielded his face. Dred laughed softly. "You think I can't break teeth through your arms?"

"I know you can," he whispered.

"Good. Forget about asylum for a few seconds. Just tell me why you're inside my border."

"I was scavenging on Grigor's orders. I didn't know I'd crossed!"

Since there were checkpoints and sentries posted anywhere territories overlapped, that was impossible. The only way Eli could be here was if he'd intentionally come through the ducts or sought some other secret way through her security. And there was no innocent reason he'd have done that, especially not on Grigor's orders.

"Bullshit," she said. "Keep lying to me, and you won't survive the hour."

"Kill him," Einar advised.

The man holding the prisoner's right arm was a tall, muscular blond with hair that looked like he had hacked it off with a rusty knife. Scars covered Einar from head to toe, his lip pulled sideways from a nasty slash to his face, and he was a missing an earlobe. Since he bathed, Einar was also one of the best catches in Charybdis.

Dred circled thoughtfully. Each time she gave the order, it got easier, like she lost a little more of her soul. She couldn't have him learning all her defensive strategies, all about her hidden weapon caches, and then reporting to Grigor. Each time there was an incursion, she had to assume the worst and react accordingly. Things had been unsettled lately, and both Grigor and Priest were daring more, pressing harder from each side.

She jerked a nod at Einar. "Do it."

"No, pl—" The giant snapped the prisoner's neck before he finished begging for his life.

"I suspect he truly was a spy," Tameron said. "You couldn't let him live."

He was a slight, dark-skinned male, younger than Dred, but it was impossible to say how much. She didn't ask people how old they were, where they were from, or what they'd done to get tossed in here. None of that mattered inside Charybdis. It only mattered how hard you'd fight to stay alive. He was also invaluable in keeping her regime on track; he supplied insights about her enemies and quiet information about the mood in Queensland, which was what the men called her territory.

The prison ship was the brainchild of some bright-eyed Conglomerate drone. *Take one of the old deep-space asteroid refinery ships and retrofit it for incarceration. We clean out overcrowded prisoners, and we can focus on those offenders who have a legitimate chance at rehabilitation.* Back when they first commissioned the prison ship, she'd heard the rationale on the bounce, like everyone else. Turns later, they had a floating city full of criminals, its orbit fixed in the middle of nowhere.

Never dreamed I'd end up here. But then, who does?

"Send the body for processing," she told Einar.

With a nod, the giant hoisted the corpse to his shoulder and headed for the chute where they deposited all organic waste. It would be processed and converted into fertilizer for use in the hydroponic gardens, which didn't work as well as they were supposed to. Half the lights had burned out, and it wasn't like they could requisition new ones. Occasionally, supplies came in with a load of prisoners and a unit of Peacemakers. None of the fish ever went after a one-ton machine armed with laser cannons, disruptors, and shredders, fortified with heavy armor. Those who had been inside longer might've chosen it as a better, faster way to die, if they could. But it was impossible to get to the docking bay. Every emergency door on Charybdis went into lockdown, and energy fields came up when a ship arrived, effectively sealing off the docking area completely. Only after the ship departed did the failsafe kick off, leaving the fish to make their own way.

Usually that meant joining with whatever territory you found yourself in. Sometimes, other sectors sent recruiters to wait just outside the first set of emergency doors to make their pitch. Though Charybdis had four would-be kings, it had only two queens, and she was the only one they called so. Silence wasn't looking to build an empire; she just enjoyed the art of death. Dred had been around enough to know that Silence had a gift because the other woman did it so quietly, so cleanly, you'd almost fail to note she'd garroted clean through your throat. She didn't often mess with Silence, who killed for pleasure, not defense, not to keep people out of her territory. And there was no predicting the behavior of someone like that.

She felt cold eyes on her. Spinning, she saw Lecass watching with a small group of his followers. He had been part of Artan's regime, but so far, he hadn't made a move. The man's inaction troubled her as much as a challenge would. Deliberately, Lecass stared until she gave him her back, a calculated insult. One of these days he would tire of the quiet drama and step things up. Dred would be ready.

Tam turned as the lights flickered. "That means a ship's coming in."

Because the machinery was so old, it stressed the circuits. The ship couldn't efficiently light the whole vessel as well as go into lockdown mode. It had been a while since she'd headed toward the docking area to wait for the new fish and look them over. She wasn't greedy for bodies like Grigor or Priest. Grigor fed on fear, sometimes literally, she thought, and Priest brainwashed his fish into thinking he was the living incarnation of some god. They worshipped him over in Abaddon, which was what he called his section of Charybdis.

She cocked her head, knowing it was a scary look. "Want to go see what the universe has thrown away today?"

Tam nodded. "We lost a few guys in the skirmish with Grigor."

Most of their daily conflicts occurred with Grigor or Priest, the two greatest threats to Queensland. Grigor had been here longest, and he was constantly pressing to see what new areas he could claim. Dred had the bad luck to be his neighbor. With Priest on one side and Grigor on the other, she was fighting constantly to maintain.

Sometimes, however, Mungo came out in search of blood; and you had to fight hard against his people. They were the hungriest in the ship. He was a short, red-haired man with a bushy beard, pale blue eyes, and rosy cheeks. By his appearance, one could be forgiven for guessing he was harmless . . . right before he ripped out your throat with his bare hands and tried to eat your face. She'd heard that Mungo liked children best . . . for all kinds of things, and such preferences had gotten him thrown into Charybdis early on.

They prey on weakness. Uncertainty.

She had little of either one left in her. Whether her decisions were right or not hardly mattered. Nothing mattered in this hole. The smart ones gave up and died; maybe they found the afterlife that the priests and holy women had promised, shortly after her arrest. At first, during the trial, she had missionaries in her cell every day, trying to save her soul, trying to sell her on Mary's grace, but after everything she'd seen, everything she'd done, she couldn't believe.

Could. Not.

Over the years, she'd learned to block it out—to read

only of her own volition. Otherwise, she lived with a barrage of other people's twisted violence drumming in her skull at all times. That was probably why she'd snapped. Maybe her sentence would've been lighter, at a different facility, if she could have brought herself to whisper those words of remorse the judge so badly wanted to hear.

But she couldn't.

And what that ancient Old Terran philosopher had written so many turns ago was true, after all. *He who fights with monsters might take care, lest he thereby become a monster. And if you gaze for long into an abyss, the abyss gazes also into you. She had become what she despised most . . . and she belonged here.*

I am the Dread Queen.

"Come," she called to Einar, who caught up to them at a jog.

"How long until docking?" he asked.

"Half an hour," Tam guessed. "When everything goes dark, then we'll know they're here."

"Let's see how far we can get."

During docking, recruiters didn't interfere with one another, even if they crossed borders. This one time, it was allowed, because otherwise it would be impossible for any group to augment its numbers, save the one in closest proximity. On this side, that would be Priest. He cared only for adding worshippers, but it often took longer for convicts to succumb to his brand of brainwashing. It wasn't the sort of thing that made for a quick pitch.

Still, she didn't linger in Priest's territory. Since they moved fast, they reached the second set of doors before the lights went down, and the barricades came up, along with the energy fields that would fry anyone who tried to cross. A few distant screams told her that some convicts had a timing problem.

Uneasily, they shared the space with Silence's people,

unusual, because the quiet killer didn't often take an interest. But it had been a while for her too. Silence must have advisers who let her know that if she killed too many of her own people out of sport, then she wouldn't have the numbers to drive off anyone intent on taking her territory. There were six in all . . . and hers was among the largest with space on all decks. The lifts didn't work, but she had shaft access, which meant her people could sneak around the ship unseen. Tam was particularly good at it.

There was a neutral zone just past the docking bay, a shantytown inside the prison ship, where fish often huddled until they realized it was worse there than when they affiliated. Townships had rules at least, enforced by the leader's people. The neutral zone had only one: take whatever you can. It was impossible to sleep safely there without being robbed, raped, or shanked, sometimes all in the same night. And so she'd tell anyone she deemed worthy of a second look.

That was the extent of Dred's pitch: *Come with me, and you may not die.* There was no reason to be more persuasive. The smart ones listened.

In the dark, it was eerie with only the red glow from the nearby shock field and the crackle of electricity. Silence's people didn't talk, even among themselves, and their behavior made for an uneasy truce. Tam kept a hand on his shiv, eyeing them with wary attention. On her other side, Einar played the role of gentle giant, but he wasn't gentle. Nobody inside Charybdis was. If they'd been sent up on a wrongful conviction, then they learned to fight, or they died.

Einar had been inside longer than Dred, and she'd been here for five turns before she got tired of etching hash marks into a sheet of metal to mark the days. Forever wasn't a number anyway. It just was. At her best guess, she was thirty turns, give or take. She had been killing for three years before she got caught. Before she got cocky. At the height of her career, she'd thought they'd never figure it out.

Ah, hubris.

At last, the vigil ended. The lights came back up and the security measures died, which meant it was safe to proceed. Pushing to her feet, Dred signaled her two men and jogged past the two sets of security doors, through Shantytown, and toward the reception area, where fish always milled around, as if expecting to be greeted by guards, someone to tell them where to go, what to do, how to get food or water. Poor, stupid fish.

This crop looked particularly sad. A few of them were crying, faces wedged between their knees. They all wore prison-issue gray, numbers and chips in the backs of their necks. Most of them had been shorn and deloused, though a few looked as though they had been dragged from the darkest hole in the system, then set on fire. The weak and wounded wouldn't last long; she ignored them.

Then her gaze lit on a man near the back. At first glance, he looked young, but his eyes refuted the initial assessment. Though he was slim and clean with a crown of shining blond hair, his summer sky eyes held a hardness that came only from turns of fighting, turns of violence and despair. He might well be the most dangerous man on the ship. *Time to find out if he's stable.* Giving Tam and Einar the order to guard her, she closed her eyes and let slip the dogs of war.

"Aguirre has a gift for creating strong characters who keep her readers coming back for more."
—*Publishers Weekly*

From *USA Today* bestselling author
ANN AGUIRRE

The Corine Solomon Series

Corine Solomon is a handler. When she touches an object she instantly knows its history and its future. Using her ability, she can find the missing, which is why people never stop trying to find her...

Blue Diablo
Hell Fire
Shady Lady
Devil's Punch
Agave Kiss

"Outstanding and delicious."
—#1 *New York Times* bestselling author Patricia Briggs

"An authentic Southwestern-flavored feast, filled with magic, revenge, and romance."
—*New York Times* bestselling author Rachel Caine

annaguirre.com • facebook.com/Ann.Aguirre
facebook.com/AceRocBooks • penguin.com

R0136

"The world Ann Aguirre has created is
a rollercoaster ride to remember."
—#1 *New York Times* bestselling author
Christine Feehan

From *USA Today* bestselling author
ANN AGUIRRE

The Sirantha Jax Series

Don't miss this romantic science fiction series,
featuring Sirantha Jax—a "Jumper" who possesses the
unique genetic makeup needed to navigate faster than
light ships through grimspace.

Grimspace
Wanderlust
Doubleblind
Killbox
Aftermath
Endgame

"I highly, highly recommend the series as it's one of
the best, if not, thee Best Sci-Fi romantic series."
—Book Pushers

annaguirre.com • facebook.com/Ann.Aguirre
facebook.com/AceRocBooks • penguin.com

New from *New York Times* bestselling author

CHLOE NEILL

HOUSE RULES
A Chicagoland Vampires Novel

At the tender age of 28, Merit became a sword-wielding
vampire. Since then, she's seen a Master fall and rise,
a city nearly burned to the ground, and discovered that
she could weather it all. But now, she'll have to test her
mettle—and her metal—once again.

Vampires across the city are going missing without a
trace. The tide is turning against the vampire houses.
And only Merit, and her friends, can stand in the way.

"These books are wonderful entertainment."
——#1 *New York Times* bestselling author Charlaine Harris

Available wherever books are sold or
at penguin.com

facebook.com/ProjectParanormalBooks

New York Times and *USA Today*
bestselling author

Karen Chance

FURY'S KISS
A Midnight's Daughter Novel

Dorina Basarab is a dhampir—half-human, half-vampire.
Subject to uncontrollable rages, Dory has managed to
maintain her sanity by unleashing her anger on those demons
and vampires who deserve killing.

Together with sexy master vampire Louis-Cesare, Dory will
have to face off with zombie vampires, fallen angels, and the
maddest of mad scientists—if she's going to get to the bottom
of a deadly smuggling ring and somehow stay alive…

"Karen Chance takes her place along with
Laurell K. Hamilton, Charlaine Harris,
MaryJanice Davidson, and J. D. Robb."
—SF Revu

Available wherever books are sold or at
penguin.com

facebook.com/projectparanormalbooks

S0444